# look
# after
a novel
# you

*To michaelea
lots of
love
George matthews
x*

# elena matthews

*Look After You*
Copyright © Elena Matthews 2014

This book is a work of fiction. Names, characters, places, and incidents either
are products of the author's imagination or are used fictitiously. Any resemblance to actual persons, living or dead, events, or locales is entirely coinci-
dental.

Cover design by ©Sarah Hansen, Okay Creations.
Edited by Jennifer Roberts-Hall
Interior by Champagne Formats

ISBN-13: 978-1497494848
ISBN-10: 1497494842

# dedications

*To my grandma who passed away on the 29ᵗʰ May 2013. And to my beautiful niece, Caitlin, NICU miracle baby, born thirteen weeks premature, who fought and survived. My little superhero …*

# chapter

1

September 2013

TWO POUNDS, TWO OUNCES. That's how much my baby girl weighed when she was born.

Ten hours ago.

This wasn't supposed to happen yet. I was supposed to have another thirteen weeks of pregnancy before I gave birth to my baby. I was supposed to have her nursery painted in pink with teddy bears surrounding the walls, her crib assembled with gorgeous soft blankets. I was supposed to have a baby shower, being showered with gifts and guessing the size of my baby. I was supposed to have time to come up with a name or at least discuss the possibility of names with my boyfriend. I was supposed to work up until my maternity leave, have at least a month of waddling around like a penguin and complaining about back pain or Braxton Hicks contractions.

I wasn't supposed to give birth to her by C-section ten hours ago without my birthing partner and my boyfriend. Without any warning. Without understanding why my body had decided it wasn't fucking good enough to carry my baby full term. Without having her in my arms like most other moms do the minute their baby is born.

Without…
Without…
Without…

A nurse is wheeling me into the neonatal intensive care unit to see my baby girl. This is the second time I'll get to see her since she was born. Well, the first time didn't even last ten seconds before she was immediately taken away from me so the doctors could work on her breathing and get her ventilated. I couldn't believe how small she was, but she was a baby, a real life baby with ten fingers and ten toes.

My baby.

Since the moment I took that pregnancy test and the window turned into a smiley face, she was a tiny thing inside of me, just a little blip. A couple of months later she was bigger than a blip, a bump, but I never really thought of her as a baby until I actually laid eyes on her beautiful face. Does that make me a terrible mother? I feel like one. I wasn't ready, and I should have been. I should have been prepared for this, but I was so naïve about the preterm side of pregnancy and birth that it hadn't even crossed my mind. But why should it have? Every parent hopes and wishes for the perfect pregnancy with zero complications and for the perfect baby. Nobody ever contemplates the worst possible pregnancy outcome until it actually happens to you.

The only thing that had worried me was the morning sickness, and surprisingly that hadn't really bothered me. God, I would do anything to swap giving birth to my premature baby with fucking morning sickness. Anything.

The nurse continues to wheel me through the NICU hallway, which consists of clinical white walls and huge glass windows that lead into the NICU rooms. There are so many incubators, each holding small and sick babies attached to tiny oxygen tubes, high dependency medical equipment and monitors.

I'm a little shocked. Considering this is a specialized ward for small and sick babies, I was expecting it to be full of crying babies and frantic doctors and nurses running around, but it is quiet, tranquil even, with the exception of the constant beeping sounds I can hear in the background.

My eyes start to fill up with panicked tears when we finally come to a stop at a pair of double doors. The nurse moves to stand in front of me with a sad smile and retrieves a small bottle of sanitizer from her pocket. She puts a small amount into my palms and I massage the liquid into my hands, ensuring every inch of skin has been covered.

"Okay, before we go in I need to warn you that when you see your daughter it will be a shock, but you have to remember that the tubes you see are there to save her life, they will not harm her. The sounds from the machines are alarming at first, but you'll get used to them after a while." She pauses briefly before asking, "Are you ready?"

She looks to me, expecting some type of verbal response, but all I can do is sob. She pushes me through the double doors and wheels me to my baby girl. Even though the nurse just warned me about what I would see, it doesn't stop me from slamming my hands over my mouth in shock.

"I know, sweetheart. I know it's upsetting," she whispers softly while placing her hand to my back, patting me gently against my hospital gown.

Upsetting? Is this woman serious? This is the worst moment of my life.

I continue to quietly sob as I take in every detail of my daughter. She's so tiny … she can't be much bigger than the size of my hand. She is naked except for the diaper that covers nearly every inch of her small body. Her body looks almost transparent; you can see the network of blood vessels underlining her skin. She is on her back, one of her tube covered arms flat beside her tiny body, and the other arm is bent with her little hand covering her face. That arm is covered with a bandage, a white foam board holding it horizontal. She has a breathing tube in her mouth with strapping that sits just below her nose and across her cheeks, keeping the tube in place. I look down her body and notice she has two blue pads with tubes coming out placed on her protruding chest and two separate long thin tubes coming from her belly button.

The nurse holds out a box of tissues in front of me. I smile up to her sadly as I accept a tissue and begin to wipe my eyes.

3

"I'm sorry, I must look such a mess," I mumble mid-sob.

"It's okay, sweetheart. I can't even begin to imagine what you must be going through. Would you like a glass of water?"

I can only nod, the lump in my throat restricting my speech. She holds out a plastic cup of water and I immediately start chugging it. After a couple of minutes, I begin to calm down and the rational side of me starts to slowly return.

"Sorry ... I ... this ... it's just a bit of a shock," I say, feeling over-whelmed with my surroundings and the sight of my daughter. The nurse nods politely at me.

"I understand. It is very daunting. Let me give you a little run down, it might ease your nerves a little. The tube you see in her mouth is called an endotracheal tube, and that is attached to the ventilator. It helps blow supplementary oxygen gently into her lungs. Because your baby is un-developed and immature, she becomes tired and stops breathing more easily, so the ventilator support is essential at this stage as it takes the pressure off her. The ventilator gives two types of pressures that help her to breathe. The PIP, which stands for Peak Inspiratory Pressure, inflates the lungs, and the PEEP, which stands for Positive End Expiratory Pres-sure, helps keep her lungs open and prevents them from collapsing."

She pauses for a brief moment before proceeding. "Did the doctor explain how your daughter has Infant Respiratory Distress Syndrome?" I nod, remembering the conversation I had with a neonatologist earli-er in the evening. "She was given surfactant replacement in her lungs within the first two hours of her life and her lung capacity has improved dramatically. It is likely she won't need the power of the ventilator for much longer."

I gasp in shock. "Will she be able to breathe on her own?" I frown at the realization of that. Surely that can't be right. "I mean she is still so tiny."

"No. She will still need consistent help with her breathing during her development. When her lungs are strong enough not to need the strength of the ventilator we will put her onto the CPAP, which stands for Continuous Positive Airway Pressure." I nod as I allow the informa-tion to sink in.

"You see the monitor to your left?" I glance over to a vital sign monitor and notice how the lines continuously move across the screen.

"That monitors her heart and respiratory rate, pulse, blood pressure and oxygen saturations. As you can see, she has two umbilical lines coming from her navel."

She opens up the door to the portholes of the incubator, then places her hands within the small space and gently takes apart my daughter's diaper. She points to two individual umbilical lines. "One is an umbilical arterial catheter which measures arterial blood pressure and allows arterial blood sampling. The second line is an umbilical venous catheter where she is given the intravenous fluids and medication." The nurse follows her finger along another wire that is passed through the nose. "And this line here is a nasogastric feeding tube. The thin tube is passed up the nose, down the esophagus and into the stomach. At the moment she isn't strong enough to feed through conventional methods, so she will be given her nutrition and oral medication through this tube until she is strong enough for the breast or bottle."

I stare at my daughter, dumbfounded at all of the information I have had to take in, in such a short amount of time. I feel even more overwhelmed than I did when I first walked in. It's all too much. Panic begins to squeeze heavily against my chest, and it makes it almost impossible for me to breathe as more tears continue to run down my face.

How did this fucking happen? I took all of the vitamins, did the regular yoga, everything that I was advised to do. I didn't even indulge in a glass of wine for Christ's sake. I was the perfect mother to be. How could this have happened?

"This is all my fault, but I don't understand how, I did everything right … I did everything right … I don't understand …" I gasp as sobs wrack through me. I continue to fight for each breath I take and through my panic I grip tightly to my gown, clenching it through with my fingers, trying to gasp for air, grasping for something, anything.

The nurse kneels down beside me and places her hand against my arm with her gentle touch. "Oh, sweetheart, this isn't your fault. You can't blame yourself. Your baby needs you to be strong. She needs her mommy. Do you hear me? I understand how upsetting this is but you need to focus on the fact that she is here and fighting for her life. She is in the best place at the moment. Of course, it's no womb, but we are definitely the next best thing. Just have faith. We are doing everything in our power to keep her alive," she says with a quiet hush.

Surprisingly, I begin to calm down. "Okay. Strong. Best place. Have faith. I can do that," I say, repeating the words as a chanting mantra through my head, over and over again. When I look at the nurse, I notice she is staring directly at me, awaiting an answer. "I'm sorry, did you say something?"

"Would you like to be alone with your daughter, Ava?"

"Yes, please. Thank you."

I watch my daughter in awe, taking in her delicate little hands as they slowly stretch, changing direction trying to get into a comfortable position. Once I'm alone, I wheel myself closer to her. My breath catches as her little toes wriggle slightly, and she kicks her legs out to the side. This happens two more times before she finds a comfortable position and stills. She looks so peaceful, so fragile, but at the same time strong. I can see that she is already a little fighter, and it's breathtaking.

"Hey, baby," I whisper. I'm not quite sure if she can hear me or not but that doesn't stop me from talking. "I'm your momma. You've put me through a lot during the past sixteen hours, baby girl, but that's okay. I'm sorry, baby. I wish more than anything that you were still inside of me, keeping you safe, but it's okay. We can make it work. I've tried to call Daddy, but he's fighting the bad guys so you won't get to meet him for a while yet. He'll be devastated that he missed this."

I bite down on my bottom lip and force the tears back, contemplating where her daddy is right now. I already knew he wouldn't be here for the birth, but it still kills me that he doesn't know his daughter has been born. I am unable to gain strength of my tears and the vicious circle of crying begins.

Sebastian is on a nine-month tour in Afghanistan. It's his third tour. He is a front line infantry officer. He has been there for four months already, so I still don't get to see him for another five months. That's five months without seeing his daughter. It was hard to accept when I thought he would be away for the first two months of her life, but now it's even worse. It feels like a life sentence. I just wish I didn't have to do this alone, without him. I miss him so damn much. I need him desperately. I called the American Red Cross earlier on, and they are currently trying to relay a message to Sebastian over in Afghanistan, but they told me it could take between twenty-four to forty-eight hours. I hate how I have to wait, but I don't have any other choice. It isn't as if I can call

6

him on his cell. I'm lucky if I get to speak to him once a week and even then it's brief.

I hadn't planned to have the birth alone. My best friend, Caleb, was supposed to be my birthing partner but as luck would have it, he was flying over the Atlantic Ocean for a business trip to London. I managed to get hold of him when I was in labor, and he is currently on standby for a flight back to the states. I wanted to tell him not to rush back, but when the tears forced through, I realized I needed him.

I'm startled when a doctor in a white coat joins me and takes hold of my daughter's chart. My heart is pounding in my chest, and it takes me a moment to compose myself. When I look up, I can't keep my eyes off him. He has the most unusual green eyes I have ever seen.

"I'm Dr. Bailey, one of your daughter's neonatologists."

"Hi," I say with a small smile.

He crouches down to the wheelchair level, and I can't ignore the patter of my heart, beating a little faster when he does. I didn't realize doctors could be so good-looking, or so young for that matter. He honestly can't be any older than thirty.

"I'm going to try and keep the medical jargon to a minimum. I know you've been through a lot, so this will be brief. Your daughter is stable, doing brilliantly. She has responded well to the surfactant replacement, and her breathing is improving remarkably. Her X-rays confirm that. Her blood pressure is normal for her gestation. She is, however, showing early signs of jaundice."

He pauses on a sympathetic smile. "In simple terms, the liver produces a yellow chemical called bilirubin. Bilirubin is a waste product of the breakdown of red blood cells, and in preemies they seem to accumulate more red blood cells than your average person. Because they have an immature liver and kidneys, it prevents them from breaking the bilirubin down efficiently, therefore, producing the jaundice and causing the skin to have yellow pigmentation. It can be fatal if not treated, so we're going to keep a close eye on her for the next twenty-four to seventy-two hours. If her bilirubin level continues to rise we will proceed with phototherapy, which will help dissolve the bilirubin and change it from fat-soluble to water soluble so that it's able to be excreted through the urine and the stools."

He stands, and I continue to stare at him, dumfounded at the information. My mind is in such a whirlwind that it's quite possible I will forget what he said in a couple of minutes time.

"I'm going to examine her now, take a blood sample and check her vitals, and then I'll be out of your hair." He smiles down at me before turning towards my daughter and opening up her medical chart.

"That's okay, I don't mind," I state softly, finally finding my voice as I follow my gaze from him to my daughter. I can see Dr. Bailey from the corner of my eye as he sets her chart back into the little pouch on the side of her incubator, and then goes to work by opening the small isolette doors on the incubator. Soon enough he begins to draw blood from her umbilical catheter, and it makes me wince slightly. I've never been great with the sight of blood.

"Have you thought of any names for Baby Jacobson?" he asks as he continues drawing blood, obviously trying to help fill up the silence.

"Um, no … it all happened a bit too quickly." *What kind of mother am I?* I haven't even come up with a name for my daughter, and I have absolutely no idea what the hell I'm supposed to call her. My tears begin to fall again.

"I didn't mean to make you cry, I'm sorry," he says sincerely. He takes the tube of blood and shuts the doors to the incubator, reaching over to pass me a tissue.

"It's fine," I say breathlessly through a sob as I accept a tissue. "It's just a sore subject. I've been like this all day." I wave my hand in front of my face as if it isn't a big deal.

It is.

It's a huge deal.

"Your body has been through a lot. It's normal to feel all of these emotions, and as for the names, you're not the only one. My sister-in-law was exactly the same. It took her about four weeks to decide on a name for my nephew." He smirks. "What I'm trying to say is you shouldn't be so hard on yourself. The name will come, and if not, Baby Jacobson isn't so bad." He raises his eyebrows. "It's better than Stir Mix-a-Lot, which was my nephew's nickname for four weeks straight."

I don't know how he does it, but he manages to get a bubble of laughter out of me. It's the first feeling of happiness I've had since before I gave birth to my baby girl. "Seriously? As in Sir Mix-a-Lot?" I ask, wiping my runny nose as delicately as possible with the tissue.

"As wrong as it sounds, yes. She changed the Sir to Stir as he was a very wriggly baby."

I smile up at him before looking back at my daughter. She is currently stretching her left arm with her tiny fingers wriggling around.

"It seems you got yourself a wriggler too. She looks as if she is trying to reach out to you." He points towards her arm that has gone all opera style with her stretching.

"You think so?" I ask, through a smile.

"Oh yeah, definitely. She says so herself." I can't help but I choke on another laugh when her forefinger curls up, as if she were beckoning me towards her. "I wish I could hold her, even if it's just to hold her hand," I say, looking intently at her.

"Well, it's a little too early to hold her, but you can definitely hold her hand."

"Really?" I graze my hand over the plastic of her incubator.

He unclips the porthole to the incubator and opens the door. "Well, as long as your hands are well sanitized, to avoid any infection for your baby, then you're good to go."

I move my arm upwards a little apprehensively and place my hand through the porthole. I look back up towards Dr. Bailey to ensure I'm doing it correctly. With a nod of encouragement from him, I look back towards my beautiful daughter and gently graze my finger within the base of her hand. I stroke it in delicate circles until she grasps my finger so tightly I actually gasp in shock.

"Baby girl, you're so strong," I say through uncontrollable tears. I can't believe it. I'm actually holding my daughter's hand, and it feels incredible. After a short while my eyes become such a blurred mess that I have to remove my hand from the incubator so I don't poke her in the eye or something. I gently close the door and turn the latch securely in place. I glance back up to the doctor and smile.

"Thank you," I whisper, in awe. He has quickly become my favorite person. He has made my day just that little more bearable and he even managed to put a smile on my face.

"No problem."

His gaze lasts a little bit longer than is usually regarded as socially acceptable; his eyes are so bright and beautiful that I could get lost in them for hours. His hand touches my shoulder, and he lingers for a few

9

seconds with a soft squeeze before walking away, leaving me winded and quite possibly electrified. His touch was like wildfire. The moment his fingers touched my shoulder my entire body almost exploded.

After a short while of just gazing contently at my baby girl, the nurse who brought me in comes back. "Sorry to interrupt, doll, but we should really get you back to your room. It's been a long day and you need your rest. Plus, your midwife said you're having trouble expressing your breast milk, so she wants to see if you have more success the second time round."

I was advised for the first forty-eight hours that I needed to hand express my breast milk rather than express from a pump, so I tried earlier on. I don't know if it was the stress of today or because I am so exhausted, but I couldn't express a drop. I've been told that breast milk is better than formula for premature babies as it helps with nutrition and can provide antibodies from infections, and I'm absolutely devastated that my daughter will have to use donated breast milk until I can express my own. My body is letting me down again.

I press my fingers to my lips and linger them against the incubator, just where my baby girl's head is resting. "Bye, baby. I'll be back soon. Momma needs some rest. I love you so much … keep fighting for your momma, please." I weep as the nurse wheels me out of NICU and towards my room.

When I get settled back into my bed, the midwife assists with my hand expressing, and even though it's still a struggle I manage to express a little. I hope with a good night's sleep I can express more because I don't know how much more of this I can handle, my body rejecting everything.

The nurse leaves me to get some sleep, and as I allow sleep to evade me, the phone I have clutched in my hand alerts me to a text message. I smile when I see it's from Caleb.

**Caleb**: *I've just boarded. I have a connecting flight into Dallas, then Dallas to Seattle, but I will be with you as soon as I can. Love you. XXX*

# chapter 2

SOFT STROKING AGAINST MY hair shakes me out of my sleep. Slowly, I open my eyes and see Caleb looking down at me with a precious smile, his fingers lingering on my cheek.

"Caleb," I croak, rubbing my fingers against my eyes.

"Hey, sweetheart," he delicately whispers. I begin to sit up in my bed when I'm brought to a halt as pain shoots across my stomach, leaving me a little out of breath. "Are you okay? Should I get a nurse?" His eyes widen with worry.

"I'm fine, it's just my stomach. It fucking kills." I clutch my arms around my stomach as I fully sit up.

"You're really okay?"

"I am now you're here." I give a half smile as my eyes fill with the build-up of tears and my chin trembles with the essence of my emotion. "I'm so glad to see you. You don't understand how hard ..."

I gulp to try and remove the lump that seems to have become a permanent fixture in my throat. My mind goes back to yesterday, and it hits me with a vengeance. "How... hard yesterday was ... I ..."

Suddenly, something inside of me snaps with anger, an anger that I didn't realize had risen to the surface. "You know what, Caleb? I fucking needed you and you weren't here!" I cry at the top of my voice, my throat crackling like sandpaper. "I gave birth to my baby on my own! I needed you here."

I slap him across his chest, the weight behind my hits striking hard and forceful as I continue to treat him like my own personal punch bag. "My fucking waters broke, and you were over the Atlantic fucking Ocean! You were supposed to be here!"

My screams become muffled in Caleb's chest as he grabs hold of me, wrapping his warm arms around my body. The hysterical tears fall down my cheeks, and I try to push him away, desperately trying to ignore the ball of fire that is currently shooting across my stomach, but his strong grip won't let me. I scream into his chest. I don't mean to take my anger out on him, but my emotion knows no bounds. Every inch of my body is trembling as I continue to claw against him.

"Let me go!"

The bed dips as I feel him straddle my legs, pinning me in place, trying to calm me down. It doesn't work. In fact, it makes me even more furious. "Get it out, get it out, baby," he encourages, rocking me back and forth in a steady rhythm as the anger continues to course through my body.

"Fuck you!"

The screams are eventually replaced with hyperventilating cries, then the cries slowly subside to allow for the hiccups and, finally, everything is silent. Once Caleb knows I have calmed down he repositions himself so he is on his back, with my head against his chest and his arm wrapped around me. His hand lazily draws shapes along my back.

"I'm sorry," I say, the whisper so quiet I almost think he hasn't even heard me.

"You have nothing to be sorry about." His lips linger in my hair.

"I know, but you didn't deserve that. None of this is your fault." The guilt of my behavior simmers around in my stomach and I feel terrible.

"I'm your best friend. If you need me to be your punching bag, then that's what I'll be."

I sigh contently, gripping hold of him more tightly, wanting to enjoy the closeness for a little while. He really is amazing. I love him so much. I would have married him if he didn't prefer men.

"When did you get here?"

"My flight landed about two hours ago. I would've been here sooner, but I went to your place first to grab you a few things. I brought some sweatpants, PJ's, some underwear, your phone-charger, and some toiletries."

I sit up from his embrace, hissing out in pain as I do. "Thanks, Caleb. Speaking of toiletries, I could really do with a shower. I feel gross." Caleb is up on his feet to help me out of bed before I've even finished my sentence. "Hold up, speedy. Could you get me a nurse? I'm not sure if I can get my stomach wet yet."

"Okay, I'll be back in a sec." He exits the room, but as fate would have it, a nurse enters moments later. Thankfully the nurse will allow me to have a shower as long as I don't get water directly over my caesarean wound.

After, I dress in a pair of loose lounge pants and a comfortable sweatshirt. Caleb is currently braiding my wet hair while I sit on the edge of the bed, clutching my agonizing stomach.

"Have you managed to contact Sebastian yet?"

His question suddenly becomes a red alert. How long was I asleep for? Shouldn't Sebastian have gotten the message by now? Panic circles through my veins as I picture bad scenario after bad scenario in my head. Shit, what if something has happened to him and he doesn't even know about his daughter? *Fuck no ...*

"Ava, what's wrong?" I can hear Caleb, but he sounds distant. Disastrous images invade my mind, and I begin to feel nauseous and light-headed. A cold sweat breaks out over my body, and before I understand what's happening I'm suddenly lying down on the bed with a panic-stricken Caleb standing over me and a doctor with a flashlight shining in my eyes.

"Miss Jacobson, can you hear me?"

I recognize the velvety strong voice, but I struggle to figure out who it is. I follow the sound with my eyes until I come across a pair of incredible green eyes, the same body tingling green eyes I saw yesterday. Strange. He's my daughter's doctor, not mine. I don't understand why he's here.

"Dr. ..."

I rack my brain, trying to remember his name, but absolutely nothing comes to me. *Jesus, what the hell is wrong with me?*

"Dr. Bailey, we met yesterday. Do you remember me?"

13

How could I not? His gaze is quite hypnotic. Wow, those eyes. They are really distracting. What did he ask me again?

"Um, yeah ... you're the doctor with the pretty eyes." Did I just say what I think I said? Oh my God. I can hear quiet chuckling, and I desperately wish the ground would swallow me up. I'm mortified.

"So, Miss Jacobson, you took a bit of a funny turn. How are you feeling?" he asks, not once looking away from me. How does he know my name? I think back to what caused my dizzy spell ...

"I um, I think it was a panic attack ... I, um ..." The horror of the thoughts that had consumed my mind earlier begins its continuous loop of devastation again, making me feel light-headed.

"Ava stay with me. Your panic attack, what's happening?"

"Sebastian ... Sebastian is hurt ... they have him ... they're going to kill him ... but he doesn't know about her yet ... my baby girl ... he can't die yet ... I need him ... she needs him ... he can't die ..."

Everything goes black.

I can hear voices begin to stir through my mind as consciousness slowly sweeps back in, but my eyes are too heavy to open. The two voices sound familiar, warm and comforting. It immediately relaxes me.

"Is Sebastian her husband?" says voice number one. I think it's Dr. Bailey.

"No, he's her boyfriend. He's currently in Afghanistan," says voice number two. Caleb. That is definitely Caleb.

"Oh, I see."

"It's his third tour. She hasn't taken it very well, what with the pregnancy, and it isn't exactly easy for her to get a hold of him. I'm worried. She isn't herself, she's having panic attacks, passing out, something I don't think she has ever done in her entire life."

Did I really pass out? Jesus, my body won't give me a break.

"This screaming, out of control Ava is not the Ava I know. She's usually much stronger than this."

*What the hell, Caleb?* It's one thing admitting your own flaws, but it's another hearing them come out of somebody else's mouth. Especially when that mouth belongs to your best friend.

"She's been through a lot during the past thirty-two hours. Her body has been through something traumatic and she seems to be under a lot of stress. I'd say her behavior is absolutely normal."

"Really? So this is normal? She'll be fine?"

"Yes, of course, she will be. Her body is in shock, so we just need to let her rest ..."

Sleep begins to pull me under again, and I'm unable to hear anything else that is said between Caleb and Dr. Bailey.

I gradually wake up after what seems like a century of sleeping. I notice a sleeping Caleb with his head resting against the edge of my bed, his hand tightly wrapped around mine. He must be exhausted. *The poor thing.* I remove my hand to stroke gently through his hair, but with a sudden start he jerks his head backwards, looking around the room as he frantically tries to find his bearings. After a short moment of trying to work out where the hell he is, his eyes finally fall on me, and a small smile lifts from his lips.

"Hey, you're awake. How are you feeling?" he asks through mid-yawn, covering his mouth with his hand.

"I'm okay, I think ..." In fact, come to think of it, I have no idea how I'm feeling. It's bizarre. It's as though I'm not in control of my emotions. One minute I'm okay but then the next I'm turning into a raging bitch. My mind and body are a walking contradiction. "I don't know," I answer honestly.

"Well, you look a little bit better, but you have to stop scaring the shit out of me like that. That's twice in a matter of thirty-six hours. I can't cope with anymore." He slides his hand into mine again, giving it a gentle squeeze, then smiles warmly at me. "I have some good news for you."

I have no idea what good news he might have. In fact, what good news could I possibly have? My life in the past God knows how many hours has been a series of bad luck after bad luck. It couldn't get any fucking worse, that's for sure. Oh, Sebastian. Oh shit, Sebastian.

"Did Sebastian call?" I ask, my voice rising with hope.

Caleb smiles. "Yeah, he did. So you can stop with your panic because he is absolutely fine."

"Did you speak to him? What did you say? What did he say? Why didn't you wake me when he called?" I raise my voice, anger crashing through my body like a tidal wave.

"The doctor gave me strict instructions to let you sleep."

"But I needed to speak to him! I wanted to speak to him …" My voice trembles.

"I know you did, but you also needed your rest. You've been through so much."

"I know, I'm sorry." My anger simmers away as I clutch his hand. "So what did you tell him? Does he know about the baby?"

"Yeah, I told him everything. He was absolutely devastated, especially the part about you being on your own during the birth."

My eyes fill with overwhelmed tears. This is why I wanted to speak to him. "Oh God," I say, gasping for air, wiping away tears that are falling down my face. "What did he say?"

"Nothing. He broke down."

He cried? In the four years I have been with him, not once has he cried in front of me. The tears fall recklessly as I picture him breaking down.

"Afterwards, Sebastian said he was going to try and come home on emergency leave, although it can be quite difficult to get emergency leave within his unit, but he said he'd try his hardest to come home." Caleb gives me a sad smile. The possibility of Sebastian being able to come home on leave lifts my spirits slightly. I miss him unbearably. "But I told him if he couldn't get the time off, I would be with you every step of the way so that you won't be alone. And you won't, Ava. You know I have your back, don't you?"

"Yeah, I know. Your goddaughter and I need you." I smile as I bring his hand to my mouth, kissing his knuckles softly.

"Goddaughter?" he utters in shock, flabbergasted by my words.

"Yes, of course. You're my best friend."

"Ava … I … I … fucking love you." He almost jumps on top of me, hugging the life out of me, which evidently causes my stapled stomach to burn straight across the incision. He must feel me flinch because he suddenly pulls away, his smile fading with worry. "Shit. Is that hurting you?" Thankfully, the pain subsides the moment he pulls away.

"I'm okay. So are you happy to take the role of her godfather then?"

Having godparents for any child of mine isn't something I ever thought about. I'm not particularly religious, but the thought of having Caleb as my daughter's godfather makes me happy. I know Caleb would be like a second father to her.

"Happy? I'm ecstatic. You've made me the happiest man alive!" He slams his pouted lips onto mine enthusiastically. "Can we go and see her now? I've been dying to see her since I arrived."

I squint with confusion. "What do you mean? Haven't you seen her yet?" I can feel my heart rate thump faster as rage begins to flood my veins.

"No."

"Not even when I was asleep?" If this is true, I'm going to hit the fucking roof.

"No. I asked, but the nurses said I weren't allowed to go in without you."

"Are you fucking kidding me?" I scramble around the bed, trying to find the buzzer to get a nurse in here, stat. I impatiently press my thumb over and over again until a nurse rushes into the room with a frantic look across her face.

"Ava, it's fine," Caleb says, his eyes narrowing on mine, urging me not to make a scene.

"It is not fine!" I roar, throwing the bed sheets off me, staring daggers at the nurse, even though it isn't even her fault. I didn't exactly explain my situation to them properly, but I don't care, I'm on a roll. If only looks could kill.

"What's the matter, sweetheart?"

"This hospital is the matter." I try to tone my attitude down, but it's no use, I'm too angry. "Caleb told me the hospital refused him access into the NICU to see my daughter, is that right?"

Her eyes widen with shock. I think she is a little scared of me. I'd be scared of me too. Well, this neurotic version of me anyway. "Um … well, yes. All visitors have to be accompanied by a parent."

"Well, let's get something straight here, okay? The dad, my partner, is currently in Afghanistan, fighting for this country, your country. The only person I have in my life right now is Caleb, my daughter's godfather, so he needs to be able to have access at all times. Do you understand me?" I stare directly at her, not even blinking. I'm actually a little shocked that I just said that to her. I don't think I've ever been so direct with anybody in my entire life.

"Of-of course, I will have the NICU informed." She hurries out of my room.

"Well, I think you made her cry," Caleb says with a smirk when we hear her wailing down the corridor.

"I don't care. She hasn't just had a baby who is currently in the NICU. I have other things to worry about than some sensitive nurse who can't handle her patients."

I slide my legs over the side of the bed, avoiding any quick movements, and slowly stand. "Will you take me to see my daughter?"

# chapter 3

**M**Y DAUGHTER TAKES MY breath away.

The moment I enter her room in the NICU, my heart misses a beat and my entire body fills with love as I walk over to her, not once able to take my eyes off her. It's a love I really can't put my finger on. It's overwhelming, it's precious, and it's unconditional. The moment she entered my life the love overpowered me, and I don't ever want to lose her. Now that I've met her, I need her in my life so much that it physically hurts with the thought of her not being in my future. She has to survive this. She has to.

There is a luminous blue light shining directly down on top of her and her eyes are covered with a white clinical eye mask. The mask looks small enough to fit a china doll. A small bout of panic rises from me until I remember what Dr. Bailey said about the phototherapy treatment for her jaundice. Her bilirubin levels must have risen since the last time I saw her. A vacant time spent passing out and screaming at innocent nurses. Oh God.

Once I relax, I turn to an unusually quiet Caleb. I look up at him as he stares down at my baby girl with tears rolling down his face. "Are you crying?" I ask, smiling up at him.

"No," he states sharply. It would have been convincing if he weren't wiping the tears away with his fingers. "I have allergies."

I can't help but laugh. I know tears when I see them, and those are real, emotional tears. "Whatever you say." I grip his hand and pull him closer to the incubator to introduce him to my daughter.

He gasps as he finally gets a closer look at her. "She's so beautiful and tiny," he says, his voice trembling as he takes everything in.

"I know." I gulp, trying to blink the tears back.

"She looks just like you."

I look intently at my daughter, trying to see the resemblance, but I can't. It doesn't help that the mask is currently obstructing her face. "Really? I don't see it," I muse as I continue to take in every single detail of her.

"Oh yeah, she's perfect, just like her momma," he says, not looking away from my daughter.

This time, they're happy tears that fall down my cheeks. I edge closer to Caleb, wrapping my arms around his waist, and nuzzling my head against his chest. We stay like this for a while, just gazing at her, taking in every little perfect thing about her. Her perfect little hands, her perfect little skinny legs, her perfect little toes, her perfect little face, just her perfect little everything. I know every parent says that his or her child is perfect, but mine really is. She may not have fully reached her normal gestational age, but to me that doesn't matter. What matters is getting her healthy and strong so we can take her home. It will be a long journey to recovery, but I will be with her every step of the way.

"Hey, baby girl, this is your Uncle Caleb."

"Hey, baby," Caleb says, smiling down at her in absolute awe. Wow, my daughter has already gotten him wrapped around her little finger.

After having stood up for a while, I start to feel a burning pressure at the top of my thighs. I release my arms from Caleb's warm hold and take a seat in the rocking chair beside the incubator. Caleb's eyes follow my movement. "You okay?"

"Yeah, I'm just feeling a little tired."

"Do you want to head back?"

I shake my head. I have been in that room for long enough. "No, I just want to sit here for a while." Caleb presses a gentle kiss against the top of my head then tells me he's going to use the restroom and find an extra chair from somewhere.

I admire my daughter from my seat. I can't get over how perfect she is. If it were possible, I would happily gaze at her perfect features for the rest of my life.

A shiver suddenly tingles down my spine, and even before he has stepped into the room, I can sense him. I keep still, barely able to catch my breath as I wait for him to approach. Thirty seconds pass and nothing happens but I know he's still behind me. I tell myself not to turn around. I tell myself to focus on my daughter, but it becomes next to impossible when my heart starts to defy me, pounding away in my chest. I painfully want to look into those brilliant green eyes of his, and the urge only becomes more prominent until I finally cave in. I glance back and I see him leaning against the door frame, his arms crossed over his chest as he looks straight at me, a look that makes my heart beat faster.

"Hi," I squeak, unable to take my eyes away from him. He is ridiculously good looking with dark hair, strong jaw line, light stubble, a dimpled chin and wonderfully plump lips. Plump lips I can't resist taking a second glance at. They look strangely inviting.

"Hi, Miss Jacobson," he says in his strong southern accent that takes my breath away. "I'm sorry, I didn't mean to disturb you." He walks into the room, closing the gap between us. As he walks towards me, the heat in the room suddenly fills and I almost gasp for air as he stands in front of me. It's uncomfortable, to say the least.

"It's okay, you're not disturbing me. And please, you can call me Ava."

He nods, his smile growing. "How are you feeling now, Ava?"

I cringe as I remember telling him he had pretty eyes. "Yeah, I'm okay. Well, I think I am. It's kind of hard to tell lately. I'd definitely keep your distance though," I say in mock warning.

"And why's that?" He raises an eyebrow, a frown appearing on his face, obviously intrigued by my comment. That's when I notice the light freckles over his nose. Surprisingly, it makes him look even sexier.

"Because apparently I like to abuse the staff in this place."

He chuckles, shaking his head, his smile spreading. "Oh yeah, I heard about that. You made one of the nurses cry, am I right?"

"Well, I didn't, the psychotic version of me did. The rational version of me wouldn't have overreacted like that. In fact, the rational version of me would like to slap the psychotic version for behaving that way. I'm not usually so forward," I confess, then shut the hell up when I realize I am babbling crap. It's a trait I have when I'm nervous.

"I wouldn't worry about it. She isn't a very nice person. She's actually ... a bitch," he whispers the last part, causing me to laugh out loud.

"Well, in that case," I sputter through laughter, "is there anybody else you would like me to unleash my verbal diarrhea on? I'm probably due a few more psychotic episodes. It's only a matter of time."

"Actually, there is this one nurse ..." He leans over, his mouth inches away from my ear. I can't help the shiver that tingles across my skin at his sudden proximity. "Who works in orthopedics, and when she thinks nobody is looking, she picks her nose and doesn't sanitize her hands afterwards." He pulls back on a smirk. I gulp nervously, feeling as if he has just told me the world's dirtiest secret.

"So by all means, you can head over to that department during your next episode and give her a lecture on personal hygiene." He gives me a hearty laugh, almost causing me to choke on my own saliva. That has to be one of the most beautiful sounds I have ever heard. Once his laughter subsides, he takes a moment to look at me, and I have a hard time taking my next breath. I look away when his gaze becomes too intense and cough nervously.

"How is she?" I ask.

This shakes him from his reverie, and his professional doctoral mask is quickly put back in place. "Her IRDS is improving, her oxygen and respiratory rate are stable. As discussed yesterday, her bilirubin levels took a turn for the worse and we had to proceed with the phototherapy. It's still early days, but she's doing okay. I'm going to check her vitals, do some bloods, and I'll leave you to enjoy your time with your daughter, but first I have a little gift for you."

*A gift?*

I give him a bewildered look as I try to figure out what it could be. That makes absolutely no sense. I barely know him. "For me?"

"Yeah." Smiling, he reaches into the pocket of his white coat and retrieves a small book, handing it over to me. I purposely avoid touching his hand with my own. I don't know how many more surprises I can handle from this beautiful stranger, and I certainly don't want to add to it, especially when I know how electrifying his touch is. It's too much. He's too much. I glance down at the book and smile.

"It's a book of baby names. I know you're having trouble coming up with a name for Baby Jacobson, or Miss Stir Mix-a-Lot," he says with a wink, "so I thought this book would be great for you."

This is one of the nicest things anyone has ever done for me, let alone a man I just met, a stranger.

"Wow, I, um, thank you," I say, struggling to find the right words, truly touched at such a thoughtful gesture.

"It's no problem, honestly." He shrugs nonchalantly. I look back down at the miniature book in my hand, and that's when I notice how pristine it looks. I turn it around and gasp when I see a price sticker on the back. He must have gone to a bookstore to buy this for me. When a person gives me a gift they usually want something in return, but with the look of sincerity I can see in his eyes, I know the gift is purely out of the kindness of his own heart.

"Thank you," I repeat, not really knowing what else to say, humbled by his sweet gesture. With a small smile, he reaches for my daughter's vital chart and turns his attention to her.

I clutch the small book of names with my fingers and watch as he checks my daughter's vitals. Caleb returns with a chair in tow. He places it beside me and takes a seat, his eyes watching Dr. Bailey warily. "Is everything okay?" Caleb questions.

"Yeah, everything's fine. The doctor is just doing her vital checks and a blood sample."

"Okay," he sighs with relief as he kisses my temple. When he pulls away from me, he notices the book clasped in my hand. He points at it as an intrigued smile spreads across his face. "Hey, what's that?"

I lift the book and pass it over to him. "It's a baby book of names, one of the ... um, nurses gave it to me." I'm not quite sure why I lie. It isn't like Dr. Bailey means anything to me. I've only just met the guy. It's just a gift. No big deal ...

My eyes shoot up to Dr. Bailey. He briefly turns to me, a smirk pulled up at the corner of his mouth. I blush furiously when he winks at me discreetly before turning back around. My heart flutters inside my chest.

"Oh awesome. Let's see if we can pick a name for my gorgeous goddaughter." He starts to flip through the pages, rolling off some names while my eyes stay solely on the back of Dr. Bailey's head, trying to understand what the hell just happened. I lose myself within my own thoughts until I'm momentarily brought back to my senses when I hear Dr. Bailey's voice through the haze.

"I'm all finished. I'll be out of your hair now." A shiver prickles its way down my spine when he brushes past me, and I gaze at him in awe as he walks away until I'm just gazing into thin air. Taking a calming breath, I turn my attention back to Caleb, desperately trying to ignore the uneasy feeling in the pit of my stomach.

During the next hour, Caleb looks through the list of baby names. However, we don't find any names I like so instead we joke around, trying to find the most outrageous names known to man; names that you wouldn't ever dream of naming your own child and if you did your child would likely be beaten to a pulp until the day they turned eighteen. Caleb did say if I named my baby after any fruit, city or cartoon character, he would disown me and have me handed over to child protective services.

There are a lot of lovely names such as Olivia, Rebecca or Megan, but those names just don't feel right for my daughter. I want something special. I want something that is out of the ordinary, but isn't ridiculously unusual. I want something that will represent the person she will grow up to be. I just don't know what that name should be.

The soft sound of snoring jolts me from my thoughts, which is an unusual sound in the NICU. I turn to my left and notice Caleb is the culprit. He is upright in his seat with his head resting uncomfortably against his shoulder, fast asleep. Oh God. He must be absolutely exhausted and probably hasn't slept for about thirty-six hours. Maybe more. I have no concept of time at all. In fact, what day is it? I have no idea if it's Saturday or Sunday. Heck, it could be Monday for all I know. I really don't want to wake him but sleeping in that position isn't going to be beneficial for his posture, and I don't think the nurses would be at all pleased with having a grown man asleep in their NICU. He needs to go home.

"Caleb," I whisper, trying to get his attention, but it's like trying to wake up a corpse. "Caleb," I whisper louder, this time punching his arm. He nearly gives himself whiplash as he wakes up with a start.

"Whoa, what?"

His disorientation makes me chuckle. "You fell asleep."

He calms down slightly, smiling weakly at me. "Oh, sorry. I didn't even realize."

"It's okay, but you need to go home and get some sleep. You're exhausted."

"No, I'm fine, honestly," he says while trying to cover up a yawn.

"Yeah, of course you are," I mutter. "Please just go home. You look like crap." That's a lie, I don't think it is ever possible for him to look like crap. He is too damn pretty.

"I don't want you to be on your own I can sleep in the chair in your room. Honestly, I don't mind."

"Yeah, but I mind. You need a good night's sleep in your own bed. Go home. I'm just going to sleep when I get back to the room, I'm beat," I lie, knowing I probably won't be able to sleep for hours yet.

"Are you sure?"

"Yes! Now let's go before I change my mind."

We say goodbye to my daughter, and once he helps me to my room, he pulls me into a hug. We don't say anything as we hold each other. His warmth has always been comforting and in a moment like this is when I cherish it the most, especially when he is all I have at the moment. He finally pulls away, and presses a kiss against my temple, his thumbs stroking delicately against my cheeks. "If you need anything just call me, okay?"

I definitely will *not* be calling him for anything, my boy needs his sleep, but I won't tell him that. If I do, he'll never leave.

"Okay, I will." He reluctantly exits the room and I'm left alone, feeling a little out of sorts. I know I should try and get some sleep, but with all the crap going on inside my head, it would just be a lost cause.

Getting into bed, I begin to contemplate the past couple of days. I still don't understand what's happened. Why was my baby born now and not in three months time when she was actually due? I understand the anatomy of what's happened, but what I don't understand is why my body would betray me like that? Is it my fault? My past? Could that have caused the rupture in my uterus?

Through my obsessive thoughts, I somehow manage to fall asleep until the sound of buzzing awakens me. I squint groggily through the darkness over to the bedside cabinet on my right and notice my phone flashing. I move carefully, holding pressure to my stomach with my arm and reach over to retrieve the phone. My heart leaps out of my chest at the name flashing on the screen.

"Sebastian," I sigh breathlessly as I answer.

"Hi, baby," he answers, a mixture of rugged emotion straining through his voice.

"I've missed you so much." It feels so amazing to hear his beautiful voice. It feels as if a lifetime has passed since I last spoke to him only six days ago. A lot has changed since then.

"I miss you too. How are you feeling?"

"I'm okay."

"Really?" Sebastian asks, questioning my honesty.

He's right to doubt me. I'm far from okay. I'm an emotional wreck.

"No." My whisper is barely audible through the receiver as my heart squeezes fist tight with a painful ache and I begin to sob uncontrollably.

"Oh, baby … it's okay, just cry it out. I'm right here."

And that's exactly what I do. I cry, letting out every emotion, crying harder than I have since my baby girl was born. And for five minutes we don't say a word, we just cry out to one another, tears full of pure sadness, hurt and frustration.

"I'm sorry—"

"No, you have nothing to be sorry about, nothing. I'm the one who should be sorry. When your life depended on me the most, I wasn't there for you and you had to go through everything alone. You deserve so much better than that."

Another pain surges through my heart, leaving me gasping for air. It isn't his fault he's not here with me, it is just the way things are. I mean yes, it's been hard without him, and even more so in the past two days. I miss him like crazy, but nobody is to blame.

"I'm no good to you or our baby in a fucking war zone where soldiers just like me are being killed on a daily basis. I am putting my entire life on the line and what happens if I die? Where will that leave you then? I'm a selfish bastard. I've chosen a job over you and our baby, and I've only just recently realized it. And what for, huh? So I can get myself blown up in a war that makes absolutely no sense? Because right now, Ava, it makes no sense to me. Not now that our baby has a fight of her own to battle.

"I don't see the point of continuing if it means being without you for any longer. You and our daughter need me. I'm coming to the end of my reenlistment contract. Once my duty has finished, that's it, I'm not continuing. I can't be away from you anymore. I want to raise our child together. I want to marry you, be your husband, a husband who sees his wife and child every single day without worry that I could be deployed at any moment."

Marriage. Leave the army. Shit.

I close my eyes as I sink further into the bed, trying to make sense of his words. My mind feels as though it's about to explode.

"Ava, are you okay? You haven't said anything," he says after a short while, an apprehensive tremble to his voice.

"I'm just thinking," I say, a little dazed by the sudden information.

"About?"

"That it's a girlfriends fantasy to hear 'I'm leaving the army' while their boyfriend is in Afghanistan. The relief to know they never have to return to a war zone ever again. The relief of knowing that every time the phone rings I won't automatically think it's bad news."

"Exactly, I—"

"But the army has been your life for the past twelve years. It's all you know and if you leave it will absolutely destroy you. We both know that if you hadn't enlisted into the army at the age of eighteen that you wouldn't be here right now."

"Ava—"

"No, let me speak. Back in high school you were a tornado of a mess, spiraling out of control, addicted to drugs, and if it weren't for the army, your first accidental overdose would not have been your last. I just worry that leaving could have a bad effect on you."

I know I'm digging at a painful sore, but if he is considering leaving the army for good, he needs to know what the cost may entail in the long run. Not only did the army save his life, he actually found something he was good at and loves, and it took him a long time to find it. I just don't want him to give it up because of me.

When I say I knew him back in high school, I mean the term loosely. I didn't know him personally; he was a senior, I was a sophomore, and we didn't hang with the same crowds. Plus, he was my brother's friend, so I stayed away. It wasn't until years later when I was celebrating my twenty-fourth birthday in a club in Seattle that we actually met again. It was a bizarre encounter really because we're both originally from Mi-

27

ami, so to see a guy I went to school with, a school on the opposite side of the country, is crazy. I don't usually believe in fate, but that night I was convinced it had to be fate because there was no other explanation.

The memory makes me smile.

The morning after my birthday we had our very first date. He met me outside Denny's restaurant for a breakfast date with a bouquet of pink calla lilies and treated me to a stack of pancakes. That was the day I fell in love with pancakes and calla lilies. It became a monthly ritual after that. Well, it *was* a monthly ritual before he got deployed four months ago.

"Babe, that's not going to happen. I'm not the person I was before."

"I know you're not, but who knows what leaving the army would do to you. I just worry that if you quit you'll eventually hold it against me, and grow to hate me."

"No, I won't. I promise you that won't happen."

"Yes, you will."

"No, I won't."

"How do you know that?"

"Because I just do. I would never put that kind of blame on you."

"You say that now but how can you be sure?"

"Because I love you, and I love our daughter. That's how I can be sure."

"But—"

"But nothing, Ava. I understand your concerns, I do, but I haven't even thought about drugs for years. I haven't wanted to take them, haven't had the urge. It isn't something I would want to do again. I've been thinking about leaving the army at the end of my contract since you told me you were pregnant, but getting a phone message from the American Red Cross saying my girlfriend had given birth to my daughter thirteen weeks early … well, it put everything into perspective. I want to give you a life that both you and our daughter deserve."

His words cause every single hair on my body to stand up, and my heart to hammer in my chest.

"This is what you want?"

"Yes, it is. I want a life with you, a family. Talking to you on the phone wasn't how I pictured discussing marriage with you. It was supposed to be under romantic circumstances, not in a hysterical mess, but

I was serious when I said I wanted to marry you. I want to propose properly, with a ring when I come back from Afghanistan—"

"Yes."

"Yes what?"

"Yes, I will marry you."

His chuckle sends goose bumps trembling up and down my body. "But I haven't asked you yet."

"I don't care. I just want to be your wife."

He clears his throat, and I don't miss the sound of excitement in his voice when he asks the next question. "We're getting married then?" He chuckles nervously.

"Yes, I think we are, husband to be."

He moans affectionately down the phone. "I like the sound of that. God, I love you."

"I love you too," I say with a smile, holding the phone to my ear with my shoulder as my thumb caresses over my ring finger, visualizing what it will look like with a wedding ring on it.

"Now, on to the other woman in my life. How is my daughter? I want you to tell me everything."

I spend the next ten minutes telling him about the fine hairs on her beautiful head as Sebastian listens quietly. It isn't long before he tells me he needs to go, and I have to ignore the disappointment that sinks to the pit of my stomach. It isn't long before he tells me he needs to go, and I have to ignore the disappointment that sinks to the pit of my stomach.

"I've requested emergency leave, but our unit is so fucked up that it can go either way. If I can't get emergency leave, then I'll get ordinary leave, but I *am* coming home. I don't care what commanding officer I have to fight with to get the authorization, I'm coming home."

I know he means well, but getting any kind of leave isn't easy. There is a possibility he won't be coming home yet, even with the severity of our current situation.

"If you can't, that's okay, I have Caleb—"

"Ava, I'll be home, whether it's in two days or in two weeks, I'll be coming home to you and my daughter."

# chapter 4

I T'S BEEN A WEEK since my little angel was born and every single day she gets stronger. And every day that she gets stronger gives me an extra day of hope, hope that she can survive this. Her strength is giving me the power to carry on, to be there for her, to be there for *me*.

From the moment I wake up to the moment I go to sleep, I spend every single minute with her. There isn't a place on this earth I'd rather be than here with my daughter. Every time I look at her, she takes another tiny piece of my heart away, expanding it to a size that I never knew possible.

It takes my breath away.

It's true when they say a child's love is like no other because this love is definitely one of a kind. Unconditional. I would give my life for her, trade places with her in a heartbeat if I could. It breaks my heart to sit here and watch, knowing there is absolutely nothing I can do and that everything is completely out of my control. There are no guarantees. I have to put my trust in a bunch of medically trained strangers and hope that she'll pull through.

At the moment, everything seems to be heading in the right direction, and for that I am truly grateful. That's not to say the past week has been easy. It hasn't, far from it, in fact.

On Monday I was told her IRDS had resolved itself and that her lung capacity was strong enough for her to be taken off the ventilator and put onto the Continuous Positive Airway Pressure, a machine where a tubing nasal mask is strapped directly over her nose and secured around her head with a special white hat that covers the majority of her face. It then blows mild air pressure through a tube to keep her airways open.

She is being given intravenous caffeine which stimulates her breathing regularly. I was told apnea—a pause in breathing—was normal for preterm babies because of how immature and undeveloped they are, but what I wasn't told was how often they'd occur. Every couple of hours the monitor triggers off an alarm, and more often than not, a nurse will have to remind my baby how to breathe with a little nudge or stimulation. It scares the shit out of me every time.

On Wednesday, the nurse allowed me to assist with her feeding. It wasn't anything to write home about. I just pressed down on a syringe that was attached to her feeding tube, but knowing I was the one feeding her made me feel ecstatic. It was the first time that I finally felt like a mother, instead of a passerby watching my daughter from afar. The nurse also showed me how to change her diaper with tiny cotton balls and warm water. I actually changed her diaper myself. I was absolutely terrified that I was going to break her somehow because of how tiny and fragile she looked. It was hard work, especially when I couldn't raise her legs like you can with a normal baby, and having to maneuver what felt like gigantic hands against her miniature bottom without causing her distress was harder than it looked. It took me a while but eventually I managed it.

On Thursday, I was discharged from the hospital. My first night away from her was impossibly difficult. I don't think I got a wink of sleep. I tossed and turned all night in a panic, thinking something bad was going to happen. As the hours went by, I watched my cell phone like a hawk, waiting for the heartbreaking call to come. Thankfully, it never did.

This morning couldn't come quick enough.

I bounce through the door just to make sure she is still in one piece. When I approach her, I slap my hands to my mouth. The CPAP mask has been removed and has been replaced by a nasal prong. The CPAP mask is no longer obstructing her pretty little face.

"Oh my God, Caleb." I grasp hold of his hand in a death grip. "The CPAP is gone."

"Holy shit, look at that little fighter." He opens up the isolette doors and caresses his forefinger against the palm of her hand.

"Language," I scold. He chuckles. I retrieve my phone from my shoulder purse, then take a snapshot of her and attach it with a quick text to Sebastian.

**Ava**: *Look who isn't on her CPAP anymore?*
*Love you.*
*xxx*

I send him a daily picture, keeping him updated on her progress. I know the pictures are the only things helping him get through everything at the moment. I know it isn't the same as seeing her in person, but he will be able to see her soon, when he comes home on ordinary leave. The emergency leave wasn't necessary considering how stable she became in such a short amount of time. He has been granted emergency leave if her condition deteriorates, but for now he should be coming home in the next week. I wish he were coming home for good, but I'm grateful that I get two weeks with him.

"Good Morning, Ava."

My heart springs out of my chest at the sound of Dr. Bailey's voice and I spin around, almost giving myself whiplash. My heart drops when I see him staring at me. I gulp nervously as I place my phone back inside my purse.

"Hi," I say shyly, trying my hardest not to look directly into those brilliant green eyes of his because when I do, I feel as if I am being fast-forwarded into the twilight zone and all I can see is him.

It's really distracting.

My skin hums at his proximity and I feel disarmed just being in his presence. I don't know if I should be worried that he is making me feel on high alert and, quite frankly, turned on. Every time I see him, I feel as if I'm meeting him again for the very first time. I can't breathe.

It's incredibly intense.

I take a nervous glance to Caleb to see if he has noticed the sudden flush of my cheeks, but thankfully, he isn't paying any attention. This is ridiculous. I'm engaged. I'm in love with Sebastian. Dr. Bailey shouldn't be making me feel like this. No. It must be the hormones. It *is* the hormones. I'm not attracted to him. I just miss Sebastian, that's all. I'm feeling like this because I miss Sebastian.

Well, that's what I tell myself anyway…

"How are you?"

I almost combust on the spot at the sound of his burly southern accent. It's the most wonderful sound in the world. Shit. Why couldn't my daughter be given an ugly doctor? Instead of this … sex *god*.

*Great.* Now I've given my libido food for thought.

"Yeah, I'm great, good, I'm good." I squirm on the spot, feeling extremely uncomfortable.

He smirks, one eyebrow raised. "Great, good, good," he mocks, and I get the distinct feeling he is teasing me. He knows he's getting under my skin. I flush under his scrutiny, and for a moment I feel dizzy with lust. I begin to lose myself within his gaze, forgetting where I am until he clears his throat and abruptly breaks our connection. "So we have good news. On Wednesday, we discussed the possibility of weaning her off the CPAP?" he asks.

I nod, remembering the conversation we had two days ago.

"With her breathing dramatically improving, we were finally able to take her off the CPAP. She is still on oxygen, but she is taking it all in her stride. Considering she didn't have the steroids at the end of your pregnancy, the strength of her lungs is quite remarkable. But she is still undeveloped, so the possibility of her having to go back on to the CPAP is still high, but for now she's stable."

I understand that a setback is possible. I don't expect this to be an easy journey because I know it won't be. I feel happy she is getting stronger and that she has pushed through a great hurdle. I am immensely proud of her for that. Even if we take one step forward and two steps back, I will take this journey for what it is, and I will cherish every moment with her.

"We will continue to keep a close eye on her, but everything is heading in the right direction. So you can breathe, for now." I let out a breath that I didn't realize I was holding. He gives me a breathtaking smile as he steps towards the incubator where my daughter is taking breath after breath.

I take a sudden step back when Dr. Bailey's elbow accidentally grazes my arm, electricity striking and humming through my body at our physical contact. He smirks at me, a smirk that tells me he felt that too, the instant chemistry. I stare up at him with a heavy mixture of heat, frustration and lust. His smile widens, his eyes sparkling with humor before he turns his head back to my daughter, getting back to his work. I take another step back, leaning into Caleb for support while I try to gather my thoughts.

He looks at me is as if he can see right through me; like he can hear my thoughts and read every secret. It's beginning to bug the hell out of me, but that doesn't stop my heart from galloping in my chest. I try and shake the feeling off, turning all of my attention back to my daughter. That doesn't work though. I can still feel him, his essence, even though he is three feet away.

"You okay?" Caleb asks, placing the back of his fingers against my cheeks. "You look a little flushed."

That statement causes my cheeks to glow fifty shades brighter. Only two out of the three of us know why I am blushing and the quick intrigued glance I receive from Dr. Bailey only confirms it.

"Yeah, I'm fine," I lie, inwardly urging the heat to die down.

Caleb smiles at me. "It's okay, just don't watch when he has to take blood from her."

That makes my blood boil. I hadn't even realized that he was taking blood from her. This is ridiculous. I hate how he makes me feel. The moment I see Dr. Bailey everybody else in the room just fades away, even my daughter and that is just downright unacceptable.

"Have you nearly finished?" I snap.

Caleb must recognize the brazenness of my question because he looks at me a little shocked. "Ava," he scolds, and I have to refrain myself from rolling my eyes.

"Yep, just finishing up now." Out of the corner of my eye I can see his mouth is curled up in a smirk. When he walks away, I'm finally able to breathe again, away from his ... intensity.

"Ava, that was rude." Caleb sounds serious, but when I look up to him, he's smiling at me.

"Whatever." I shrug.

"He is sexy though, huh?"

A rising heat seeps through me. "Who, the doctor?" I feign ignorance, but the look on Caleb's face calls me on my bullshit. Is there anything I can't hide from him?

"Don't play dumb with me. You know what I'm talking about. The doctor was the one who was making you blush. I know it. You know it. He knows it. He couldn't take his eyes off you."

Why are we talking about this? I don't want to talk about him or think about him but, of course, my brain doesn't allow that, or Caleb for that matter.

"Then why did you call me on it, me blushing right in front of him?" I place my hands on my hips, staring up at him.

"Because I'm *mean* like that." He smiles. "I can't blame you though. He is ridiculously good looking. Have you checked out his credentials? I'm sure doctors aren't supposed to be that hot."

That makes me chuckle. "Discrimination is frowned upon you know." I don't add the fact that I had the very same thought myself.

"And?" he questions, like he isn't bothered.

I roll my eyes. "You're an ass, you know that?"

"Language," he scolds mockingly, causing me to laugh.

I reach into my purse, take a ten-dollar bill out of my wallet, and thrust it into his hand. "Shut up and get me a drink. Momma is thirsty." I smirk, looking down at my daughter. Momma. It's still strange using that terminology.

"Yes, Momma."

I laugh to myself as he wanders off, leaving me to have a moment alone with my daughter. A moment where I can thank the God above that my baby girl is still alive and continuing to fight for her life. Once I sanitize my arms and hands again, I open the isolette door to her incubator, placing my finger inside her hand and tracing gentle circles against the softness of her skin before allowing her to take hold of my forefinger. She makes me gasp as she tightens her grip, clinging to me. It isn't the first time she's done it, but it takes my breath away every single time.

"Hey, baby girl. I'm so proud of you. You're no longer on your CPAP, way to go, baby. It was hard being away from you last night, but we managed it, huh?" I continue talking to her in a quiet whisper, talking about anything and everything. I like the idea that she can hear everything I'm saying and that the sound of my constant voice is keeping her tiny heart beating.

I turn to Caleb, who is mumbling profanities under his breath. "What's wrong?" I ask, concerned by the frustrated look etched along his face.

He reaches into his jeans pocket and retrieves his phone. "Somebody keeps calling. I'm going to have to answer it. I'll be right back."

When he returns he has a face like thunder, mumbling something about incompetent bastards. "I can't fucking believe them," he whispers as he approaches me. "Sorry, gorgeous, I have to go into work for a couple of hours. Apparently nobody can do my job except me. Are you going to be okay on your own for a while? It's just for a few hours."

I stand up from my seat, stretching my legs as I try to ease the cramp from being sat down for too long. "Yeah, I'll be fine, what's the emergency?"

"Just idiots who can't get things right. Are you sure you'll be okay?"

"Yeah, just go."

He leans in to give me a quick kiss on my forehead. "I'll be back soon, I promise."

Not long after he departs, a nurse approaches me with a smile. "I have some good news for you. I've been speaking to the doctor, and I can confirm that you can finally hold your baby." I stare at the nurse in disbelief. "Would you like to hold your baby, Ava?"

I could cry. "Really? She's strong enough for that?"

She nods, a pretty smile spread across her face. "Yeah, honey, she is well enough to be held. Have we spoken to you about the kangaroo care?"

I nod. They spoke to me about it briefly just before I was discharged from the hospital. I was told that kangaroo care is skin-to-skin contact with the parent and baby. In the neonatal books I've been reading, they've all mentioned that the method of skin-to-skin contact is beneficial for a preterm baby. It can stabilize their heart rate, breathing and oxygen; develop a deeper sleeping pattern and a more rapid weight gain. It also explained that it's a great technique to help parents bond with their baby, but I'm here so often I doubt that will be a problem.

"Okay, that's great. Well, let's get you into a comfortable position.

Considering this is your first time it's probably best if you sit down in the rocking chair. I will disconnect the oxygen tubing from her and then reconnect it through the side port on her incubator. Then I'll rearrange the rest of the wires so we can have a smooth transfer from the incubator to you."

I prepare myself by going for a quick restroom break which was greatly recommended by the nurses. The last thing I need is nature calling when I'm holding my baby for the first time. After thoroughly washing my hands and arms again, I make myself comfortable in the rocking chair beside my baby's incubator. I watch as three of the nurses do their final preparations: checking her temperature and other medical necessities to ensure she is still strong enough.

I unbutton the first three buttons of my blouse so my baby girl can get to my chest without restrictions, then I'm told to sit back against the chair. They delicately remove her from the incubator and transfer her over to me, wrapped loosely in a thick pink blanket. I look down at my chest in apprehensive terror when they finally place her vertically against my bare skin, removing the blanket in the process. Her little arms rest gently against the top of my chest while her hat covered head is turned to the side and nestled against the middle of my breast bone. Her neck is positioned into a sniffing position to avoid obstruction to her airways, or so I am told.

I barely move an inch as they continue with their calm transfer, their hands securely on her at all times as I watch with fascination. One of the nurses fastens two of the buttons of my shirt back up so my baby is inside the material while a second nurse arranges her tubes securely under my clothing. They ensure the oxygen prongs are attached correctly to her nose. The nurse who buttoned up my shirt covers her securely with the blanket and the third nurse positions my hands so they are now the hands holding her securely.

Oh my God.

I'm holding my baby.

I am actually holding my baby.

There are no words to describe how I'm feeling right now. I'm speechless.

"How are you doing?" the third nurse asks reassuringly.

I nod as a single tear rolls down my cheek. The experience is overwhelming but absolutely beautiful. Seven days I've been waiting for this one moment, to be able to hold her in my arms, and now it's finally happening.

"I will be nearby at all times, carrying out visual inspections, so if you have any problems just let me know."

Again I nod politely at the nurse as I look down to my beautiful daughter, clutching her against my chest. I smile as I look down at her intently, another tear escaping. I take a second to appreciate this moment. From the instant she was placed on my chest, she immediately took another piece of my heart, and I fell deeper in love with her.

My thoughts suddenly travel to Sebastian, and I desperately wish he were here. He is missing a crucial moment of her life, and he isn't here to witness it. Her father should be here for this. When I have finally found my voice again, I ask the nurse to take a snapshot with my phone and to send it to him.

An hour passes and even though my arms are aching a little from being in the same position for such a long time, I don't want to let her go. She is lying so peacefully against my chest that I desperately want to stay like this forever. However, nothing lasts that long, and the three nurses come back and help transfer her back into the incubator. I instantly feel a chill when the nurse picks her up from my chest and transfers her back to her temporary residency.

They carefully place her back into her incubator, readjusting all of the wires into the right positions, ensuring her oxygen is in correct working order and that her vitals are stable.

"Well, that went better than expected. She definitely loved being in her momma's arms," the nurse says softly as she gazes down at my daughter. Her words make me smile with comfort. "Most preemies can find this process a little distressing at first, but your little one was a real trooper." I smile again at my daughter before turning to look at the nurse.

"It was incredible ... she's incredible."

For the next hour I continue to stare down at the miracle that is my daughter, feeling so blessed to have her in my life.

# chapter 5

A T SOME POINT DURING the evening I must have fallen asleep because one of the nurses has to wake me up.

"Sweetheart, it's nearly ten o'clock. You should head on home and get some rest," she whispers. I sit up, craning my neck from side to side and moaning as a cramp shoots up my neck, massaging the knot away with my fingers. For a moment, I actually forget where I am until the beeping of the machines brings me back to reality and I stand up in mid-panic, looking down at my daughter.

"Is she okay, have there been any changes?"

"No, there's no need to panic. She's doing brilliantly. Now, go." She smiles encouragingly at me before walking away to check on a baby on the other side of the room. I stay for another five minutes, saying goodbye and taking extra glances, crying a little that I have to leave her. I don't want to leave her, it breaks my heart, but I force myself to.

As I make my way out of the hospital, I check my phone and realize I have two text messages.

**Caleb**: *Sorry, Ava. This emergency has actually turned into a fucking catastrophe. It looks as though I'm going to be here all night. Make sure you grab a cab when you're ready to go home. I* *don't want to hear that you walked home alone! x*

"Yes, sir," I mumble under my breath. I go through my second text message, and I'm instantly uplifted.

**Sebastian**: *Babe, that is amazing. My baby girl is a little fighter. That pic is awesome. Can't wait to see her. I miss you. xxxxxxx*

There is a picture attached to the text message, so I tap on the image with my forefinger and smile when the image enlarges. It's a self-portrait of him blowing a kiss to the camera. I'm so wrapped up in the photograph that I don't see the person in front of me until I slam into the back of them. It whips the breath out of me.

"Oh my God, I am so sorry!"

When the person turns around, I'm silenced to submission.

"Ava, are you okay?"

I make the huge mistake of looking into his emerald green eyes. I am suddenly engulfed within the warmth of them, and everything else begins to fade away.

"Um, yeah … sorry, I wasn't looking where I was going …" My heart hammers away in my chest.

"Figures."

He smirks, then glances down at my hand that is currently clenched into a tight fist around his sweatshirt. I didn't even realize I was holding him. I pull away quickly, smiling up at him apologetically. That's when I realize he isn't in his usual hospital attire. He is in dark washed jeans hung deliciously low at his hips, a regular white T-shirt and an unzipped dark navy Abercrombie and Fitch sweatshirt. He looks incredible. *Damn.*

"Are you only just leaving?" he asks before my perverted thoughts go a step too far. His smile tells me he caught me checking him out.

"Um, yeah," I say, slightly flustered and feeling a little drunk with lust.

"Where's your friend?"

"He had to leave earlier." My hormones must be in their element when I take a glance down at his chest and my mouth almost waters at how incredibly toned he looks.

40

"I'm actually just heading out myself. Can I give you a ride?"

Did he just say what I think he said? "Excuse me?"

"I asked if you wanted a ride home?" He chuckles, causing the heat against my cheeks to quadruple.

Jesus, what the hell is wrong with me? I clear my throat. "No, that's okay, thank you, I was just going to call for a cab. Plus you've probably been working for like, fifteen hours straight, no doubt you just want to crash." I make an attempt to move past him, but he stops me in my tracks by placing a hand gently against my right arm. I pretend his touch doesn't affect me, but as the tingles shoot up my arm, it's hard to ignore.

"Make that twenty-one hours but my diet pretty much consists of nothing but caffeine, so I'm wired. Besides, it's late. You shouldn't be walking the streets or catching cabs on your own at this time of night. Come on, I'll give you a ride."

He's right; it is late, and I am exhausted. I ignore my gut feeling and follow him out of the hospital.

"So, have you thought of any names yet?" he asks as we walk at the same pace through the courtyard.

"No. It's hard. They all suck."

He laughs. "So Stir Mix-A-Lot is still a contender then? I hear it's a really popular name."

I smirk in response.

"Your boyfriend, has he thought of any names?"

The thought of Sebastian makes me feel a little guilty for having a conversation with Dr. Bailey, let alone having him drive me home. "Fiancé, actually," I say sharply. He blinks at the sharpness of my tone, but he doesn't say anything. If anything he looks almost amused. "And no, it's hard to make decisions without him being here," I add more softly.

"He's in Afghanistan, right?"

"Yeah, he is." I smile.

"My brother was in Afghanistan. He was a surgeon. Doctors kind of run in the family." He smiles.

"Was?"

He gulps heavily, taking a brief glance past me before returning his eyes back to mine. "He died on duty."

My heart plummets down to my feet at his words. "I'm so sorry." I feel like the world's biggest jerk for bringing up something that is no doubt painful to him. I can understand that pain; it is actually my worst nightmare.

"Thanks, he was an amazing brother." He doesn't elaborate any further, and I don't push.

We arrive at the parking lot and stop at a red, mean-looking Chevy.

"Nice car," I compliment, lingering my fingers on the red shiny exterior.

"Thanks. She's my baby."

I smile softly as I walk over to the passenger side of his car. Boys and their toys. "Not to bruise your ego or anything but isn't it a bit predictable? Typical guy's car?"

His eyes light up with excitement. "Predictable yes, typical no. It's a top of the range 2012 Camaro Z1 with a 6.2L supercharged V8 engine, six-speed manual transmission, alloy wheels, keyless entry."

He comes over to my side and opens the passenger door without his key fob. "See?" He gives me a quirky smirk.

"Impressive." I chuckle. I climb in and sink into the leather interior as he shuts the door gently after me.

"Oh, and it has visual assist parking," he says as he finally enters the car, pointing to a screen when the engine rumbles to life on its own, the noise growling throughout the parking lot. Immediately the sound of Lauren Hill vibrates softly inside the car.

"You must really be bad at parking, huh?" I grin as I place the seatbelt around me, locking it in place with the buckle.

"Not a car girl, I see?"

"I'm probably into cars as much as you're into Glee."

He nods as he reverses out of the spot, much to my surprise not using his ridiculous parking sensors. "Yes, point taken." He chuckles. "So where are we headed?"

I tell him my address and he types it into his GPS. We slowly make our way out of the parking lot, and he's quiet as we exit the hospital grounds. I don't know if it's the confinement of his car or the sexy beat from the vibrating sound system, but the tension seems noticeably thicker than it did before we entered. I use the silence to take a calming breath, urging my heart rate to slow the hell down.

"How are you doing, with everything?"

I turn to answer him, and at that moment I wish I hadn't. He looks like something from a Fast and Furious movie: lean, sexy and cool as shit. His left hand is clasped around the top of the steering wheel, and his right hand casually holds onto the stick shift; it has to be the sexiest thing I've ever seen in my goddamn life. I have to pry my eyes away from his masculine hand to answer his question.

"Um, yeah I'm doing okay. I'm still trying to adjust, but I actually got to hold her for the first time today." I smile.

He briefly turns in my direction with a sincere smile before turning his eyes back to the road. "I know, I was the doctor who authorized it. How was it?"

My eyes widen at this information, but then I feel ridiculous because of course it would be him. He is her doctor after all.

Laughing nervously I reply, "Scary because she's so tiny but incredible. Thank you."

"You're welcome. There is nothing I like to see more than a parent holding their baby for the first time." His smile almost turns dreamlike and I wonder if he's a father. "Have you got any children of your own?" Jesus, I'm not usually this nosy. Blushing, I immediately say, "Sorry, that isn't any of my business."

I can see a distinct smirk etched against his mouth through the darkness of the car. "No, it's fine, Ava. And to answer your question, no, I don't have children. I'm single." I can't help the joyous feeling that shoots through my body at this new information, but it's a ridiculous emotion to feel considering I'm engaged.

After a moment of silence, he points towards his stereo system. "You can change the song if you want." I look down at the state-of-the-art navigation with confusion. I wouldn't even know where to start. Chuckling lightly I say, "That's okay, I wouldn't want to break anything in your top of the range 2012 Camaro Z1 with alloy wheels, keyless entry and ridiculous visual assist parking."

My words cause a fit of laughter to echo through his car. "And you said you weren't a car girl." Once his laughter dies down, he briefly turns to look at me again before returning his attention back to the road. "Okay, so it seems I know approximately two things about you. One, you're a new mom and two, you never leave your daughter's side. So tell me something about yourself. What do you do for a living?"

"I'm a book editor."

"What kind of books do you edit?"

"Fiction mostly. Romance, new adult—"

"Adult?" This seems to spike his interest to another level and he shakes his head, a half smile rising from his mouth. "Wow, you have a job most guys would dream about. It's practically porn!"

"It isn't porn," I say through my laughter.

"Hey, a friend of mine let me borrow that book, you know the one they're doing a film about? And I can tell you now—that was straight cut porn."

I roll my eyes. *Typical guy response.* "Well, that's because it's classed as erotica. What I edit isn't, it's not ... you know ... well you know ..." I find it impossible to say the word 'hardcore' or anything else that is remotely sexual because if I did my mind would go to that perverted place in my brain, especially when he turns and looks at me with a glimmer of heat in his gaze.

He clears his throat. "I'm sorry. That was really inappropriate."

I pivot my body towards him. "No, don't apologize. You actually made me laugh, and I haven't been a barrel of laughs lately, so thank you."

He turns and gives me a brief, heart-stopping smile. "Well, in that case, you're welcome. Again."

"Anyway, you're a doctor. Aren't you supposed to read stuff that is more sophisticated?"

He raises his eyebrow as he takes a left turn. "What, like The New York Observer? That kind of shit?" He shakes his head. "No, thanks. I'd rather stick pins in my eyes. I'm a guy's guy. You know, football and beer."

"Cars," I add teasingly. He laughs. "Okay, my turn. What made you choose to work in neonatology?" I ask with the purpose of changing the subject, *and* to stop the crazy thoughts trailing through my mind. Plus, I'm intrigued.

"I always wanted to work with children. I felt more passionate about helping sick children and babies than I did about helping sick adults, so after Med school I did my pediatric residency at Seattle Children's Hospital where I worked closely with the NICU and I fell in love with it. After my residency, I went on to do my neonatology fellowship and, well, here I am. My first year of being a fully fledged neonatologist." He

44

smiles as he continues to face forward, concentrating on the road.

I didn't think it was even possible for him to get any sexier but talking like that, about working with sick children, it makes my heart flutter. "That's a good answer. I'm glad they don't just have anybody looking after my baby." I smirk half-mockingly at him.

He looks at me seriously. "Yeah, not to blow my own trumpet or anything but she's in the most capable hands. I promise."

His words leave me speechless. I barely know this guy from Adam, but the look of honesty that he has in his eyes—a pure, heart-wrenching look of trust—has me believing every word. I believe him with every ounce of my heart.

Eventually, we come to a stop directly outside of my apartment complex. He turns to look at me, his smile never escaping from his lips. "Here you go, home sweet home."

"Thanks, it was really sweet of you to drive me home," I say honestly. Another piece of my heart has been taken away, but this time by the guy staring contently in my direction.

"It was my pleasure."

The way he says the word 'pleasure' sends a shiver trembling down the center of my spine. Oh God, his accent. "Where are you from? Just you don't sound like you're from 'round here," I ask as I unclip my seatbelt.

"I'm from Dallas, Texas."

That explains that incredible twang he has to his accent. "And you moved to Washington? The state that always rains?" I ask. I know *I* moved from sunny Florida to Seattle, but it wasn't the weather I wanted to escape from. I actually miss the Miami sunshine.

"What can I say, I like rain."

"That's crap. Nobody likes rain."

"You're right, the rain sucks, but Washington has a charm about it that I love. And not to mention there isn't a friggin' cow in sight."

We both laugh. It's scary at how at ease we are together. I don't have any friends other than Caleb, and I've never had a bond like this with any of my friends from my past. Instant, fun, and flirty; you can flirt with your friends, right? I flirt with Caleb all the time, but Caleb doesn't make my heart do somersaults like Dr. Bailey does.

"Well, I better get going. Thanks again for the ride. I'll see you tomorrow?" I ask.

"Yeah, I'll see you tomorrow." He smiles.

I open the door and get out. Just as I'm about to close the door behind me, I suddenly remember I don't know his first name. I lean over, popping my head back into the car. "What's your name? Your first name, I mean?"

He gives me one of his panty dropping smiles as he leans back into his seat. "It's Ashton."

Dr. Ashton Bailey.

"Ashton." I smile. I really like how his name sounds rolling off my tongue. "Thanks." I close the door behind me, waving at him while he watches me through the car window before I walk off into my apartment block.

I've barely let myself into my apartment when I hear a knock on my front door. To my surprise, I see Ashton through the peephole. I open the door with a smile.

"I tried to shout, but I guess you didn't hear me. You left your phone in my car."

Thank goodness he noticed. "I thought it was in my purse, thank you." He passes it to me, his fingers gently grazing mine. I jerk at the electric shock that his touch brings.

"No problem, Ava," he drawls. "It's a good job I spotted it."

We stand looking at each other for a moment, and I feel as if I should invite him in, but I don't. I can't. It would be wrong. I don't know if Caleb has come home yet, and I don't want to explain why my baby's doctor is inside my apartment.

"Well, I better get going. Sweet dreams, Ava." He turns and walks away. I lean my hip against the doorframe with my arms crossed, checking out his impressive ass as it swings side to side with every step he takes. Then suddenly, he turns around and a look of surprise crosses his face when he notices me watching him. Embarrassed that I've been caught checking him out, I rush back inside and slam the door as hard as possible, finally taking a breath of relief.

I'm officially going to hell.

# chapter 6

THE NEXT WEEK PASSES by in the blink of an eye.

Before I even know it, my daughter—who still needs to be named—is now officially two weeks old and improving drastically by the minute. We've had one minor setback during the past week. She had to have a blood transfusion for the anemia caused by her prematurity because her red blood cells were dangerously low. I was told that preterm babies experience heavy blood loss with the frequent blood sampling, and considering she has to go through them on a daily basis, it was hardly surprising she had a decreased number of red blood cells. I was devastated when I was told they would have to perform a four-hour blood transfusion, but like the trooper my baby girl is, she took it all in her stride.

Her strength takes my breath away.

The next day she dramatically improved, and her red blood cells are finally at a stable rate. She is naturally putting on weight, weighing just less than three pounds, a perfect weight for a baby of her age. It doesn't seem like a lot, but knowing how far she has come in such a short amount of time leaves me feeling overjoyed with hope. Two weeks ago I thought I'd lost my baby, but now she continues to fight for her life, and I can't help but thank my lucky stars that she hasn't been taken away from me.

Caleb's leave ended, and he had to go back to work, so I'm on my own for the majority of the day now. It's incredibly lonely sitting here on my own, but there is nowhere else on this earth I'd rather be. Once he finishes work for the day, Caleb always comes to the hospital and spends at least four or five hours sitting here with me. When I'm on the brink of absolute exhaustion, he drags me away from her.

I'm always reluctant to leave.

Several times during the day, my mood is favorably improved when Ashton makes time out of his busy schedule to see me. I always catch him on his morning rounds, but knowing he personally wants to take time out to make sure I'm okay makes me feel things I know I shouldn't be feeling. Shamelessly, it is my second favorite thing I look forward to every morning when I arrive at the hospital.

My first is obviously seeing my daughter. Once I've been assured by the nurses that she has had a successful night with no damaging complications, and I've stared mindlessly at her for ten minutes straight, checking that every strand of hair on her tiny little head is still intact, my mind automatically goes to him. I can't help but smile as I count down the minutes until I see his handsome face again. The anticipation of waiting for his presence sends me into an unruly frenzy, but when he eventually surprises me with a visit ... I swear to God that his smile—his big, bright and dazzling smile—gives me the impression that coming to see me is one of *his* favorite parts of the day, too.

He makes it his mission to make me laugh, and he always succeeds. The first thing he does is suggest a name that could be a great candidate for my baby. The names he comes up with are incredible, and it tugs at my heart that he has taken it so seriously. This morning's name is Lola-Rose and I smile at him as I shrug. That is my daily response. It *is* a beautiful name, but I won't tell him that. I never do.

He sighs with frustration, then laughs at my response. "Ava, you're killing me here."

"Well, you should try harder then." I cross my arms and lean back into my seat, chuckling under my breath.

"You're a tough woman to crack, did you know that?" he says, exasperated at my obvious stubbornness. I nod, and my eyes follow him as he finally approaches me. An audible gasp leaves me as his forefinger lightly strokes my bare arm. My heart leaps out of my chest. "You okay?"

I gulp and glance down at his beautiful finger as it continuously caresses my arm. His touch affects me immediately as a tremor of goose bumps feather up and down against my sensitive skin, leaving me breathless. I look up and meet his gaze. "Yeah, I'm, uh … great … perfect."

He looks deep in my eyes with a mixture of hunger and affection. "Yes, you are."

I almost swallow my own tongue at his compliment, and I have to turn away from him, smiling as I try my best to compose myself. My heart is on dangerous ground with this beautiful man, and I'm extremely worried about the way he makes me feel. I know I should ask him to back off, but I can't. He has become my daily addiction. I feel a pull, a magnetic pull that is too strong to stay away from, but our new friendship is totally innocent and I will make sure it stays that way.

I purposely try and avoid his gaze as he walks over to my daughter, looking down on her. "The nurses weighed her today. She is two pounds, fourteen ounces," I announce proudly when I finally find the courage to speak again. "Although you probably already knew that."

He smiles. "It's awesome. Way to go, baby girl. You'll be a little porker before we know it," he says to my daughter, and I can't help but swoon over how amazing he is with her. He steps away and traces his eyes over my features. Then, after a long uncomfortable assessment of me, his mouth turns into a frown. "When was the last time you had a decent meal?"

I frown in return. I honestly can't remember the last time I ate anything other than Cracker Jacks. I haven't been that hungry lately, plus the hospital food isn't that great. When I don't answer, he sighs. "Tell me to mind my own business, but you must have lost at least nine pounds since last week. That isn't healthy."

"Mind your own business," I retaliate as I rise and go to stand beside my daughter, but he comes up from behind me, pressing his incredibly firm chest against my back. I lean into him and close my eyes, enjoying the way his body feels against mine.

"I'm sorry," he whispers. "I didn't mean any offense, Ava." The way he drawls my name almost has me in a puddle at his feet. "But could I take you for some lunch? You really do need to eat."

I sigh. It is very tempting, but I can't leave my daughter. If something happened …

"I can't leave her," I whisper painfully. Gosh, the idea of leaving her is unsettling. I don't even like leaving her when I need to use the restroom. Tears begin to build-up in the corner of my eyes. I can't leave her, I just can't.

"It's only for half an hour, Ava."

"I can't leave her, I'm sorry." It might be irrational on my behalf, but I don't care. I'm her mother, and it's a mother's job to stick by their child through thick and thin.

He sighs and I can feel his breath tingle against my neck, causing me to shiver. "Okay, but I'll be grabbing lunch around two if you change your mind." He walks away, leaving me yearning for his touch.

I understand that it isn't normal to spend more than twelve hours a day at the hospital, but I feel that any fraction of a second I'm away from her she'll be taken away from me. I constantly have an anxious pit of sickness in my stomach, a feeling that something bad is going to happen, and for the sake of my sanity I'd prefer to stay here.

"I'm not going anywhere, baby," I mumble. I ask the nurse if I can hold her and she assists with the wires that are attached to my daughter. I take her out of the incubator and clutch her gently to my chest before taking a seat in the rocking chair. Looking down at her tiny body snuggled perfectly between my breastbone takes my breath away. She's truly incredible and absolutely mesmerizing to watch.

Once she is tucked safely back into the cocoon of her incubator, I find myself falling into the Ashton mind trap. I glance up to the clock in the middle of the room and notice it's five minutes after two. *Oh good, I might still be able to catch him for lunch.* That is if I actually have the courage to leave my daughter for a little while.

I fidget nervously with my fingers. "Um, would I be a terrible mother if I left her for a little while to grab some food? I'll be twenty minutes, half an hour at the max, I promise," I ask the nurse. God, I sound like a bad mother even contemplating it.

"Of course not, you need to eat." She smiles, then frowns as if my words have only just registered. "Is that what you think? If you leave her side to grab some lunch, that you're a terrible mother? Oh, Ava."

She takes a step towards me and places a comforting hand against my arm. "Listen to me, you're a fantastic mother. You're here every morning by eight o'clock, without fail and then you don't leave until at least ten o'clock most nights. Do you hear me? You're like superwoman to that beautiful child of yours. I see how much you love her and how much you're fighting along with her. You're entitled to a break. So go, grab some lunch. Have a moment for yourself."

I can't help but wrap my arms around this lovely nurse and squeeze the hell out of her. "Thank you."

She grabs my purse from the floor beside the incubator and shoves it in my arms. "Now, go."

After a brief emotional goodbye to my daughter, I finally make my way down to the cafeteria. As I walk through the cafeteria doors, it takes me a moment to find him, but when I do my heart does a double take. The moment my eyes fall on him, he turns to look at me as if he can sense my presence. He looks surprised at my sudden appearance but then his mouth turns up into a smile. I would feel extremely jealous of the pretty female doctor sitting with him if it weren't for the bright and affectionate smile he is throwing my way.

He glances down at his wrist as if looking down at a watch, then shakes his head and mouths, "You're late." I laugh. He says something to the doctor beside him before standing up and heading in my direction. The other doctor looks far from happy as she watches him approach me, but I couldn't care less.

"Hey," he says, meeting me halfway, placing his tray on an empty table.

"Hey to you." I smile as I pull out a seat and sit down. He follows my lead and sits next to me. I look down at his tray and laugh at the array of food he has piled on it. It could feed a small army. "You hungry?"

He chuckles. "I'm starving, but this isn't all for me. It's for you too. I knew you didn't want to leave Miss Stir Mix-a-Lot, so I was going to bring you up some food and leave it in the family kitchen, just in case you got hungry. So you changed your mind, huh?"

I nod, a little sheepishly. "Yeah. I overreacted earlier, sorry."

"Ava, there isn't anything to be sorry about. I understand your reasoning, but I'm glad you changed your mind. The doctor I was sitting with wouldn't shut the hell up."

I glance back towards the table he was originally seated at, and chuckle under my breath. "Hmm, would that be the doctor who is currently staring daggers at me, probably wishing I was dead?"

He takes a glance in her direction in shock, then grumbles something inaudible, shaking his head. "Yes, that would be the one. I'm sorry, she … kind of has a thing for me," he says, taking a bite of his sandwich.

"Do you have a thing for her?" I blurt out.

He almost chokes on the sandwich. "Hell no."

"She's that bad?" I ask half amused, half intrigued.

He finally swallows his food and takes a sip of his drink through a straw. "Let's just say she has a bit of a reputation in this place … with the other doctors."

I chuckle. "Hot, incredible sex in the on-call rooms?"

He howls with laughter. "Yeah, something like that."

"Sorry, I couldn't resist. I have the box sets of Grey's Anatomy and hot, steamy sex in the on-call rooms are a frequent pastime for the surgical residents."

He raises his eyebrow, giving me a quirky grin. "Really? I'm gonna' have to check it out on Netflix," he says flirtatiously, winking as he pops a potato chip into his mouth.

"So what did you get me? Something good I hope. A friend of mine told me I wasn't eating properly."

He smiles as he pushes the tray of food in my direction. "I wasn't sure what you liked, so I bought you a club sandwich, a tuna-fish sandwich, two flavored bags of chips and a water."

*Oh wow, he's supplied a little picnic for me.*

"Thank you." I reach for the club sandwich; I don't have the heart to tell him that I despise fish after he's gone to so much trouble.

"You're welcome. And just for the record, your friend is a very wise man."

"I bet." I smile as I take my first bite. It isn't the best sandwich but my stomach sure does appreciate the food.

As soon as I've demolished half of my sandwich I look up briefly at Ashton, who is outright staring at me. "What?"

He doesn't answer as he continues to stare at me. I wipe my mouth with paranoia. "Have I got something on my face?"

He shakes his head with a smile, looking a little flustered. "No, I just … I can't seem to take my eyes off you."

My eyes widen at his forward confession, and I suddenly feel very aware of my racing heartbeat. Then the racing hitches up a little further when he adds, "I don't think you realize how beautiful you actually are."

"Do you say that to all of your patients' moms?" I ask through a nervous laugh, trying to make light of the situation, but it does nothing to deter my heart rate when shivers erupts up and down my body as his hand gently reaches over mine, covering it delicately.

"No, just the ones I can't stop thinking about. You're the first."

His words pierce through my mind. My heart is past being in a dangerous territory and has fallen head first into a minefield, moments away from detonating. This doesn't feel innocent anymore.

I tell myself to create some space but instead, I make the mistake of looking directly into those hypnotic eyes of his. I'm frozen to the spot. My heart throbs as he starts to move closer to me and for a moment I think he's going to kiss me. In fact, I'm certain he is going to kiss me when his lips linger over mine, but it seems fate has other ideas when his beeper goes off, freezing us in time. He sighs as he reluctantly lets go of my hand and looks down at the offending beeper.

"Shit, I gotta' go." He looks conflicted as he rushes up from his seat, almost as if he doesn't want to leave me. I just nod in a daze, unable to find my voice. "I'll come and see you later, okay?" He turns, and jogs out of the cafeteria, leaving me breathless and overwhelmed.

It takes me a short moment to tear my gaze away from the double doors he just rushed through. Feeling deflated, I slump back into my chair, contemplating what almost happened. Taking a deep breath, the guilt takes residence in my stomach at the realization of my near betrayal, and I'm thankful his beeper went off just in time. I don't know what I would have done if he'd kissed me. In fact, I know exactly what I would have done, and *that's* what scares me.

Shit.

I take a glance down at my half-eaten sandwich; suddenly, I don't feel hungry anymore. I head over to the food counter in search of a 'to go' bag, ignoring the daggers from the doctor who'd sat with Ashton earlier.

I'm in an absolute daze as I walk through the hospital and back to the NICU. I'm so lost in thought, I don't even recognize the man dressed in a US Army uniform until I hear my name being called out. I drop my bag of food on the floor in shock as I stare at the man I haven't seen in over four months.

"Sebastian?" I whisper as I walk slowly over to him, trying to work out if he's an illusion or not. He nods, confirming that he's real as he smiles at me with a look of absolute worship. "Sebastian," I repeat, then move towards him at full speed and jump into his strong arms, ignoring the burning sensation I feel against my cesarean wound, my lips slamming against his.

# chapter 7

"I TAKE IT YOU'RE happy to see me?"

Happy? That's the understatement of the year. I can only answer with a kiss. The feel of his wonderful tongue coaxing the tip of mine fuels the fire of how much I've missed him, and I devour him with our first kiss in months, clutching him tight, inhaling his wonderful scent.

He chuckles against my mouth as he pulls away, breathless, gazing lovingly into my widened eyes. He presses his lips against my nose. "I've missed you so much," he says, his eyes taking my entire face in.

I smile, still a little shell shocked to find him here, so I press my lips against his again as I consume him with every force in my body. I don't think I could answer him even if I wanted to; I've been struck silent by his presence.

After I've had my fill of kisses, I finally pull away and slide down his body until I'm standing back on my own two feet. "I can't believe you're here," I say in disbelief as he wraps his arms around my waist. I close my eyes as I feel his lips brush gently against the top of my head. "I've missed you so, so much."

The emotion of seeing him takes its toll. I try to force the tears away, but it's useless. My body breaks down in unbearable sobs. I grip him as I unleash the pain and heartbreak of the past two weeks into his chest.

"Shh, it's okay, sweetheart, I'm here. I'm here now. Everything's going to be okay," he soothes as his hand strokes delicately against my back, his lips pressing against my hair.

The guilt from earlier churns at my gut and the sobs intensify until I am to the point of hyperventilating. I almost kissed another man. Oh God, I'm a horrible person. Sebastian is comforting me yet he doesn't know half of the reason why I'm crying. If only he knew the truth of my inner battle, he wouldn't be here right now, comforting me the way he is. He deserves better.

As I continue choking on my sobs, I feel Sebastian lift me up into his arms and carry me a few feet until he sits us down on what feels like a wooden bench. He starts to pull away from my embrace to look at me, and I have to clamp my eyes closed. I don't deserve his sympathy, and I can't bear to look at him, it's too hard. As I choke on another sob, I feel his calloused fingers linger against my cheek, wiping the tears away.

"Baby, look at me." Tears stream down my face as the guilt rockets through me, and I shake my head furiously. I can't look at him. It's too painful. "Baby, I want to see your beautiful eyes, please. Sweetheart, look at me."

Eventually, I lose the battle with myself and reluctantly open my eyes. I'm met with a concerned and pained looking Sebastian and once again the guilt crashes through my body; so violently that it almost has me doubling over in excruciating pain.

"I'm so sorry I wasn't here," he says. I shake my head, trying to convey my thoughts. I don't deserve his apologies. "No, Ava, let me finish. I can't imagine what you've been through, and it kills me knowing you've had to go through it alone. I won't ever forgive myself for that. But for the next two weeks, gorgeous, I'm all yours, one hundred percent. Then I only have to go back for another four months, and that's it. My contract will end, and I'll come home. I will only belong to you and our daughter, do you understand?"

I nod as I try to catch my breath. He presses a calming kiss against my lips before pulling away slightly, his head lingering against mine. "I love you," he whispers, causing my heart to double over at his words.

"I love you too," I whisper back honestly.

He pulls me into a tight embrace, and we stay like that for a while. Eventually when my tears have subsided, I pull away, and he gives me his adoring smile. He sweeps a piece of stray hair from my face and caresses his fingers across my cheek and down my neck.

"Are you okay now?"

Smiling softly, I reply with a simple, "Yes."

"Good," he says, pressing a kiss against my lips. "Do you think I can see our daughter now? I've been dying to meet her."

With a mock sigh, I pull away from his embrace to stand. Taking his hand, I pull him up to his feet. "I forgot I have to share you now."

"You don't need to get jealous. I still love you."

"Lucky for you, I don't mind sharing, especially with our daughter. She's incredible."

We make our way to the entrance of the NICU, but Sebastian unexpectedly stops me in my tracks, chuckling under his breath. "We better pick that up." He bends over, grabbing the paper bag that I'd dropped on the floor. The *same* paper bag with the lunch Ashton bought me earlier, a haunting reminder of my near betrayal. I swallow the bile that is threatening to escape as I take it out of his hands and dump it in the nearest trashcan, hurriedly disposing of it. Pushing the guilt away, I take Sebastian's hand and lead him to our daughter.

As we make our way along the clinical corridor of the NICU, I bump into one of the regular nurses. Her eyes widen in obvious surprise at Sebastian. "Well, this must be your wonderful fiancé Sebastian."

I smile, clutching hold of his hand a little tighter. Sebastian looks down at me with a look of honor. "So everybody knows who I am, huh?" He smiles.

"Oh my, she doesn't shut up about you, Sebastian this, Sebastian that. You've definitely got yourself a keeper here." Again, I have to force the guilt-ridden bile back down that continues to rise from my stomach. I feel sick. I doubt he would feel the same if he knew the thoughts that had been circling my brain of late. His smile widens, obviously unaware of my inner turmoil.

"Well, that's good to hear."

I smile gently, pushing myself further into his side. Even with the lustful thoughts I've been having of Ashton lately, my feelings for Sebastian haven't changed. His smile still makes my pulse beat faster, his touch causes the butterflies to flutter around in my stomach, and the feel of his mouth makes the goose bumps prickle through my body.

I am still in love with him.

Looking up at the man I love, I come to realize the feelings I thought I was beginning to have for Ashton must have been a figment of my imagination, a meaningless attraction. I was in a vulnerable place and unbelievably lonely, and he was there, in the right place, at the right time.

The nurse asks Sebastian when he arrived home and how long he's staying.

"I came back today on special leave for two weeks to spend some quality time with my family." He gently lifts my hand to his mouth and presses a soft kiss against the back of it.

"Well, make the most of it while you're here." She starts to walk away but turns back to us, a small professional smile curving her lips. "And before I forget, thank you for your service."

I smile proudly up at him as she walks away and he gives her a courtesy nod. Once she's out of earshot, he chuckles, shaking his head. "I still find it awkward when I'm thanked for my service by a stranger. It's so surreal."

"Well, you *did* come to the hospital in your military uniform, looking sexy as hell." I turn to face him and caress my hands over his chest, inching closer to him, feeling his hands trace the edge of my arms.

He smiles seductively down at me. "Sexy as hell, huh?"

His smile falters as he leans down and presses his soft lips against mine, lingering for a few seconds before edging his tongue between my lips. I sweep my tongue against his, then laugh as I hear the sound of wolf whistling. I pull away to see Valarie, one of the regular nurses, wink at me before walking in the other direction.

"Come on, you're distracting the nurses."

He laughs as I lead him to the door of the shared NICU room. Once we're well sanitized, we enter and walk straight to our daughter. The moment we approach her, I hear Sebastian's breath hitch, and like magic, our baby girl opens her eyes as though she is looking directly at him.

"Oh wow …" Sebastian pulls me into his arms with my back to his chest, holding me tight. "You did amazing, baby. I love you," he whispers happily in my ear. I know without even looking at him that tears are falling down his face. My bottom lip trembles and I have to turn my head to kiss him against his neck.

"I love you too," I whisper against his soft skin.

We stay wrapped in one another's arm as we continue to gaze at our daughter, unable to take our eyes away from her. It's the first time since Lily was born that I've felt like we're a real family. The last time I remember feeling this whole was before I turned eight years old. I frown as painful thoughts of my daddy come to the forefront of my mind.

"You okay?" Sebastian's voice cuts through my saddened thoughts.

I sigh. "I was just thinking about my dad." I was eight when he died of a brain hemorrhage. He was my favorite person in the whole world, but he was brutally taken from me, turning my life upside down for the worse and leaving me with a screwed up family.

"He'd be proud of you. I bet he's looking down on us now."

My smile widens when I realize that he's probably looking down on our daughter as we speak. It's a comforting thought to know that my daughter has a guardian angel in the form of her grandpa. "I hope so."

He kisses the side of my head, his lips lingering against my hair. "God, she's so beautiful."

I snuggle closer to him. "I know. She's just perfect," I say, looking up at him. "So how are you feeling, Daddy?" I squeeze his arms tight against my chest.

"Overwhelmed, trying to take everything in, but I'm good, baby, I'm really good." He presses another kiss against my head. I sigh with contentment, glad to have him back if only for a little while.

I go on to explain everything, well everything to the best of my ability. I show him how to change her diaper with the tepid warm water and the cotton balls. Once we've finished, a nurse comes by to check on our daughter's vitals and sets her up with her next feed through her feeding tube. Eagerly, Sebastian takes the small tube of my breast milk from the nurse's hand, and presses down on the syringe, feeding our daughter for the first time. He spends a long time by her side, her small delicate hand clasped tight around his forefinger, and I watch from the rocking chair with tears in my eyes, letting him have his moment with her.

Caleb arrives, but they can't let him in because we're already at capacity; two visitors at our daughters bedside only. Hospital regulations. I leave Sebastian with our baby girl and find Caleb at the reception desk.

"Hey, what's going on? Why aren't they letting me in?"

"I'm sorry, I was supposed to text you. Sebastian came back just a couple of hours ago. I've been a little caught up," I say as his panicked frown turns into an enormous smile.

"No shit. How's he doing?"

"Good. Tired, but good. You want to come in and say hi to him?"

"No, it's okay. I'll catch up with him later. I'll leave you guys to it."

I press a kiss against his cheek. "Are you going to be at mine later or are you heading home?" I ask, taking a few steps back. He's taken up temporary residence with me while Sebastian has been away in Afghanistan, so I don't know what his plans will entail now that Sebastian is back for two weeks.

"I'll go home. I'm obviously not needed for the next two weeks anyway." He sighs dramatically, making me laugh out loud.

"Don't worry. You'll always be my number one, Caleb." I smirk, continuing to walk backwards.

"Hell yeah, I'm your number one. You're one lucky woman, Ava Jacobson, having all these men constantly at your beck and call." He walks off, leaving me gasping for air as thoughts of Ashton suddenly surface and the guilt rears its ugly head again. I force the thoughts of him to the back of my mind, and head back in the direction of Sebastian and our daughter.

When I return, he's sitting down in the rocking chair, his elbows resting against the top of his knees as he gazes lovingly at our daughter. He smiles as I approach, bringing his hands up to my waist and dropping me onto his lap in one smooth transition.

"Everything okay?" he asks, a hint of concern to his voice.

"Yep, it was just Caleb. I forgot to text him, what with all the excitement this afternoon." Minus all the drama, it has been one of my favorite days to date. If it were possible to put your memories in a bottle, I would lock in today's memories in a heartbeat so I could go back and watch it over and over again.

"Why didn't he come in?"

"They only allow two visitors, hospital policy," I explain. "He said he'd catch up with you later."

Returning our eyes back to our daughter, Sebastian seems lost in thought until he shakes his head with a bemused look on his face. "We really need to come up with a name for her. We can't keep calling our daughter, 'her' or 'baby girl' for the rest of her life."

Or Miss Stir Mix-a-Lot …

*Jesus, I really need to stop thinking about Ashton.*

Inwardly, I slap myself for getting carried away with my thoughts. "I know, but I don't like any names. All the names suck." I pull out my bottom lip in a frown.

Sebastian rolls his eyes at me. "Now you're just being ridiculous. You must like some names?"

"Yeah, of course I like *some* names, but nothing sounds good enough for our daughter. Do you have any ideas? Please tell me you have an idea or we're screwed."

He chuckles as he plays with a strand of my hair. "I have thought of a few actually. How about Lily-Mai? A lily after your favorite flower and Mai after my mother. Or Ava-Grace, after you and my grandmother …"

I stop listening as soon as I hear the name Lily-Mai. That is perfect. It's beautiful, unique and it seems to fit her effortlessly. "Wait. Lily-Mai, I love that. Lily-Mai," I repeat, testing how it sounds on the tip of my tongue. A sob escapes when I realize this name is perfect.

"I love you so much, it's perfect, so perfect!" I smack a full-blown kiss against his lips through my falling tears. Happy tears. With a breathless sigh, I pull away.

His eyes are wide with humor. "You actually love the name? I thought you said all names suck?" he mocks.

"That was until you came up with Lily-Mai. It's beautiful."

He smiles his award winning smile before pressing yet another kiss against my mouth. "So we're going with Lily-Mai?" he whispers against my lips.

I nod enthusiastically as I press a kiss against his lips. I pull away and smile affectionately between my fiancé and my daughter, my daughter who finally has a name. Lily-Mai. "Yes, we're calling her Lily-Mai Gilbert."

"No, we're calling her Lily-Mai *Ava* Gilbert."

I launch my arms around his neck, pressing my body deeper into his. "I love you," I murmur into his neck, smiling happily against his skin.

"I love you too."

My smile suddenly falters when I look up and see a distraught set of green eyes looking back at me. Ashton stands there motionless, the hurt evident on his face as he looks between Sebastian and me.

My heart slams down into my stomach as I notice what he currently has clasped in his hand. I have no idea how he knew that was my favorite flower or that I named my daughter after it just moments ago, but in his hand is a single cut pink and white calla lily. There is no mistaking it. I have no idea where he could have possibly gotten it from, here in the middle of a hospital, and I'm pretty certain flowers of any kind are prohibited in the NICU. Before I can react, he turns and rushes away, leaving me speechless and guilt-ridden.

# chapter 8

A S MUCH AS I want to say I had a better sleep last night, with Sebastian beside me for the first time in months, I can't because I'd be lying. I spent the majority of the night tossing and turning, racked with internal guilt. I couldn't get the image of Ashton's distraught face out of my head.

It makes no sense. I've only known the guy for two minutes. Why should I care that he saw me with my fiancé? He knows I have a fiancé, so why did he look so hurt by it? Why did he look almost heartbroken?

To say that I'm confused would be the understatement of the year. I'm so far-off being confused that I'm pretty sure there isn't a word in the English dictionary that describes how I'm feeling right now. However, there is one word that has been circling my brain for the past fifteen hours—tease. Well, more specifically 'dick tease,' and I can't help feel that I've led him on somehow. It would explain his reaction yesterday ...

"Hey, you okay?"

I'm abruptly brought back to the present with the sound of Sebastian's voice. I look up to see him staring down at me, a bemused look on his face. I clasp his hand tightly in mine, giving him a reassuring smile. "Yeah, I'm fine. Sorry, I was miles away."

"Come on," he coaxes, pulling me in the direction of Lily in her NICU room.

Putting everything else to the side for a moment, I'm blissfully happy to be walking hand in hand with Sebastian, and I have to thank my lucky stars he's safe and here with me right now. Knowing I have him all to myself for the next two weeks leaves me feeling somewhat giddy, until I remember the war zone he has to be subjected to for another four months when he returns. The thought makes me feel violently sick.

Once Sebastian and I have thoroughly cleaned our hands at the communal sinks, I round the corner and my heart comes to a stop. Ashton is doing his vital checks on Lily. With my hand clasped tightly in Sebastian's, I approach with apprehension. Oblivious to my inner turmoil, Sebastian engages him in conversation. I stand back, and it suddenly feels as if my vocal chords have been ripped out of my throat.

"How's my daughter?"

I watch Ashton intently as he looks up from Lily's chart and over to Sebastian with a professional smile, subsequently avoiding all eye contact with me. I hate to admit it, but my heart takes a brutal hit as he ignores me.

"She had another successful night, no problems at all. You must be Sebastian?"

Sebastian smirks knowingly down at me. I smile back uncomfortably, noticing in the corner of my eye the dubious look on Ashton's face. "Yes, I am. Ava must have told the entire hospital about me. It's good to know she didn't forget about me while I was gone." He chuckles while my gut churns inside out with unruly guilt. I purposely avoid looking at Ashton and focus solely on Lily.

"No chance of that." Ashton gives a feigned laugh, my heart almost shattering into a million pieces at the underlying jealousy I can hear in his voice. I clench my eyes shut, feeling like the worst human being in the entire world. To make matters worse, Sebastian wraps his arms around me, bringing me closer to his chest and kissing the very top of my head. Usually I'd embrace this kind of affection from Sebastian, but with Ashton only two feet away, I feel as if I'm flaunting my relationship.

"So I hear you've been in Afghanistan. Are you back for good?" Ashton asks.

"Unfortunately not. I'm only back for two weeks special leave, then I have to head back out there. But it's only four more months, then I'll be back for good. I need to focus on my family, you know?"

I watch as Ashton gives Sebastian a subtle smile and I swear for just one moment I see a flash of resentment in his eyes but it quickly disappears again as if it were a figment of my imagination.

"Well, it was nice to meet you. I'm Dr. Bailey, one of your daughter's neonatologists. If you have any questions, I'm always around, so don't hesitate to ask." He holds his hand out to shake Sebastian's hand, a genuine smile on his lips.

"Thank you. Likewise, Dr. Bailey." Sebastian accepts his hand eagerly.

Ashton goes back to Lily's chart, Sebastian watches over Lily, and I'm left to stifle through my thoughts of utter confusion.

Sebastian left the hospital early this afternoon to run some errands, so it's just Lily-Mai and me at the moment. As I caress her tiny little hand, I smile at the memory of this morning when Sebastian held her against his chest, wrapped gently in his arms. It was the most precious image I've had the liberty of witnessing and even thinking about it now gives me light goose bumps. When a single tear rolled down his cheek as he gazed proudly down at her, the moment became perfect.

They are two of the most important people in my life and the similarities between them are uncanny. The same darkened hair, similar shaped lips, chin, and nose. I can't see myself in her at all. They're definitely two peas in a pod that's for sure.

As I continue to gaze at Lily-Mai, I feel the presence of Ashton beside me. I gulp nervously, letting go of my daughter's hand and adjusting it back into a comfortable position before closing the isolette door. I take a step back, slowly glancing in his direction. Immediately, I feel the awkwardness radiating from him. His face is unresponsive, and the way he stands with his body positioned as far away from me as possible gives me the impression he wants to feel the distance. This saddens me.

"Hi," I say, hoping to get some kind of reaction from him. He doesn't so much as throw a cursory glance in my direction as he pulls on a pair of latex gloves. The angry sound of the latex snapping against his hands causes me to flinch.

"Hi," he answers in a clipped tone, again expressionless. This side of him is a trait I didn't realize he carried and I don't like it. He opens the isolette door and uses an alcohol swab to clean Lily's heel.

"How are you?" I ask, hoping to entice him into at least having a conversation with me, but I have a feeling it's going to be a lost cause. My mouth feels dry, and my palms are sweating with nerves. It's unpleasant.

"Good."

I feel my heart sink in my stomach at his standoffish attitude. I take a huge gulp, trying to salvage some saliva to avoid choking on my own tongue. I watch as he opens up a pink disposable lancet from its packet. I have to look away when he uses the lancet to puncture the skin of Lily-Mai's heel and begins to collect the blood specimen as it still makes me feel queasy. I gaze at his beautiful face, and surprisingly, it relaxes me.

"We came up with a name, by the way. Lily-Mai," I say, hoping to improve the conversation, or lack thereof. I smile proudly before his less than enthusiastic reply wipes it off my face.

"Yep, I noticed." He tilts his head to the pink elephant name tag that hangs loosely from her incubator. "That's ... um, that's great, Ava. It's a beautiful name." He tries to smile, but the look of pain in his eyes slashes deep at my heart.

"I just thought you'd like to know," I whisper. He doesn't respond. The awkward silence becomes so unbearable that I have to ask the first question that pops into my head; a question I'm pretty sure I already know the answer to. "Have I done something to upset you?"

He freezes, his jaw clenching at the sound of my voice. He's silent for a moment and just when I think he isn't going to answer, his heated words startle me. "No, Ava." He sighs exasperatingly. Avoiding me at all costs, he keeps his eyes down on Lily. "I'm just ... busy."

"If I haven't upset you then why won't you even look at me?" My bottom lip trembles at his blatant disregard for me.

He glances into my direction. "I'm fine, see?" but the evident pain I can see in his eyes isn't that of a person who is fine.

"I can see you're not fine, Ashton. Can you just tell me what I've done wrong, please?" I have to take a few deep, calming breaths to help keep the tears at bay.

"Ava, you haven't done anything wrong." He flinches as I rest my hand on his arm.

"Is it because of yesterday, because if it is, I'm so—"

I stumble backwards when he cuts me off, snatching his arm away from me with lightning speed, so fast that you would have thought my touch had physically stung him. I pale on the spot, feeling moisture begin to dampen in my eyes.

"Don't, okay? Just don't." His sad eyes plead, giving me an intense glare that has my heart cracking under the pressure.

"Ashton, I—"

With a dark and haunted look, he hastily cuts me off with a whisper. "Just drop it, Ava, please. Leave it alone. And, for the record, it's Dr. Bailey."

I double over in excruciating pain, completely breathless at his words. "I-I thought we were friends?" I question with a trembling breath.

"No, I'm your daughter's doctor. Now, if you'll excuse me, I have things I need to be getting on with." I watch dumbfounded as he turns back to my daughter. On a shaky inhale, I reach over to the rocking chair for my purse and hastily place the strap against my shoulder.

"I'll be back soon, sweetheart," I say to my daughter, pressing my fingertips against the incubator. Pushing my humiliated tears back, I turn to him one last time. "Look after my daughter, *doctor*."

Wiping angrily at the tears that trail down my face, I walk away, not taking a second glance. If he wants to be an ass, then he can be my guest. Actually he'll be doing me a favor. He was overwhelming, and he was beginning to confuse the hell out of me. At least now I won't have any more distractions, and I can just concentrate on what's important. My family. I don't need Ashton … sorry, *Doctor* Bailey.

It's late when Sebastian and I arrive back at our apartment. Ever since he came back from his errand this afternoon, he's had a goofy grin on his face. As we approach our front door, Sebastian's smile grows, and I become more suspicious.

"You've got that goofy grin on your face again," I state with a small smile of my own.

"What do you mean?" He smirks, making me roll my eyes.

"The goofy grin you've been wearing all afternoon." Placing my hands on my hips, I squint my eyes, putting him under scrutiny. "What are you up to?"

"I have a surprise for you."

"A surprise, for me?"

He nods as he takes something out from his jeans pocket. It happens to be a black silk blindfold. "Yeah, but first I have to blindfold you or it will spoil the second surprise."

Now I'm intrigued. This day has just dramatically improved. "A second surprise?"

He chuckles at my bewildered response while moving to stand behind me. He doesn't say a word as he places the black material over my eyes, instantly blocking my sight as he fastens the blindfold securely around my head. I feel the warmth of his body move in front of me.

He takes both my hands in his. "Can you see anything?"

"Nope."

I hear the sound of the front door opening, then a gravity pull as Sebastian leads me over the threshold by our hands. My heart starts beating a little faster at the loss of my senses, and a small bout of panic begins to consume me as he leads me through the apartment.

"Don't let me walk into anything," I say, and he laughs as we come to a stop. I expect him to take the blindfold off, but he doesn't. Instead, I feel the presence of his lips lingering against mine. Immediately he deepens the kiss and I relax into him, moving my hands up against the solid ripples of his chest, moaning at the incredible sensation his kiss brings to me. The darkened environment heightens my senses and makes everything seem much more erotic, causing nerve-ending vibrations to jolt through my body at the anticipation of the unknown. I moan inwardly when his lips pull apart from mine but that is quickly replaced with an audible moan as I feel his tingling breath hover over my ear.

"I wouldn't let anything happen to you, I promise."

The mixture of my hidden eyesight, my body on high alert and the sensation of his mouth against my ear, almost causes me to combust on the spot. "We're keeping this blindfold," I state breathlessly.

I feel his mouth move tenderly just below my jawline. "Is this turning you on?" He trails his fingertips along my arm, and I can't stop the shiver that escapes when I feel the early signs of a sensual heat pool within the confine of my panties, my clit throbbing violently against the material.

"Hmm," I moan as his fingers trail delicately along the top of my hands, over my protruding hipbone and down towards my pulsating area, skimming over my sex. As he brushes over it a second time, his forefinger burrows against my clit, bringing me dangerously close to the brink with two touches alone. His lips press against my ear, causing me to whimper.

"Later, gorgeous, or you're going to ruin my surprise," he whispers teasingly as his finger moves from my clit.

"Sorry, I'm under strict instructions. No action for at least six weeks, so four more weeks of abstinence," I say with a breathless sigh.

"Are you serious?"

I smile, desperately trying to hold my laughter in. "So you're telling me I haven't seen you in over four months, and I can't even fuck my fiancée senseless." He lowers his mouth over my ear. "Well, shit, that sucks," he whispers.

"Well, I'm sure we can think of something, I was only told to refrain from sexual intercourse. The nurse didn't tell me to refrain from the other stuff."

His lips linger against mine. "Like I said ... later, babe."

"You're such a tease," I murmur, a breathless hitch to my voice. My pulse continues to skyrocket as he leads me through the room. "This surprise better be amazing."

He chuckles. "It's beyond amazing, baby," he boasts arrogantly, and I softly laugh. We continue our steps forward, and my ears prick up when I hear the sound of a door opening and then closing from behind. We come to a final stop.

Chills tingle down my back as his knuckles brush gently against the back of my hair. His fingers pull against the material that lingers over my eyes and the blindfold falls. I blink as I adjust to the bright light. Once I have my 20/20 vision in correct working order, I gasp at the sight I see in front of me.

Standing in the center of the kitchen, the entire space is surrounded in multi-colored birthday balloons. Above the dining table is a multi-colored banner with another birthday wish in huge printed letters, balloons covering each corner. I gasp out loud again when I notice an array of different sized gifts scattered around a huge buttercream iced cake that reads,

*Happy 28th Birthday, Ava*
*Sorry I missed it x.*

Feeling overwhelmed by my surprise, I turn towards Sebastian with a smile. He holds my face in his hands. "I know your birthday was a couple of months ago, and I'm so sorry I couldn't be here for it, but I'm here to make it up to you. Happy birthday, babe."

He presses a gentle kiss against my lips before pulling away. He leads me to the table and I take a seat as he sits beside me.

Go on, open them," he urges and I don't hold back. I pick up the smallest gift; a tiny square box covered in beautiful gold glittered wrapping paper. As I rip it open, I burst out laughing as fine gold glitter particles erupt everywhere, covering me in the process. I open the small box to reveal a pair of sparkling purple-studded earrings in a gemstone cut surrounded by fine silver.

"They're so pretty, thank you," I say as my fingertips stroke gently over the gemstone.

He picks up a long, slender box and hands it to me. "Open this one next."

I go to work on ripping the wrapping paper when more clouds of glitter dust erupt everywhere. "Glitter? Really?" I laugh as I continue to rip open the paper.

"Yeah, I didn't think that one through when I bought it, but it will be fun to clean it off you later." He winks.

Once I successfully open the paper, I grin as I'm greeted with a matching purple-studded necklace that hangs loosely on a fine silver chain. I gasp at the intense color of purple as the light reflects from the captivating gemstone. It really is beautiful.

I open the rest of my gifts: a brand new dark navy zip-up hoodie, new perfume and a Kindle Touch which will be perfect for my countless hours at the hospital. As I familiarize myself with the electronic device, Sebastian cooks me a birthday dinner of pancakes. We celebrate everything with breakfast food; it started on our very first date and has become a rite of passage for the two of us ever since.

Once we've eaten our all day breakfast, and a plateful of delicious birthday cake, he heads out of the kitchen for what I assume is my second surprise. He emerges seconds later with an enormous bouquet of white calla lilies and places them in front of me on the table, pressing a soft kiss against my temple.

"Happy anniversary, baby. I'm sorry I couldn't be there for that either," he whispers against my neck, causing goose bumps to prickle against my skin. I reach for my beautiful flowers, the sweet aroma wrapping around my senses like a blanket as I trace my fingers against the soft petals of one single cut lily. I pick up the card that is standing tall against the bed of lilies.

> *Happy four-year anniversary, beautiful.*
> *Sorry I had to miss this along with your birthday.*
> *I will make it up to you.*
> *I love you.*
> *Sebastian*
> **xxx**

I rise up from my seat and throw myself into his arms carefully, wrapping my legs around his thighs, wanting to feel as close to him as possible. "I love my gifts and my flowers. They are amazing, thank you. I love you so much." I gently press my lips to his, before tracing the edge of his mouth with my tongue and pressing it against his, sweeping against the moist texture of Sebastian, moaning at the wonderful feeling that coaxes through my body.

He starts to pull away. "Are you ready for your second surprise?"

I look in his eyes, confusion engulfing me. "I thought my flowers were my second surprise?"

He shakes his head, then kisses the very tip of my nose. "That was the second part of your first surprise. The second surprise is waiting for you in the living room."

I smile at the thought of a second surprise. What else could he possibly have in store for me? He carries me from the kitchen and leads me through to the living room. Just as I'm about to ask him if I need to close my eyes, I burst into laughter at the sight in front of me. It seriously looks as if a care bear has thrown up all over my living room.

"Oh my God," I say through my laughter, slipping through his arms and standing on my own two feet. Plain pink balloons cover the entire ceiling; not a stitch of white can be seen through the pink. A pink, baby shower banner covers one wall above the sofa, with balloons in the shape of pacifiers in each corner. A pink elephant sits in the middle of the coffee table surrounded by hundreds of pink ribbon strands with tiny little footprints embedded on the material. Intermixed between the scattered ribbons are more gifts, in pale pink glittered wrapping paper.

"I know you didn't get a chance to have a baby shower, what with Lily-Mai arriving so early, so I decided to throw you one, just the two of us."

I have no words.

I can't believe he did this for me.

He guides me towards the sofa and once we take a comfortable seat he places a hot pink sash around my neck. 'Yummy Mummy to be', but 'to be' has been crossed out in thick black marker.

"Sorry." He chuckles. "They didn't have anything else." He scoops my hair out from underneath the sash.

"It's perfect."

Everything is perfect. From the insane amount of pink balloons that could quite possibly light up the Space Needle, and the glitter that I'm covered in, to the incredible guy sat next to me. It's perfection at its best. I'm so lucky to have him in my life, and I can't believe I almost ruined it.

I accept the gift that Sebastian passes to me. "More gifts?"

"Yeah, gifts are pretty much a given at a baby shower. Now open it," he says encouragingly. I rip through the paper like a six-year-old child on Christmas day, except I have pink glitter floating endlessly around me.

I burst into surprised tears as I open the gift. It's a tiny pink sleep suit with a matching pink hat. The perfect size for our daughter. "Oh my God, Sebastian, where did you get these?" I pick the tiny baby suit up in my hands, holding it out in front of me with a look of awe. I didn't realize they made baby clothing this small. Even after two weeks of being beside my daughter, little things like this still take me by surprise.

"I looked online last night when you fell asleep, and found a shop that specializes in preterm wear. They had everything from tiny pacifi-ers, micro diapers, neonatal T-shirts and diaper wraps to accommodate with the wires, blankets, everything. I picked them up earlier. They're all in here."

He picks up a large sized box and places it in-between our legs on the sofa. I open it up, and I'm amazed to find tiny baby clothing, unbe-lievably small pacifiers, a cuddle wrap, mittens and what looks to be a thin pink teddy called a Cuskiboo.

"These are incredible," I whisper quietly as I look down at this extraordinary hamper of preemie baby clothing and accessories. I pick up the small teddy bear and feel the soft texture between my thumb and forefinger.

"The woman in the shop said this is ideal for the incubator. You're supposed to sleep with it for a couple of nights, and when you take it to the hospital, the babies can keep the familiar smell of their mother with them. It will be as if you've never left Lily."

I spend the next fifteen minutes sifting through the gifts from cute teddy bears to baby memory boxes and baby journals. He even got me my own breast pump. He didn't think it was particularly hygienic to share the hospital's pump even though I'd explained more than once that they disinfect them after every use, but his main reasoning behind the gift was that my perfect breasts (his words, not mine) need as much gentle care as possible, and the state-of-the-art electric breast pump is the only way to receive that care. It is sweet—in a totally perverted way, of course.

Once everything has been opened, and my living room is covered in pink glitter—Sebastian, and me included—I crawl over to him and straddle against his legs, kissing him hard until we're both gasping for air.

"You're perfect, you know that?" I ask between gentle kisses.

"Well, I have my moments." He smirks with a sexy arrogance.

"Thank you for everything. It's been incredible." I pepper delicate kisses up and down his face. He has always been sweet with me, but today's surprise has to be the most incredible thing he has ever done for me. Nothing could top today.

"Well, that isn't the end. I have one last surprise in store for you."

Another surprise? Oh hell.

As we make our way through the hallway, I see a faint trail of rose petals on the wooden floor leading directly to the door of our room. I turn my head to look at him with a smile as I continue my steps, and that's when I notice how nervous he actually looks.

When I approach the door, I anxiously look back up at him. He gives me a timid smile and I take that as my cue to turn the handle and open the door. The rose petal trail continues, leading directly to the bed that sits in the middle of the room, against the back wall, and the bed has been scattered with hundreds of rose petals in an arrangement of both our names. Between our names is a heart shape.

I turn around to Sebastian and have to hold back a sob.

He's bent down on one knee and holding a ring box between his thumb and forefinger with an anxious smile on his face. "Ava, you made me the happiest man on earth when you agreed to be my wife over the phone two weeks ago, so today I am doing it again, properly, with a ring, the traditional way, my way. So, Ava Jacobson, will you marry me?"

I stare down at him, tears streaming down my face. It is the most beautiful diamond ring I have ever set eyes on. It's a simple white gold band with a single princess cut diamond dominating the center. I push down the lump forming in the core of my throat, and kneel down to his level.

"Yes, I will marry you," I say through my tears. He takes the ring out of its box and places it on my ring finger, then smiles at the elegance that is sitting perfectly on my finger and kisses the diamond. He slides both hands to the back of my head, tangling his fingers through the silky strands of my hair. Pulling me forward, he places his lips to mine and kisses me with a gentle force.

God, I love him.

# chapter 9

I GLANCE DOWN AT my diamond ring, twirling it with my fore-finger as it hangs loosely against a silver chain around my neck. I decided to put my engagement ring on a necklace for now until Lily finally comes home and I can wear jewelry on my hands again. I have to take my necklace off when I hold her, but other than that it stays with me, resting perfectly over my heart. I gaze down at the beautiful reflective colors, hoping that it might take my mind off the fact that Sebastian is currently packing his life away, but it doesn't. I have to face the fact that he has to go back to Afghanistan tomorrow.

I look up from studying my engagement ring, forcing the excruciating lump back down my throat. Sitting cross-legged in the middle of our king-sized bed, I smile sadly at my fiancé. "I wish you didn't have to leave tomorrow," I murmur like a sullen child as he adds boxer shorts to his rucksack.

"I know. I wish I didn't have to go either."

Sebastian looks up and gives me a grim frown as he continues to pack his bag. He stops placing everything into an organized 'military space-saving' way and places the rucksack gently on the floor beside the bed. He crawls over the quilted bed sheets until he finally reaches me. It feels as though it were just yesterday when he came home, and now I have to say another goodbye. The first time was so painful; it broke my heart into a million pieces having to watch him walk away from me. I don't think I can cope with it a second time around. But at least this time will be for the last time.

Four months.

Then he will be home, and he'll never have to endure that horrific warzone ever again.

"Then don't," I say with a smirk, wishing it could be as simple as that.

He kisses my nose, grasping my fingers in a tight lock. "I wish I could, but if I did, then I would be reported AWOL. And quite frankly, that isn't something any soldier would want on his record."

"It sounds pretty romantic though, going AWOL for the love of your life." I try to use humor as a defense mechanism, a way to conceal the pain that is currently ricocheting through my body, but it's useless. I feel sick to the stomach at the mere thought of tomorrow.

"Four months, then I'll be home. And then you'll probably get sick of seeing my face every day."

I shake my head in immediate disagreement. "Never. I can't wait to see your face every day. It's just cruel that I've had you all to myself for the past two weeks, and now I have to let you go back for another four months. I hate it. I wish you didn't have to go." I pull out my bottom lip with a trembling cry. He looks at me with such heartbreak that I feel my own heart shatter with the sadness of his turmoil.

His hand gracefully grazes my chin, his thumb stroking gently against the softness of my skin, forcing me with a telepathic gaze to look directly into his glistening tear-filled eyes. "Trust me, there isn't anything I want more in the world than to stay here with you and Lily. I wish that I could stay so much."

I don't say anything. I can't say anything because anything I might say could cause me to burst into tears at any second, and I want to leave the hysterical craziness of sobbing until tomorrow, when I'm on my own and I can wallow in my own misery.

"Do you think it's going to be easy for me to leave you both for the next four months? Do you think I want to go back to that war zone and witness people dying?" I wince at the disturbing visual thought that just erupted inside my brain, and I try with all the strength possible to push it to the back of my mind.

"Do you think I don't know that there is a tiny possibility that I might not return home? That I could be one of the unlucky ones who come home inside a wooden box? That I might not get to see your beautiful face again? That I won't see my daughter's beautiful face again? It's all I've thought about."

I shake my head frantically as the tears run painfully down my heated cheeks. "Please … please don't say that. You have to come home." I wipe my falling tears with the back of my hand as I look desperately into his eyes, the possible truths hitting me hard. It's almost too much to bear.

"I'm sorry, babe. I didn't mean to upset you. I'm just scared."

I hold onto his hands in a death grip, feeling my tears gradually subsiding. "It's okay. It's okay to be scared."

He smiles sadly at me, pulling me onto his lap. "I'm not usually this much of a wreck. I'm just going to miss you so much, and now that I've decided to leave the army, I wish I could just leave without having to go back."

I trace patterns along his chest with my finger as I look up at him. "Well, if it's anything like these past two weeks, the time will fly by." I smile, trying my best to make light of the whole situation, even though my heart cracks at the physical thought of being apart from him for another four months.

"You think?"

"Yes, and if it doesn't, just keep in mind that when you come home, Lily will most likely be at home with us." I have to send Sebastian away with a positive thought, or I think he might break down. Lily is getting stronger, but she isn't out of the woods just yet. I have faith in her though.

"You're amazing, you know that?"

He slams his lips onto mine, and a battle of ecstasy instigates immediately. I'm on my back as he deepens our kiss. A moan of pleasure leaves my lips at the feel of his arousal pushing against my overly aroused sex, his fists gripping tightly in my hair.

"Usually I'd fuck you senseless right about now, but seeing as I can't do that, I'm going to kiss you senseless for the rest of the night instead. Is that good with you?"

"Yes," I breathe out as he kisses me deeply, his tongue melting into mine. And we do just that. We kiss for the rest of the night.

The perfect way to say goodbye.

The next morning comes around agonizingly fast, and once Sebastian has had one last cuddle with his daughter, it's time for him to go. I can already feel my chin trembling with the build up of tears as he says goodbye to Lily, telling her how much he loves her and how much he'll miss her. Then I nearly lose it on the spot when he promises Lily that he'll come back to her and her momma. I grind my teeth together, swallowing the lump that is lodged deep inside my throat as I try to clamp down with every muscle in my body, urging myself to keep strong until I'm out of the NICU and away from the prying and sympathetic stares of the medical staff.

I feel my heart double over when we eventually find ourselves outside the main building, gazing at each other intensely, awaiting the doom of our goodbye. He drops his bag beside his feet and pulls me into him, enveloping me in the warmth of his strong arms.

"Are you okay?" he whispers in my ear.

Of course I'm not okay. How could I be? I'm sending my future husband into a death trap, and I don't have any guarantees that he'll come back to me. I shake my head as heat fills my face and tears furiously fall down my face as I cry into his arms. He pulls me closer and his hand caresses my hair as he places lingering kisses against the side of my head. "Four months and then everything will return to normal. We can be a family, be husband and wife. I love you so much. I'm coming back, okay? I'm coming back."

I nod even though I'm not convinced, but I know what I have to do. Put my trust in faith. It's what I've been focusing on to help Lily-Mai fight through this intense battle of her life since day one, and what I continue to focus on in order to get her out of the hospital. I have to believe that he will come back to me. If I don't, then what will that leave me with? Nothing. Faith is I all I have, and I plan on grasping it with both hands, praying with the universe that I can have my happy ending;

praying that my life won't suddenly be crushed into a thousand pieces.

"I'm coming back," he repeats in my ear, and I grasp him as tight as possible, desperately not wanting to let go of his loving arms. I want to cherish his hold with every essence of my body.

And I do.

I learn by heart the distinctive smell of his cool fresh scent, the warmth of his body against mine, the feel of his mouth against my lips and his tongue sweeping against mine. I memorize the way he is huskily breathing against my ear right now, saying how much he loves me, and as I glance up at his beautiful blue eyes, I memorize how incredible he looks in his Army uniform, with his name standing proudly on the badge against the right side of his chest. I'm extremely proud of his selflessness and how brave he is to return, even though I desperately don't want him to leave.

"I love you too," I croak.

He brushes his lips against mine, and I lose myself in his mind-blowing kiss. Everything and everybody dissolves around us as his kiss consumes me until all I can feel are our pounding hearts beating as one. I feel light on my feet as I kiss him back with an equal intensity. I feel heat radiating deep within me as he puts every last drop of emotion into our gut-wrenching embrace. It says everything words could never express.

I stumble backwards as Sebastian pulls away from my lips just a fraction and chuckles breathlessly against my mouth. "Wow." He brushes another longing kiss against my swollen lips, then pulls back, bringing his hands up to my face and caressing both thumbs against my flushed cheeks. "If I hadn't had already proposed to you, I'd be on my knees begging you to marry me in an instant. That was some kiss."

I smile as I glance over his shoulder, noting that his taxi still hasn't arrived. "Well, stop talking and kiss me until your taxi comes."

He doesn't argue. He gently presses his lips back to mine, sucking against my moist lips as I eagerly accept his beautiful mouth. My tongue sweeps lightly against his as tingles erupt up and down every molecule of my body. We enjoy the closeness of our embrace for as long as physically possible, but I know it will only be a matter of seconds before he has to leave me.

I sob against his mouth as soon as I hear the distinctive sound of a car horn, and I know that our time is up. My tears fall as I cry into his chest, clinging onto him as though my life depends on it. He holds me tight against his body and presses his lips against the top of my hair, caressing the ridge of my spine with his fingers.

"I have to go," he chokes with a whisper. I nod as tears continue to flow against my weeping face and I pull away. I die a thousand deaths when I look up to him. His face is haunted with a look of despair that I feel crippling at the center of my own heart.

"I'm going to miss you so much." I press a final kiss against his lips, trembling as I pull away for one last time. "I love you. Go be a soldier."

He takes a step back, a sad smile fading on his face. "I love you too."

I close my eyes, trying to force the tears back as he walks into the direction of the cab. Once he's safely inside the taxi, I take hold of my engagement ring that is draped around my neck on a chain and kiss the diamond, then blow the kiss to him. He smiles and returns the gesture. I choke on a sob as his taxi begins its descent.

Then he's gone.

Unable to hold back, I burst into tears in the middle of the outside courtyard. I drop to my knees, allowing the heart-wrenching tears to shake through me.

I don't know how long I'm bawling into my hands, but eventually the tears start to dry up and I take my first step of courage forward without Sebastian. I have to go back to my daughter. Wallowing in self-pity isn't going to be helpful to Lily-Mai.

I stand up, taking a deep breath as I wipe the concrete dust away from my knees with the palm of my hands. Once I feel a little more composed and less likely to break down at the thought of my heartbreak, I turn around and make my way back into the hospital.

As I approach the double doors, I notice a familiar face walking in my direction and I pause for a moment as my heart jolts to a stop when his gaze falls on mine. I sniff and wipe my eyes from the moisture of my salty tears. For a moment, I think he's going to say something, but instead he looks at me with a hint of sympathy in his eyes. I grind my teeth in agitation. He can't just suddenly start talking to me again now that Sebastian is gone. No, no way. Plus, I haven't spent the past two weeks trying to get him out of my head just for him to confuse me again. No, it isn't fucking happening.

With the dirtiest look I can muster, I glare at him as I walk away, ignoring the heated stare I can feel directed at the back of my head as I stride in the direction of the elevators.

# chapter 10

WALKING UP THE STEPS to my mother's mansion, I can feel the vibrations under my feet as the pounding music practically rattles through the house. My brother must be having one of his 'parties of the year' which he throws at least four times a year. A shiver crawls slowly up my spine at the thought of him as I approach the glass covered double doors. I take a deep breath as I grab the gold door handle that reverberates against my fingers, counting down from three before I enter the pandemonium.

Three, two, one ... enter.

My heart beats erratically against my chest as I squeeze past the drunken idiots, despising the very feel of their sweaty heated bodies pushing and clawing against mine. I fight among the limbs of others, desperately wanting to get back to the surroundings of my bedroom. The only room he doesn't enter.

Thankfully, I don't see him as I climb over the comatose junkies, slide past couples sucking face, and kick my way through drunken perverts as I make my way up the stairs. I look over my shoulder in rising panic as I continue down the hallway until I finally reach my bedroom. I put the key inside the lock and turn it, opening my door. I breathe out a sigh of relief once I'm inside my dark room. Just as I'm locking my-

*self inside my safe haven for the night, I feel two hands curl around my waist, and I yelp out a scream of absolute terror. My heart is hammering beneath my skin as a hand covers my screaming mouth, the sound of chuckling against my ear.*

*"Shh, it's just me."*

*Tears fill my terrified eyes as shivers convulse through my entire body at the sound of his voice. He isn't supposed to be here. He doesn't come in here. My door was locked. I don't understand how he got in. I got the lock specifically for this very reason. I knew it would have only been a matter of time ...*

*"I missed you, where have you been?"*

*I squeeze my eyes shut in disgust as I feel his lips nuzzle against my neck, the cool air of his mouth sending disturbing chills against my skin. I clench and grind my teeth against my jaw, anger coursing through every vein of my body. My hands feel clammy with sweat, my mouth feels dry of saliva and as I try to swallow my throat tightens, restricting my breathing. A whimper escapes and I feel something hard against my back as he pushes his hips into me. His hand spreads along my stomach, continuing downward, pursuing towards my groin area. Bile rises from my stomach as my heart continues to thrash against my chest.*

*"Well?"*

*The room begins to spin and heat covers me like a blanket when he cups the most private part of my body. He isn't supposed to be in here. I want to make him stop, but I'm too weak.*

*He has made me weak.*

*"Out," I manage to croak.*

*He spins me around so I'm facing him, my back against the door. The moment I have to look into those evil eyes of his through the shadows of darkness. My internal organs are shutting down on me, one at a time and I can't feel anything. I am numb.*

*"Out?" he questions as he strokes my stomach with his fingertips. He sounds almost angry.*

*I nod pathetically, afraid of what he might say to me.*

*"Who with?"*

*My teeth chatter together as I shake my head, my entire body shaking with fear. "Nobody." I slam my eyes shut as I try to hold the tears. I can't show him how weak he makes me feel.*

*"Are you lying to me?" he spits in my face.*

*I shudder at his wrath as I shake my head hysterically. I'm not lying. I really was on my own. I don't have any friends. He doesn't allow it. He has me trapped.*

*"Have you been out fucking?" he whispers, spitefully. He knows me. He knows I don't fuck around. I haven't been with anyone else and he knows that. He is the only person who has ever touched me, and the thought makes me sick.*

*He is sick.*

*"No ... I promise," I stammer urgently as tears spill from my eyes. I take a strained gulp at the terrifying man that is staring down at me with an obvious look of lust.*

*"Good, because you're mine."*

*He looks up and down my body and the gaze alone has me quaking in my boots. It's a look of pure evil. His hands trace my curves. I clamp my eyes shut as his fingers begin to unzip my jeans. I desperately urge myself not to vomit as the bile continues to rise.*

*Oh no, please no, no, no ...*

*"My gorgeous Ava ..."*

I jerk up out of bed, screaming hysterically. Sweat is drenched through my pajamas and my heartbeat is accelerating in my chest as I look around the room, looking for him. I shiver with a cool sweat as Caleb runs into my bedroom with only a tiny towel wrapped around his waist, water dripping down his body. The sound of the shower running fills the silence.

"Ava! What's wrong?"

I claw at my face with my hands, sobbing against my fingers. It's been years since I've had that dream. What the hell? Why am I suddenly being haunted by that vision, again? It was bad enough to live through it the first time.

Caleb's strong arms wrap around my body, but with the vision of *his* arms around me still fresh in my mind, I stiffen and bolt out of Caleb's arms, running into my ensuite, slamming the door shut as the terrors continue to replay in my mind. I stumble into the bathtub, turning the shower on at the press of a button, yelping out loud as the icy water thrashes against my face and body. I allow the water to assault my face, mixing with my tears as sobs gurgle from my mouth. I turn away so my back is pressed against the cold tiled wall and shrink down inside the tub, the water soaking through my pajamas. Shakes convulse through my body and goose bumps shudder against my skin as the cold water covers every inch of me.

I sense a body coming into the bathtub. I know it's only Caleb, but I cower in the corner, sinking my head to my knees as I try desperately to force the fucked up dream out of my head.

Caleb yelps as the freezing water covers him. He must turn the heat up on the water since it immediately begins to warm up, helping to ease my shivers. I feel him bend down to my level, his hand stroking gently over my soaked hair.

"Are you having nightmares again?"

By nightmares, he means the post-traumatic dream where my brother raped me for the first time, taking away my innocence at fifteen years old and continuing to rape me until I turned eighteen, until I ran away from home. I nod through my choked cries. He reaches out for me, his fingertips stroking my face as he comes closer, but I shudder from his touch. All I can see is *his* evil face. I just want it to stop.

"It's me, Ava. I'm not going to hurt you. It's just me." Caleb's words sink in. I know he would never hurt me. He loves me. He's my rock.

I launch my soaking wet body on top of his and cry into his naked chest. I feel his soothing arms wrap around my body, his fingers caressing delicately against my back, speaking softly in my ear. "It's okay, it's okay. I'm here. It's okay."

"It won't go away," I whimper, *his* evil eyes and smug smile haunting my mind as I close my eyes tight.

"Well, let's get that bastard out of your pretty little head okay? Just imagine you're on a beautiful beach, white sand between your toes, clear blue skies, the sea is a perfect color between green and blue with the sun shining down on you. It's paradise, and the only thing you can hear is the crashing of the waves. Can you see it? Can you feel it?"

I feel myself begin to relax in his arms as I visualize the quaint surroundings of a paradise island, somewhere like Jamaica …

Yes, Jamaica. Jamaica is perfect.

I can still see *his* face, but it is gradually fading as Caleb continues to talk in gentle tones. I imagine the heat from the shower is the heat beaming down on me from the scorching sunshine. It actually feels wonderful. Relaxing.

"Imagine the arms you feel around you right now are Sebastian's. He's holding you, softly kissing your silky brown hair, whispering in your ear how much he loves you, how much he cherishes you, how much he can't wait to marry you. He can't wait to call you Mrs. Ava Gilbert."

I smile into Caleb's chest. I can't help but caress his stomach, loving how warm he feels under my fingertips. My stomach fills with tingling butterflies, each time his mouth lingers against my hair.

"You're watching your beautiful three-year-old daughter. She's dressed in a bright pink all-in-one swimsuit so she doesn't burn in the sun. Her wet, curly hair bounces perfectly against her shoulders. She's trying to build a sandcastle, but instead she covers herself with the pure white sand. She giggles as she runs in the sand, a smile so bright and beautiful it makes your heart melt. "Mommy, can you help me make a sandcastle?" she asks you with such an adorable smile you couldn't possibly dream of saying no. Then you stand on your own two feet and chase her around the deserted beach until you catch her and tickle her arms and ribs until she is giggling hysterically in your arms."

I laugh softly at the wonderful picture I see fold out in front of me, of my daughter. It feels so real in my head that I don't want to open my eyes to the reality, so I keep my eyes closed, clinging to Caleb's wet body as if my life depends on it. The remainders of my dream have vanished from my head and I finally open my eyes, smiling sadly at Caleb's concerned face.

"How you feeling?" he asks, concern circling in his eyes.

"Okay, I guess. He's gone now."

"Is this the first time you've had one in a while?"

I nod as I sit up out of his arms and backcomb my wet hair with my fingers.

"Yeah, not since college. I don't understand what triggered it. It was so real, Caleb, I felt as if I was back there." I wipe my wet eyes frustratingly. "God, I thought I was past this shit." I shake my head with anger. It's been thirteen years, yet the bastard keeps ruining my life.

I hate my brother to hell and back.

Even before the first time, he would give me weird looks, touch

86

me in inappropriate places, whisper inappropriate things to me, and it was always when my mother wasn't around. It was as if the bloom of my puberty lured him, but when my mother was around, which wasn't very often by all accounts, he would act like any regular brother. I knew it was wrong, I knew it was evil, but I was only fifteen years old at the time, and I was too frightened to tell anyone. He was a very influential person. Everybody knew who he was. His status on the high school basketball team meant he was practically a celebrity in our small town in Miami, so the probability of anybody believing their precious shooting guard was abusing his little sister behind closed doors would have been next to impossible.

He was a god in their eyes, flawless and perfect, whereas I was just plain old Ava. A loner. A geek with an overbearing asshole brother who was hell bent on pushing all my friends out of my life. I never understood why he did the things he did to me. He had girlfriends his own age, he was ridiculously popular, and I heard through the grapevine that he was a player, sleeping his way through half of the girls in high school.

He took my virginity like it was his for the taking. But once wasn't enough for him. He kept coming back for more and continued to force himself on me as if it was normal to be raping his fifteen-year-old sister. I craved my period because it meant he wouldn't touch me. I could walk around without my heart constantly thundering away in my stomach, without looking over my shoulder every second, trying to determine when or where he would come for me.

It was easier when he moved away to college, I could be myself again, only having to worry about him during the holidays and a few weekends here and there. He brought a girl home with him one weekend, and I desperately hoped his infatuation with me had finally stopped. I almost believed it. He was so affectionate with her, so loving, extremely loud in the bedroom. In a twisted way, I even felt happy for him. I honestly thought it had stopped, that he'd finally leave me alone ... until he came into my bedroom during the second night of their stay and proved me wrong. I despised myself for being so fucking gullible and stupid that I didn't leave my room for the rest of their stay. I was afraid that she'd be able to sense what he did to me right under her nose. That somehow she would be able smell him on me even though I scrubbed myself bloody in the hottest shower I could endure, removing all essence of him from my body. I harbored such heavy guilt that I loathed myself.

It wasn't long after my seventeenth birthday that I began to make my escape plan. I applied to every college in the Washington State, desperate to get away from the only place that haunted every one of my nightmares.

Money wasn't a problem for me. My mother came from an extremely wealthy family. My brother, sister and I were each given a credit card with a limit of fifty- thousand dollars, and a generous monthly allowance.

I had everything organized. My flight was leaving early the following day from Birmingham, Alabama. Instead of catching a flight in Miami or any other airport around the Florida vicinity where I could have easily been tracked, I decided to rent a Hertz car from Miami airport, drive the eleven hours to Alabama, and catch a flight from there.

I left Miami with one suitcase packed with basic necessities, clothing, photographs of my father and sister, and a teddy bear my father gave me when I was little. I also had my passport, my boarding passes and a bankcard with two hundred and fifty-thousand dollars. I left, not once regretting my decision to leave, but feeling guilty for leaving without saying goodbye to my sister. That hurt tremendously. I had contemplated taking her with me, to take her away from this hellhole called life, but it was one thing for me to disappear from the face of the earth; it was another thing to be responsible for the abduction of my twelve-year-old sister. Instead, I left a small, pink, heart-shaped post-it note on her desk in her bedroom.

I just hoped she knew how sorry I was. I hope she still does.

After two months of being in Seattle, I finally met Caleb.

*For the two months I've been here, I've come to one conclusion: it rains. A lot. I've had to invest in a waterproof coat and an umbrella. On the plus side, the temperature has kept in the steady eighties, so at least I haven't had to purchase a whole new wardrobe.*

*Today, however, is a beautiful day. The sun is shining, the heat is blazing, and like the majority of the students at Seattle University, I welcome the last of the summer spell. I walk across the school gardens, my aviators on and an iced-coffee in hand as I look around the various extra curriculum stands during orientation. The school grounds are crowded with freshmen, and that is quite possibly why I don't see the huge jock running towards me trying to catch a football until he slams against me, knocking me off my feet and spilling my entire iced-coffee over me.*

*The stranger immediately pushes himself off me. "Holy shit, are you okay? I'm sorry, I didn't see you!"*

*I'm in a slight daze as I look up at him. It takes me a moment to realize what happened. Then I feel downright humiliated as my ass starts to throb from the sudden fall. Son of a bitch, that hurts.*

*"What do you think?" I feel a little woozy as I stand up, but I manage to stand on both feet without any aid. Then I stumble backwards, and I think I might fall back down, but the stranger's arms manage to catch me just in time.*

*"Whoa, careful." He helps me over to a wooden bench that is close by and sets me down. He runs off to grab a bottle of water and is back within seconds. Sitting down beside me, he holds the bottle of water for me, the top already unscrewed. I snatch it from him and bring it to my mouth. Then I panic. What if he put something in it?*

*"You haven't spiked it, have you?"*

*He chuckles and shakes his head. "No, you're safe." I take this as a perfectly acceptable answer and take a drink, almost gulping the entire bottle in one. "I'm not really into that kind of thing, but even if I were, you wouldn't have to worry about a thing. You're not my type." I gape at the 'not my type' comment. What the hell does he mean by that?*

*"First of all, you knock me down, spill my drink on me, and now*

*you say I'm not very pretty. Gee, thanks. This is a great welcome com-mittee that's for sure."*

*He laughs hysterically. "It isn't because you're not pretty, you're quite the opposite actually. But I'm gay."*

*"Oh ..." I smirk, feeling a little shocked. I'm certainly not his type. "You don't look gay." Oh crap, I wasn't supposed to say that out loud. I feel the heat cover every inch of my face, embarrassment deepening as I drain the rest of my water. He chuckles nevertheless.*

*"What do you want, rainbows and fairies? Sorry to disappoint you, gorgeous, but I like football, not handbags."*

*I laugh. I suppose that was a very naïve thing of me to say, but the only gay references I have are from television and they all seem ex-tremely camp. I've never met anybody who is openly gay before. "Sorry, I didn't mean it like that ... I just meant—"*

*"I'm just messing with you. Don't worry about it."*

*"So what you're telling me is that you were messing with me when you said you were gay? That, in actuality, you are straight and that you may have actually spiked my drink?"*

*His eyes widen in shock and I have to hold back my laughter. "No, I'm gay, I swear. I ... um," His face pales at my accusation.*

*I burst with hysterical laughter. "I'm messing with you," I say through my laughter.*

*His eyes brighten at my confession, smiling at me with affection. "I like you. You're funny." Someone shouts at my new friend, something about getting his ass back over there and finishing the game of football. "I better get back to them. How are you feeling now? You good?"*

*"Nothing that a hemorrhoid cushion won't fix."*

*"Again, I'm really sorry about that. Let me take you out to dinner tonight, to make it up to you. What do you say, my treat? I'll even bring the cushion," he adds with a smirk.*

*It would be nice to go out. I haven't made any friends since I moved to Seattle and I think it's about time I started to live my new life. "Yeah, that sounds like fun."*

*"Okay, great. There's a bar just out of campus called Shelly's Tav-ern. Their food is pretty awesome. You want to meet me there about seven?"*

*I nod as he stands up. "Yeah, okay."*

*"Oh, and I'm Caleb, by the way."*

*"I'm Ava," I say with a smile.*

*"Well, Ava, I will see your pretty little face later. Again I'm really sorry I nearly gave you a concussion and ruined your shirt."*

*I glance down at my coffee covered white tee and shrug. "No problem, I have other shirts."*

*He waves and jogs back to his friends.*

*When I meet him later that evening, I'm pleasantly surprised to find how much we have in common. We have the same ridiculous taste in television programs, the same sarcastic sense of humor and the same bizarre fixation for anything with ketchup. There's a constant flow of conversation as he introduces me to a few of his friends and makes me feel welcome. But most importantly, he makes me laugh, and laughing isn't something I've done in years. A piece of my heart is gradually healing back into place, and I have Caleb to thank for that.*

*I've only known him for approximately six hours, but already I've fallen in love with him. Plus, he isn't exactly bad to look at either.*

*I'm starting to feel Seattle was definitely the right choice for me.*

I glance up to my best friend, smiling as the water from the shower continues to fall over us. I honestly wouldn't know what I would do without him.

"Thank you."

He seems surprised by my words. "Thank you for what?"

"Just for being you. Since the moment I met you, you have always been there for me. Just knowing you has changed my world completely."

He smiles as he places a tender kiss on my forehead. "I will always be there for you, Ava, no matter what. Hoes before bros and all."

Laughter bubbles from me. "I love you, Caleb."

"I love you too. Now, are we ever going to get out of this shower?"

I move from his lap, standing up on both feet, and reach over to turn the shower off. With a smirk, I jump out of the bath, eyeing his towel as he stands. I suddenly remove the drenched towel from around his waist and playfully slap it against his bare ass.

"Ava!" he shouts in humored alarm.

Taking the towel with me, I head out of the bathroom into my bedroom to dry off and get dressed for a day at the hospital with my Lily-Mai.

I check my text messages and smile when I notice a message from the early hours of this morning. It's from Sebastian. He sends me a text whenever he can with a countdown. I just wish the countdown didn't sound like a life sentence.

**Sebastian**: *Only 119 days until I come home. I love you. X*

# chapter 11

*I* STIR FROM MY *sleep as I feel the bed dip. Even in my sleepy unconscious state, I can feel the heat from his body pressed up against my back, the feel of something hard pushing against me. I squirm uncomfortably, edging away from him, my brain screaming for him to get the hell off me, to get the hell away from me. But even in the dark haze of my thoughts, I know I can't do a damn thing to stop him. Chills cover my body as the warm bed sheets are peeled away from me and replaced with something less comforting.*

*I wake with sheer terror, my dream state mind slowly fading away. I screw my eyes shut, praying that the darkness will take over, to engulf all of my senses as deep as possible so I don't have to be a witness to my unwanted torture. An evil tingle spreads through my body like wild-fire as a whisper is pressed against my ear, a touch pressed against my crotch.*

*"I've missed you."*

*A single tear rolls down my face, confirming my fears; sleep isn't going to take me away. Hell, I would easily take death if I could escape the inevitable. His touch turns aggressive as he rips my pajama bottoms and panties off in one. Then without any warning he slams into me, and an agonizing burn spears inside of me causing an inaudible scream to escape ...*

*Suddenly my bedroom isn't my bedroom anymore. Instead, I'm in my bathroom back in Miami. A strange heat soars through my veins as a cold sweat covers my half-naked body. My panties have been discarded, leaving me in my own bloody discharge. I try to stand, but I double over in pain, collapsing against the tiled floor, my hands clawing at the edge of the bathtub. A scream strains from my throat as I glance down; blood gushes dramatically from me, and something pushes from inside, trying to escape. I feel with my hand, and my heart drops when I realize it's a head, a bloody head stretching me, ripping me apart.*

*HELP.*

*Help... help ... please.*

*I hear my name in the distance, and I turn around. Sebastian is running towards me. I feel immediately happy, and the pain suddenly stops ...*

*Everything magically disappears. The bathroom isn't my bathroom anymore but a scorching hot desert instead. He continues to run at me, stomping footprints in the sand. He screams, but he doesn't get any closer; he seems to move further away. The screams become louder and more urgent as an Afghan soldier dressed in a khaki uniform comes into view. A camouflage shemagh covers his head and face, only revealing black haunted eyes. The blood-curdling words, "Ava, run!" echo through the lifeless desert, the urgency in his voice alerting me to this new danger. The sounds of deafening gunshots pierce through my eardrums as angry bullets hit Sebastian's chest over and over again until the light goes off in his beautiful eyes and his limp body crashes heavily on top of the grainy sand. I run towards him as screams erupt from my mouth but death catches up with me.*

*I hear another loud gunshot and something sharp and excruciating hits directly over my heart.*

*Darkness clouds my vision ...*

Screaming wakes me from my nightmare, and I shoot straight up from the bed, my heart thrashing against the inside of my chest. The sweat has drenched through to my tangled sheets.

Fuck.

I glance around my darkened surroundings, taking deep inhaling breaths as I hear heavy footsteps rushing through my apartment. The light from the hallway suddenly illuminates my room when the door opens, revealing a concerned Caleb.

"Ava?" He strides over to my bed and crawls over to me, enveloping his arms around me. I welcome his comforting arms while my nightmare still swirls around in my mind.

"Another dream, sweetheart?" I nod as he swipes a piece of hair that is stuck to my cheek with a cold sweat. "Gosh, you're drenched, Ava. This isn't healthy. This is the fifth night in a row that you have woken up screaming. Maybe we need to get you some help."

Since my first nightmare five nights ago, they haven't stopped, and each night they continue to grow worse and even more bizarre. They always start off with *him*, and then gradually morph into my worst nightmares and undeniable fears. Tonight's nightmare was even more terrifying than usual.

"When am I supposed to get help, huh? When? I spend all my time at the hospital. I haven't got time to talk to a stranger for an hour at a time about how fucking screwed up I am."

I shift my body away from his, unwrapping myself from the wet tangled sheets. Standing up from the left side of the bed, I walk over to the window. I calm slightly as my eyes focus on the early morning city of Seattle in the distance.

I feel Caleb's presence from behind as I continue looking at the scene, my fingers lingering against the cool glass as I watch the light rainfall. "You're not screwed up, Ava. You've just had a lot of shit to deal with."

"Yep, I'm pretty much the definition of screwed up."

I hear him sigh behind me. "Do you want to talk about it? Your dream?"

"No."

I just want to forget about it. I don't want to have to go into the depths of my screwed up mind to explain the reasoning behind my fears. Honestly, I don't think I could explain it even if I wanted to. That dream was so screwed up that it would take a lot more than a few psychologists to help fix me up.

"I just want to forget about it." Even as I say the words out loud, I know there is no way the lifelike visions of my dreams are ever going to go away, especially when they keep repeating in my head on playback.

"Okay, if that's what you want. You should try and get some sleep."

"No, I'm going for a run instead. The rain looks refreshing." I go over to the wardrobe, looking for my running leggings and sneakers.

"Running? It's two AM, Ava," He says half alarmed, half bemused.

"And?" I continue to search through the closet until I finally find my leggings and roughly drag them off the hanger.

"*And* it's October, *and* it's raining, *and* you're going to freeze to death. Plus, I'm pretty sure you shouldn't be running in your condition."

I remove my sweat soaked pajama bottoms and replace them with my leggings. "Exactly. It's perfect weather for a run to help clear my head. I'll be fine." I pull my pajama top off from my body, replacing it with a sports bra and an old band T-shirt. Once I have my sneakers on, I head over to the bedside table and retrieve my pink iPod shuffle.

"Well, give me a second and I'll come with you."

I shake my head as I clip the shuffle to the bottom of my T-shirt, and place the earphones in each ear. "No, I want to be alone, Caleb."

I turn and head out of my bedroom, snatching my keys from the small table beside the front door, and jog out of my apartment.

I turn my iPod on, and the sounds of Papa Roach's *Last Resort* blast through my ears. Once I'm outside in the cold Seattle rain, I run at full speed with no destination in mind, just endurance and adrenaline. The song choice seems quite fitting, so I allow the music to take over my senses, and the anger from the lyrics soars through my veins. I continue to run, allowing the screwed up lyrics to push me to the brink. I play this one song on a constant loop as I try and sort through my own shit, heavily propelling one foot in front of the other, desperately moving forward, urgently running through the streets of Seattle, trying to push the disturbing images of my haunted dreams out of my head. As I continue running to the beat of the metallic drums and the loud guitar riffs, my visions become more extreme and five days worth of dreams come at me all at once.

Unwelcome hands touching ...

Screaming ...

Sobbing uncontrollably ...

Babies crying ...

Gunshots ...

Sebastian dying ...

Lily-Mai struggling for breath ...

My brother ...

I lose all concept of time. I don't know how long I've been running for, but by the time I return to my apartment I'm exhausted. I launch myself through the main doors of my apartment complex and race up the stairs, practically crashing into my front door. The moment I stop running, I hunch over and gasp for air, gripping the doorknob tightly as I start to hyperventilate. Struggling to catch my breath, my heart thrashes recklessly inside my chest. Every muscle in my body burns excruciatingly as a cramp tightens against my hamstrings and thighs. My cesarean scar is throbbing, and I feel nauseous. I try to fit the key inside the lock, but I struggle to find the keyhole as dizziness takes over.

I weakly slam my hand against the wooden door to alert Caleb of my presence as I try to catch my breath. With every second that passes, I feel extremely lethargic and the urge to vomit is prominent. My head throbs with an oncoming migraine, and my soaked body begins to shake violently. I can feel bile rising up my chest, my heart racing as it reaches my throat.

The moment Caleb opens the door, I lose the contents of my stomach all over his bare feet, up the door and down myself.

"Ava!"

I wipe my mouth with my trembling fingers as he reaches for me, cradling me in his arms. He carries me into the low-lit living room, gently sitting me down on the sofa, and covers my shivering, vomit-covered body with a blanket. I shiver uncontrollably under the blanket, my heart continuing to beat erratically against my chest.

"Jesus, Ava, you're fucking soaked," he says before rushing to the kitchen. Within seconds, he bounds back into the living room with a large glass of water. I'm suddenly very aware of how dry my mouth feels and how unbelievably thirsty I am. As soon as he brings the glass to my mouth, I eagerly gulp down the refreshing water, enjoying how easily it glides down my throat. Once I've finished, he places the empty glass on the coffee table, pushing the wet hair away from my eyes, giving me the 'I can't believe you' look.

"Are you trying to kill yourself?"

Tightening the blanket around me, I shake my head as tears begin to fill up my eyes.

"Then what was that?" He points his head into the direction of the door, indicating my meltdown.

I shrug my shoulders as a single tear glides down my cheek. "I just wanted to clear my head."

With a sad look, he pulls my shivering body onto his lap, rubbing me down with both hands, helping me warm up. "And running yourself to the brink of exhaustion and dehydration was the way to do that?" I snuggle into the warmth of his neck, squeezing tight against the inside of my blanket.

"Did it work?"

"No," I mumble quietly into his neck. I just want to forget about *him*, forget about my dreams, forget about everything. But even running, the only therapeutic thing I had going for me, the only thing that helped me cope with my demons, has finally stopped working. Running used to calm me. I would grab my sneakers and run for miles, allowing the tranquility of my surroundings to captivate my inner thoughts. The heavy thoughts and the bad demons would float away, always allowing me to forget how shitty my life was, at least for a little while. Now it seems that I can no longer forget.

I'm beyond repair.

"What the hell is wrong with me?" I sigh frustratingly as shivers pass through my body, my fingertips numbing with the chill of my wet clothes.

Caleb presses me closer to his chest as he continues to rub me down with his warm hands. "Nothing, baby girl. You're just going through a lot."

"I wish Sebastian was here. I miss him so much." I smile sadly at the thought of him. I wish I could hear his voice right now. I just want him to tell me everything will be okay and that he loves me. My heart physically hurts, and knowing that it will be another one hundred and fourteen days until I get to feel him in my arms again kills me.

God … I don't know how much more of this shit I can cope with.

Caleb drops me off at the hospital, and I give him a sad wave as he drives off. I'm practically a walking zombie. My head and heart are still pounding from dehydration, and no matter how much water I consume, it doesn't make me feel any better. I almost wish I could have stayed within the walls of my apartment, crying myself into a miserable sleep, but I know I can't wallow in my own self-pity. I have my daughter to think of. She is the reason why I got out of bed this morning. She needs me.

The first person I see is Ashton and my heart plummets down to my feet at the look of concern on his face. "Ashton, what's happened?" I gasp urgently as I grip his white coat in a tight vice.

He gently takes hold of me by the arms. "Ava, I've been trying to get hold of you for hours. Lily took a turn for the worse during the night." My eyes widen in panic as I slap my hand over my mouth, choking on a sob. My phone. Shit, where is my phone?

"A turn for the worse? Wha-What's happened? She was absolutely fine when I left her last night." If it weren't for Ashton's tight grip, my knees would have buckled under me.

"Come with me," he speaks softly as he guides me to a sofa in the private family room just outside the NICU.

"She's doing okay," he says, smiling sadly. "She was having a few issues with her breathing during the night. She had symptoms of apnea, bradycardia, desaturations and increased work of her breathing. She had a high temperature, she was extremely lethargic, and her blood sugars were low. We took some blood, did an x-ray—"

"Jesus, Ashton, just get to the point. What the hell is wrong with her?" All the venom from the stress of the past week comes pouring out with every word. What is it with doctors? Can they not just get to the point?

He pulls away, looking a little taken aback by my outburst. "She has pneumonia."

My heart drops to my stomach and the tears come on even stronger. "Oh my God ..."

Ashton moves in closer, delicately taking hold of my hand, looking at me with a sweet look that I don't deserve, especially after the way I just spoke to him. "Ava, it isn't as bad as it sounds—"

"It isn't as bad as it sounds?" I question astoundingly, cutting him off again. "She has an infection in her lungs, tiny lungs that are still developing. How can that not be as bad as it sounds? Because from where I'm sitting, it sounds worse than bad, it sounds downright catastrophic."

I look away, concentrating on a bit of invisible lint on my jeans, desperately urging myself to calm down, to ease my tears.

"Pneumonia is just a fancy medical word for a chest infection. Of course, pneumonia can be serious, life threatening if not caught early enough, but we noticed the signs immediately, and because we acted fast, we determined she has a severe lung infection quickly. She is now on a very strong course of antibiotics. I have put her back on the CPAP for a short while to prevent the possibility of her lungs collapsing from the infection. She is stable, her temperature has come down, it is still a little high, but she is doing great. I'm confident she's going to be just fine."

I choke back a cry, my hand tightening into his. "Really?"

"Yes. She's a little weak now, but with the help of the CPAP and the intravenous antibiotics, she'll recover in no time. This is common with a lot of preemie babies due to the poor development of their respiratory system. They are more prone to infection, especially babies like Lily who have suffered respiratory distress syndrome. Early detection is easy, so it's rare that it results in further complication. I'm not saying her recovery will be easy, but I'm guessing you already know that."

I give a gentle nod, sucking in a deep breath, sniffling through my runny nose. "Yeah, I think I know it too well." I feel as though I'm drowning in the deepest of waters without a life jacket and with no way of survival. I abruptly pull my hand out of his and bury my face deep into my hands. "I don't how much more I can cope with."

"Hey."

My eyes water at his sympathy and that only makes me feel worse. I cry hysterically, wishing for just one moment that I wasn't the poor girl with the preemie baby daughter. That I wasn't the poor girl whose fiancé was in Afghanistan. That I wasn't the poor girl who was being tormented by her demons and fears. I want to be a normal girl without a worry in the world.

Of course, the perfect life doesn't exist for me. It never has.

I feel the sofa dip beside me, and when a pair of strong arms wrap around my shaking body, I accept them and bury my face into the incredible warmth of Ashton's chest. After a few deep breaths, the steady beat of his heart begins to create a calming effect, and I don't ever want to let go.

Ashton rocks me back and forth as I grip his white coat, pain ricocheting through my body, causing me to wail through my ugly cries. I feel a comforting tingle move down my spine as he lightly strokes his hand through my long hair. Somehow I've lost my ponytail holder during my hysteria. He doesn't utter a word as I lose control of my emotions. He just lets me break down into his arms.

I know how inappropriate this would look to an outsider, how bad this would seem to Sebastian, but right now Ashton's arms are all I have, and I like how he is making me feel. I finally realize how much I've missed him, how much I missed the friendship that we developed during the confined environment of this hospital. I hate to admit it, but I love the way his arms feel around me; it feels natural. It feels perfect.

My tears eventually dry up, and the only sound in the room is the drumming of Ashton's heartbeat and his soft, light breathing. I know I should let go of him, but I don't. I remain locked in his embrace. I feel safe.

"Are you okay?"

I moan out my reply. Ashton squirms uncomfortably under me, slowly pulling away. I blush as I unwrap my arms from him.

"Sorry about that. You're just extremely comfortable." I cringe as soon as the words come out.

"It's okay."

He clenches his jaw, looking a little tense, and I take this as a hint that he is uncomfortable being in such close quarters. I shift away from him and sit back against the corner of the sofa, tucking my feet under my bottom and brushing out the odd few knots in my hair with my fingers. I notice the single ponytail holder sitting between the creases of the futon, so I pick it up and tie my hair back in a messy bun. I wipe at my swollen eyes with my fingertips, sighing as I remove all presence of my tears.

"I must look a mess."

He gives me a warm smile, shaking his head. "No, you look beautiful."

That takes me by surprise.

I cough nervously, desperately wanting to move away from the heavy subject that involves our obvious attraction to one another and, more importantly, I need him to stop looking at me as if I'm the most beautiful woman on this planet. Not because I don't like it; quite the opposite. But I'm not supposed to feel this way about anyone other than Sebastian. It's wrong on so many levels.

No. It's wrong on *all* levels.

"So, where do we go from here?" I ask.

The lines of his forehead crease. "We?" he answers, his voice thick with emotion.

"Yeah, with Lily."

He looks momentarily lost, then snaps out of his spell. "Of course, Lily. Well, we'll keep her under close observation for the next forty-eight hours, keeping check of her vitals, her breathing and inflammation of the lungs. The trauma from the ventilation has caused the inflammation in the lungs and the CPAP is there to help stop them from collapsing. Plus, the oxygen from the CPAP certainly helps with her restricted breathing. We'll see how she responds to the antibiotics and once we begin to see dramatic improvements, we can think about taking her off the CPAP. I'm confident she will start improving within the next twenty-four hours."

I let out a long jagged breath at yet another hurdle we have to face. As much as I hate that she is back on the CPAP, I'm grateful that it isn't any more serious than this. She can fight through this; she can push through to the very end.

"Just when I thought this intense week couldn't get any worse, it outright punches me in the face. God, when I saw your face … I thought I'd actually lost her. I can't lose her, Ashton, I just can't." I roll my eyes at my endless amount of tears that continue to fall, and wipe frustratingly at them with my fingertips. "God, my emotions are all over the place."

Ashton's eyes darken with an intensity that scares me. "What do you mean by intense week?"

Shit. "Er, um … uh …"

He shifts closer to me until our knees are touching; his accidental touch makes the hairs on the back of my neck stand. "What's going on, Ava?" I shrug. "Look, I know I haven't known you for very long but something is going on, it's written all over your face. Is it Sebastian?"

I laugh. "Believe me, that's just the tip of the iceberg."

"Then what is it?"

I purposely avoid eye contact with him. I'm afraid that if I look into his incredible green eyes he'll see right through me; see the demons that are embedded in the deepest part of my brain. Or worse, blurt out every single secret that has riddled me from the age of fifteen. Every time I look him in the eyes, I physically want to tear my heart open and pour every secret to him, bleeding myself of vulnerability.

It terrifies me.

"Look, I shouldn't have said anything, it's nothing I can't handle."
*If only that were true.*

He winces as he shifts a little closer. "I get it, okay, I get it. I'm the last person you want to speak to about your problems. For what it's worth, I'm really sorry I was such a dick. That wasn't fair. But I like you, okay? And if you're going through something, I'd like to help. Even if you don't trust me enough to tell me, I can refer you to a professional if that's what you need."

My heart rate skyrockets at his words, and I can't help but focus intently on his choice of words—*"But I like you, okay?"*

Instinctively, I reach out and clasp my hand in the warmth of his as I find the courage to look him in the eye. They widen at my intimate gesture, but he doesn't hesitate, his hands tightening around mine.

"That isn't it. I promise. It's more complicated than that, but I don't think a therapist would help. In fact, I know they wouldn't. I've been there, got the T-shirt, but you're sweet for suggesting that, so thank you. What I would like is a friend. You make everything disappear when you make me laugh and I want to laugh again. As it happens, I like you too." I don't add how much, but it is hardly necessary, not when my body language makes it obvious.

He smiles. "I want to make you laugh. So much. I'm here, and I'm here if you ever want to talk. You have my cell number."

I wrinkle my eyebrows. "I do?"

He chuckles. "Yeah, the night you left your phone in my car, I quickly put my number in your contacts before I brought it to you. Just in case."

I'm not quite sure what to say to that and luckily I don't have to respond as his beeper suddenly goes off. I slide my hand out from his and he glances at the black device before looking back at me. "Sorry, I need to go. Are you okay?"

I nod, smiling weakly. "Yeah, I'm okay, thank you. I needed that cry more than I realized." I lean in slowly and gently press my lips to his cheek, causing his breathing to abruptly stop. I linger a little longer than is probably classed as appropriate. He smiles, then takes my hand and we stand together.

"So … Ashton, I guess were back to a first name again, huh?"

He gives a small smile. "Yeah, Ava, I guess we are." We leave the room and say our goodbyes.

As I'm about to walk through the double doors to the NICU, I hear my name being called. I turn to see Ashton looking at me, a concerned smile on his face.

"She's going to be okay," he says.

I nod, giving him a half smile before turning back and walking through the doors of the NICU. Once I head into Lily's room, it takes a lot of strength to keep the tears at bay. The majority of her face is covered with a blue nasal mask that's attached to the CPAP.

She's sound asleep and even though the equipment and wires look frightening, she looks relaxed, almost happy. It's as if these setbacks are just a walk in the park for her, and that she's simply going with the flow. I love how she continues to fight, even after six weeks of constant hurdles and complications. I have never known strength so powerful before, especially from someone so tiny.

And to those who say superheroes aren't real …

You're wrong.

Because I'm looking at one right now.

# chapter 12

I'M SO IMMERSED IN the story I'm reading that for the first time since I've known Ashton, I'm unaware of his presence. His masculine hand grazes gently against my shoulder, jolting me to my senses, and when I say jolt, I mean an eruption of tingles explode up and down my body. Breathlessly, I turn around and smile up at him.

"Hey, Ashton," I say as I press the button at the bottom of the e-reader with my forefinger to turn it to sleep mode.

"Hey to you. You looked miles away. Good book?" He glances down at the device in my hands before returning his eyes back to mine.

"Yeah." I smile. "Sometimes it's nice to get away from everything and be somebody else for a little while, especially with what's been going through my head lately." My eyes widen at my own honesty. Jesus, I keep forgetting how easily my words just slip out when I'm in such close quarters with him. I'm going to have to keep an eye on that, just in case something more secretive slips out, something that can't be taken back.

Noticing the uncomfortable flush glowing against my cheeks, his sad eyes suddenly turn mischievous. "If it's anything like the literature that you edit, I'm guessing you were channeling a submissive, maybe a dom or a pole dancer. So which one was it?" Ashton winks.

I laugh. "None of them actually."

His own hearty laugh trails away, and I feel my heart constrict at his penetrating gaze, swept away by the intensity of it. "How are you?" he asks, shoving his hands into the pockets of his white medical coat, not once taking his eyes from me.

"Yeah…I'm doing okayish," I say with a weak smile, desperately wanting to change the subject. I don't want to spend any more time speaking about my weaknesses. Although yesterday morning was less talking and more sobbing uncontrollably in his arms.

"You were called away pretty quickly. Was everything okay?" I say, successfully being able to steer the conversation away from me.

"No, but it's all part of being a doctor." He shrugs his shoulders, but the sad look he gives me tells me everything without actually telling me.

My heart drops. "I'm sorry."

"For every success story on the NICU, there is always a traumatic ending for another. It's a vicious circle, but that's the way it is."

He looks at Lily for a moment. "It's hard because as much as I would like to be able to save every baby who comes into this unit I know that isn't possible, but it's the preemies like Lily-Mai who give me a reason to push on as a doctor. The incredible babies who do nothing but fight from the moment they are born."

I stare at him, furiously scanning the perfect contours of his face as I search for confirmation he's as amazing as he looks because if he is I'm in trouble.

His breathing noticeably deepens as he looks at me with the same intensity. His mouth turns up into a sexy smile, his eyes twinkling with a look of lust, and for just one moment I have the urge to bite against those incredibly swollen lips of his. They are ridiculously inviting. And what I wouldn't do to run my fingers through every strand of his hair, gripping it tightly in my fists …

"What?" he whispers, the movement of his chest rising and falling in a quickened pace.

I have to shake my inappropriate thoughts away from my head before I can find my voice. "Nothing, I … um, you're just one of the most selfless people I have ever met. You're pretty incredible." This time I actually meant to say what I said, but it still doesn't stop the blush from glowing against my face.

His eyes are wide, momentarily stunned at my words, then he gives out a nervous clipped laugh. "I don't know about that."

Not only is he sexy as fuck, sweet, and selfless, but he's modest too. "I do. A selfish person wouldn't do what you do. You work crazy hours, crazy shifts, practically live in this place twenty-four seven as you save the lives of babies. If that isn't selfless, then I don't know what is."

I earn the most charming smile from the most charming man. "Selfless or not, I didn't sign up for the job for self-gratification or a ticket to the golden pearly gates of heaven. I just wanted to make a difference. And for your information, I don't practically *live* in this place twenty-four seven. I'm actually heading out soon, *and* I have a day off tomorrow," he says matter-of-factly, chuckling quietly.

"Okay, that I retract, but the rest still applies."

"That I'm pretty incredible?" he asks, mocking my words.

"Don't push your luck. I might retract that if you're not careful."

He continues to laugh, his shoulders shaking slightly. "I don't think my ego could cope with the deflation of that retraction."

"I wouldn't want to do anything to deflate you in any way," I mock, adding a dramatic eye roll. It takes a moment to realize the content of my words and how easily they could be taken out of context. He doesn't say anything but the smirk on his face tells me he understood the accidental hidden innuendo behind my words.

For the second time in two days, Ashton has made me feel light again. He has made me forget the weight I've been carrying on my shoulders, and I feel I can breathe. The airy, weightless sensation I'm feeling right now is exactly what I was trying to find in the solace of my run yesterday morning. And even though I know it's wrong on a thousand different levels, I can't hide away from the fact that Ashton makes me feel this way.

Not Caleb.

Not Sebastian.

Ashton.

The mere thought of Sebastian hits me like a tidal wave, and I despise myself for having these strange feelings for somebody else while he's risking his life fighting a bloody war.

"Hey, where'd you go?"

Ashton's burly voice suddenly brings me back to reality, and I realize I've been staring at him. I shake my head, blinking rapidly through my tired eyes, hoping to refresh my mind. "I'm sorry, I was in a world of my own. I think I'm just exhausted," I lie, even though exhaustion isn't far from the mark. That and I'm still feeling a little crappy with the dehydration from yesterday. I confirm my exhaustion with an all mighty yawn that has my eyes brimming with tears.

A velvet chuckle vibrates from Ashton as he takes one step forward, closing the space between us. "You can say that again. Well, I'm off duty in an hour. I have a few rounds to do, my first being this beautiful girl here," he says, smiling affectionately at my daughter. "Then I can take you home if you like." As soon as the words escape his lips, I notice Caleb's head bob up through the glass door, smiling warmly once his eyes stop on mine.

I point towards Caleb as he pushes the door open, entering the NICU room. "Um, it looks like my ride has arrived, but thank you for the offer," I say quietly as I glance nervously in Caleb's direction.

Ashton must sense my growing anxiety in the presence of Caleb as he takes a much-needed step away from me, but never once unlocking his gaze from mine. However, it seems the intense gaze currently coming from Ashton doesn't go missed by Caleb as his forehead wrinkles.

"Am I interrupting something?"

"I was just discussing Lily-Mai with Ava here. I'm going to do some vital checks, then I'll be out of your hair," Ashton says, giving us a polite smile before turning towards Lily-Mai.

Caleb turns to look at me, his arms crossed and his eyebrows raised. When I mouth, "What?" he doesn't say a word, so I sink into the rocking chair and go back to my novel.

When Ashton finishes his vital checks on Lily-Mai, he tells Caleb about her current situation and prognosis then gives me his sweet smile, his eyes gazing almost lovingly towards me. I have to swallow down the lump that has formed at the back of my throat as my heart races faster. I smile back at him as he exits the room, leaving me a little winded by the lack of his presence, even though he's only just left. I don't realize I'm staring at the door until Caleb moves into very same space, shaking me out of my daze.

"That dude is totally into you," he says matter-of-factly. I laugh. The mere thought of Ashton being 'into me' is absolutely ridiculous.

"He is not." I look back down at my e-reader, pretending to be engrossed in the literature even though I've spent the past ten minutes rereading the same sentence.

"I saw the way he was looking at you, Ava. He wants you. Bad."

I don't look up. I continue to stare down at the words that glare uncomfortably at the screen.

"Ava?" he snaps at me quietly.

My head whips up, my eyes narrowing in silent question.

"You're blushing."

"No, I'm not," I say furiously, my cheeks disobeying my body in the worst possible way as I feel heat filling my entire face.

"Do you like him?" he demands, his eyes piercing into mine.

"I'm engaged to Sebastian," I say quickly, brushing off his accusation, anxiously wanting to steer away from this conversation.

He scrunches his face. "That wasn't the question I asked, Ava. I'll ask again, do you like him?"

I purposely avoid eye contact with him as I concentrate on my daughter. I do like him, a hell of a lot. I'm so attracted to him that the thought of him melts me to my core, and I hate that I feel that way, yet at the same time I love it.

Shit. It's confusing.

"You say a lot with your mouth shut."

I roll my eyes, glaring towards him. I go to say something, but my words get caught at the back of my throat. He steps forward, crouching down in front of me. "It's okay to be attracted to him, you'd be blind not to, but I'm a little worried about his intentions. He wasn't looking at you as if he wanted to get into your panties, it was more than that. It was as if he would walk over hot coals for you."

I shake my head. "He's just friendly. He doesn't like me, not like that." I brush it off for the benefit of Caleb, but deep down I know it's anything but an innocent friendship.

"Just be careful. You're vulnerable at the moment, and I don't want anybody taking advantage of that. You're still recovering from the last asshole who took advantage of you." The calming warmth that had surrounded me when Ashton was near has suddenly faded, and all I feel now is a heavy weight reigning over me, dragging me back down into the darkness.

"Well, thank you very much for reminding me what an absolute head case I am. I may be at the most vulnerable I have ever been in my life, but I will never let anybody else treat me the way my brother did. Ever," I hiss at him, my body quaking with anger as I stand up from my seat, and storm out of the room. The NICU is not the place where I can vent my anger. Lily doesn't need the fucking stress of it. She has enough on her little plate. Once I remove myself from the unit, I pace up and down the corridor, urging myself to calm down, and my anger begins to subside as I keep my focus on Ashton. Caleb walks towards me, with his face a look of concern.

"You're an asshole, you know that?"

Instead of being offended by my words, he laughs. "You can call me whatever the hell you want, sweetheart, but if I'm an asshole for being protective of you, for worrying about you, then fine, so be it. I'm an asshole."

"That's not why you're an asshole, asshole. You're an asshole because you mentioned my brother. You're an asshole because you're asking me these fucking stupid questions, judging my feelings just because a guy was looking at me. And you're an asshole for thinking less of me! Yes, he's gorgeous, it is pretty hard to miss, but just because a guy gives me some attention, you think I'm going to jump into bed with him? We've developed a friendship, and in case you haven't noticed, I don't have a lot of friends around! In fact, I don't have any friends except you. It gets lonely in this place, and with you at work and Sebastian in fucking Afghanistan, all I have is Ashton to talk to."

"Ashton? You're on a first name basis now?" He clicks his tongue. "Does Sebastian know about this friendship you have developed with another man?"

"You know what, Caleb? It's been a couple of especially shit days, to add to my especially shit week, so a bit of slack would be great!" My eyes fill up as I lift my head to the ceiling, taking a moment to gather enough strength so that I don't have a mental breakdown.

I hear him sigh as he pulls my frigid body into his arms. "You're right, I'm sorry. I just worry about you. Seeing the way he was looking at you, as if he was about to declare his undying love for you, it concerned me. The last thing you need is confusion from the opposite sex."

"I still think you're wrong, but even if he did declare his love for me, it doesn't mean that I would. You have to trust me."

He presses a kiss against my forehead. "I do trust you, it's other people that I don't trust."

"I know, but you can trust him. He's an incredible doctor, and he's amazing with Lily."

He pulls away slightly to look down at me. "I know he's a great doctor, and I'm not disputing that, just be careful. He may be Lily's doctor, but he's still just a guy, okay?"

"You have nothing to worry about. I wouldn't do anything to jeopardize my relationship with Sebastian. I promise."

# chapter 13

I SHOULD FEEL GUILTY.

Not only was Ashton the last person on my mind moments before I fell asleep, he is also the first person I see when I wake.

But I don't feel guilty.

Last night was the best night's sleep I've had in weeks. I didn't wake up in a cold sweat, screaming. Instead, I wake up to a flushed sweat, throbbing and satisfied, my body tingling from the memory of my pleasurable dream. I smile dreamily as I flutter my eyelids shut, hoping to get another glimpse, but that is quickly interrupted by the sound of Caleb's voice entering my thoughts.

"Rise and shine, sleeping beauty."

I peek out of one eye, watching Caleb walk towards me, freshly showered and dressed in a crisp gray suit, with a hot, steaming mug in hand. The distinct aroma of delicious coffee filling the room has me sitting up against the headboard, my bed sheets wrapped around me luxuriously.

"Good morning. I hope that's for me," I say, eyeing up my favorite pink and green pastel striped mug. It says, 'The Best Mom In The World' under a white heart.

He smirks, looking down at the mug. "Not unless I've suddenly become the best mom in the world during the night."

I chuckle as he sits down on the edge of the bed, passing me the decaffeinated coffee. "Thank you," I say softly, bringing the mug to my lips and taking a soothing sip.

"So is it safe to say you had a good night's sleep?"

I pull the mug away from my mouth, cradling the heated coffee in my hands. "Yeah." I stretch my legs. "Best night's sleep I've had in a while."

"No dreams?"

I'm not admitting the filth of my dream to Caleb, especially when it wasn't Sebastian I was dreaming about. I shake my head with a smile as I take another sip of coffee. "Nope, nothing."

His eyebrows burrow with a frown. "Huh," he muses.

"What do you mean, huh?" I ask suspiciously.

He shakes his head. "Nothing. I'm just happy that you've finally had a peaceful night's sleep." He smiles as his hand affectionately massages the right side of my sheet-clad leg. I know there's more to that than he is letting on, but I decide to let it go. It's too early to argue with him.

"So what's on the agenda today?" I ask casually, taking another drink.

"Just meeting after mind-numbing meeting. Honestly, I wish I could stay tucked up in your bed all day. It looks awfully comfortable." His fingers crawl inside the bed sheets, his cold hand causing me to jump when they latch on to my bare leg.

"Get off me! Your hands are freezing!" I shriek through laughter, thankful that the mug of coffee is already half empty or it would have spilled everywhere.

He chuckles as I hastily finish the remainder of my coffee in one gulp. "Well, if you weren't such a tight fisted bitch with the heating bill, I'd be toasty warm instead of freezing my ass off. My penis is the size of a cashew nut."

I burst out laughing at the vivid image my best friend just conjured, no doubt tainting my already chaotic mind. "If you don't like it, you know where your own apartment is. In fact," I begin to say, all joking aside, "you don't have to stay here with me every night. I'd probably manage on my own, you know."

"Are you saying you're getting tired of having me here?" He grins.

"No, of course not. I love having you here. I just … I don't want you to feel like you have to babysit me."

"I don't feel like that at all. You're going through a lot, and as your best friend it's my duty to look after you. Plus, I promised Sebastian, so you're stuck with me, kid." He leans over and drops a sweet kiss on the top of my head.

"I've been thinking," he starts as he sits back, his hand continuing to caress my leg through the bed sheets, "we haven't been out in ages. In fact, you haven't been out at all in over six weeks and I don't think it's healthy. You need to start taking your life back. So tonight, me and you, what do you say?"

I cringe at the thought of continuing everyday things when my daughter is fighting for her life in hospital. It feels wrong. "No, Caleb, I can't, and I'm a little pissed that you would even suggest a night out, considering the current predicament I'm in."

He shakes his head in exasperation. "I mean dinner and maybe a movie. Just a couple of hours to take a time out from everything, my treat. It would do you good. What do you say?"

Well, I suppose a couple of hours wouldn't hurt. In fact, it would be nice to eat a proper meal that didn't come from a plastic cup in the form of noodles. "Okay."

He blinks. "Okay? I thought it would take much more convincing than that."

"Well, I haven't finished. I have one condition. If Lily hasn't improved, I'm not going anywhere. But if her condition has improved by the time I get to the hospital then yes, dinner and a movie would be great. Oh, and we're having Mexican," I state confidently as I set my empty coffee mug on the bedside table. I crawl out of the warm quilted sheets, heading over to the closet to get dressed for my day ahead.

"Whatever you want."

I pull out a pair of skinny gray sweatpants, tossing them lazily onto my bed before I continue my closet search.

"And Ava?" I turn to look at him. "No sweats. We might only be going for dinner and a movie, but please, no sweatpants."

I roll my eyes as I reach into my organized wardrobe, taking out a cute, sheer, mint-green pullover. "Fine. I'll take a change of 'Caleb approved' clothing with me to the hospital. Happy?"

He stands up and walks over to me, placing yet another sweet kiss against the top of my head. "Very. I'll pick you up at seven-thirty."

When I arrive at the hospital, I'm pleasantly surprised to find that Lily has had a really good night. She's responding brilliantly to the antibiotics, and if her breathing continues to improve she should be able to come off the CPAP machine in the next couple of days.

I spend the rest of the day just sitting with her, talking about anything and everything, even reading to her. When I notice the time has just gone seven, I say an emotional goodbye to my daughter. I almost call Caleb to cancel when the daily panic of having to leave Lily's bedside consumes me, but then I remember what he said about staying cooped up in the hospital and how unhealthy it is. He's right, of course; my life outside this hospital is bordering on none existent. Plus, I did promise him I would go out if her condition had improved, which it has.

I don't qualify for any excuses.

As per Caleb's wishes, I change into suitable sociable clothing. I spend a good fifteen minutes in the restroom freshening up, applying a light amount of makeup and giving my hair a quick brush, leaving my chocolate brown, wavy hair hanging over my shoulders. I change into a pair of plain black leggings, and my favorite loose-fitted, short-sleeve, tan shirt-dress that has faux buttons at the chest and a ruffled skirt that flows from my waist to my mid-thigh. I add my three-inch wedge black knee-length boots and a spray of fruity body mist.

Glancing at my reflection in the mirror one last time, I come to realize that this is the first time I've taken time on my appearance since giving birth to Lily-Mai. Lily has been my priority. Every morning, I wake up, throw on some comfortable clothes, brush my teeth and then I'm out of the door. I don't even think about it.

I'm beginning to feel a little more confident in myself, like a tiny piece of me has returned back into place. Smiling, I grab my purse, quickly zipping it up as I make my way out of the restroom.

As I approach the foyer, I feel the vibrations of my phone coming from my purse. I frown when I see Caleb's name flashing. "Hey, are you on your way?" I ask as I approach the brown sofa chairs in the center of the foyer, placing my bag in the middle of one of the cushioned seats.

"I'm really sorry, but I'm going to have to take a rain check on tonight. There has been another fucking screw up at the office, and I'm the motherfucking idiot who has to fix it. It looks as though I am going to be here all night. I'm so sorry. I'll make it up to you, I promise."

"It's fine. Don't worry about it," I say nonchalantly, although I would be lying if I said I didn't feel a little disappointed.

"Are you sure?"

I twist the cushion from the back of the sofa, kneading the material through my fingers. I look down at my clothes, sighing inwardly at my wasted fifteen minutes. "Yeah, of course. I'll just stay here for a little bit longer, then head home."

"Are you going to be okay getting home?"

I smile at his worrying. "Yes, I'll get a cab home. I promise."

"Okay, sweetheart. I'll see you when I get home. Don't wait up though. It's going to be a long night," he says with a loud sigh.

"See you later." I press end on my call, quickly placing my phone back inside my purse. I put my purse back on my shoulder, turning back in the direction of Lily-Mai. I was looking forward to a night for myself, but at least now I can spend a little more time with my daughter. I start to make my way over to the elevators when I hear my name being called out. It's a familiar voice that has the hairs standing at the back of my neck. I turn around to see Ashton walking towards me with an irresistible smile.

"Hey." I smile as he finally steps in front of me. My heart flutters inside my chest as he looks my body up and down, approvingly.

"Hey to you," he says, taking in another hungry gaze before coming to a final stop at my eyes. "Wow, you look ... you look ... wow."

I blush as I take a quick opportunity to check him out. He is in casual dark washed jeans, a dark navy and white striped T-shirt, a thin navy jacket, and converse sneakers. After thoroughly inspecting him, I manage to tear my gaze away from his body and lock onto his eyes.

"What are you doing here? I thought it was your day off?"

"It is, I just came to pick something up from my locker. Are you on your way out?" He smiles, his eyes penetrating the curves of my figure, drinking me in. I gulp nervously at his attention.

"Yeah. Well, I was. I was supposed to go for dinner and a movie with Caleb, his way of pushing me back out into the real world, but he had to cancel. Some kind of work emergency came up. I was just heading back to Lily-Mai for a little while before I head home."

He smiles. "Well, that's just a shame. How about I take you out instead?" I jerk my head back in shock. Did he just ask me out? Almost as if he can read my mind, he quickly adds, "As friends."

An odd sensation of disappointment flows through me as his words sink in, which is an absolutely ridiculous emotion to feel, considering I have a fiancé. Nevertheless, I still feel it. "No, I can't ask you to do that. It's your day off, and you probably have better things to do with your time."

He shakes his head, his expression serious. "Better than dinner and a movie with a beautiful woman? Trust me, this will be the highlight of my day."

I smile when he calls me beautiful. It's a word I don't hear very often, especially aimed at me, but coming from him it has my heart in a heated frenzy.

"Are you sure?" I know deep down that this is not a good idea, the worst idea ever, but I can't seem to stop myself.

"Absolutely," he says eagerly. "Let me just head to my locker then I'm all yours. I'll be right back."

I watch as he jogs to the elevators, and my eyes zone in on his perfect ass, the creases of the denim moving sexily from side to side. I lick my lips, my entire body tingling with anticipation, clenching with sexual need.

I cannot have those kinds of feelings for him.

It is extremely bad to have such sexual thoughts about a human being while being committed to another.

That doesn't stop me visualizing what he might look like naked in the shower, in bed ...

I shake the R-rated thoughts out of my head before I need to take a cold shower, especially after visualizing how sexy he could look sprawled naked on the top of the red hood of his car, perhaps with me under him ...

Shit.

I am with Sebastian, I am marrying Sebastian. I love Sebastian.

Ashton comes back, all smiles and seductively kissable. "You ready?" he asks.

"Yes," I say with a smile.

He leads me through the open foyer. "So where would you like to go?"

I look up at him as we walk through the cool Seattle breeze. "How do you feel about Mexican?" I smile when his eyes light up with excitement.

"I love Mexican food."

We approach his car and like a gentleman he opens the passenger car door for me. I blush when I glance at the hood of his car, remembering the naughty thoughts I was thinking minutes before. Once I'm safely seated, he gently closes the door behind me, then rounds the car to the driver's side with a gentle jog.

He starts the engine up and reverses out of the parking space. "I know of this great Mexican place in downtown Seattle. Shall we head there? Or do you have a preference?"

I smile, turning towards him as I buckle in my seatbelt. "No, no preference. I'm happy to go anywhere."

"Okay then." He turns to me briefly, giving me his panty-dropping smile.

"So Lily has improved even more since yesterday, they should be able to take her off the CPAP machine in the next couple of days."

He glances at me for a brief moment before turning his attention back to the road in front of us. "I know, I spoke to the hospital this morning. It's awesome news."

I stare at him with my mouth gaped open in surprise. "Really?"

"What? That it's awesome news? Because I—"

"No. That you called the hospital on your day off."

He smiles as he turns to me for a brief moment. "Yeah, of course, I wanted to make sure she was doing okay. She's one of my favorite patients," he says with a wink.

The smile practically explodes from my face. I'm pretty sure my feelings for him just skyrocketed. The flutter in my heart confirms it.

We chat idly until we're parked in front of the restaurant. Even before I've taken my seat belt off, he has my door open. I laugh lightly at his eagerness. The palm of his hand lightly touches the bottom of my back as he leads me to the entrance of the restaurant.

We're told it will be a twenty minute wait for a table, so the waitress leads us to an open bar in the center of the restaurant. We take a seat on the bar stools and I take a moment to have a look around the restaurant, immediately feeling as if I've been transported to Mexico. The walls are covered in bright paintings and there are coat stands filled with bright sombreros in every corner of the restaurant. Instrumental guitar strings create an acoustic folk sound in the low-lit room.

"What would you like to drink?" Ashton asks me as I turn towards the bar, picking up a drink menu and skimming through it.

"Well, I'd love a margarita," I say, looking down at a mouth-watering picture of a strawberry margarita on the menu, "but I'm breastfeeding, so I'd better stick with water," I place the drink menu down on the bar.

His eyes flicker down to my breasts for a brief moment. "Would it really suck if I ordered a beer?" he says with a sly smirk crossing his face. I raise my eyebrow wryly, in mocked annoyance. He chuckles. "I promise I'll keep it to the one."

Once we have our drinks, Ashton turns his full attention back to me. "So what's your story?" he asks, taking a generous swig of beer from the bottle.

I'm lost in a trance as I stare intently at the way his neck sexily constricts and flows with each swallow. I have to clench my legs together at the heavy, pounding heat I feel at the thought of my lips on his neck, sucking against his tanned skin.

It takes a long moment for his question to register. "My story?" I ask, taking a refreshing sip of my iced water through the straw.

"Yeah. I only know a handful of things about you. I want to know who Ava Jacobson is. The real Ava."

A shudder runs up my back as he leans towards me, his knee brushing against mine. I nervously take another mouthful of my drink through my straw, taking the moment of silence to gather my thoughts. It isn't a question I've had to answer before. I shrug my shoulders as I place the glass back down on the bar. "There isn't much to know."

He takes another casual sip of his beer. "Now, we both know that's bull, Ava. I know there's so much more to you, and I'm not talking about the sadness you try to hide behind those beautiful eyes of yours. I'm not asking you to delve into your deepest and darkest secrets here. I'm asking about the normal Ava things. In fact, while we wait for a table, let's play twenty questions. My turn first. What's your favorite color?"

For a moment I think he must be joking because why on earth would he want to know something so mundane like my favorite color? "Are you being serious?"

"Deadly."

I smirk. "Well, it depends. I change my mind all of the time. At the moment, my favorite color is mint-green. My turn. What's your favorite color?"

He raises his eyes, mocked humor soaring through his smile. "Hmm, how predictable and easy."

"Just answer the question."

He smiles. "Well, if I haven't already made it obvious," he points to himself with his beer bottle, "blue. Navy to be exact."

During the next nine or so questions, I find out that he was fifteen when he lost his virginity during summer camp and that it lasted a whole fifteen seconds. When he was six years old he wanted to be a cowboy when he grew up, but actually formed a phobia of horses in his later years, so didn't follow through with that career. His most embarrassing moment was during his freshman year in college when he got so wasted at a frat party that he woke up the next morning in a pair of women's hot pink panties, and his chest hair shaved into the superman logo. That image had me laughing hysterically for five minutes straight. I would have given up my right arm up to see that.

His favorite food is his mother's roast. Ever since moving to Seattle nine years ago, it's her mashed potatoes that he misses the most, and no matter how many times he makes his own, they never taste the same. His childhood pets consisted of two hamsters, a goldfish and a choco-late Labrador. However, the goldfish only lasted a week. His younger brother Christopher flushed it down the toilet. I learn that he is one of three boys. Ashton is the oldest at thirty-three, Christopher, the brother Ashton lost at war three years ago, would have been twenty-nine, and then there is Tyler, who is the same age as me.

I couldn't stop myself from reaching out to him, my hand grasp-ing his at the mention of Christopher, understanding only too well the excruciating pain of his loss. Ashton gives me a sad smile, his hand tightening around mine. There's a moment of silence, and just when he is about to say something else, the waitress appears to move us to an available table.

We follow her to a cozy little section of the restaurant as she leads us to a two-person table. Once we're seated, and we've ordered our food, he takes another drink of beer, resuming with his next question for me. "So, where were we? Oh yeah, my turn," he states with a sly grin. "What's the most reckless thing you've ever done?"

The question hits me in a vulnerable place, and I don't know what the hell possesses me to do it, what possesses me to give the answer I give him, but it seems to spew out from my mouth before I actually have a moment to register what I said.

"I ran away from home," I blurt out, immediately regretting it.

At first he gives me an amused smirk, then when he notices my serious stance, the smile quickly fades. I look down at my glass filled with mineral water, the contents of it suddenly becoming the most intriguing thing I've ever set eyes on as tension fills the air. I hear the concern in the croak of his voice immediately. He knows this is no joke. "You're serious, aren't you?"

I don't answer.

"Ava?"

I desperately want the ground to swallow me up into nothingness, but the way my name slides off his tongue, all husky and warm, I can't resist looking up at him. It's like a magnetic force, the pull too strong to stay away.

He leans forward, placing his hand on mine. "Ava, talk to me."

I shake my head, trying to pull his hand from mine, but his grip is too powerful to loosen. "I shouldn't have mentioned it. Just forget I said anything." I look down as his thumb strokes the top of my hand, shivers covering me from head to toe.

"You can talk to me. You can trust me," he urges, almost desperately. When I glance up, my heart constricts when I see the look in his eyes. The green hues show the purity of Ashton's words and I find myself falling into them, opening up to him, effortlessly. I tell him my story of running away, but I leave out the why. I'm not ready to talk out loud about my demons with him, if ever. He never pushes the question and I'm grateful for the space he gives me.

"Thank you for telling me, Ava," he says gently as he continues to caress his thumb against my hand, lulling me into absolute calmness.

"Can I ask you one question though? Why run away? Why didn't you get help? Surely there was somebody you could have gone to, somebody who would have helped you."

I ponder over his words for a second, understanding his curiosity. I desperately try to rack my brain for somebody who could have come to my rescue, to save me from the monster, but I come up blank. "There was nobody. I ... I just ... running away was my only option. If I hadn't run away, I probably wouldn't be here right now."

He shakes his head slowly, his jaw locked in a tight vice. He's quiet for a moment, his somber eyes tracing my face as if trying to memorize every fragment of it. Then he says something that will be inscribed in my mind until the moment I die.

"Well, that isn't even worth thinking about. A world without you is a world not worth living in."

My heart slams against my chest, and for a moment it feels like cupid has just taken a shot with his bow and arrow, zeroing straight for my heart, filling me with love.

The waitress appears with our food, evidently ruining our moment. After one last gentle stroke against my hand, he pulls away, but not once taking his eyes off me. I hate how cold my hand feels.

I miss his touch already.

We dig in, and the moment I put a piece of enchilada into my mouth, I moan as the flavors explode. We eat in comfortable silence, but Ashton keeps glancing at me with an odd passionate glare in his eyes, shifting in his seat uncomfortably.

Blushing furiously, I try to ignore him and just concentrate on eating, moaning in appreciation when I take another bite. It's so damn good. As I look back up, Ashton is glaring at me again with his penetrating gaze and that one look alone has my insides clenching, a heat rising to the surface. I gulp nervously as my heart rate starts to pick up.

"What?" I croak, my cheeks flushing red at the sudden attention.

"Nothing," he mumbles with a slight smile, quickly concentrating on his own food.

I cut into the enchilada with my knife and fork, taking another eager bite. As I am in a mid-chew moan, Ashton drops his own cutlery against his plate. The metallic sound echoes around the restaurant, followed by a grunt, then a hearty chuckle. "Ava, you're killing me here." His words

122

strain through his voice.

I squint in confusion as I swallow my food. "What?"

He picks up his bottle of beer and downs the rest of it in one, then slams it back onto the table. "You're eating your food as if it's the sexiest thing that has ever passed your lips." I widen my eyes with shock, my cheeks turning the heaviest shade of pink. "It's a damn turn on, Ava," he adds with a sexy smirk, almost causing me to choke on my food.

"Oh, God," I say in a whispered shriek, my flush covering my entire body.

"That's what she said." He chuckles.

I shrink down in my chair, my hands covering my face with embarrassment. "I can't believe I was moaning out loud like a damn porn star," I say into my hands, purposely avoiding his gaze.

"It was better than porn," he says with a mouthful of food. I peek at him through the gaps between my fingers like a naughty child. He winks at me as he takes another bite, moaning out loud for maximum effect, mocking me, causing a laugh to bubble from my chest.

For the next ten minutes, all you can hear through the restaurant is our laughter. It's the first time in a long time that I've just let go and laughed for laughing's sake. It feels nice.

Before I know it, the evening has come to an end and Ashton is walking me to the front of my apartment block, his fingers gently brushing against mine. I have the urge to close the distance and feel his embrace, but the way his hand lingers against mine seems more intimate.

We come to a subtle stop, facing each other. His smile has my heart in a heated frenzy, which frightens me as much as it excites me, and I physically stop breathing when he reaches over and tucks a loose strand of stray hair behind my ear, his thumb stroking against my cheek.

"I've had an amazing night, Ava."

I shiver as he says my name, the velvet tones reaching the sensitive peaks of my body. I nod in a daze, whispering, "Me too."

"I wish I could kiss you." I gasp as his thumb comes to a rest against my bottom lip, my heart thrashing unabashedly against my chest. "But you're not mine to kiss."

I gulp painfully at his statement, and I fully expect him to move away from me, but he surprises me by moving even closer to me until his chest is flush against mine.

"We're just friends," he whispers inches away from my lips, his thumb stroking the small gap between my lips, his fingers holding my chin in place. I'm finding it impossible to breathe having him so close. I'm dizzy. I'm overwhelmed. I'm drunk with lust.

I blame this for my next question.

"But friends can kiss, right?"

He blinks. "Yes," he says in a deep, strained, sexy voice as he edges even closer to me, so close I can feel his heart racing against my chest. "A friend kiss is okay, right?"

*No, no it isn't okay.*

But that isn't the answer I give him. Instead, I nod eagerly, desperate to have his lips on mine.

"One little kiss, one little peck isn't going to hurt, right?"

I shake my head in agreement as my eyes zone in on those beautiful plump lips of his. His hands glide through my hair, sliding up the back of my neck, eventually coming to a stop just below my ears, his thumbs drawing circles against my cheeks, my entire body shuddering at his touch.

"You're so beautiful," he whispers.

Then, in what feels like slow motion, he gently presses his lips against mine with the lightest of kisses. I stumble backwards at the powerful sensation his lips create. He applies more pressure, and I moan lightly against his mouth. He keeps his lips on mine and then all too quickly he pulls away, breathless. My eyes flutter open as I struggle to catch my breath …

Well, that is how it happens in my head.

Instead, when I think he's about to press his lips against mine, he briefly presses his lips against my forehead. "But I'm not going to kiss you. If I kiss you right now, we both know that it'll be more than just two friends kissing. I want more than anything to be able to kiss you, to blow every other kiss you've ever had out of the water, but I can't be that guy. I can't be that guy who breaks up a family. It just wouldn't be fair."

He steps away, pushing his hands deep into his pockets. "Goodnight, Ava." He walks away, leaving me shaking with adrenaline as I replay the kiss over and over again in my head.

Eventually, in a half daze I make my way up to my apartment.

When I see the door to the home I share with Sebastian, my heart lurches into the pit of my stomach as guilt consumes me. What the hell was I thinking?

I scramble furiously through the contents of my bag for my phone, knowing how I might have missed a call from Sebastian, especially since I haven't heard from him in days. I feel my eyes water with unshed tears as I pull out my phone and press my thumb impatiently against the middle button, the glorious picture of my daughter popping up on the bright screen along with the time.

My heart drops.

No missed calls.

# chapter 14

T HE DAYS ROLL BY, but I don't receive a call or text from Sebastian. Panic begins to set in. I know that communication with him is rare at the best of times, and I'm lucky if I get more than five minutes with him, but twelve days without any communication is unusual.

What if something has happened to him? I'd hate to think of the dangers Sebastian could be in while I'm here having more than friendly dinners with Ashton.

Falling for him …

"Hey, are you okay?" Ashton asks, pulling me aside. "You look a little out of it today."

I shake my head, worry continuing to rack my brain. "No, not really. Um …" *I wonder if this is inappropriate, discussing anything Sebastian related with Ashton?*

"It's Sebastian."

"Has something happened?" he asks, worry lines creasing his forehead. My brain starts to get a little foggy when his thumb lightly caresses my arm. Apparently my body is still overwhelmed by him, even when the life of my fiancé could be hanging in the balance.

"No, um, well I don't know actually. I haven't heard from him in over a week and I'm kind of worried. It's so unusual for him not to call me."

He gives me a saddened smile. "I'm sorry. It's normal to be worried, but I honestly think you're worrying over nothing."

"How can you be so sure?"

"When Christopher was deployed in Afghanistan, it could be days or sometimes weeks before he could call or email. The units regularly have something called commo blackouts, usually when a soldier was injured or killed. All communication is off limits until the army can get in contact with the family."

"Sebastian mentioned that a blackout could happen before he left the first time. Oh God …"

Ashton takes my hand, comforting me. "Shit, I didn't tell you that to freak you out. It's just that the blackout is probably the reason why you haven't heard from him, not because something has happened to him."

"But, but?" I ask in a slight panic until his warm eyes gaze down at me, immediately calming me.

"But, nothing, Ava. I'm sure he's absolutely fine. No news is good news, okay?"

Sebastian finally calls me and I'm hysterical with delight when I finally get to hear his voice after fifteen excruciatingly long days. Ashton was right about the blackout. Once Sebastian tells me how much he missed me and how sorry he is for not calling, he explains to me how his unit was under a communication blackout because of the brutal death of two troops. I want to feel sad for the two fallen soldiers, but all I can feel is relief that it wasn't Sebastian. Of course, he can't stay on the phone for long, but he promises to speak to me soon.

I text Ashton as soon as the calls ends.

**Ava**: *You were right. Sebastian is absolutely fine. Thank you xx*

His reply is almost instant.

**Ashton**: *I told you he would be. Just sucks that you have to go through this. I wish there were something I could do, but I'm here* *for you, day and night. Sleep tight, beautiful.*

As the week goes by, Lily continues to get stronger. The pneumonia has completely cleared up, and her immune system is becoming stronger by the day; she is now eight weeks old and gaining weight at an appropriate rate, her last weigh in coming in at five pounds. She's still on oxygen but breathing completely on her own. She is now receiving her milk by breast and bottle now, which she absolutely loves. It took her a few times to learn how to latch onto my nipple, but once she was able to coordinate her sucking, breathing and swallowing, it became natural to her. She found my breast easier to control than the bottle at first, but with a little practice she got the hang of that too.

The first time I breastfed was interesting. The moment I removed my breast from my nursing bra, Ashton decided to come in for his usual friendly visit. He stopped dead in his tracks and just stared at me. I blushed, then giggled quietly as he quickly looked away. I turned my attention back to my daughter as he turned his attention to anything but me.

The doctors and Ashton are confident that it might only be a matter of weeks until she'll be allowed home. I'm terrified as I still haven't given a single thought to her nursery or even baby proofing the apartment. The sickening pit in my stomach reminds me of how much I wish Sebastian were here to help with the important stuff like decorating the nursery.

I look down at the color samples I picked up at the local DIY store this morning. I hold up the samples, pointing to the lightest of pinks as if I might get some kind of response from Lily.

I hear light chuckling and turn just as Ashton saunters over to me, a grin plastered on his face. "What are you doing?"

"We are trying to pick out a color for the nursery," I state confidently, holding out the samples with pride.

"We?" He looks down at me, his arms crossed in front of his chest, still smiling.

"Yes, Lily and I. She happens to know a thing or two about the art of decorating," I say with a smirk, causing him to laugh.

"I bet. And what did you and Lily choose?"

"Well, we're deciding between these two shades of pink."

He squints for a moment, examining both colors, then shrugs his shoulders. "I honestly can't tell the difference. They both look the same to me."

I roll my eyes. "Useless."

"Ouch, you really know how to bring me down a notch." He smirks, moving his hand up to his heart, feigning hurt. He steps past me and places his hand through the isolette door to hold Lily's hand with his forefinger. "How you doing, baby girl? You good?" Lily looks up to him with her big brown eyes. "So when were you thinking of decorating Lily's nursery?" he asks as he continues to look down at my daughter, stroking his thumb against the skin of her delicate little hand.

"As soon as possible, although I'm debating whether or not to get a decorator in. Both Caleb's artistic ability and mine begin and stop at stick figures, so the end result of her room would likely be a disaster."

He turns to face me. "Well, you're in luck, I happen to be pretty great at decorating, and I have a few days off starting Friday, so we can make a start on it then." He turns back to Lily briefly, before returning his gaze to me. "What, you think I don't have skills?" I laugh.

"Because I'll have you know," he says, pulling his hand out from Lily's incubator, closing the isolette door shut, "I do amazing things with these babies of mine and I'm yet to have any complaints." He shows me his hands, palms up, as he winks at me.

That one flirtatious gesture has me tingling from the inside out.

After spending the morning with Lily, Ashton picks me up from the hospital and we head over to my apartment. The moment he steps through the threshold, a moment of uneasiness flows through me. The thought of him entering a home I share with another man suddenly makes me feel uncomfortable, almost as if I'm flaunting my friendship (if I can even call it that) with Ashton under Sebastian's nose. I shake the uneasiness from my mind, convinced that I'm doing nothing wrong. I'm simply having a friend of mine over to help with some decorating. It is completely innocent.

*At least that's what I tell myself.*

"Wow," Ashton says as he takes in my living room. "This place is immaculate. When the hell do you have time to clean? You're always at the hospital."

I chuckle. "Oh, I don't. Caleb does. If it were down to me, I wouldn't even have any clean underwear. In fact, I don't remember the last time I did laundry."

"You should just do what I do," he says with a shrug.

"And what's that?"

"Go commando."

The idea of Ashton with absolutely nothing on is an image I can't deal with right now. I smack him against the chest. "You," I say pointing my finger into his chest, looking up at him. "Head out of the gutter. We have decorating to do."

"Yes, boss." He salutes with a grin. "But FYI – I don't really go commando." He raises an eyebrow. "Or do I?" I roll my eyes and shove him out of the living room.

We walk out of the living room through an adjoining hallway on the left that leads to three bedrooms and a bathroom. I head into the second door on the right. The room is only half the size of my bedroom, but it's perfect for a nursery.

We make a start. Luckily we haven't got any furniture to move or cover up as I still haven't purchased anything. We cover the plush cream carpets with plastic to avoid any accidental paint spillage because as long as I'm involved, spills will happen.

While Ashton gets the primer ready, I retrieve the portable wireless speaker from the living room and place it in the corner. The sound of music fills the room immediately as I press shuffle on my iPhone.

When the second coat of primer is complete, Ashton crouches down to the paint tray as he prepares the paint, but his shoulders begin to shake with laughter and he looks up at me with a shit-eating grin. I'm confused for a moment until it suddenly registers and I smirk, heat covering my entire face.

"Are you kidding me? Footloose?" He shakes his head at me in mock disgust as the guitar riffs and country beats of Footloose fill the room.

I shrug. "So? This happens to be the best song from the best 80's movie ever."

"Ava, baby, no 80's movie is the best 80's movie ever. It was the 80's," he says through a chuckle.

I retrieve my phone out from my pocket, turning the volume up so that the song begins to reverberate around the room. He stands up from his crouching position, shaking his head in mock-horror. "No!"

I point to my ears. "I can't hear you over the best 80's song ever! You'll have to speak up!"

I start to move my head to the rhythm of the beat, smiling devilishly at Ashton. Then I bounce on my feet to the beat, moving my hips from side to side. Without any warning, I jump to the rhythm with my arms in the air, dancing over to Ashton, dramatically mouthing the words of the song to him. He shakes his head as he backs away from me laughing, waving me off, but I ignore his cautionary glare and just continue moving towards him, jumping like a lunatic, waving my arms from side to side. I reach out for his hand, twisting his arm to the music as I continue to dance on the spot in front of him, shaking my entire body.

"You're crazy!" he says, laughing.

I shrug my shoulders mid-dance, not phased. "Who cares!" I grab his other hand, swinging both arms to the beat, shaking my loose hair in his face, moving my feet from side to side while he remains completely motionless, still wearing his grin.

"Come on, dance with me!"

Instead of agreeing to my embarrassing version of eighties dancing, he pulls away and heads towards the paint tray that is full of pink paint. A shrieking laughter escapes me when he reaches for the paint roller and rolls it through the wet texture. Standing back up, he follows me with the offending weapon.

"No, Ashton!" I cry out, laughter bubbling from me as my head shakes furiously at the threat of his attack.

He gives me a playful smirk and quickly pulls the roller down my front, covering my chest and stomach with pink paint. I gape at him in shock. I notice a small looking paintbrush in the far corner of the room with a few other supplies, and I try to make a run for it. I only make it two steps before being swooped up into his arms, his chest flushed with my back.

"I wouldn't do that if I were you."

"And why not?" I gasp breathlessly, my heart racing as I try to ignore how incredible his body feels pressed up against mine.

"Because then I can't do this."

In lightning speed, he brings the roller round to my front and rolls the remaining paint down the front of my face. I gasp in shock as the sound of his laughter vibrates down my neck. I elbow him in the stomach playfully, recovering my momentum just enough to turn around to face him, noticing a smile curving around his mouth.

Another song has begun to play, so with full purpose I pull my phone out, careful not to get paint on it and go back to the previous song. Ashton groans at the sound of Footloose filling the room again. My smile widens as I put my phone back in the rear pocket of my jeans and resume dancing. I swing my arms side to side, dancing towards the paint tray. Skeptically, Ashton follows, not trusting my motives. I approach the paint tray and dance around it for a moment, smiling deviously.

"Don't even think about it," he warns, shooting an evil glance my way.

I shrug my shoulders. "I don't know what you mean." Then I bend down, press both hands into the tray, covering my hands with the wet substance, then run at him. He drops the paint roller to the plastic covered sheets, causing paint to splatter against the covers and grabs hold of me at the elbows, my arms sprawled against my chest, stopping me in my steps, almost making me fall into him. I groan out loud, hating how much stronger he is than me.

"You don't play fair!"

He pulls my body further into his, chuckling, never once letting go of my elbows. "Neither do you."

His laughing falters as I look up into his bright green eyes. The mischief that was there only seconds ago has turned into something else, something more intense. I notice how his eyes trace down to my lips in a way that causes my pulse to race. I nervously gulp, my mouth suddenly dry as he loosens his hold on my arms. The sound of Footloose is replaced with the sound of my own heart beating recklessly in my ears. I feel light-headed as his lips move closer to mine while his eyes continue to trace the rest of my pink streaked face. When I can feel the warmth of his breath across my lips, I jolt out of my drunken haze in a panic, realizing exactly where we are, and exactly why we can't do what he is initiating, what my body is craving.

Smirking inwardly, I bring my paint-covered hands up to his face and take a quick swipe, covering both cheeks as I jump out of his embrace, giggling. He blinks in confusion, losing momentum for just a second, then his lips curve up into an evil smile. "Right, that's it, you're getting it now."

I scream out loud through a hysterical giggle as I move away from Ashton and he chases me around the room, covering me in even more paint.

After our paint fight, where we probably covered ourselves with more paint than the actual walls, we pull together and finish all four walls with one coat. Waiting for the first coat to dry, we decide to take a break, hunger taking priority. As we head to the door, covered head to toe in pink paint, I turn around, giving him the best stern look I can muster, the one that threatens him within an inch of his life.

"Off," I demand, pointing to his paint drenched jeans and T-shirt. "You're not walking through my apartment like that. So strip."

He smiles, a little too hungrily, his eyes lighting up with amusement. "You want me to strip?" he asks in a surprised tone.

"Yes," I reply curtly. I am not removing myself from the doorframe until he has removed his paint-ridden clothes.

"Okay." He shrugs, a hint of a smile curling against his mouth.

Only thinking of ways to avoid the disaster of getting paint all over my apartment and furniture, I just about lose the ability to speak when he removes his T-shirt, revealing a taut chest and smooth stomach. I follow my gaze downwards, and my heart rate picks up as I notice a valley of dark hair that begins at his navel, gradually disappearing inside the confinements of his waistband. I avert my eyes, purposefully trying to look elsewhere, but moments later my eyes return. I feel a shiver of heat spread through my body like wildfire as he reaches down to the button of his jeans, deliberately pulling his zipper down in slow motion. My eyes widen in disbelief as he slides his jeans over his hips. Then I think I forget how to breathe when he fully removes them. I gulp nervously as I unashamedly stare at him in only his underwear, knowing now that asking him to strip was such a bad idea.

"You okay?"

It takes me a couple of seconds to register his question and then a couple more seconds to peel my eyes away from his body. "Ah, yeah …

I am great, just great," I stutter as my body goes into a nervous frenzy, unable to string a viable sentence together.

"Are you sure? You look a little flushed," he taunts me, his smirk growing on his cocky face.

As I continue to struggle with each breath, I realize I can't have him this naked while under my roof. "One second," I mumble, becoming more flustered as I take one final gaze at his half-naked body before making my way towards my bedroom. I chuckle when he yells after me, "If I have to strip, then so do you. You're covered in more paint than me!"

In desperation, I try to find something of Sebastian's for him to wear, trying to be extra careful not to get a single smudge of paint anywhere. Not feeling particularly comfortable dressing Ashton in my fiancé's clothing, I find a pair of basketball shorts and a plain white T-shirt that I know Sebastian doesn't wear anymore. Without looking or even speaking to him, I just throw the clothes at him from the doorway of the nursery, blushing furiously. When I rush back into my bedroom to change, I can I hear him chuckling.

I walk into the living room to find Ashton looking at a photograph of me and Sebastian on our first-year anniversary, running his thumb over the image of me. I cough lightly to make him aware of my presence. He turns to me, his hand dropping from the picture frame, and his eyes widen with humor. "Um, you seem to have missed a bit," he says as he continues to laugh, making his way over to me.

"Shut up. I wouldn't even be in this mess if you hadn't have painted my entire face. It won't come off," I complain, a smile plastered on my face.

"It was funny though," he states, continuing to laugh at my expense.

"I don't know what you're laughing at. Have you looked in a mirror?" I smirk at the hand shaped prints against his cheeks. "Hey, shall we order a pizza?"

Just as he's about to answer me, the sound of the phone in my apartment begins to ring. I smile, holding my finger up. "Hold that thought for one second." I walk towards the telephone on the table beside the sofa and pick it up. "Hello?" I say with a smile.

"Ava?"

I feel the blood drain from my face when I hear the voice; the voice

I prayed I never had to hear ever again. *My gorgeous Ava.* I shiver inwardly as his voice triggers a memory.

*I'm in my bedroom, he's standing in front me, touching me, taunting me ...*

"Who is this?" I say through the churning of my own stomach, but I know exactly who it is.

"I think you know who it is."

I feel the phone begin to shake in my hand, the feel of bile rising up my throat. "How did you get this number?" I ask as calmly as possible, even though the heavy pounding of my heart ensures I'm anything but calm.

"It was only a matter of time until I found you again. You can't run from me, Ava. How is Seattle, by the way?"

I stumble backwards against the armrest of the sofa, gasping for air. No, no, no. He wasn't supposed to find me. It has been ten years. Why, after all of these years is he tormenting me now?

"What do you want?" I seethe, the shock of hearing his voice after all these years quickly turning into anger.

"It's Fran."

I close my eyes, clutching my hand to my heart, hoping that the turmoil I can hear in his voice isn't what I think it is.

"What about Fran?" I question painfully. And when I think my world couldn't possibly get any worse, in two simple words, my brother changes that for me and my world crumbles beneath me.

"She's dead."

I choke on a silent sob. Dead? Then to rub salt into my wound, he adds, "She killed herself. Hung herself, to be exact."

"What the fuck did you do?" I pant, anger coursing through my veins. He just chuckles on the other end of the phone, a sound that has the hair on my arms spike up with sickening shivers.

"Ava Jacobson with a potty mouth. Who would have thought, huh?"

"What. The. Fuck. Did. You. Do. To. Her?" I repeat, venom pouring out every word.

"And why would you automatically assume it had anything to do with me?"

"Because I know you. I know what a fucking monster you are."

Ashton crouches down in front of me, a worried look on his face, but I ignore him. It's hard to pay attention to anything else when I'm on the phone with a monster. A bastard.

"You're very brave all of a sudden aren't you? Well, I'll let you into a little secret, my gorgeous, *Ava*." My insides clamp down with hatred, shuddering at the very mention of my name. "I'm outside your apartment right now." My gaze flies in the direction of my front door as terror consumes every sense, my body convulsing with intense fear. I hear Ashton calling out to me, reaching for my hand, but the terror has captured all of my senses, and not even Ashton can ease me out of this nightmare. Not this time.

"Not so brave when you think I'm stood behind your front door, are you, Ava?" He laughs evilly knowing the effect he has on me, even after all of these years. I slam my eyes shut, hot tears rolling down my face.

"Fuck you." I hiss angrily, causing another laugh to erupt from his perverted mouth.

"Now, now there's no need for the foul language. That's no way to speak to your brother." He chuckles down the phone, and I shiver at the very sound. "Tell me, Ava, would it make you jealous if I said I touched my gorgeous Fran?"

I feel the utmost urge to heave and vomit at his words. "I swear to God if you even … I'll—"

"You'll what, Ava? What will you do?"

I can't form a single word, but I wouldn't think twice about putting a bullet into that sick and twisted head of his.

"I thought so," he answers, obviously mistaking my silence for weakness. "You won't do anything. And do you know why? Because I still own you, just like I owned your sister until her very last breath."

I can't stop the flashes of him forcing himself upon her, hearing her begging cries as she urges him to stop. I can see the internal pain on her face, wishing death to cover her. I've been there. Death always seems like an easier way out.

A new pain cripples me. I led him to her. I left to get away from him without fully comprehending what I was leaving behind for her. "Why couldn't you have just left Fran alone?"

"It's pretty simple really. You were gone, she was there. Do the math."

"You sick bastard!"

"Well, if you hadn't have left, none of this would have happened."

"Don't you dare put the fucking blame on me, you sick, twisted bastard!" My anger causes my insides to shudder from the impact of my own words. His sadistic laughter sounds through my phone, the very sound causing me to crush it within the palm of my hand.

I try to make myself calm down enough to ask the next question, even if it makes me want to hurl. "When's her funeral?" I ask through gritted teeth, hatred pouring out of every single word. Once he has given me the details, I end the call and throw the phone at full speed against the wall. I don't even flinch when the plastic device smashes open against the wall and falls to pieces.

"Ava, who was that?" Ashton asks, sounding worried.

I shove my pumps on my feet and grab my purse from the cushioned sofa. "I've got to go."

I can hear Ashton calling for me, but I ignore him and rush out of my apartment.

Right now I need my best friend.

# chapter 15

I BARREL MY WAY into Caleb's workplace, startling the receptionist as I make a sudden stop in front of her, my bag making a loud clanging sound against the wood of her desk. "Caleb Summers, please," I pant, trying to catch my breath.

"He's in a meeting for the rest of the afternoon. Would you like to schedule an appointment?"

I grasp hold of the desk, my hands turning white with the intensity of my grip. "No, I need to see him now." My chin trembles as tears threaten to spill.

"I'm sorry, miss, but that isn't possible. I suggest that you schedule an appointment. The earliest you can see him is on Monday morning."

"No, I need to see Caleb right this fucking minute. If you could tell him Ava Jacobson is here, I'd appreciate it. Greatly." I growl the last word, staring down at her with a scowl. As I turn around, I see a security guy approaching the reception area, eyeing me in particular. I turn to face her, shaking my head at her audacity.

"Are you kidding me?"

She shrugs her shoulders and continues with her mundane task of typing, ignoring me as if I don't even exist. I let out an angry exhalation, and I take a quick look towards the corridor where I know Caleb's office is before flicking my eyes back to where the security man continues in my direction

"God, why can't my life ever be simple," I mumble to myself breathlessly, then I make a run for it. I only make it half way before I'm being hauled to a stop.

"Miss, you can't be back here."

"I just need to see Caleb Summers. I'm Ava Jacobson. I need to see him, it's urgent." I look up at the bald chubby man, his face impassive as he stares down at me.

"I don't care who you are, or who you've come to see. If you don't have a visitor's pass, then you can't be back here."

Becoming even more exasperated with the situation by the second, I try to force his tight grip from my arm, but when he doesn't budge, I'm reduced to screaming Caleb's name at the top of my lungs. My behavior has me utterly mortified, but considering nobody will help me, I don't have any other choice.

Caleb comes rushing out of his office with a look of alarm and confusion flitting across his face. "Ava? What's going on?" Security loosens his grip, then removes his hand from my arm when he notices the stern glare coming from Caleb. Seeing his beautiful face sets me off, and the tears begin to run down my face. I rush into his arms, sinking my face into the crook of his neck.

"Jesus Christ, what's wrong?" he says into my hair, his arms holding me close to his body as I continue to cry. "Shit, is it Sebastian, Lily-Mai?"

I shake my head into his neck, and then manage to breathe out a shuddered, "No," through my continuous cries. I feel him visibly relax, his hands stroking gentle patterns up and down my spine.

"Then what is it? You're starting to freak me out."

My throat feels like hot razor blades when I take a gulp, preparing for the words of pure devastation, words I never thought in a million years would pass my lips. "Fran, my sister, she's dead." As I say the words out loud for the first time, I gasp at the very realization of it, setting off a new set of sobs.

Dead. My baby sister is dead.

I throw myself back into the comforting arms of my best friend, returning to the safe cocoon of his neck. Caleb lifts me into his arms and carries me into a room, setting me down on the couch. He kneels at my level, unraveling himself from my tight hold, and pushing the hair that is welded to my cheek by my wet tears.

"Stay here, I'll be right back."

I nod as he exits the room, shutting the door securely behind him. Moments later, Caleb comes back with a glass of water. He sits beside me, holding out the water for me. "Here you go, sweetheart. Drink that."

I accept the glass of water with shaky hands and take a few small sips. "Your receptionist is a bitch, by the way," I say through a hiccuping sob, glancing up at the concerned expression of Caleb.

"I'll deal with her later," he says in a stern 'I'll-take-no-shit' attitude. "I just want to focus on you. What happened?"

I bite against my lip, forcing the tears back, but it doesn't stop the tears from falling down my face. "She killed herself. She killed herself to get away from my brother."

I try to shake my head free of the horrific images that continue to build in my mind, all of the painful images inflicted by the monster himself. Caleb is shocked into silence, opening his mouth only to close it again, his face paling on the impact of my words.

"Caleb, he's found me."

Then the shock suddenly turns into anger. "That motherfucker," he growls, his eyes turning to a deadly black.

"He called the apartment. He-he's the reason why she's dead."

"Please tell me he didn't? He hasn't?"

I press my trembling lips together as I look into his eyes, the feel of a powerful cry building up from inside my chest. "Yes!" I shriek, my shoulders rising up and down with my sobs.

"Oh, Ava," he soothes. He quickly takes my glass away, surrounding my body within the warm embrace of his arms as he rocks me back and forth, comforting me through my howling cries.

"It's all my fault," I mumble into Caleb's chest, my brother's words circling my brain.

"It's not your fault, baby. You're not the molesting bastard. He needs fucking castrating," he hisses as he holds against me tightly, kissing the hair on my head.

"But I ran away from him without thinking about the possibility of him turning to my sister, of hurting her, and he did. He fucking did! I should have known. I should have fucking known!" I scream, teetering on the edge of sanity, but it doesn't stop me. "She was fucking twelve years old when I left! Twelve! Shit!"

I feel Caleb's soothing hands at the nape of my neck, cradling me in his lap as he continues to rock me back and forth, his lips gently planted at the top of my head.

"I could have stopped it. I could have told somebody. I could have protected her. I could have saved her! It's all my fault!"

"Hush, baby, it's okay. It's all okay, just cry it out." Caleb says, but it isn't okay at all. My baby sister is dead because I was too scared to tell somebody. If I had, my sister would still be alive. I was supposed to protect her from him but instead I ran. And now she's dead.

"I hate him! I hate him! I hate him!" I repeat over and over again, my voice cracking at the intensity of my screaming cries.

Stirring from a heavy sleep, my eyelids flutter with disorientation as a comforting sensation of fingertips caressing my hair overwhelms me. I open my eyes to an upside down Caleb. I squint through my confusion, then realize I have my head in his lap.

"Hey, streaky," he says with a frown, which is actually just an upside down smile, and continues to stroke my hair. Streaky? I rack my brains for a moment until I come to realize he's referring to the pink paint streaks covering my face from the earlier paint fight. I must look a fright. If I weren't so distraught, I might actually give a crap.

"Hi," I attempt but with the closing up of my throat, I can barely manage a whisper.

"Water?" he questions.

I reply with a wispy, "Yes." I sit up as he retrieves the glass of water and passes it to me. I give an attentive groan as the water glides down my throat painfully, but after a few more gulps, it slowly begins to ease.

"Thank you," I whisper once I've finished my last drop of water. "Did I fall asleep?"

Caleb nods, reaching for me, pulling me into his chest. I accept easily, crawling into his lap. "Yes, you were asleep for a good hour. You tired yourself out."

After a few minutes of silence, Caleb asks, "When's the funeral?"

"It's on Sunday," I respond quietly, still having a hard time processing the news.

"Are you going to go?"

I shrug my shoulders. "I don't know," I sigh. Then an image of my beautiful girl flashes before me, taking the decision away from me immediately. I can't leave her. "No, I can't. I can't leave Lily."

"I think you might regret not going," he says with a sympathetic tone.

"But what choice do I have? There's no way I can leave my daughter to fly to Florida. I wish I could be in two places at once, but I can't. Plus, the thought of having to face him ... I ... I just can't." It's one thing to speak to him on the phone but to be in his presence for one moment is just too much for me to stomach. I feel nauseous just at the thought of it.

"Yes, you can. You shouldn't have to dictate your life around that low life scumbag. If you want to go and say goodbye to your sister, then you should. I know that if you don't, you will regret it for the rest of your life. I know you." He touches my nose with his forefinger, making my nose scrunch up. I know he's right. I will regret it but what am I supposed to do? My daughter is still in the hospital. I can't just leave her.

"But what about Lily? I can't just leave her for a couple of days. I need to be here."

"You have been by her bedside for nine weeks, day in, day out, twenty-four hours a day, seven days a week. A couple of days away from her will not replace that. You're a brilliant mom, but you need this. You need to say goodbye to your sister," he says firmly.

I want to go, I want to say goodbye to my sister one last time, but a hundred different things continue to stop me. "But what if something happens and I'm not here? I just ... I—"

He places his index finger against my mouth, stopping me midspeech. "Stop it with the insecurities. She'll be fine. I promise."

"But—"

He places his firm finger across my lips again. "But nothing," he says, gently pushing a piece of hair away from my face. "Lily is doing amazingly well. She is healthy and strong. You have nothing to worry about. And on Monday, she will still be healthy and strong, even more so. It's just two days. Two days, so you can say goodbye to the other little girl who holds a piece of your heart. She might not be here anymore, but she still needs her big sister. Go, say goodbye. I will be with you. You won't be alone in this. You have me."

The sound of jingling keys wakes me up from my solemn haze. I sigh sadly, not even remembering how we got home. I shuffle my way through my front door, dragging my almost lifeless body through the small foyer. I hear the door close behind me, and feel Caleb's hands stroke the top of my arms.

"I'll go and run you a bath." He kisses my cheek, then continues through the living room but stops dead in his tracks as Ashton stands up from the sofa, an anxious look on his face.

"Ava," he breathes, a sigh of relief rolling from his lips. I see Caleb's scrutinizing look between the both of us, confusion etched across his forehead. Ashton walks towards my limp body, ignoring the baffled glare he is receiving from Caleb, his eyes only focused on me. I want to smile at his beautiful face, but all I manage is a feeble frown as the devastation continues to bubble through me, making me feel paralyzed from the inside out.

"Hi," I whisper as he stands in front of me, his eyes shadowing with worry.

"I'll start your bath, Ava," I hear Caleb say, giving Ashton and me a moment alone.

"You're still here."

He takes my hand, gently stroking it with his thumb. "Yes, of course. You ran out on me. I was worried sick and I needed to make sure you were okay."

"Sorry," I mumble through my distressed state, my vision blurring with tears.

"Hey, come here." He pulls my body into his and I cry weakly into his chest, his strong arms keeping me from collapsing into a heap on the floor. He whispers calming words into my ear while his fingers run through my hair in a continuous motion, comforting me.

"She's dead, my baby sister is dead," I mumble into Ashton's warm chest, my heart breaking into a million pieces.

143

Slowly the tears subside but Ashton's hold does not. I feel the softness of his lips brush my hair. "I'm so sorry," he murmurs gently against the top of my head, his crackling words cutting through the silence. "If she was anything like you, she must have been beautiful."

This makes me smile into the warmth of his chest. "She was," I agree as I finally find the energy to bring my arms up, my fingers crawling at his back, clutching against him as tight as possible. "So beautiful," I whisper.

We continue to stand in silence, enveloped in each other's arms, the feel of his beating heart pounding against my ear, settling me into a comfortable stance.

"You're so comfortable," I sigh dreamily, my fingertips scratching delicately against the bottom of his bare back, my thumbs tracing the naked space between the waistband of his boxer shorts. I know it's pushing the boundaries, but at the moment I don't care. It feels right. It feels perfect. It feels comforting.

"I'm glad you think so."

"Hmm, like a cuddly squishy bear."

To my dismay he pulls back slightly to look down at my face, a smile surrounding those plump lips of his. "Are you saying I'm fat?"

I shake my head on a small smile. "Nope," I say sleepily, my hands sweeping round to his front, my fingers taking a clump of his T-shirt in my hands, my thumbs stroking the front of his stomach, not ready to let go of him. He raises one hand to my face and he brushes a piece of hair away, tucking it behind my ear.

"When's the funeral?" he asks gently, palming his hand against my cheek. I take a calming breath as I lean into his hand. "Sunday."

"Is Caleb going with you?"

I give a gentle nod. "Hmm, he won't let me go alone, but I really want him to stay with Lily. I don't want to leave her on her own."

"I'll go with you."

It takes me a moment to register what he said, but when I do, I pull my head away in confusion. "Why?"

He gives me a serious look, closing the gap between us. "Because you're important to me," he states confidently as if it were the most obvious answer in the world.

"What about work?"

He gives me a comforting smile, his thumb working gentle patterns against my cheek. "I'll sort it. Now go take that relaxing bath and get some rest. I'll call you in a little while." He places a kiss against the corner of my lips, causing my heart to skip a beat, before pulling away and leaving my apartment.

My eyelids immediately fall, heavy exhaustion taking over. I tiredly drag my sleepy body towards my bedroom, lazily strip my clothes off and make my way into the bathroom. I lower myself into the steaming hot bubble bath, closing my eyes as I lie back and allow the fruit aromas and heat to relax my muscles.

I hear a light knock on the door. I mumble an incoherent response, squinting through my tiresome eyes. The vision of Caleb appears through the cloud of bubbles in front of me. "How's the bath?" he asks as he kneels beside me, his fingers tracing over the foamy white bubbles.

"Hmm," I reply, too comfortable to give a spoken answer.

"Ava?" I hear him question. I open both eyes, noticing a jug in his hands. "Sit up. Let me wash your hair."

I push my relaxed body into a sitting position, my arms wrapped around my knees, my eyes closed, unable to keep them open. He begins to wash my hair gently, softly massaging the shampoo into my scalp, unrushed. It feels wonderful.

"I overheard you and Ashton," he says as he dunks the jug into the bath water and gently pours the water over my hair, rinsing the soap out. He repeats the process. "Do you want him to go to Miami with you?"

I nod, unable to answer verbally as sleepiness continues to cover me like a blanket.

"Okay. I'll stay here with Lily then. If that's what you want."

There isn't anyone in this world, other than Caleb, who I'd trust to leave with my daughter. Except for Sebastian, but he isn't here.

"I know you're tired. Just one more rinse, and then you can go to bed."

Once he has rinsed my hair, I hear the gurgling sound of the plug being pulled out from the bathtub. "Up you get." Caleb lifts me out of the bath, setting my feet down onto the fluffy bath mat, surrounding my drooping body with a soft towel. Once Caleb dries me off, he carries me to the softness of my bed.

"Sleep tight, princess."

I moan a wordless goodnight before I feel the relaxing darkness envelope me.

# chapter 16

THE NEXT SIXTEEN HOURS are a blur to me.

I slept through twelve of them, but you wouldn't know it considering how exhausted I feel. I wake up feeling disorientated and lethargic, as if I've been hit by a freight train, but then it all comes back to me. My sister is dead.

Once I'm fully awake, and yesterday's heartbreak has fully sank in, I'm surprised by the pleasant image of Ashton walking through my bedroom door with a tray of breakfast. I don't question why he's here at seven-thirty in the morning; I'm just grateful to be greeted by his beautiful smile.

I don't have much of an appetite. I almost feel like I'll never have an appetite again. The thought of my baby sister not existing in my world is more than enough to turn me off food forever. As I nibble un-enthusiastically at the slice of toast, Caleb gives me my travel itinerary. I have a direct flight booked for one-fifteen this afternoon, and a twin room booked at the Hilton Miami airport for a two-night stay, returning Monday afternoon. He even packed a bag for me, leaving me with only one task: to get myself ready.

I shower, change then head to the hospital. I only have a couple of hours to spend with Lily until we had to head to the airport, so I want to make the most of my time with her. The thought of not seeing her again until Monday breaks my heart. If it weren't for the fact that I have my best friend here by Lily-Mai's side, I probably wouldn't have the courage to leave her. I kiss Caleb on the cheek and blow a kiss to Lily. Then I spend another couple of minutes gazing at her, trying to commit every feature of her to memory. As I begin to walk away, I can't stop myself from rushing back to her to tell her I love her, tears falling down my face. This continues for a solid five minutes until eventually Caleb has to push me out of the door, saying I'm going to miss my flight.

Ashton and I board the plane, taking our allocated seats. Once I've buckled and secured my seat belt into place, I glance at my phone, smiling down at the picture message of Lily that Caleb just sent me.

**Caleb**: *Already missing you mommy. xx*

**Ava:** *Miss you too, both of you. I've just boarded, will call you when I land. Love you x*

I put my phone into flight mode, quickly putting it back inside my purse and placing the purse under the seat in front of me. I sit back, pulling at my seat belt, ensuring it is as tight as possible, then pull the inflight magazine out from the seat pocket in front of me and start flicking through it apprehensively, not really reading it. It's purely a diversionary tactic, something to try and take my mind away from taking off.

I jump out of my skin when I feel the plane jolt backwards, my hand clasping tightly to the armrest. God, I forgot how much I hate flying.

"Are you okay?" Ashton asks.

I turn my attention to Ashton who is sat on my right next to the window, pursing my lips into a tight smile. "Yep. Fine."

I return the magazine to the pocket, then sit back again, my hands automatically moving to the armrest, my fingers wrapping securely against them. My breath hitches slightly, and my heart pounds heavily as the plane continues to move, taxiing towards the runway while the flight attendant goes through the safety procedures. Safety procedures I conveniently block out.

"Are you sure? You look white as a ghost."

"Yep. No." I feel my hands begin to clam up with sweat, panic beginning to set in.

"Yep, no, which one is it?" he asks with amusement.

I turn to look at him, my tight grip never loosening. I let out an exhaled breath. "I'm kind of afraid of flying," I say honestly. I yelp as the plane goes over a bump, causing my heart to race even faster.

"Give me your hand."

Without a second thought, I peel my clammy hand from the armrest and clasp it into his. The intimate contact of his hand in mine momentarily makes me forget the panic I'm experiencing. After a few short minutes, my heart wallops even harder when the plane comes to a complete stop, an obvious indication that we're ready for takeoff.

Great.

I slam my eyes shut, almost forgetting how to breathe.

"Ava, look at me."

When I refuse to open my eyes, he places his other hand gently against my cheek. "Ava, look at me." This time I obey, opening my eyes and looking at his perfect face.

"Do you trust me?"

I nod, then clench my eyes shut as I feel the plane suddenly pick up speed, then launches into what can only be described as rocket speed. My stomach lurches with the sudden change.

"I'm going to try something. Just don't slap me," he says with a light chuckle.

"Are you going to slip me a valium?" I joke through an inhaled breath, a nervous laugh escaping from my lips.

"No, something much better."

I feel his lips on mine, and I can't help the deep moan that escapes at the impact, my fear of flying forgotten. The edge of his tongue sweeps across my lower lip, and I eagerly accept, opening my mouth to his. He deepens the kiss, the softness of his tongue brushing against mine, and the whole world disappears in front of me. My stomach flutters with a thousand tiny butterflies, my heart pounding furiously as he kisses me like I've never been kissed before.

Breathlessly he pulls away from my lips, his eyes dark with sheer passion, leaving me panting heavily. "You're welcome," he whispers inches away from my lips before pulling away from me.

Sitting back against his seat, his hand tightens around mine, leaving me feeling shell shocked. My lips tingle from the unbelievable aftermath of his kiss, the takeoff at the very back of my mind. In fact, I'm on such a high that I barely register the increase in altitude as we continue to climb thousands of feet into the air. For the next six hours, the only thing that gets me through this flight is the replay of that kiss.

I'm staring at the reflection of myself in the mirror—the sad woman dressed in black—and I can't remember a time when darkness wasn't a part of me. Darkness has always been a constant companion, even from an early age. With every happy moment I've ever experienced, tragedy has always been close behind, reminding me that I can never truly be happy.

I take an inhaled breath as I smooth down the front of my pencil dress with trembling hands, then exit the bathroom. Ashton is sitting at the foot of his bed looking ridiculously handsome in his black attire. He rises from the bed when he sees me.

"I'm sorry if this is inappropriate on an incredibly sad day like this, but you look beautiful, Ava," he compliments. I would have blushed if I weren't so pale from the nausea, but his words still make my heart flutter.

"Thank you."

"Are you all set?"

I shake my head, my bottom lip trembling with sorrow. "No."

He gives me a sad smile, his hands clasping mine. "I know, Ava, I know. But I will be there with you every step of the way. I won't leave your side."

I nod, taking a deep breath as his words give me enough strength to take my next step. He escorts me from the hotel to a sleek blacked out Mercedes S class that Caleb generously hired. A chauffeur dressed in a smart black suit, black cap and white gloves stands patiently with his hands held in front of him, the rear passenger door already open. I say a polite thank you, then slowly slide in.

Once the door closes behind Ashton, he slides in as close as possible to me, his hand automatically taking mine. I lean my head against Ashton's shoulder and watch the bright Miami sunshine passing by through the tinted window. This makes me smile. Fran loved the sunshine. She would spend hours on a weekend riding her bike, jumping in and out of the pool, running around a playground—anything that would keep her outside until sunset. She even had a sunshine themed bedroom— a beautiful image of a sunrise on one wall and a beautiful image of a sunset on the opposite side.

She was just like sunshine: beautiful, bright, and colorful.

The tears begin to spill from my swollen eyes, knowing that somewhere along the line she must have lost her sunshine. Though it seems fitting that on the day of her funeral, on a beautiful bright day like this, that she can finally have her sunshine back.

A glorious tingle shudders through my body as Ashton's lingering lips press against the top of my head. I'm so glad I have Ashton here with me. Even with the tragedy, the sorrow, and the heartbreak, Ashton is the only person who gives me the belief that there might be light at the end of the tunnel.

My heart goes into overdrive when the car comes to a stop in front of a stunning renaissance Italian white church. Mourners stand idly along the church steps and entrance. As I glance around my heart stops violently when I see *him* for the first time in ten years, his arms around the waist of a blonde haired woman and kissing the side of her face. He hasn't changed much. He's still the same handsome, tall, well-dressed man I knew ten years ago—*with the same fucking smug sparkle in his eyes*.

I hate him.

I hate that we're related. I hate that he's my brother.

"I don't think I can do this." I shake hysterically, squeezing my eyes shut at the thought of having to confront my brother, not to mention the questioning stares and whispers at the sudden reappearance of the sister who ran away.

"Listen to me," Ashton demands in a soft but authoritative tone, cupping his hands against my cheeks, my eyes opening at his forceful words. "You can do this. You're here for one person and one person only. Just ignore everybody else. You can do this, I know you can."

His encouraging words speak volumes as his eyes stay locked onto mine. Knowing Ashton will be by my side comforts me greatly. I grasp his hand and tighten my grip around his fingers. "Thank you for being here with me," I whisper gently as I lean my forehead against his, the feel of his minty fresh breath doing crazy things to me.

"Of course," he whispers back, placing a single kiss against the top of my head. He pulls away, both of his palms covering mine. "Ready?"

I take a few deep breaths, then nod of my head. "Okay, before I change my mind."

The driver opens the door and I close my eyes, count to three, then slide out of the car. Moments later I feel Ashton behind me, lacing his fingers through mine. A squeeze of my hand and a smile is just enough reassurance to help me walk through the front door of that church.

As I walk up the steps, I let out a breath of relief, noticing that *he* must have gone into the church already. It gives me a few more seconds before I have to be within distance of him. I walk through the throng of people and they turn their heads with recognition in their eyes, but I continue walking, ignoring the stares as Ashton's words repeat over in my head.

*I'm here to see one person and one person only.*

I take the most terrifying step of my life as I step over the threshold into the beautiful, brightly lit church, but I don't stop. I walk, my heart thrashing against my chest, swallowing the nausea that continues its pursuit up my esophagus.

When we approach the crowded row of pews, Ashton leans into me, his mouth close to my ear. "Shall we see your sister now or after the ceremony?"

"Now," I say calmly despite my frantic racing heart. He leads me down the aisle, his hand clasped firmly in mine. Ashton whispers in my ear, "Breathe, just breathe, Ava," and that calms me until I notice Avery with our mother at the front of the church, a shocked look on their faces. Instead of giving them the satisfaction of my attention, I ignore my mother's glare and Avery's smug smile and continue in the direction of my sister's open casket.

At the top of the steps sits an open silver metallic casket with a colorful funeral cross laid against the closed section of the casket. To the left of the casket stands a golden memorial frame of a beautiful Fran standing in front of a spectacular orange tinted sunset. She has the same beautiful glow in her eyes and the big bright smile I always remembered her having.

Smiling sadly, I quickly push the tears away. After taking a deep breath, I count to three and with the strength of Ashton beside me, I force my feet to move up the marble steps towards the casket.

Once I've made my final step, I stand in front of the casket and look down at my sister. I burst into tears as I take in her peaceful beauty. She's dressed perfectly in a red-orange silk dress and matching silk scarf fastened around her neck, her long dark hair in loose waves, her soft, flawless face applied with just the right amount of makeup. My trembling eyes trace over the scarf, and it doesn't take a genius to know why it was placed around her neck.

My legs quickly turn to jelly and I feel them start to sway as my feet fall out from under me. Luckily Ashton catches me just in time, scooping me into his arms. "I've got you, I've got you, baby," he says gently into my ear, his arms holding me upright.

"She's dead. My baby sister is dead." Ashton's hold loosens around my waist as I lean forward, tracing my fingertips against the coolness of her cheek.

"I'm so sorry, Fran," I whimper as the guilt consumes me, guilt for leaving her, guilt over my bastard brother, guilt over her death. Guilt for the years I missed watching her grow up.

Unable to stand here any longer, I press my lips against her forehead then pull away, wiping softly at my fallen tears. "I love you."

Ashton gently leads me down the marble steps towards the rows of pews. We take a seat in the front row on the opposite side from my mother and brother. I curl up against Ashton's chest and wait for the funeral to begin.

The ceremony only lasts around twenty-five minutes before we all rise to exit the church and make our way to the cemetery for Fran's burial. As we approach the Mercedes, I hear the sound of my name being called and my body turns to steel, the hairs on the back of my neck on red alert. I clench my fingers forcefully against Ashton's arm as panic threatens to take over. Taking a deep breath, I slowly turn around to confront my brother.

"Avery," I say, my voice void of any emotion or eye contact, almost vomiting as his name falls from my lips.

"I can't believe you're here. It's been a long time."

I shudder at the irritating nasally sound of his voice, the worst sound in the world. Instinctively I clutch harder against Ashton's hand, cowering closer to him, visibly shaking in his grasp. Ashton glances down at me with a questioning look before returning his attention to my brother, his eyes darkening with irritation, sizing him up, clearly not happy.

"I'm here for Fran," I say through gritted teeth, giving him a darkened glare, hatred pouring from me, wishing I had the power to kill him with just one look alone.

He arrogantly nods his head and then moves his eye line to Ashton. He holds his hand out. "Hey, I'm Avery Jacobson, Ava's brother."

I shudder at the use of his word 'brother,' my fingernails clawing deep into Ashton's chest. Ashton raises his eyebrow in suspicion as he glances down at me, then quickly returns his gaze to my brother's hand, sizing him up again. Reluctantly he accepts his hand and gives it a firm shake. "Ashton Bailey," Ashton says sharply, eyeing him up with disapproval. Avery notices this and an amused smirk lifts on his face. He glances to me briefly before turning his gaze back to Ashton. "It's nice to meet you, Ashton Bailey."

He's joined by the blonde woman I had seen him with earlier. She links her arm with his, beaming us with a smile. "Are you going to introduce me to your friends?" I hear her ask as she looks up at him with Bambi eyes.

He smiles. "Sorry, babe. This is my sister, Ava, and her boyfriend, Ashton."

I don't bother correcting him; he can think whatever he likes. It's none of his goddamn business. Her eyes light up as she zones in on me with familiarity. "Oh, hi! It's so nice to finally meet you, Ava. I've heard so much about you!"

I shudder inwardly at her words, despising her already for being associated with a monster. "I bet," I mumble, wondering how much she knows. I feel a painful crack in the center of my heart.

"This is my wife, Rebecca," Avery announces, causing me to choke with disgust. Ashton looks down to me, concern written on his face. I can't believe he has a wife. He doesn't deserve a bag full of piss, let alone a beautiful doting wife, a doting wife who is supporting a smallish bump.

She notices me looking at her bump and smoothes her hand over her stomach. "We're pregnant, three months," she beams, her eyes dancing with excitement. "Have you any children?"

My insides clench with fear at the thought of my daughter being in close range to my brother, even in mere thought. I don't even want her existence known to him. It's bad enough to find out that he might have a daughter of his own. I can't even contemplate the things he could unleash on his daughter as a father.

I elbow Ashton in the ribs gently, clearly indicating that I'm uncomfortable with this conversation and want to leave. Now.

"It was nice to meet you, Rebecca," I say in a grim tone, a contradiction to the actual words. Ashton gets the hint and turns us towards the car, ushering me into the cool exterior. I'm shaking hysterically by the time the car begins its journey to the cemetery.

Ashton pulls me into his arms, seeing the evident tremors. "Shit, you're shaking." He holds me to his chest, his arms tightly compressed against my body.

"I'll … I'll b-b-b … be … o-o-o … okay … in a-a-a … m-m-m minute." Ashton continues to hold me until the spasms finally come to a stop.

He pulls me from his embrace, to look down at my face. "Can-can I ask you a question?" I know with the hesitation of his words that I'm not going to like it. I nod with caution.

"Your brother," he says with a grimace. "Is he the reason you left town, the reason you ran away?" I clench my eyes shut, hating the question. I nod my head sadly, unable to give him a verbal answer.

"What did he do to you?" His voice is laced with anger, the green in his eyes nearly turning a solid black. I shake my head as panic begins to escalate up my chest, causing my breath to constrict. Only one person knows my secret, and I'm not ready to delve into my demons, not today. I just want to say goodbye to my sister.

"Ava, look at me. Whatever it is you can tell me."

I try to force my escaping tears away, but they just keep coming back with a vengeance. *"Even if you did want to tell somebody, nobody will believe you."* It would kill me if I told Ashton and he thought I was lying. The thought of losing him almost cripples me. That feeling in itself confuses me. I don't know what it means for my feelings for him or what it could possibly mean for my relationship with Sebastian. All I know is that Ashton's friendship is something I want to cherish for a little longer.

I wipe furiously at my falling tears. "I just want to say goodbye to Fran." My voice trembles with a vulnerable whisper, another tear slowly rolling down my cheek. Ashton catches it with the pad of his thumb, a somber smile lifting at the corner of his mouth.

"Okay."

He nods with understanding. He pulls me back into his comforting chest and holds me in his arms until we come to a final stop at the cemetery. We make our way to the allocated spot where her burial will take place. As I struggle to walk through the grass in my six-inch heels, I suddenly freeze. I can see my father's headstone not too far from the open grave.

Ashton stops still in front of me, his fingers brushing against the top of my forearms. "Hey, what's wrong?"

"Fran," I say, taking a deep breath. "She's being buried beside my dad." It has been over ten years since I last visited and even now the pain of missing him still hurts.

"Shit, Ava, I didn't know. I'm so sorry."

I wipe my tears away with a handkerchief that the chauffeur had given me as I exited the car. "Thank you," I say, giving Ashton a weak smile through my sadness. "Would you mind if I made a quick visit before the burial begins? It's just … it's been a while since I've visited him."

He takes my hand. "Of course not. Come on."

I lead him towards my dad's grave, stopping a foot away from his headstone. "I wish I'd brought some flowers," I muse.

# IN LOVING MEMORY OF
# PATRICK MATTHEW JACOBSON
## A DEVOTED HUSBAND, FATHER, SON,
## AND BROTHER
## 01.04.1960 – 04.13.1994

I look up to find that Ashton is no longer standing beside me. I turn around in confusion to find him jogging towards me with a handful of bright orange flowers.

"Here you go," Ashton says, handing them to me. I stare at him dumbfounded as I gently take them. "I noticed a bed of wild flowers when we walked in."

I can't help but smile, a small laugh bubbling from me. "You're not supposed to take these from the gardens, Ashton." I smack his arm, shaking my head at him. "But it's very sweet, thank you."

I turn back to my dad's headstone, gently taking a crouching position and laying the flowers down. I remove a fleck of dirt from one corner of the headstone with my thumb, then sit back on my heels.

"Hi, Daddy. I'm sorry it's been a while since the last time I visited, but I'm sure you understand. I hate how it's under these circumstances, but I do have great news. You're a grandpa. Yes, I've had a baby. She's called Lily-Mai, Lily after my favorite flower and Mai after Sebastian's mom, but I'm sure you already knew that. I'm pretty positive you're the reason she's still here with us. Thank you for that because she is my entire world."

I wipe at my tears. "This is Ashton. He's my … friend," I struggle, not knowing how to introduce him because friend doesn't seem fitting enough for how much he means to me. My eyes widen as Ashton speaks up.

"Your daughter is incredible, sir." He winks at me, quickly returning his gaze back to my father's grave. "She's being well looked after, your granddaughter too."

I smile before turning back to my father's headstone. "I miss you so much, Daddy. I think about you every day. I just wish you were here to see Lily because she is amazing."

"Ava."

Ashton nods towards the front of the cemetery where a classic black hearse with Fran's casket is driving slowly through the entrance gates. My chin wobbles knowing that this is the final goodbye. I nod weakly, turning my attention back to my daddy's grave.

"I have to go and say goodbye to Fran now. Please look after her for me. She's been through enough. She needs her daddy." I press a kiss against my fingertips and place them softly over his name.

"I love you."

I stand up and turn to Ashton, entwining my fingers with his. We walk over to the open grave where people are beginning to gather, and watch as the hearse comes to a stop on the paved cemetery road. Six pallbearers approach the hearse and my heart skids to a stop when I notice one of them is my brother. My blood begins to boil with anger. How fucking dare he? After everything he put her through, after everything he did to her, he has the fucking nerve to carry her casket as if he's the mourning brother.

"He has no fucking right," I murmur angrily to myself, my entire body shaking with fury.

Ashton turns to me, his other hand coming to a rest on top of our entwined hands. "Just ignore him. He isn't worth your wrath, baby."

I clench my eyes shut, my tears burning. I calm slightly as I feel Ashton's arms hold me to his chest, whispering gently into my ear, "Breathe, just breathe."

I watch as they slide Fran's closed casket from the hearse, using their strength to carry her casket over to the open grave. They slowly march until they approach the open grave draped with green cloth. They carefully place the casket on top of a metal frame situated around the open grave and step away. The pastor says a few final words and then the bastard decides to say a few words as well.

"I just want to say a few words before we say a final goodbye to my sister. I'm still trying to come to terms with her death. It came as a shock to us all. It happened suddenly but instead of us remembering how she died, and the tragedy behind it, I want us all to remember her for the happy, incredibly kind human being she was. When you say goodbye, think of the last happy memory you have of her and then go on with your lives. That is what she would have wanted. She wouldn't want you mourning for her, shedding tears for her. If she were here right now, she would be trying to make you laugh with some lame ass joke, anything to help take your mind off your sadness. She didn't like seeing people upset. She used to say life was too short to be sad, and she was right. She proved just how short life can be. As much as we will miss her, we will always remember her happiness. Rest in peace, Francesca."

Then her casket is slowly lowered to the ground.

I hate him. I hate how he is tainting her funeral like this. She can't even rest in peace without him pissing all over her grave. My falling tears are for the lies he's feeding to everybody. I want to scream, tell everybody the reason why she's dead, but I don't. Instead, I turn my head into Ashton's chest, not wanting to see the lie continue as Avery takes a clump of soil and scatters it over her lowered coffin.

Soon enough, I step up to the open grave. Sadly, I scoop a handful of the earth in my hand and throw it over her casket. Ashton follows after me, speaking softly, "Rest in peace, Fran." Without another glance at my brother or mother, I take Ashton's hand and walk away. As we walk towards the exit, I hear a female voice in the background hollering my name. I'm surprised to find a sad girl in her early twenties, tall with platinum blonde hair, approaching me.

She smiles warmly as she comes to a stop in front of me. "Hi, Ava, you don't know who I am, but I was Fran's best friend. I'm Darcie."

I smile as I loosen my tight grip in Ashton's hand. "Hey, Darcie. This is Ashton," I say, introducing him to her. She politely smiles before looking back at me.

"I have something for you. It's a letter." My eyes widen in shock, my grip tightening unconsciously in Ashton's hand again. "It's from Fran. I found it with a bunch of stuff she'd left at my place. She … stayed with me quite a lot. I didn't know it was there until after she'd died. I guess she knew I would find it and would be able to give it to you. She didn't trust a whole lot of people, especially towards the end."

*Does she know?*

"The letter, do you have it with you?"

She shakes her head. "No, it's back at my place. I can go and grab it for you before everybody heads back to the Jacobson's."

I furiously shake my head, emphasizing my feelings on ever stepping foot in that house again. "I'm not … I can't … I can't go back there. We're going to the hotel."

She nods with a small smile. "Of course, I understand. Where are you staying? I can drop it off for you in the morning if you like."

"Are you sure? I don't want you to go to any trouble."

"It's no trouble at all," she says with a kind smile.

My face drops as my mother stomps over, an ugly ass snarl across her face. "You have a fucking nerve turning up here, girl." It's obvious she's drunk and I have no idea how she is keeping herself upright. Ten years later and she is still a raging alcoholic, go figure.

"I came to say goodbye to my sister. I was just leaving." I pull on Ashton's hand, turning to leave, but her evil words stop me in my tracks.

"You lost the right to call her your sister the moment you walked away. We thought somebody had abducted you but instead you were just a selfish bitch who ran away! I gave you everything, and that was how you repaid me!"

I flinch as she screams at the top of her lungs. The scene she is creating is attracting quite the audience as people start to crowd around us, most with the look of intrigued amusement. I snatch my hand out from Ashton's and take a step forward, anger flaring. "I'm not doing this here. It is Francesca's funeral. Have some respect," I hiss calmly and quietly as possible, not wanting to attract even more attention.

"You had everything money could buy. A car, a phone, a maid to do your cooking and cleaning. You had a life most girls would dream of, and you walked away from it! And for what? A poor life with a middle-class boy on your arm," she snarls towards Ashton.

Okay, so we *are* doing this here.

My nostrils flare with continuous anger as I take a step closer to her, so close I can smell the alcohol on her breath. "You gave me everything except for your love. I didn't care about materialistic crap or expensive cars. Your version of love was throwing a credit card at each of your children, then fucking off to the Caribbean to find your next toy boy. You were so busy on your next adventure that you had no idea what was going on back home." I take a moment to glare at my brother as he approaches my mother. "I'm surprised you even noticed I was gone, to be honest. So well done, you actually became the caring mother Teresa after I left. At least that benefited two of your children." Then I give out a loud sinister laugh, feigning amusement. "Oh wait. No, you didn't. If you had then you wouldn't have just had to bury one of them today, bravo, Mother. Fucking bravo."

I blink in shock, when her hand meets my face with a sharp slap. The power behind it has me stumbling backwards a little disorientated. Immediately Ashton is at my side, gripping her drunken hand in a tight fist, stopping her from slapping me again. "If you so much as lay another drunken finger on her, I will not hesitate to hurt you. You don't fucking touch her. Do you understand me?" he says in a southern drawl, his eyes darkening with anger. He gently lets go of her arm and takes hold of my hand.

"Ava, let's go," Ashton whispers in my ear, pulling me gently towards him.

"Come on, Mom, she's not worth it," I hear my brother's ugly voice as he struggles to steer her intoxicated body away.

We begin to walk away from the crowd, when my mother's screeching screams echo through the cemetery. "Yes, walk away! That's what you're good at! It should be you in that casket! You! You're good as dead to me anyway! Dead to me!"

I walk away with my head held up high, pretending that her words don't cut like a knife or that each word doesn't feel like a bullet to the chest.

# chapter 17

AFTER I'VE HAD A long and refreshing shower, I emerge from
the bathroom with a white fluffy bathrobe wrapped around me,
my hair still damp and hanging loosely down one shoulder. Surprised to find that I'm alone, I walk over to the table on the other side of
the hotel room, noticing a scrap of paper.

GONE TO GET
SOMETHING FOR
DINNER
BE BACK SOON.

ASHTON X

At the mention of dinner my stomach growls, swiftly reminding me that I haven't eaten since yesterday morning. Given the private moment, I decide to call Caleb. I grab hold of my cellphone from the bedside table and guilt kicks me in the chest when I notice I have a missed phone call from Sebastian. I close my eyes, the kiss I shared with Ashton yesterday coming to the forefront of my mind and how I've conveniently forgotten to tell Sebastian that my sister has died. It isn't as if he could have done anything about it even if I'd told him. He's a million miles away, so what's the point in worrying him? He has enough to deal with.

*At least that's what I'm telling myself.*

Pushing the guilt aside, I find Caleb's name in my contact list and press call. It takes a while to connect but the sound of his voice on the other side when he does answer is like home to me. "Hey, sweetheart, how are you doing?"

"Shit," I say with a sigh as I walk over to the bed on the right and perch myself on the edge.

"That bad, huh?"

"Let's just say I'm glad it's over. It's been a long day." I fall backwards on the bed, looking up at the white ceiling.

"I bet you turned some heads while you were there."

A small sadistic chuckle escapes. "Oh yeah. I was the pinnacle of entertainment to the entire city of Miami. Not only did I have to bury my sister today, but I also had to endure the whispers from strangers, and witness my brother's deceiving and pretentious bullshit. And then, to top it off, I was bitch-slapped by my mother."

I wince as I delicately palm my sore left cheek where she slapped me. "Who, by the way, wishes I was dead."

"She slapped you? And what do you mean she wishes you were dead? Jesus, Ava."

"I mean that she wishes it was me who died, not Fran. For a drunk, she has remarkable aim. Oh, and that's not everything. My brother has a wife, and they have a baby on the way."

"No!"

"Yes."

"Fuck me," he breathes out. "Do you think she had a good send off? Without all of the bitch slaps and bullshit."

"Yeah, I think she did. She looked beautiful."

"I'm glad, after everything she must have gone through. It's nice to know she doesn't have to suffer anymore."

I inwardly sigh with frustration when the tears begin to fill up again, and I slam my eyes shut, trapping the moisture behind my eyelids. "Anyway, enough of the funeral. How's my baby?"

"She's doing amazing. She's missing her mom though."

This causes me to cry out, my attempts at forcing the tears at bay failing drastically. "I miss her too, so much," I say as I let the tears fall. "God, I wish I was there. I hate Miami."

"Don't cry, you'll be back here tomorrow."

"I know, I know." I wipe my tears. "It's been one of the worst days of my life, and I just want to be able to hold Lily in my arms and forget about everything else."

"I know," he says, his voice full of sympathy. I hear the door open and close. I sit up from my lying position to see Ashton walking through. He's still dressed in his funeral attire but without the jacket and tie. My stomach growls when I spot the large pizza box he is carrying, and I quickly wipe my remaining tears.

"Can I call you back? Ashton's back with dinner." Once I've ended the call, I stand and follow Ashton to the table at the far end of the room.

"Caleb?" he questions as he kicks his shoes off.

I nod, looking down at the beverages and pizza. "Why didn't you just order room service?"

"I wanted to give you some space while you showered. I know today has been hard for you." He walks over to the cabinet in the corner of the room where the mini fridge sits and takes hold of a wine glass, then comes back over. He unscrews a bottle of rosé wine and pours a generous amount into the wine glass. To my surprise he hands it to me. I shake my head immediately.

"I can't drink that. I'm still breast—"

"Breastfeeding," he cuts me off. "But after the day you've had, I know you could do with a drink. One drink won't hurt."

I look at the glass of wine and then back at him. "Are you sure?"

"I'm positive. One drink won't affect the milk. Promise. Now drink up. Doctor's orders." I smile, accepting the glass of wine and bringing it to my lips, taking my first sip of alcohol in eight months.

"Good?" he questions as I pull out a chair.

"So good," I praise dreamily. Taking a seat, I curl my feet under my bottom in a half kneeling position and enjoy another satisfying sip. Ashton sits in the seat facing me, taking a bottle of beer from a six pack. Twisting open the bottle top, he flicks the crown cap against the wooden table, causing it to rattle against the table. Once he has taken a well-deserved chug of his beer, he settles the bottle onto a coaster and places a napkin in front of me.

"How you holding up?" he asks as he opens the pizza box. He places a slice of pepperoni on my napkin, before grabbing a piece for himself.

I swap my wine glass for my slice of pizza, taking a small bite against the corner edge, chewing thoughtfully. "I don't know," I gulp. "I'm just glad it's over, and we can go home tomorrow. Miami holds too many bad memories for me." I shake my head from the horrific images, forcing them to the very back of my mind. I take another bite, concentrating on the beautiful features of the man sat in front of me, only to burst out into laughter as he wolfs his slice of pizza down.

"What?" he questions with a mouthful of pizza.

"You're a pig. You know that, right?" I say, managing to swallow my pizza, once my laughing has died down.

"What can I say? I'm a guy, and if it keeps that smile on your pretty face, I will continue eating like a pig. Sexy right?" he says, flashing his eyebrows up and down, shoveling another gigantic piece into his mouth and causing me to laugh for a second time.

Once we finish our food, I shuffle my exhausted body over to the twin beds and collapse into the middle of one with my head leaning against the headrest and my legs crossed at the ankles. I watch as Ashton walks over to the bed after cleaning up after dinner, a fresh bottle of beer in one hand and his phone in the other, scrolling through it intently. His brow creases with concentration as he begins typing out a message.

"Everything okay?" I ask, taking a small sip of my half empty glass of wine.

He tips his head up to me, a small smile shifting on his lips. "Yeah, why do you ask?"

"Oh, you just looked a little confused."

He plops himself on the edge of the bed, chuckling as he turns towards me, one knee bent. "Oh, it's my mom." He rolls his eyes as he holds the phone up. "She asks the most bizarre questions. She thinks that because I'm a doctor I'm the go-to person for knowledge."

He hands me the phone and I read the text out loud. "Question. If you immerse yourself at the bottom of a swimming pool with scuba gear on, do you think you could survive a tornado?" I burst into laughter in utter confusion.

Ashton laughs with me. "I honestly don't know what goes through her head some days." I read his response, which makes me laugh further.

**Ashton**: *Mom, I'm a neonatologist, not a rocket scientist. But no, I don't think you could survive.*

Throughout my laughing, I accidentally swipe my thumb against the front of the screen, and I come across a message that clearly isn't meant for me to read. My heart suddenly stops.

*She's incredible. I'm falling for her. Hard. I don't know what I'm supposed to do. She's ...*

I quickly swipe back to the bottom of the messages to his mom without reading the rest, handing him back the phone as if it's hot coal. My mind goes into overdrive, wondering if he's talking about me. Is he falling for me? I take a large sip of wine from my glass as the information begins to sink in. Ashton's falling in love with me? Unless, it's another girl? But he hasn't mentioned seeing anybody. Oh, God what if he is seeing somebody?

I drain the rest of my drink, in one gulp as I begin to picture him with some gorgeous blonde with a body that hasn't been inflicted by the impact of childbirth ...

A persistent clicking sound awakens me from my thoughts, and I see Ashton hovering over me, clicking his fingers in front of my face, trying to hold my attention.

"Hey, where'd you go?"

I shake my head of my thoughts, giving him a perplexed look. "Um, sorry, it's just been a weird day," I say sullenly, gazing down at my empty glass, wishing I could have it filled back up again.

He takes the glass from me and places it on the bedside table, along with his bottle of beer. Sitting in the middle of the bed, he lifts my bare feet up, and places them in his lap, his firm hands holding my left foot.

"That it has. You're not ticklish are you?" he says, pointing his head into the direction of my feet. I shake my head, sinking further into the mattress as his thumbs begin to draw small circles along the ball of my foot with medium pressure. Concentrating exclusively on the ball of my left foot, a small whimper escapes me as his glorious thumbs begin to knead against the arch of my foot. His fingertips delicately massage the top of my foot, keeping in rhythm with his thumbs, and my entire body tingles with delight.

"That feels good," I mumble with appreciation as I feel my body sink into the mattress. I almost feel as if I'm floating on air.

He chuckles as he continues his work on my foot. "Well, lucky for you, back in college we did a seminar in reflexology, so I'm pretty good with my fingers."

"Hmm," I moan in delight, wriggling with satisfaction.

A comfortable silence covers us as he continues to massage my foot with precise movement. With each tingle that evaporates through my body, my muscles continue to loosen up. I begin to feel delirious with comfort. I'm drowsy, but instead of allowing sleep to overtake me completely, I let my previous thoughts consume me, questioning who Ashton might be in love with. I don't know if it's the one glass of wine that I've just gulped down, or how ridiculously relaxed I feel, but I blurt out the question that was supposed to stay confined in my own head.

"Are you seeing somebody?"

I inwardly groan as his fingers suddenly stop their movement. He's quiet for a moment, and I automatically take his silent response as a yes. I keep my eyes clenched shut.

"Um, no. Why do you ask?"

I want to kick myself for asking the question. Now he expects me to answer. As I mentally berate myself for being such an idiot, he places my foot onto his lap, exchanging it for my right foot. Expecting him to continue with his heavenly massage, I feel a little agitated when he just holds my foot still within his hands.

Secretly sighing to myself, I realize I need to answer. "No reason, just curious," I mumble, coming up with the first thing that popped into my head, avoiding opening my eyes at all costs.

"Ava?" he questions, obviously not buying my bullshit excuse.

I sit up on my elbows, opening one eye to him. "What?" I ask, sounding pissy.

He looks as if he wants to say something, but shakes his head as if the very thought is too ludicrous to say out loud. "No, I'm not seeing anybody else." Immediately flushing crimson, he quickly realizes his own mistake. "I mean, no I'm not seeing anybody."

His mistake makes me smile.

"Why?"

As he contemplates his answer, he presses his thumbs against the ball of my foot, moving the medium pressure into a sweeping motion. He shrugs his shoulders, looking me straight in the eye. "I don't know. I guess I haven't found the right girl yet."

My stomach drops as he dazzles me with his penetrating glare. He continues with his foot massage and concentrates solely on my foot, uncomfortably so. I smile sadly, my gut instinct telling me that he has found the right girl, but he can't do a thing about it. I suddenly remember things he has said to me, certain looks he has given me. That one time after dinner when he said he desperately wanted to kiss me but how he couldn't be the guy who breaks up a family.

"Why?"

He raises his head, a confused smirk etched along his mouth. "Why? Why what? Why haven't I found the right girl?"

*No, why are you falling in love with me?*

"I don't know, Ava," he says sounding exasperated. "I guess we're not all as lucky as you. You've found the person you want to spend the rest of your life with. You have a beautiful daughter who loves you. You're lucky because not a lot of people find that kind of happiness."

That one statement has my heart shattered in a split second and I find it hard to catch my breath. I want to reach over and put the bright smile back into his sad eyes, but instead I allow the silence to settle over us.

I spend the remainder of our awkward silence thinking about what he said; how even with my "lucky happiness," I still find myself remembering how amazing his lips felt on mine when he kissed me yesterday and how I wish he would kiss me again. A part of me wishes that I'd met

Ashton before Sebastian. He's an incredible person, so sexy, so perfect …

But if I hadn't have met Sebastian, then he would have never given me Lily, and that thought is almost crippling. She is my world and I can't imagine my life without her. Plus, I love Sebastian. I can't allow myself to go there with Ashton. Even if it means denying myself of him …

I lift myself up onto my elbows when I feel his hands settle my feet back down gently onto the bed, and I watch as he moves himself off from the bed. He blinks in surprise, a small smile playing on his lips. "I thought you were asleep."

I shake my head as I sit up crossed legged, enveloping my fluffy white robe around me to avoid flashing him. "No, I was just thinking."

"About?" he inquires, no doubt his turn to ask all of the questions.

I purse my lips, before answering. "Nothing. Everything."

"Hmm, cryptic," he muses as he sits beside me. I flinch slightly when the pad of his thumb brushes delicately against my tender cheek where my mother so *kindly* slapped me this afternoon.

"Sore?" he questions, a painful look upon his face.

"Yes, a little." I gently nod, the sting a little unbearable now that he's mentioned it.

"Let me grab some ice to help reduce the swelling. I'll be back in a second."

Minutes later he returns with an ice bucket full of ice and a small white towel from the bathroom. He sits on the edge of the bed with the bucket perched between his legs. He grabs a handful of ice cubes and places them into the center of the towel, folding the edges over the ice cubes and fisting the towel in the palm of his hands. He gently brings it up to my left cheek, the ice immediately beginning to ease the sting.

"Thank you." I smile as he keeps the ice held securely against my cheek. He traces my face with an intense gaze for a moment. "Are you going to tell me what happened today?"

"What? With my mom?"

He shakes his head. "No. Of course, I could have fucking throttled her, but I was talking about your brother."

The relaxing foot massage Ashton just spent the last hour giving me suddenly feels wasted as every single muscle in my body tenses at the mention of my brother, my calm mood vanishing in a second. "Nothing, it doesn't matter now," I say, waving it off like it isn't a big deal.

But it is a big deal and he knows it.

"That would have me convinced if you didn't suddenly just tense up, and not to mention your reaction to him earlier. I think I still have some fingernail marks somewhere," he says, pointing to his stomach for full emphasis. "What has he done for you to be so damn scared of him?"

I deliberately shy my eyes away from his, picking at an invisible mark on the sleeve of my robe, desperately wanting to talk about anything other than my brother. As I continue avoiding him, he takes actions into his own hands and crawls on top of me, his knees straddling the top of my legs, his hand still holding the ice pack to my cheek. I gape at him in shock.

"Why did you run away from home, Ava? Did he hurt you? Is that it?"

I look away, sucking my bottom lip into my mouth, desperate to stop my chin from quivering. He delicately removes the ice pack from my cheek, placing it beside his knee while his right thumb and forefinger tilt my chin up, forcing my eyes in place with his.

"You can tell me. Whatever it is, you can tell me. You can trust me with anything. I promise."

Hot tears fill my eyes, blurring my peripheral vision. I shake my head hastily, wishing he would just leave it alone. "I can't ... you won't ... you won't ..."

The words get stuck in the back of my throat, becoming more difficult to speak with each given breath.

"I won't what?" he encourages, his deep voice shaking with determination. I feel more tears disperse down my face, my face reddening with unpleasant heat at his obvious struggle.

"You won't ..." I clench my eyes shut as I push through the lump lodged inside my throat. "You won't believe me. You'll h-h-h-hate m-m-me," I manage to stutter through my exhaled breaths, my body shaking with uncontrollable shivers.

"It isn't possible to hate you, ever. What I'm feeling for you right now, Ava, is the very fucking opposite of hate. So try me," he growls animatedly.

My eyes snap wide open as his powerful words begin to register, encouraging me. For once in my life, I feel I can let go of my secret with somebody other than Caleb.

A secret I have kept buried for thirteen years.

I take a deep breath and then force the words I never thought I would get to repeat. "He r-r-raped me."

His face instantly pales, his eyes turning a solid black, a hundred different emotions of shock and anger rousing his facial features. "D-did I just hear you right?"

I nod my head in one fluid motion, a silent sob striking painfully through the core of my body. His body tenses on top of mine, the hands at the side of his legs clenching into angry fists.

"No, no … if I would have heard you right, then I wouldn't have just heard you say he raped you," he growls with a shake of his head.

*Almost like he doesn't believe me …*

He moves away from me in one swift movement and angrily paces the length of the room, his hands gripping harshly at the tendons of his neck. I watch in absolute heartbreak, wishing I could take my words back, to take the angry look from his face.

"Ash-Ashton," I say through my panicked sobs. "P-please, you have to b-believe me."

He snaps his head back at me, sorrowful shock widening his eyes. "Oh, baby." Immediately he is at my side, his gentle hands cupping my face, taking extra care with my tender cheek. "I do, baby, I do believe you. I'm just really fucking angry right now but not at you, never at you." I gulp heavily in relief, clutching at his wrists as if I'm holding onto him for dear life. A look of terror fills his eyes as he searches my entire face.

"How many times?"

I look at him with tears filling my eyes, unable to give him an exact number of times.

"More than once?" he utters with sickening shock.

I nod.

He clenches his eyes shut, and quickly reopens them again, his body trembling. "How old were you?"

"Fifteen," I whisper, dreading his response.

His shoulders rise and fall as he chokes on a silent heave, a look of pure disgust registering on his face. He clutches tightly against my robe.

171

"I can't … I can't even … comprehend … I mean fifteen … you were just a child …"

He slowly brings his hand up through my hair, sliding a loose strand behind my ear. "Does Sebastian know?"

I shake my head. "No, only Caleb knows."

"I'm so sorry, baby. You should never have had to go through that, not at fifteen, not at any age." He catches a falling tear with his thumb. "How long?" he asks with anger laced in his voice.

"Until high school graduation, and then … I ran away," I say through a hiccup, struggling to catch my own breath.

"Three years?" he whispers in added shock, still trying to come to terms with what I'm telling him. I close my eyes on a nod, tepid tears flowing from my eyes.

"Oh fuck, baby. God, I want to fucking kill him," he states angrily through gritted teeth. "Sick twisted bastard," he mutters under his breath, causing my eyes to reopen. Then a sudden look of realization crosses his features. "Your sister … please, tell me he didn't?" The one tragic look I give him as I cry hysterically gives him the answer that he needs.

"Oh, God no. Is that why she?" he asks frantically, his fingers physically shaking.

"Yes," I whisper through my sobs.

He bolts up, charging angrily to the dining area, forcing his shoes onto his feet. "I'm going to fucking kill him!" he roars angrily, every muscle of his body clenched tightly together. His fists are bound together at his sides, and a look of indescribable anger is pouring out from him.

"What are you doing?" I rise onto my knees in sheer panic.

"I'm gonna' go and chop that guy's dick off and feed it to the fucking dogs!"

*Oh shit, he's going to go and find him. Oh fuck, no.*

"That so-called *brother* of yours needs to be taught a fucking lesson." He grabs his wallet and phone from the bedside table, then places a chaste kiss against the top of my head. He lowers his head to my eye level, looking at me with his possessed demon eyes. "I promise he's not going to get away with this."

He hastily makes a step to move but at a frantic pace I scramble up onto the bed, standing unsteadily on both feet, and rush towards the edge, gripping forcefully against his arm and pulling him towards me. "Ashton, no, please no. Please, you'll get yourself into trouble!" I scream, my face drenched with tears.

"Ava, let go of me." He tries to force his arm away from me, but I just tighten my grip against his arm, determined not to let go of him.

"No! I won't let you do this. Please."

"Ava, he hurt you and your sister! He's a monster, and I can't just sit here and do jack about it. I won't let him get away with this."

I fist my fingers through his hair, gripping the strands with more force than is probably necessary, using my two-foot leverage of height to force him to look up at me.

"No, please. Stay here. Stay here with me."

In one fluid movement, I jump into his arms, straddling my legs against his hips, locking my feet together at the crook of his ass, my arms clinging tightly against the back of his neck. With the sudden loss of momentum, he stumbles backwards, his hands clutching my ass cheeks firmly to keep me from falling.

"Please, just stay here. Don't," *kiss*, "leave," *kiss*, "me." *Kiss*. "Stay," *kiss*, "here," *kiss*, "please." *Kiss*. "I," *kiss*, "need," *kiss*, "you."

I press tiny delicate kisses against the edge of his lips, still sobbing and clutching desperately against him. Then, without taking a moment of consideration, I kiss him fully on the lips.

And everything changes.

# chapter 18

ASHTON GROWLS AND A cry of surrender vibrates through his chest. Suddenly, I'm being charged backwards and pushed onto my back, bouncing against the softness of the mattress. I gasp at the sudden gravity change, clutching my fingers against his back, fisting his shirt into my hands. I kiss him back with full force, unconsciously grinding my hips against his, my bare feet pushing against his ass. I greedily accept his tongue, devouring him with every stroke.

His left hand slides through my hair, gripping securely at the wavy strands while his right hand travels down my robe-covered body. His fingers subtly skim through the gap of my robe, causing my breath to hitch and my nipples to pucker at the brief contact of his fingers against the curve of my breast.

Heat courses through my body. My heart thrashes with unbridled passion, matching the thumping pressure I suddenly feel between my thighs. Arching my back, I grind my hips against his, trying to ease the painful throb. The bottom of my robe has somehow opened up, leaving me exposed and vulnerable, and I'm greeted with a hard bulge pushing against my naked crotch.

My hands scramble to his shirt, ripping abrasively at his buttons, desperate to get him out of it. Breathlessly, he pulls away from my lips and his dark hooded eyes glare down at me in worship. My fingernails scratch against his skin as I rip the shirt from his back furiously, earning a sexy growl.

He slams his lips hungrily back onto mine before nipping and caressing over my chin, pursing tiny kisses along my jaw. He moves down to my neck, zoning in on the sweet spot just behind my ear, his hot breath sending shivers through my body. I assault his back with my hands, covering every inch with eager caresses and forceful scratches. My own back arches as he kisses along my chest, licking and kissing down to my breastbone, the top of my robe unraveling at his command.

He thrusts his hips into mine, his cock filled bulge sliding against my overly sensitive clit. The delicious sensation rockets through my body, causing a whimpered moan to escape my lips. In one swift movement, he unties the fabric belt of my robe and it unravels open, revealing my naked body. Ashton lifts himself up to hover over me, his masculine arms outstretched on either side of my head to take a full sweep of my nakedness. He looks ready to self-combust as he ravishes my body with his eyes, suddenly making me feel like the sexiest woman alive.

"Ava," he growls fiercely as he shifts down my body, his right palm trailing a path down my chest, over the curl of my breasts, and down towards my stomach. His fingers come to a lingering stop at my cesarean scar. His thumb follows along the six-inch scar, his eyes gazing intently at it. Kissing it once, his hand continues downwards to the sweltering area between my thighs.

His fingers hover over my most sensitive part, not once taking his indulgent eyes from mine. I widen my thighs, desperate for him to touch me. I'm seconds away from begging when a finger slides against my wet folds. My entire body bucks against his touch, but when his thumb flicks against my clit, I close my eyes, moaning as the pleasure pulsates through my body.

I open my eyes to see Ashton gazing at me, his hooded eyes looking as if they could drink me in. He has me spellbound, and I'm unable to take my eyes from him. He looks so damn sexy.

I bite against my bottom lip eagerly when he presses a soft kiss against my pelvis just below my scar. With his green eyes still trained on mine, he lowers his mouth to set a lingering kiss against the very tip of my pubis. A shiver courses through my veins when he sucks delicately at the skin and I nearly come undone when he slides his finger inside my entrance. Instinctively, I clutch greedily against his finger, sucking him tightly into me. His finger pulls out of me only to be pushed back in, setting a slow rhythm, in, out, in, out. Through my moaning gasps, he slips in a second finger, pressing his lips over my swollen clit, sucking it into his mouth.

"Oh, God," I moan out loud, my fists desperately gripping his hair, pulling against the strands as he assaults my clit with his mouth, his tongue sucking and lashing against the bud. At my responsive moaning, his fingers thrust harder into me, hitting me in just the right spot. My hips buck against his face as my body continues to rack with waves of intense ecstasy.

My heartbeat is thrashing against my chest.

My breathing has increased.

Waves of pleasure take over my every sense.

I'm so captivated as I watch him eagerly fuck me with his mouth that I can't take my eyes off him. It's highly erotic. My moans are coming closer together, and moments before I'm pushed over the edge, he stops and rises up onto his knees. My body sags irritably at my near release being taken away from me.

I watch as he quickly removes his shoes and socks, then goes to unfasten his belt clasp, unzips his slacks and hurriedly slides them down his legs, revealing a highly aroused cock bursting at the seams of his black boxer shorts, a wet patch of arousal evident at the head. As he moves closer to me, I drag my palm down his defined chest, following his happy trail of hair down to his lower stomach, coming to a satisfying stop over his cock. When I grasp my fingers tightly against his length, he's on top of me, crushing his lips onto mine with a growl. I meet his growl with a moan, sucking against his tongue when he thrusts against my thighs. The feel of his rock hard cock as it presses against my overly sensitive pussy creates a fiery pressure and I can't keep the cry from escaping when the feeling only becomes more prominent.

Impatiently, I slip my hands into the back of his boxer shorts and squeeze against his ass cheeks with the palm of my hands, then furiously pull the boxers down his hips. He complies with a lift of his hips, allowing me to pull them over his protruding cock. I force the material down his legs by the tip of my toes, kicking them from his own feet. I eagerly open my legs to him, a moan escaping my lips as his cock slides easily against my wet folds. I clasp my nails deep into his ass cheeks, rocking my hips into his.

"Damn, Ava," he groans huskily against my mouth, before biting down sharply against my bottom lip. I rock my hips against his again, desperate to have him inside me.

"Fuck. Me. Now," I breathe out urgently while my fingers scratch up and down his bare back.

My heartbeat constricts when I hear the telltale sound of a condom wrapper being torn open, and I stop breathing when he sits back on his heels. I watch in fascination as he slides the latex over his impressive length. Once the condom is covering every inch of his cock, he crawls back over me, pushing deep inside of me. I cry out at the sudden movement, and then groan devilishly as he hits me straight to my core.

His elbows are bent at either side of my head, his hands scrunched tightly into my hair. His beautiful green eyes are captivating me with his intense stare as he thrusts into me again, this time a little slower as if relishing in this very moment. We begin to move together as one, meeting each thrust, each moan, each kiss, becoming a frenzied mess.

I wrap my legs around his waist, locking my ankles against his ass and the sudden switch in position has me screaming with the heightened intensity. The pressure builds quickly, my body climbing to a climax within seconds. I lose the coherence of my speech as my body begins to tremble, and my limbs shake uncontrollably under Ashton as I come around him, falling apart, slamming my eyes shut to allow my climax to consume me. I hear Ashton curse as his hips slam hard into mine.

Not even thirty seconds from my last climax and I can feel my orgasm building again. I mumble something illogical as my second climax hits me with more force than the first and my body shudders, colorful fireworks exploding around me. I slam my eyes shut as I come for the second time. I swallow Ashton's groan as he slams his mouth onto mine, sucking against my tongue as he pumps furiously through his own climax.

As we come down from our high, Ashton still inside of me, I moan contently as he presses gentle butterfly kisses against the side of my cheek, moving down to my throat, nuzzling against the crook of my neck. I sigh happily as I draw lazy circles against his back with my fingertips. He chuckles against my skin, as his fingers caress against my breast and over my nipple.

Suddenly the image of Sebastian pops into my head and my entire body freezes under Ashton's.

"Oh, God," I panic, as heavy guilt courses through my entire body.

Ashton looks down to me as I tense around him. "Ava, what is it?"

"Oh, God. Oh, God," I repeat in horror, tears blurring my vision. I scramble from under Ashton, hiding my naked body with my robe.

"Ava?" His eyes turn from blissful to sad in a second as he watches me move away from him.

"That should not have happened. I love Sebastian. I love him!" I shriek as tears flow down my face. I stand and rush to the bathroom, but not without witnessing the broken look on Ashton's face as his eyes shut, his head dropping down in painful defeat.

Slamming the door shut, I lock it and sink my half naked body to the floor against the door and violent sobs rack through my body.

What have I done?

The dull invasive burning sensation I'm currently feeling downstairs is enough of a reminder. I've been unfaithful to my fiancé with another man. And not just with any man; the man I'm falling in love with.

Oh, shit.

This isn't me. I'm not a woman who cheats on her fiancé. I have *always* valued the sacred constitute of a committed relationship. I have *always* condemned those who are unfaithful to their loved ones, never understanding why you would hurt them in such an unthinkable way like that, but I guess I'm not that different after all.

I have *never* been so damn reckless in my life.

The next hour is spent alternating my guilt over Sebastian and Ashton.

Sebastian's beautiful face and his selfless ways …

Ashton's beautiful face and his selfless ways …

Sebastian's pure love for me …

Ashton's pure love for me …

Sebastian holding Lily in his arms …

Ashton holding Lily in his arms …

Then I crumble.

Lily.

My stupid, idiotic, reckless decision doesn't just affect Sebastian. It affects my daughter.

I have let her down.

Once I shower the betrayal from my body I exit the bathroom to find an empty room. Ashton didn't leave a note this time. Through my disappointment at Ashton's absence, I crawl onto the other twin bed—the bed we didn't have sex on—and cry myself to sleep.

I'm jolted awake at the sound of quiet cursing. Groggily, I sit up to see Ashton's silhouette sat on the edge of the accompanied twin bed.

"Ashton?" I whisper, rubbing the sleep from my eyes.

I see his head pop up from his crouching position. "Shit, sorry. I didn't mean to wake you. Go back to sleep. Shit," he hisses painfully.

Ignoring his request, I switch the bedside lamp on. I squint for a moment adjusting to the bright light, then gasp when I see Ashton's bloody fists. I am at his side in a flash. "Ashton, what the hell? What's happened?"

He gives me a brief look, not quite meeting my eyes. "Nothing." His eyes fall to the crumpled bed, the same crumpled bed we'd had sex on only hours before.

"It sure looks like something to me." Then it suddenly comes to me. Avery. "What did you do?"

He hears the alarm in my voice and looks up at me. "Not what you think. Well, not for the lack of trying anyway," he states with a hint of broken frustration to his voice. "I just had a run in with a brick wall. And as you can see," he holds out his hands, "the wall won."

I look back down at his fists, wincing at the very sight. I shake my head sadly. "Those cuts look really bad, you probably need stitches. Your knuckles might even be broken. Maybe we should go to the hospital and get them checked out."

He shakes his head. "No, I'll be fine, it looks worse than it is." He clenches his fists open and closed, indicating no broken bones, although the grit of his teeth through the obvious pain isn't missed by me. "See? Not broken."

"Okay, but we need to clean them up. Did you bring a first aid kit with you?"

He nods. "Yes, it's in my luggage."

I head over to the closet to retrieve his small suitcase, and take out a travel-size medical bag. I walk back over to the bed, sit down and set the first aid bag on the sheets. Unzipping the medical bag, I reach for an alcohol wipe and rip at the packet, unraveling the folded wipe. I place his hand on my knee and gently wipe at the blood.

"Shit," he hisses as I tend to his wound.

"Sorry," I whimper apologetically. I have to fight against the urge to heave as I look down at the blood. I wipe away at the heavy layer of blood; the scrapes and cuts don't look as bad as I first thought.

"What were you thinking? You're a doctor for Christ's sake."

He closes his eyes for a brief moment as if contemplating his own idiocy. "I wasn't."

I sigh sadly as I reach for another alcohol wipe and clean his other hand. With the guilt still sinking heavily inside me, this makes it feel ten times heavier. It's my fault that he isn't thinking properly. It's my fault why he rushed out of the hotel room full of anger and turmoil looking for my brother and punching goddamn walls.

"I'm sorry," I whisper, keeping my eyes trained on his hand as I continue to wipe the blood away.

"Why?"

Still avoiding his eyes, I answer. "Because it's my fault. I shouldn't have told you." I take a quick glance at the ruffled bed sheets, the reminder of what we did. "And *that* shouldn't have happened."

Feeling satisfied that his bloody wounds are completely clean, I rummage through the first aid kit in search of a tub of alcohol cream. A shiver erupts along my body when he places his hand over mine, stopping me in my tracks.

"Look at me," he says softly. I take a heavy gulp, and then glance up at him, but I still don't meet his eyes. "First of all, I'm glad you told me and secondly, was what we did so bad or is that just the guilt talking?"

I bite the inside of my lip as I let the question linger for a moment and for the first time since it happened, I allow the memories in. Pleasant memories. I desperately want to say that it was horrible, that it was the worst sex I've ever had, that it doesn't give me tingles at the very thought, but it would be a lie.

It was incredible.

"So it's just the guilt then?" he answers for me and, of course, he is absolutely right, but it still doesn't mean it wasn't wrong.

Feeling extremely uncomfortable with where this conversation is going, I ignore his question and gently pull his hand away from mine. I feel the heat of his eyes bore into me as I resume my search for some alcohol cream. Eventually, I come across a miniature tub and I unscrew it, still ignoring his glare. I dab some cream against my forefinger and gently apply it against his cuts. Once I have thoroughly applied it to both knuckles, I screw the top back on and place it back into the first aid bag.

"Band-aid?" I ask, still avoiding the question at hand.

"You feel it don't you? What I feel for you, you feel it too?"

My heart halts as he tilts my chin up with his thumb and forefinger, forcing me to look at him. I'm trembling under his intense gaze, and I have to slam my eyes shut to stop the tears from spilling.

"Ava, look at me. Baby, please, look at me." I shake my head, clenching my eyes tighter. I can't look at him. If I do, I won't be able to look away. "Please look at me so I can tell you that I love you."

My eyes blink open, shock coursing through my veins as I let his words register. My heart races and I find it next to impossible to catch my breath. "W-W-W-What?" I stammer as the words echo through my mind.

Ashton moves closer to me and carefully palms my hands into his own. "I love you." His voice cracks with the emotional strain as he repeats those three words, and with one look into his eyes I know without a doubt his words hold truth.

"When?"

He smiles at my obvious flustered state as I can't even string a sentence together. Luckily he understands. "I don't know, maybe since the first time I saw you in the NICU, in your wheelchair, looking at Lily. It may sound cheesy or cliché, but the moment I laid eyes on you, I couldn't breathe. You just blew me away, you still do," he says with a gentle caress of his thumb against my cheek.

"You love me?" I question with disbelief, still trying to come to terms with his words. Of course, I kind of figured his feelings out for myself earlier, but I still find it hard to understand. "But why?"

He smiles. "You don't even realize how beautiful you are, do you?" he says, his thumb tracing gently over my lips. "Yes, I love you. I'm so in love with you."

I shake my head furiously. "No, but you can't. You can't love me. Sebastian … we're getting married, we're engaged," I whimper desperately to myself, reaching for the necklace around my neck with my engagement ring, but my heart drops when I come up empty. I suddenly remember taking it off on Friday before decorating, and with the sudden change of events, I must have forgotten to put it back on.

Ashton grips my hand against my chest, holding me with his intense stare. "Where is he, Ava? If he loves you, where is he?" I want to defend Sebastian, defend his love for me, but for some reason I remain silent. "If he really loves you like he says he does, then he wouldn't be at war, risking his goddamn life. It's unfair to you and Lily."

"Ashton ... he has a contract, it's his career—"

"I know. Shit, I know. This isn't coming out right." He takes a deep breath, clutching hold of my hand tighter. "I didn't mean that the way it came out. I respect him and every other soldier, but knowing how it feels to lose somebody so close to me in the same fucking war ... I just think you deserve better, Ava. You don't deserve any more heartbreak. He has everything I've ever wanted, and this is probably my jealously talking right now, but instead of cherishing his life and the people in it, he's gambling it away. You deserve better and deep down you *know* that. I know you know that." I am stunned to silence as the power of his words slice through me.

"You're amazing, so fucking beautiful. I would marry you in a heartbeat. I love you. Yes, I might have only met you nine weeks ago, but it feels as though I've known you my whole life. I'm here. He isn't. You've opened up to me, in a way you haven't ever opened up to him. How can he love you, when he doesn't even know the real you? Not like I do. I love you, Ava, and I know you love me too."

I stare at him in awe, unable to respond. I want to defend Sebastian but my mind is spinning, and my pulse is racing as I allow Ashton's words to sink in.

"You feel guilty because it isn't in your nature to be cruel. I said I wouldn't kiss you, that I wouldn't break up your family, that I couldn't be *that* guy, but I've changed my mind. I will be that guy since your guy is doing a shit-ass job of protecting you, of loving you. I want you, and I'm not letting you go. I will cherish you. I promise you."

I forget the mechanics of breathing as soon as he presses his lips to mine, leaving me breathless and overwhelmed. He pulls away slightly, his eyes urging me to take the next step. My mind is in a spin, battling between my fiancé and the man I'm falling in love with, knowing I need to pick one and let the other go.

After a moment of emotional deliberation, I go with what my heart is telling me and press my lips to his, unable to deny Ashton any longer.

# chapter 19

## ASHTON

I SHATTER INTO A million pieces on top of Ava, coming the hardest I have ever come in my entire life. I press gentle kisses at the side of her cheek, gingerly nibbling down her neck, worshiping her skin with my lips.

I can hear her sigh with satisfaction, and the feel of her arms mauling my back is almost making me rock hard again. As I kiss along her collarbone, I stroke against her breast, brushing over her nipple. I chuckle against her skin as I swirl my tongue against the dip in between her collarbone.

Suddenly her entire body tenses around me. "Oh, God."

"Ava, what is it?" I ask cautiously. Tears are pooling in her eyes, a clear indication she is freaking out.

"Oh, God. Oh, God."

My heart drops to my stomach as she desperately scrambles from under me, covering herself up with her robe, becoming hysterical as she crawls to the other side of the bed, away from me. My heart drops further when I realize it's because she regrets it. She regrets what's happened between us.

"Ava?" My voice trembles as tears fall down her face. It breaks my heart to see her in such physical turmoil.

My heart cracks straight down the middle with her next words.

"That should not have happened. I love Sebastian. I love him!" she shrieks as she rushes towards the bathroom, away from me.

I shut my eyes with a grimace as I drop my head down in defeat, grasping the bed sheets in devastation. When I hear the bathroom door slam and her hysterical cries from the other side of the door, I decide that staying in this hotel room is not an option. Each distraught cry is too hard to bear. I never thought I would be the person who would cause her to make that sound, ever, and I hate myself for it.

Why couldn't I have left her alone?

She'd just told me her brother fucking raped her, and before I'd even realized what was happening, I was kissing her and throwing her on the bed with me between her legs, practically attacking her with my mouth. Yeah, way to fucking go, Ash.

I rip the condom off my dick, throw it in the trash can, then change into my crumpled clothes and rush out. Too impatient to wait for the elevator, I rush down the six flights of stairs, through the lobby and out into the cool Miami air. The fresh air does nothing to ease the anger that soars through my body. Every muscle tenses two fold and I desperately look for something to take my anger out on.

I can see his goddamn face, and I can see *it*, the image of him touching her with those dirty, incestuous hands of his. It's enough to send me over the edge. Without any hesitation, I pull my phone from my pocket and pull up a web page. I search his name in the white pages within the Miami Beach area. It comes up with four people with the same name, but looking closer there is only one who fits the age criteria of the Avery Jacobson I am looking for. I save the address to my phone as I hail a taxicab. It takes a good twenty minutes to get to my destination and when we finally come to a stop, I almost swallow my own tongue as I look up at the big-ass white beach house.

"Um, are you sure this is the right address?"

"Yep, sure is, son. 4236 Bay road, Miami beach."

I grit my teeth with rage as I realize this is the house he lives in. It doesn't seem right that he gets to live in luxury while Ava has had to live in hell on the other side of the damn country. I hand the driver a fifty-dollar bill and step out of the vehicle, shutting the door behind me.

As I walk towards the front of the house, I realize there is an electronic security gate, and I'm going to have to speak to someone through the intercom. When I hear his voice, I have to use every ounce of strength I have inside of me to control my anger.

"Hi, I'm sorry to disturb you. It seems my car has broken down, and as luck would have it, my phone battery has died. Would it be possible to come in and use your phone?"

"Sure, head on in."

The security gates begin to open up for me and just stepping foot on the driveway causes every muscle in my body to tense up with anger. The rage I'm currently feeling is something I've never felt before, but as I stomp my way through the graveled driveway—past the ridiculously expensive 4x4 Land Rover—it takes everything I have not to scratch the side of it with my fucking keys.

But I'm not here for that.

I'm here to break his face.

When I walk up the steps to the front door, my entire body is trembling so much with pure anger that I accidentally end up pressing the doorbell more than once. The moment the door swings open and he emerges, I fucking lose it. I launch for him, wrapping my hand around his neck, fist tight, and throw him a good ten feet through the lobby. I almost shock myself at my own strength. I glare at him as I stride over to him, watching as he tries to gather his bearings in confusion.

When he looks up, and realization crosses his face, he suddenly turns angry. "What the fuck, man?" He tries to stand up, but I grip him by the collar of his shirt and pull him up and slam him against the wall.

"You sick motherfucker!" I spit in his face, aggressively slamming my forearm against his chest, causing him to hiss in pain. He fights against my hold, but I force my arm deep into his chest while my other hand wraps around the base of his throat. All I see is red.

I hear a female panicked voice shouting from behind, but I ignore it.

"You're a fucking disgrace, do you hear me? I should have you fucking castrated after what you've done. Or even better, chop your dirty little dick up into tiny little pieces. You like raping fifteen-year-old girls? Is that what turns you on, what you get your kicks from? Or do you only have a preference for siblings?"

As I spit out the word 'siblings' I squeeze my hand tighter around his neck, causing him to choke with restricted breathing. He coughs and splutters for a moment, his fists trying to swipe at me. I ease my hold on his neck for a moment to hear the bastard's response, glaring at him with full anger. My entire body is shaking with adrenaline as the fury pumps through my veins.

"Get off me! What the fuck are you talking about? What has she told you?"

I force my fist into his stomach, causing him to double over with a curse. And just for good measure, I do it again. "You know exactly what I am talking about or do you need me to spit it out for you?"

I let go of him forcing him to drop heavily to his knees with his arms wrapped around his torso as he topples over in pain. I grip him forcefully by the hair, forcing him to look up at me. He grunts in pain, and it gives me great joy.

"I'm talking about you raping your own sister. Ring any bells?" I clench tighter at the strands of hair that are embedded within my fist, and I pull more vehemently, to the point his eyes begin to water. "Or how you raped your other sister, to the point where she had to kill herself just to get away from you?"

I glare at him, hoping to see some recollection or some kind of response, regret, anything, but there is nothing.

"She's lying."

"She's lying?" I question, and I can feel my anger becoming more futile by the second. "Oh, okay then." I palm my left hand into a fist, and I drive it into his nose with such a speed that blood gushes down his face. "Do you know how sick you are? You should be locked up for what you've done." I punch him straight in the jaw, almost laughing out loud when I hear a crack. Good that's a broken nose and jaw. What next?

The guy suddenly gets a backbone and grabs my legs from under me, causing me to lose balance, and I fall heavily onto my back, against the marble floor. I grunt painfully as I feel a dull shooting pain from my coccyx all the way up my spine.

Motherfucker.

He straddles me and lifts his fist to my face, but with the pain only fueling my anger even more, I'm too quick for him. I duck to my right, causing him to miss my face and punch the marble floor instead. Crack. This gives me an open opportunity, and I take a quick swipe of my fist against the right side of his face. As he loses sudden momentum, I twist my legs around his waist and slam him onto his back, crushing his chest with my knees, and I punch him over and over again. I ignore the burning in my knuckles as my fists continue to drive into his face. All I can think of is destroying this asshole.

The normal, rational Ashton is nowhere to be seen.

He has been replaced with a raving lunatic.

"You sick scumbag!" I scream as my fists propel against his bloody face. "You motherfucker! You dirty motherfucking asshole!"

"Let go of him! You're hurting him. Stop it!"

When I don't stop, she becomes more hysterical, striking me against my back as she screams for me to get off him, threatening me with the cops.

Finding the hidden strength to pull myself away from his semi-conscious body before I get myself thrown behind bars for attempted murder, I stand and hover over him. Then I spit on him.

"Call the cops. Then I can tell them what a sick and twisted bastard your husband is! Tell them how he raped his sisters, over and over again!" She gapes at me in shock, and this only makes me smirk. "I take it you didn't know that tiny bit of information when you married him, huh?"

"Why are you saying all of this? We've just buried his sister! Have you no respect?" she whimpers as she strokes gently against his hair.

"I'm saying it because it's true. Your husband is a monster."

She shakes her head as a bloody Avery begins to stir in her arms. "No, no, he wouldn't. He loves his sisters. He would never have done anything to hurt them."

"If that were true, then would I be here right now? It's the very same reason why today is the first time you got to meet Ava and the very reason you had to attend Fran's funeral." Her entire face pales as she looks down at her husband in doubt.

I kneel beside her and smile sadly, taking a quick glance down to her bump. I feel terrible for her. She doesn't deserve this. "If I were you,

I'd get as far away from him as possible. If he can do that to his sisters, he probably won't think twice about doing the same to his daughter."

She gasps at the very thought, cowering away from him, clutching desperately to her bump. I inwardly smile because it reminds me of Ava and how protective she is of her daughter. Then when I look at the morphed version of her brother, I'm swiftly reminded of why I am here. I lean over him, yanking him by the hair and force him to look me in the eye. I can see his eyes flicker open through the small slits of his newly swollen lids.

"If you so much as look at Ava, get within a mile of her or lay a fucking hand on her ever again, I will track you down and I will kill you. Do you understand me? I will not hesitate, motherfucker."

He nods pathetically as I shove his face away with a growl. "And just to avoid any misunderstandings, that was a threat."

Then I walk away.

Oh, and I key the fucker's car.

When I get back to the hotel, I head straight to the bar for a much-needed beer. I take a seat and a look of suspicion crosses the young bartender's face as he looks down at my blood-covered fists. He places a bottle of beer on top of a coaster in front of me, and I give him a twenty with my best 'don't ask and we'll get along just fine' glare as I tell him to keep the change. He walks away with his generous eighty percent tip. *Good boy.* I down the entire bottle in one gulp, gasping on a satisfying breath. I slam the empty bottle down on top of the bar, indicating to the bartender for another.

As I make my way through my second beer, this time at a reasonable speed, I start to process my actions. God, the last time I fought like that was when I was about sixteen years old and I'd wrestle with my brothers, usually over shit like who was hogging the PlayStation or who ate the last bag of potato chips. Christopher would be left with a bloody nose, Tyler with a kick to the groin and I'd end up with a dislocated shoulder. But never in my thirty-three years have I felt the kind of anger that has made me lose control to physical violence like I did today, to the extent that I could have easily killed a man. *Maybe I should have ...*

I have no idea where my strength came from, but I just kept seeing him touch Ava, and I lost it. I saw red and became somebody I didn't even recognize.

It was frightening.

Jesus, since the moment I met her my life has turned upside down. The woman is driving me insane. Everything about her consumes me; everything from her smell, her laugh, and those beautiful brown eyes. She is perfect. I love her so much it physically hurts.

I tried to stay away, especially when Sebastian came back for those two weeks. That gave me the wake-up call I needed. She wasn't mine, and she would never be mine. I was an asshole to her after that. I was angry, I was upset with her, so a lot of it came naturally. But there was never a moment that I didn't hate myself for the way I spoke to her, for the way I just cut her out of my life. I was frustrated as hell, too. I couldn't understand why I was so upset with her in the first place.

I knew she had a boyfriend, I knew she was committed to him. Hell, the woman just had his kid! But I could see the worry in her eyes. The same worry that all army wives and girlfriends have. She was so panicked with worry that she even collapsed with the stress of it, and immediately I hated the guy. He has this beautiful woman who cherishes the fucking ground he walks on and where the hell is he? In the middle of a fucking war zone.

She'd just had her baby, thirteen weeks premature. On top of the distress and absolute heartbreak of wondering if Lily-Mai would survive the first forty-eight hours of her life, she was also racked with worry, wondering if that was the day she would finally receive *the* phone call. The same call my own mother received only a couple of years ago. Every time I'd call to check in before Christopher's death, I'd hear the panic in my mom's voice when she would answer. She was always a nervous wreck, and I hated it.

I might sound like a dick, but from where I'm standing it seems to be one of the most selfish things to bring onto a family. I've been there. I've witnessed the heartbreak.

It's brutal.

I knew how much she loved him, but it didn't stop me from falling head over heels in love with her. The very first moment I laid my eyes on her beautiful face, I knew I was a goner. I'm surprised I haven't been reprimanded at the hospital for my friendship with Ava because I haven't done a very good job of hiding it. We have this incredible connection that makes me forget all of my inhibitions. I even forget my own name most days. Just being in her presence is enough to throw me off balance.

I tried to stay away from her. I even had a few one night stands just to try and get her out of my system, but it didn't work. I might have physically been with those other girls, but it was always Ava I was with.

The day I had to tell her Lily had gotten pneumonia changed every-thing for me. Having her in my arms, sobbing the way she did, I couldn't stand it. I wanted to look after her and take all her pain away. She looked exhausted, her eyes almost lifeless. I made a promise to myself that I would put the light back in her eyes, if only as a friend. And I did …

Until she got that call on Friday.

So that pretty much lead me to this moment where I'm picking at the label of my empty beer bottle, my hands covered in blood. What a fucking mess.

I've visualized making love to her, how it would feel to be buried deep inside of her, how amazing it would be to watch her crumble to a million pieces around me … but not once did it compare to the real thing. She was so responsive, so eager, so damn turned on that I never expected her to react the way she did. It was like I physically repulsed her, and the way she couldn't get away from me fast enough killed me. That intimate moment we experienced together was the best moment of my life, but she obviously didn't feel the same way.

And I'm confused.

I saw the dazzle in her eyes. I saw the heated passion, the look of adoration, and even a hint of love. She liked it; she liked the way I made her feel. I know that for sure.

*Fuck.*

Why did I have to go and fall for the one woman who isn't avail-able? Why has everything got to be so damn complicated?

I'm not going to get any answers from an empty bottle of beer, so I set the bottle on the bar and make my way back upstairs. I quietly let myself in the room. Ava is on the bed nearest to the door, and I can't ignore how much that hurts. She chose to sleep on the bed we didn't have sex on.

I take my shoes off, leaving them by the door, and tiptoe towards the bedside table to place my phone and wallet on the side. I accidentally walk into the bed, stubbing my toe painfully. "Shit," I hiss as I sit on the edge of the bed away from Ava, gripping my toe to try and ease the throbbing. Completely forgetting about my swollen knuckles, I let out another curse as the pain ricochets across my fists. Now that the adrenaline has evaporated, the pain of punching the shit out of Avery's face has intensified. *Shit.*

"Ashton?"

I look up from my crouching position to see her sitting up in bed, her hands rubbing against her eyes.

"Shit, sorry. I didn't mean to wake you. Go back to sleep. Shit," I hiss out. A burning sensation stretches over my knuckles as I go to pull my phone and wallet from out of my pocket. Ava switches on the table lamp, and I blink as I adjust to the light that illuminates the room. She gasps when she notices my bloody fists then practically throws herself onto the bed beside me, gaping in horror at my bloody hands.

"Ashton, what the hell? What's happened?"

I barely give her a side-glance, shrugging my shoulders as if my blood-covered hands aren't a big deal. "Nothing," I murmur sullenly. I look away from her, allowing my eyes to fall onto the bed, following the lines of the crumpled bed sheets, my heartbeat racing just thinking about being inside her again.

"It sure looks like something to me." Then a second later I hear her voice pick up in a panic. "What did you do?"

I look up and immediately want to take the worried look off her face. So I lie. "Not what you think. Well, not for lack of trying anyway. I just had a run in with a brick wall. And as you can see … the wall won." I hold out my swollen hands, hoping she'll buy it.

She gives me a saddened look, gazing intently at my hands. "Those cuts look really bad, you probably need stitches. Your knuckles might even be broken. Maybe we should go to the hospital and get them checked out."

I shake my head immediately, not having the heart to tell her that the majority of the blood isn't actually mine. "No, I'll be fine, it looks worse than it is." Just for her benefit, I open and close my fists to show her I still have full movement in my hands, an indication of no broken bones. It hurts like hell though, and that is evident through my hiss of pain.

"See? Not broken." I smile through a grimace.

She gives me a skeptical look. "Okay, but we need to clean them up. Did you bring a first aid kit with you?"

I nod and point to the closet beside the bathroom. "Yes, it's in my luggage."

I watch her intently as she pads over to the closet to retrieve my medical bag. I have a tendency to take it everywhere with me. I'm unable to take my eyes off her when she sits back down and starts rifling through the bag. She's just so damn beautiful. I trace her entire face, immediately getting lost within the beauty of her ...

"Shit," I hiss, momentarily being shaken out of my Ava bubble as a sharp sting cuts through my skin at the swipe of an alcohol wipe. *God, I'm such a baby.*

"Sorry," she murmurs. I almost chuckle as her face pales at the sight of the blood. She looks as if she might be seconds away from throwing up. With her back rod straight, she wipes at my hand as gently as possible, a little too gently, almost as if she's scared to touch me. As I watch her face intently, I notice that the lines across her forehead wrinkle with frustration.

"What were you thinking? You're a doctor for Christ's sake."

I clench my eyes shut so I don't have to witness her look of disappointment. I didn't for one moment think of the consequences that this could have on my career. I have to use my hands for a living; they are my tools so to speak. But the moment the anger coursed through my veins, any rational thought was erased. Even though my hands hurt like hell, I know there will be no permanent damage.

I must admit it was a pretty stupid thing to do, but do I regret kicking the shit out of him? Hell no! And I'd do it all again in a heartbeat if I had to. When it comes to Ava, there probably isn't a thing on this earth I wouldn't do for her. I'm probably insane for being so willing to fuck up my career for a woman who isn't even mine and quite possibly never will be, but I can't help the way I feel.

"I wasn't," I sigh as she reaches for a clean alcohol wipe, rips it open and begins to clean my other hand.

She is quiet as she intently wipes against my bloody wound, and then in the quietest of whispers she says, "I'm sorry."

"Why?" I ask, baffled by her apology. She has absolutely nothing to be sorry about.

Keeping her eyes focused on my hand, she answers. "Because it's my fault. I shouldn't have told you." For a split second I notice her eyes flick to the bed before they return to my hand. "And *that* shouldn't have happened."

The way she describes what we did together as *'that'* hurts in the most indescribable way. But remembering the way she responded to me, the way her eyes flickered closed when I brought her to her first climax, then her second, I know it must be the guilt talking. She's guilty because she thinks she has betrayed Sebastian which, strictly speaking, is true but she can't deny what we just shared together was amazing.

Placing the bloody wipe on the wet towel that was left on the bed from earlier on, she goes to grab something from the first aid bag, but I grasp her wrists before she can go any further. "Look at me," I demand, softly. I watch as her throat constricts, taking a bracing gulp. She finally looks at me but doesn't quite meet my eyes. Realizing this is probably the best I'm going to get from her, I go on.

"First of all, I'm glad you told me and secondly, was what we did so bad or is that just the guilt talking?"

Her eyes widen at my question, while she bites subtly against the inside of her lip. That one tiny move has my mind in a spin. She is so damn sexy, and she doesn't even know it. She looks thoughtful for a moment, then suddenly her eyes turn from expressively concerned to turned on. The way her pupils dilate and the way her breath constricts tells me everything I need to know.

"So it's just the guilt then?"

She blinks unevenly as my question breaks her from her thoughts. She blushes uncomfortably as she gently pushes my hand away from hers, avoiding me at all costs as she searches for something in the first aid bag. With an amused smile, I keep my eyes trained on her, watching as she pulls out a small tub of alcohol cream and gently applies it to my swollen knuckles. The way her gentle fingers trace across my skin feels incredible. My body is on high alert, and if I'm not careful, something a lot less subtle will be on high alert too.

Once she has thoroughly covered every inch of my wounds with the cream, she screws the lid back in place and puts the tub of alcohol cream back inside the bag. "Band-aid?" she asks quietly, still not meeting my eyes.

Ignoring her question, I change the subject and ask her the question that can no longer be avoided. "You feel it don't you? What I feel for you, you feel it too?"

Asking the question out loud has my heart pounding erratically inside my chest. She freezes when I lift her chin up with my thumb and forefinger, forcing her eyes to mine. I can feel her shake between my fingers and I know my question hits her in just the right place when she slams her eyes shut, pools of tears spilling from the corner of her eyes. I know I'm getting to her.

"Ava, look at me. Baby, please, look at me," I ask with raw desperation to my voice. She shakes her head, clasping her eyes even tighter. My heart breaks as she continues to avoid my gaze. I desperately need her to open her eyes and look at me. The only way to get her to open her eyes is to shock her, and I decide there is only one way to do that.

"Please look at me so I can tell you that I love you." My chin is trembling when I say the words out loud to her.

Her eyes flutter open, with a look of shock that pales her complexion in an instant. "W-W-W-What?" she stutters incoherently, a dumbstruck look upon her face.

I bring myself closer to her, clutching her hand in mine despite the agonizing pain it sends across my knuckles. "I love you," I repeat, desperately trying to convey my love for her in three simple words.

"When?"

I can't keep the smile from my face, knowing I'm the one who has her all flustered as she struggles to string along a rational sentence.

"I don't know, maybe since the first time I saw you in the NICU, in your wheelchair, looking at Lily. It may sound cheesy or cliché, but the moment I laid eyes on you, I couldn't breathe. You just blew me away, you still do," I say wholeheartedly, stroking my thumb against the softness of her cheek. It's amazing to tell her how I truly feel. I know there's a chance that this might backfire on me, that she'll reject me in an indescribable way, but I'm glad I can finally let it off my chest and tell her that I love her.

"You love me?" she asks in disbelief. "But why?"

I love that uncertainty about her; that she has no idea how incredible and perfect she is. "You don't even realize how beautiful you are, do you?" I say with a smile, brushing my thumb over her beautiful plump lips. "Yes, I love you. I'm so in love with you."

Her eyes widen even more as she shakes her head furiously at my words, then like a knife to my chest, she brings Sebastian up again. "No, but you can't. You can't love me. Sebastian ... we're getting married, we're engaged."

She clutches desperately to her chest, and I can see a look of panic cross her face when she realizes her engagement ring isn't there. I grasp her hand that is sprawled across her chest, and gaze intently into her eyes.

"Where is he, Ava? If he loves you, where is he? If he really loves you like he says he does, then he wouldn't be at war, risking his goddamn life. It's unfair to you and Lily."

"Ashton ... he has a contract, it's his career—"

"I know. Shit, I know. This isn't coming out right." I take a deep breath, trying to find the right words. I clutch her hand tighter in mine.

"I didn't mean that the way it came out. I respect him and every other soldier, but knowing how it feels to lose somebody so close to me in the same fucking war ... I just think you deserve better, Ava. You don't deserve any more heartbreak. He has everything I've ever wanted, and this is probably my jealously talking right now, but instead of cherishing his life and the people in it, he's gambling it away. You deserve better and deep down you *know* that. I know you know that.

"You're amazing, so fucking beautiful. I would marry you in a heartbeat. I love you. Yes, I might have only met you nine weeks ago, but it feels as though I've known you my whole life. I'm here. He isn't. You've opened up to me, in a way you haven't ever opened up to him. How can he love you, when he doesn't even know the real you? Not like I do. I love you, Ava, and I know you love me too.

"You feel guilty because it isn't in your nature to be cruel. I said I wouldn't kiss you, that I wouldn't break up your family, that I couldn't be *that* guy, but I've changed my mind. I will be that guy since your guy is doing a shit-ass job of protecting you, of loving you. I want you, and I'm not letting you go. I will cherish you. I promise you."

196

Breathlessly, I press my lips against hers gently, just once. Pulling just a fraction away, my lips hover over hers, leaving the ball entirely in her court to decide our next move. Her breath hitches and her hands grip tightly against my biceps as she searches my eyes. Tracing my fingers down her neck, I can feel how fast her pulse is racing, and it's thumping just as fast as mine.

After what seems like an eternity of searching, battling with her inner self, she closes the space between us and finally presses her lips to mine. Taking my time, I savor her mouth with my tongue, cherishing her with each sweep. She moans softly into my mouth when I suck against her bottom lip.

Sweeping the first aid bag, and towel with my blood-covered wipes onto the carpeted floor, I gently push Ava onto her back, covering her body with my own, my lips never straying from hers. Stripping her from her robe once again, she eagerly complies by removing my clothes. Peeling my lips from hers for one moment, I take the opportunity to take in her nakedness as I search my wallet for a second condom. Her eyes do the same to me, tracing along my face, all the way down to my cock. Her eyes widen with lust, and she bites her bottom lip in anticipation as I harden even more. Eventually, her eyes come full circle back to my face. I slip on the condom and slowly I slide inside of her, taking my time with her sweet, sweet body, whispering how much I love her, over and over again.

# chapter 20

I WAKE UP TO the sound of distant voices and sit up, the sheets wrapped securely around my naked body. The door is slightly ajar, indicating Ashton must be speaking to somebody. I make a move to stand, but Ashton walks back through the door with a letter in his hand. I stop breathing. He looks delicious with his messy 'just got out of bed' hair, and even more delectable in his slacks from yesterday and his open shirt that doesn't leave much to the imagination.

*He loves me.*

The words 'I love you' echo around my mind as I still struggle to come to terms with them.

*He loves me.*

He's *in* love with me.

My heart races as I think back to last night and how he opened up, pouring his entire heart out to me. He tore his heart wide open, and the raw vulnerability I saw in his eyes broke my heart. In that one moment, my entire world shifted, and all I could see was Ashton.

Everything is clear to me now.

I love him too.

"Morning."

A tingle erupts through my body as his southern twang greets me.

He walks towards me, and I smile. "Morning," I reply quietly, feeling shy. I realize what a horror I must look like, having just woken up, and I brush my fingers through my hair, desperately trying to smooth it out.

His fingers grasp mine. "Stop it, you look perfect." He leans down and presses a single kiss against my lips. I feel dizzy with lust when he pulls away, his eyes smiling down at me with passion.

*He loves me.*

"How'd you sleep, baby?" he asks, sitting down beside me.

"Yeah, okay, I think. Did you sleep okay?"

The smile on his face makes him look like a child on Christmas morning. "Like you wouldn't believe."

I lean over and kiss him on the lips. When I start to bring my hands up to his hair, I have to reel myself back in before I get too carried away. His eyes glaze over when I pull away, and I look down, noticing the constrained bulge against the crotch of his slacks, straining at the seams and desperate to escape. I have the impulsive urge to press my hand against him, to wrap my fingers around his thickness and bring him to the brink like he'd done to me several times during the night.

"Um, who was that at the door?" I decide to turn a full one-eighty on the conversation when I notice him adjusting uncomfortably. He smirks at my obvious change of conversation, then his face turns serious.

"It was your sister's friend, Darcie. She came to drop this off." He hands me an envelope, and I have to swallow the bile back as I look down at the letter.

"Oh." I'd almost forgotten about it. Yesterday was a whirlwind, from the funeral to Ashton declaring his undying love for me, and not to mention everything in between. It was one of the worst, yet best days of my life, a mixture of good and bad, but right now the hell of yesterday is staring me dead in the face. The last memory of my baby sister.

"I'll go and get a shower, leave you to read it alone." He makes a move to get off the bed, but I reach for his hand, clamping my fingers tightly around his. "No, don't go. I don't ..." I swallow the lump in my throat. "I can't read this alone."

He grimaces slightly, and I realize I have my fingers wrapped around his red raw hand, and I let go immediately. "Shit, I'm sorry. How bad are they?"

"A little sore but I'll be okay." Changing the subject to the letter he adds, "Are you sure, baby?"

I nod because I know if he doesn't stay with me, I am fairly confident that this envelope would stay sealed. "Yes."

I look down at the envelope with trembling hands. I go to rip it open, but chicken out at the last minute and hand it back to Ashton. "I can't do it. Can you read it to me?"

He nods once and sits back on the bed against the headboard. He pats the space between his legs and I crawl over to him. With my back to his warm chest, I nuzzle my head into the crook of his neck.

"Together, okay?"

I nod against his neck. "Together," I whisper.

I watch him open the envelope and take out a folded up letter. He unfolds it, and I have to hold back the tears when I look down at the pages filled with my sister's beautiful handwriting. Her written words make it feel like she's still alive.

I close my eyes as Ashton begins to read.

*To Ava,*

*I don't know if my letter will ever reach you, but I hope that someday you will get to read it.*

*When you first left home, I was really angry with you. I hated you. At twelve years old, I couldn't understand how you could just up and leave like that without saying goodbye. You simply left a post-it note saying, 'I'm sorry,' and I spent a long time trying to work out exactly what you were sorry for. Sorry for leaving? Sorry for leaving me with a joke of a mother or sorry for just being a selfish bitch? I went with the latter and I spent a good four years of my life hating you for leaving. I missed you every single day. You were my big sister. You were my world.*

*It wasn't until the day after I turned sixteen that I came to realize why you had left. Suddenly, I wasn't angry with you anymore. I understood. I really fucking understood.*

*The first time it happened, I had just come home from school and Avery was in the living room watching television. It was the first time that I'd seen him in nearly ten months. He had been working in Australia on some business development so it was safe to say I was pretty excited to see him.*

*During those ten months I had changed a lot, and I was finally getting attention from the boys at school. I had even been on my first date and was dating a boy named Adam Kavanagh. What I didn't expect was to receive the same attention from my own brother, our brother. He gave me a once over, lingering his eyes over my curves. Then he began to say really inappropriate things to me, touching me in places he had no business touching.*

*He raped me.*

*Once he'd finished, I remember his words exactly, "If I hear that you have told anybody about this, I will kill you." Then he placed a kiss on my cheek and walked out of the house, leaving me naked. My entire body wracked with self-loathing sobs in the middle of the living room floor. I had never felt so disgusting in my own skin until that moment he stole my virginity.*

*The next day, I'd convinced myself that I must have dreamed it; that there was no way in hell that my brother would have done those things to me. So I continued with my life as normal: going to classes, hanging out with my friends and boyfriend. But two weeks later reality hit me in the face once again and I realized that it was real, that my brother really was a monster.*

*It became obvious to me why you had run away. It was to get away from him.*

*It went downhill from there. He would take advantage of me at any given opportunity and every single time I could feel another part of my existence just fade away.*

*For the next six years, his constant torment and abuse were the bane of my life. The only time I actually looked forward to was when he was away on business, but he'd always return, and I hated it. I hated him.*

*Last year, I even tried to take a leaf out of your book and run away, but I only made it as far as Georgia before he found me.*

*I had been hitchhiking with this married couple, but they were only going as far as Georgia. I walked to the nearest bus station to catch the earliest bus out of there to anywhere. I just wanted to get as far away from Florida as possible. I bought a ticket to Chicago and boarded the bus. What I didn't anticipate was that Avery would be in the front row of the bus waiting for me.*

*My life came tumbling down on me when my eyes fell on him. My first thought was to run, so I pushed my way through the throng of passengers and ran, desperate to get away from him. But, of course, he caught up with me. Threatening me within an inch of my life, I followed him to his car. I didn't have a choice. But do you know what the worst thing about him finding me was? I had been given a taste of freedom only to have it snatched away from me again. It destroyed me.*

*After that, things only got worse. It seemed after I pulled the 'Ava trick' as he liked to call it, he watched me like a hawk. Wherever I would turn, he would be there, texting me constantly, reminding me who I belonged to and that without him, I was nothing.*

*What life did I lead? I went to college and came home. That was it. He dictated everything I did.*

*The bastard even got married and forced me to be a fucking bridesmaid in the wedding party! Do you know how hard it is to help plan a wedding with my sister-in-law to be, knowing what a sick scumbag her fiancé is?*

*But even on his wedding day he couldn't keep his filthy hands off me. It wasn't even two hours after the ceremony when he forced himself on me in the restroom. That was the day my best friend Darcie heard everything. She had just moved back to Miami and attended the wedding as my plus one.*

*She texted me a couple of minutes earlier asking me to meet her in the ladies' restroom (she had missed her period and needed some moral support while she took a pregnancy test). As soon as I walked into the restroom, Avery was right behind me. He locked the door and barricaded me into a toilet cubical. Then as if nothing had happened, he walked out, leaving me perched on the toilet seat, trying to gather up enough strength to go back to the wedding party and pretend that my brother hadn't just raped me in the middle of his "special day."*

*Darcie had been in the disabled cubical listening to everything. Through my hollow cries, I could hear Darcie's soft voice, asking if I was okay. I couldn't keep it in any longer; I opened the cubical door and told her everything. She allowed me to tell my story, and it was a tremendous weight lifted from my shoulders.*

*She wanted me to go to the cops but who would have believed me? I had allowed it to go on for far too long. I was scared of him. Going to the cops wasn't an option for me, it just wasn't. I guess this is something you can relate to. I can only make that assumption because he isn't in jail.*

*I don't blame you.*

*Darcie wasn't happy, but she'd let it go on one condition: I got as far away from him as possible. I told Darcie it wouldn't be easy, but I would take the chance. At this point what did I have left to lose? He'd already taken everything else from me.*

*I need to tell you something—I'd been trying to find you. I'd looked high and low, searching the Internet desperately, and last month all my hard work finally paid off. I'd found you, so Darcie booked us two tickets to Seattle.*

*I wrote your address down in my diary, the diary that was always kept in a small safe inside of my closet. On the day we were scheduled to fly out, I couldn't find my diary. The panic didn't set in until after he came into my room, holding my diary in his hand. I had just given him access to your exact location.*

*I'm so sorry, Ava. I just wanted to see you. I never thought he would find my diary, but I should have known. I know the lengths that man can go to and I couldn't believe how careless I was. I am so sorry. I truly am.*

*He was so angry. He said he couldn't allow it; that he would destroy anybody who tried to get in his way. That he would stop at nothing. I knew that it would only be a matter of time before he'd come after you, and I just couldn't let that happen. I told him that if he left you alone, if he didn't hurt you, then I would stay and I wouldn't try to run away again. Once he'd had his way with me, and he'd left, I called Darcie. When she didn't answer, I drove over to see her at her parent's house, where she had been staying.*

*It seemed I misunderstood Avery's threat.*

*When Darcie opened the door, she seemed different. Her eyes were bloodshot, her usually bright complexion was a pasty white and her entire body was shaking. She told me that Avery had been to see her earlier in the day and that he had been really angry.*

*He had raped her.*

*As I emptied the entire contents of my stomach, I came to realize that his previous threat wasn't about you. It was about Darcie. He re-*

*ally wouldn't stop at anything, and he had just confirmed it for me in the form of my best friend. It was my fault. If I hadn't had gotten her involved in my mess, then none of this would have happened.*

*Three days later she had a miscarriage. She was sixteen weeks pregnant. Our brother took her baby away from her, and I was an accomplice. I was the one who led him to her, all because she was trying to help me.*

*That pushed me over the edge.*

*Six years.*

*Six years I've had to endure his abuse, and now he is hurting the people that I love.*

*I can't do this anymore. My life is non-existent, and I may still be breathing, but I'm not living anymore.*

*I am saying goodbye. I can't go on any longer. He has taken everything from me, and I cannot continue on this road to hell. It has to stop, and the only way is if I'm no longer here. I don't want to be here anymore, I don't want to live anymore. It's too hard.*

*Please promise me one thing. Please don't put any of the blame on yourself. It isn't your fault. It's Avery's. I'm so glad you got yourself away from this life, away from him, and I hope you're living life to the fullest. If you're not, then please just start living it. For me, please. When I leave this earth, I want to know that my sister is living a good life; that Avery hasn't taken away yours too.*

*Get married, have children, travel the world, walk every step of the empire state building, get a tattoo, swim with dolphins, free fall from a plane, go skinny dipping. Anything. Everything. Just go and live your life, grasp it with both hands and cherish it. I'm begging you.*

*I love you, and I'm sorry to leave you, but I want my daddy. I want to be with him. He is the only person who can protect me now.*

*Even though you haven't been a part of my life for the past ten years, you're still an amazing sister, and my biggest regret of all is not saying goodbye to you in person. The only thing that gives me comfort is the knowledge that I will get to see you again one day.*

*So until then …*

*Goodbye Ava.*

*Love Fran xxx*

***P.S.***

***"Heaven is such a magical place. The clouds are made of marsh-
mallows and the rain is made up of chocolate and skittles. Every Disney character you can imagine will be there, and you will get to live
in your own Cinderella Castle just like the one at Disney World, but it
will be even bigger. You will find your prince, and you will become a
princess of your own kingdom and you will live forever and ever, and
ever."***
*– (Ava Jacobson, 1995, aged 10)*

The last part of the letter cripples me.

I can't believe she remembered. God, she was just four years old
when I told her that silly made-up notion about heaven. I'm left clutching desperately against Ashton as I let the grief of her life and her death
drive through me, consume me, and bury me.

My life compared to Fran's doesn't even scratch against the damn
surface. What she had to endure—years of constant pain and torment
from the hands of one person—is too much to comprehend. I should
never have fucking left. My leaving just made her life even more unbearable to the extent that she had to end her own life. My mother was
right. It should be me buried in the ground, not my sister.

I should have gone back for her. I should have taken her with me. I
should have done something. I should have done anything.

Ashton's arms curl around my trembling body, hushing me. Being
in his arms is the only thing getting me through this.

"Poor Darcie," I whimper, understanding all too well the pain she
must be going through. "Not her too." I look up at Ashton. "I had a miscarriage when I was sixteen."

His mouth gapes open, then his nostrils flair with anger. "He got
you pregnant?"

I nod. "Yes, and I lost the pregnancy in the very same way."

He shakes his head, almost as if his head might implode with the
information, then suddenly he grips me, pulling me into his lap and kissing me. He pulls inches away from my lips and leans his head against
mine. "I'm sorry you had to go through that, baby. It's something a
woman should never have to go through, ever."

I nod through my tears, hoping these will be the last ones for a while.

"What do you say we get out of this shit hole? I fucking hate Miami."

I nod eagerly. "Yes, please. I need to see Lily-Mai. Two days is way too long without seeing her."

He gives me another lingering kiss, one that leaves me breathless. As I pull away, the question I constantly asked myself when Lily was about to be born comes to the surface.

"Can I ask you a question?" I ask, wrapping my arms around his neck, my thumbs caressing against his skin. He nods, his hands moving down to my naked hips, the bed sheets that were wrapped around my body discarded on the bed. "Do you think he might have caused damage to me internally? The miscarriage and the abuse ... do you think they're the reasons why Lily was born early? Has he damaged me?"

A mixture of pain and anger crosses his face, his fingers tightening around the flesh of my hips. "It's possible. Your cervix and uterus could have sustained severe trauma and caused long lasting gynecological problems, but it's hard to be a hundred percent sure. It isn't even worth thinking about, baby. Just be thankful Lily is here with us and is doing brilliantly."

I smile at his words, internally shivering when he says 'us', almost as if we're a family. I want to be. I want to be with Ashton, even though I know I'm going to hurt Sebastian when I tell him I've fallen in love with somebody else. For now though, I'm not going to think of how this news is going to kill Sebastian. I'm going to concentrate on returning home to my daughter.

"I love you."

His eyes widen at my sudden declaration. Honestly, it just slipped out, but I mean it. I do love him. I chuckle as I bury my head into his chest.

"That wasn't what I was going to say." I look back up to him, his face an image of pure shock. "I was supposed to say thank you and take me home to my daughter, but then it came out I love you, which I do, by the way, but it just slipped out. I—"

"Shut up, Ava." Ashton interrupts with a growl, slamming his lips onto mine. Suddenly, I'm on my back, and he's looking down at me.

"Say it again," he demands, and I'm happy to oblige.

"I love you."

"Say it again. This time, *slower*."

I laugh. "I. Love. You."

His hands clutch my hair, working through the strands as his eyes bore into mine, locking me into place. "I love you too. And as much as I want to make love to you here in this bed right now, I can't bear to do it again in the place that holds all of your nightmares and fears. Will you let me take you home?"

"Yes, take me home. Please."

# chapter 21

THE WHEELS OF THE plane barely touch down in Seattle before I have my seatbelt off, eager to get off this moving contraption and desperate to see Lily. I drag Ashton off the plane and run through the airport, not even bothering to apologize to the other passengers who I barge in front of in my hurried state.

Before we know it, we're hailing a cab in the cool Seattle sunshine. After a little prompting to the driver, we make it to the hospital in record time. Ashton walks me through the foyer.

"Wish me luck?" he says with a smile, but his smile doesn't quite reach his eyes. He has to see his boss to discuss the repercussions of his injury.

"You don't need luck. Everything will be fine." He edges towards me, almost cornering me against the wall, his hips flush with mine. My eyes dart to our busy surroundings in panic at the sudden intimacy between us.

"I hope so."

He leans in to kiss me, but in fear I push at his chest, shaking my head, darting my eyes to see if anybody saw the near-kiss between us. A look of confusion, then hurt, crosses his face, until understanding painfully ignites.

"Oh, yeah. Sorry," he says sheepishly, pausing awkwardly. I take a step forward, when my stomach lurches with sadness, but he steps away from my grasp, grimacing through a smile. "I forgot where we were. I'll ... um, catch you later."

My eyes widen at the hostility in his voice. I watch in shock as he turns and walks away from me. I shout out his name in desperation, and he comes to a reluctant stop at the sound of my voice, turning around to face me. I smile and walk the distance to him, pressing my lips against his. I rise on my tiptoes, pressing my mouth to his ears.

"I love you."

I pull away, noticing the scowl has disappeared in place of a smile. He nods and mouths, "I love you too."

I'm so giddy with excitement that I almost skip through the corridors, eager to set eyes on my little girl for the first time in two days. I've missed her so much, too much. I do my usual sanitizing when I get onto the NICU, then wash my hands and arms. Caleb is sitting comfortably in the chair beside Lily's bedside, but when I look at Lily, I halt my steps. Before I'd left for Miami, she had been in her incubator, but now she's in a white metal crib.

I laugh quietly as I approach, taking my first appreciative look at my Lily in over forty-eight hours. "Now what's going on here? I go away for two days, and I come back to you in a crib? Way to go, Lily." I adjust her little pink hat and press a kiss against her little head. "I've missed you so much, sweetie pie, and you," I finally say to Caleb with a smile, pulling him into a hug.

"How was your flight?" Caleb asks once he pulls away, looking down at me.

I glance down at Lily for a moment, my heart swelling at seeing her in a crib, then I move my eyes back to Caleb. "Too long. I couldn't get off the plane fast enough. I'm glad to be home." I glance back down at my daughter, placing my forefinger into the crook of her little hand, my heart tingling when she latches on fist tight. "I can't believe she's in a crib. When did this happen?"

He goes to stand on the opposite side of her crib and takes hold of her other hand. "Yesterday.

"Why didn't you text me?"

He smiles. "I wanted it to be a surprise. Her vitals have improved so much that the neonatologist wanted to see if she could maintain her own temperature, and so far she's doing well. It's still early days, but if she keeps it up, it could just be a couple more weeks in this place."

I cannot keep the smile off my face at the prospect of taking her home. "I guess I had nothing to worry about, huh?" I say, unable to take my eyes off Lily, admiring her beautiful little face, looking every bit like her father. At that thought, I have to fight away at the penetrating guilt that simmers in my gut. I can't deal with that right now.

"I told you she would be fine."

"I know, I know. I'm a mom. It's my job to worry." I smile when her big bright brown eyes open, exploring her surroundings. I stroke gently against her soft cheek, unable to keep my hands to myself. She's so delicate.

The magnitude of having to bury my sister makes me feel even more blessed to have Lily in my life. She is my life, and I will protect her until my last dying breath, something I never did with Fran. I will regret that for the rest of my life.

"It seems your mom didn't get that memo," he says with a roll of his eyes.

"Yeah, let's not go there. She isn't even worth my thoughts. I just want to concentrate on Lily."

Lily's nurse comes over, smiling when she notices me. "Hey, Ava, I didn't realize you were back. How are you doing?" she asks with a hint of sympathy, which tells me Caleb's been telling her my life story while I've been away.

"I'm okay. All the better for seeing my baby girl though. It's been a long two days without her."

"I bet," she says, taking a glance down at Lily, before looking back up at me. "How was Miami?"

"Depressing. Let's just say I'm glad to be home."

"I'm sorry for your loss, sweetheart."

I give her a sad smile and look back down at my daughter. "Do you think I can hold Lily? I desperately need her in my arms." I must sound pathetic, but I've missed her so damn much.

"Of course you can. Go ahead." I smile eagerly as I adjust her white-fleeced Winnie-the-Pooh blanket, gently maneuvering her body until she is lying central to the blanket and then I wrap it loosely around her entire body. Once she is cozy, I pick her up with one hand supporting her head while placing my other hand under her bottom and lifting her up to my chest. It feels perfect.

I make myself comfortable in the rocking chair and admire her in complete silence. Overwhelming tears blur my vision at the feel of her little body in my arms.

"You're so perfect. I love you." I press a tender kiss against her head, then latch onto her hand that has escaped the blanket with my pinkie finger.

Caleb crouches down beside me. "You're a natural."

I smirk, laughing lightly at his hushed tone, watching as Lily's eyes wander over his face, almost entranced. "I don't know about that, but I'm trying."

I see Caleb take out his phone from the back pocket of his jeans, slides his thumb against the touch screen, then lifts it up. "Let's take a picture. I'll send it to Sebastian." I can't help but tense up at the mention of Sebastian's name.

"What was that?"

"What was what?" I ask, acting the innocent.

"The tension at the mention of your fiancé's name. What's going on?" He gives me an inquiring look, but I brush it off.

"Nothing's going on. Are you going to take our picture or what?" I press on, giving him my cheesiest smile.

He just holds his phone limp in his hand, his forehead wrinkling with suspicion. "Not until you tell me what's wrong."

"There's nothing wrong, I'd tell you if there was. I promise," I say, with my most convincing smile. He gives me one last suspicious look before lifting his phone and snapping a couple of pictures, discarding his worries. I hate lying to him, but I have to until I get my head around everything.

During the next two hours, I feed Lily, then bathe and dress her before placing her back into her crib. She falls into a peaceful sleep, and it isn't long after when I start to feel the effects of the last two days. I'm exhausted. I kiss my daughter goodbye, and without any arguments let Caleb take me home.

The first thing I do once I get home is take a long and refreshing shower which wakes me up a little. I change into a pair of purple sweats and a white tank top, leaving my wet hair hanging over one shoulder and head out into the living room. Caleb is on the sofa pulling out take-out boxes from a paper bag and placing them on the coffee table. My stomach growls as the aroma of Chinese food hits my senses, swiftly reminding me that I haven't eaten since last night.

"I hope there's some orange chicken in there for me?" I ask as I sit crossed leg beside him, gently elbowing him in the side of the ribs.

"Of course, and your usual fried rice and egg rolls. It's not as if I can forget. You've ordered the same thing since college." He laughs.

"What can I say, I'm predictable." I dish out a small portion of orange chicken and fried rice onto my plate and take out an egg roll from the carton, biting a small piece off and moaning as the flavor hits my taste buds. The innocent moan triggers the memory of when Ashton took me to that Mexican restaurant and how he could barely control himself around me with my appreciative sounds for food. Then *that* triggers the memory of last night and the moans that rolled off his tongue when he was buried deep inside of me. The thought has my insides clenching and shuddering with sexual need, and a blush covers my face and neck as I feel myself becoming damp with arousal. I pick up my bottle of water and take a refreshing sip, hoping the liquid will cool down my libido. Finally, feeling composed, I continue with the delicious Chinese meal while chatting idly.


"Your phone keeps beeping in your purse. Do you want me grab it?" I hear Caleb shouting from the living room.

"Yeah, please!" I shout through to him without any thought as I push the dishwasher door closed with my hip.

I walk back into the living room, and see Caleb reading something on my phone. My heart skids to a stop when I see the scowl on his beautiful face. He turns to look at me, his head shaking with disapproval, an angry glint in his eyes.

"You. Got. A. Text."

My eyes widen at his angry growl. He throws the phone at me in anger, but I manage to catch it with both hands.

"You lied to me."

"W-What?"

212

"Don't act innocent, Ava. You told me nothing was wrong!"

I shudder as his voice becomes louder with each furious word. "I don't, I don't understand …" My eyes fill up with unwelcome tears. Glancing down at my phone, I realize it's a message from Ashton. Just seeing his name is enough for my heart to flutter but I understand why Caleb is angry with me. He has every right to be. My heart drops.

**Ashton**: *Hi, baby, Everything went okay with my attending. Just had to tell a little white lie. Can I see you later? I can't stop thinking about last night. I Love you. x*

Slamming my eyes closed, I allow the tears to run down my face, despising the look of disappointment I can see in Caleb's eyes. This boy is the brother I should have had, and the disappointment from family hurts the worst. I've disappointed him in the worst possible way.

"Caleb I—"

"I knew this would happen, I just fucking knew it. Jesus, the way he was looking at you. It was blatantly obvious from the start. He couldn't keep his goddamn hands off you! I should have *never* let him go to Miami with you. He took advantage of you, just like I knew he would have. Jesus, Ava!"

I startle at his outrage. This is a side of Caleb I rarely see, and I don't like it. He should be bad mouthing me, not Ashton. I'm the one in the wrong, not Ashton.

"He didn't take advantage of me, Caleb. I wanted it to happen." It feels good to get my feelings for Ashton out in the open after weeks of inner struggle, a struggle that has been boiling away in the pit of my stomach.

"Did I just hear you right?" Caleb asks, a dumbfounded expression on his face.

I nod. "We have this connection, Caleb, I can't describe it, but he helps me forget all the bad in my life. When I'm with him, I can truly see the light at the end of the tunnel. He makes me feel like me again, the old me before … well, you know."

He's quiet as he lets that information sink in and for a moment I think he has calmed down, but then his scowl reappears, clearly still furious with me. "Oh, well that makes it all right then," he mocks. "What did he mean "he couldn't stop thinking about last night"? Did you sleep with him?"

I don't need to give him a verbal answer. The guilty look on my face says everything.

"Fuck me, Ava. Of all the people I know, I never pegged you as the cheating type. Has Sebastian even crossed your mind? I mean, he's only your fiancé and all."

I purse my lips as I struggle not to burst into tears. I know I've done a truly fucked up thing, but he's my best friend. He should have my back. "God, you make it sound like some sordid little affair. It isn't like that! And of course I've been thinking of Sebastian! He's all I've been thinking about."

"Yeah, well it doesn't seem like it."

His dejected tone just irritates me further.

"I have! I've been fighting my feelings for Ashton since the day I met him! The guilt of it has buried me for weeks and weeks. I can't help that I've fallen in love with him."

Sarcastic laughter echoes through the living room. He shakes his head irritably at me as he throws himself into a sitting position on the couch. "Oh, well this just gets better and better. Next you're going to tell me you're pregnant."

I grit my teeth, crossing my arms in front of my chest with an angry exhale. "Don't be so ridiculous, Caleb. I'm not stupid."

"Oh, well I'm glad you still have some sense in that brain of yours. And Lily, have you even thought of how your actions will affect her?"

He's suddenly forgotten our ten-year friendship; he doesn't even know me. I feel as if I'm talking to a stranger.

"You know me from the inside out, yet you're making me sound like I'm a heartless bitch who only cares about herself. Nothing will affect her in the slightest. I'll make sure of it."

He's on his feet in a split second. "You're so fucking naïve, Ava. It's unreal! You've gone behind her father's back with her doctor. Plus, you've inevitably just broken this family up. *Your* family."

"Well, it doesn't feel like a fucking family! I've been at this alone—"

"Alone!" His face reddens and the vein at the top of his head almost erupts as he roars. "Who the fuck was I then? I've been here since the fucking beginning, so don't you dare say you've been alone!"

"I was talking about Sebastian, you asshole!"

"How can you even say that you don't feel like a family?"

"Because it's the truth! He isn't here, and if he really loved me, then he'd be by my side, fighting for the health of our daughter, not fighting a war in another goddamn country." I regret the words as soon as they leave my mouth.

"Wow. That's a new low. Especially for you, Ava," he hisses through gritted teeth. His eyes darken with fury, and I get the distinct feeling he'd like to slap me senseless right about now. "I can't believe you just said that."

"I didn't mean … I don't really think—"

"You know what? I can't even stand to look at you right now. I've never been so disappointed in you. I don't even know who you are right now." With a shake of his head, he storms away towards his room.

"I don't know what you want from me. I'm trying … I'm trying …" I murmur to the back of Caleb's head as he continues to walk away. The tears fall fast as the sky continues to fall on top of me.

I call Ashton. He answers on the second ring. "Hi, baby."

"Hi," I sigh.

"Hey, is everything okay?"

I love how he can sense my uneasiness through the other side of the phone. It's ridiculous how in-tune we are with each other after such a short time. "I had a fight with Caleb, it was pretty ugly. Can I see you? I need you." My lips tremble at the end of my words.

"I just got out of the shower. Let me get changed, and I'll be there in fifteen."

My stomach lurches. He can't come here. God knows what Caleb will do if he sees Ashton right now. "No, that's not a good idea. I'll come to you instead. Just text me your address. I can get a cab. I just really need to get out of here."

As soon as we disconnect the call, I dial a cab, then head into my room. Tossing a change of clothes into a bag, I pull a sweatshirt over my head, and slip my pumps onto my feet. Once I grab my purse, I'm out of the door, not wanting to stay here for another second longer. Thankfully, when I make it downstairs, the cab is already waiting for me.

We pull up in front of a two-story townhouse with a blue and cream wooden façade that complements perfectly with the matching town-houses in this cute little neighborhood. I pay the driver, and eagerly jog to Ashton's house. He has the door open before I come to a stop. He looks fresh from his shower, and my heart takes off when I rake my eyes over his body, noticing how delicious he looks in only a pair of gray sweatpants and nothing else. He gives me a sexy smirk as he takes a step forward onto the porch, pressing a lingering kiss against my lips before pulling away, leaving me a little breathless.

"Come on in," he says softly, and like a gentleman he carries my bags through. I follow him into a small entryway, then I'm led up a small set of stairs that follow through to a modern open floor plan room with dark hardwood floors. The sitting area is to my left, and I take in the neutral beige color arrangement, with minimal furniture. This place looks so damn tidy that I'd have sworn it was a show home.

Ashton places my stuff on the coffee table in the middle of the room, then turns to me, pulling me into the warmth of his arms, strok-ing the length of my hair. I wrap my arms around his waist and nuzzle my head into the crux of his neck. I sigh with content, the sound of his beating heart reverberating through me, calming me into a state of tran-quility. I love this. I love being in his arms. Warm, loved and safe. It's perfect. He's perfect.

"Are you okay?" he asks, pressing a soft kiss within the loose ring-lets of my hair.

"I am now," I whisper against his bare skin, pressing a gentle kiss against his pulse, smelling his enticing aroma of citrus fruits and cool water.

He pulls away slightly, brushing my hair from my eyes as he stares down at me. "You want to tell me what happened? You sounded really upset on the phone."

I shake my head, my hands lingering down his silky soft chest, lust pulsating its way through my veins at the very touch. "No, not yet. I will, but first I want you," I confess, standing up on my tiptoes to press a forceful kiss onto his desirable plump lips. "I need you," I mumble against his lips, taking a subtle nip against his bottom lip with my teeth, then slide my tongue across the flesh, causing Ashton to shudder under my touch. "I missed you."

He groans under his breath, then sucks my tongue, pulling me deeper into him, whetting my appetite for what I anticipate will come soon. My fingertips wander over the ripples of his chest, traveling south as the passion erupts around us, our kiss deepening, our bodies melting into one. I reach for the waistband of his sweatpants, and the heat doubles when my fingers sweep under the material and I'm met with hard flesh. He jerks at the sudden hand contact, and I groan into his mouth as I latch my fingers around him.

"It seems you've missed me too," I whisper against his lips.

"Like you wouldn't believe, baby."

"I love it when you call me baby. Sounds sexy as hell."

"Baby," he whispers, earning a shiver of delight that shudders through my body.

I instinctively squeeze against his length, and he slams his lips back onto mine. Without breaking our connection, we fall back onto the sofa into an upright sitting position, my legs straddling comfortably around his thighs. I gyrate my hips into his, the friction of his strained cock causing an explosion to rocket through me.

We break our kiss, our eyes burning with a lust-filled passion. He peels my Seattle Redhawks sweatshirt off, pulling it over my head. Discarding it to the side, he slides his fingers through my hair, lovingly massaging my scalp as he kisses me, leaving me breathless when he pulls away all too soon. His eyes trace my chest, his hand sliding downwards until his thumb traces my puckered nipple through my white tank top.

"Baby, you're not wearing a bra," he says through a breathless exhale, adding fuel to the fire that is quickly igniting. "Damn ..."

With a satisfied growl, he quickly discards my tank top, leaving me naked from the waist up. A shiver tingles along my spine when the cold air hits my bare skin, but I feel the heat when he leans down and presses a single kiss against my left nipple. He sucks it into his mouth, causing me to jerk against his lap, then he pulls a little with his teeth, and I hiss at the impact. His lips slowly move up the valley of my breasts, pressing tiny kisses without missing a trace of my bare skin, goose pimples replacing each kiss. I arch my back, letting my head fall back as I feel his lips glide effortlessly up the center of my neckline. He is taking his sweet time adoring every inch of my skin, relishing my body like it's our very first time all over again.

His lips eventually find mine. With the pent up desire that is currently coursing through my body from the sexual tension from his kisses, I attack his lips, claw my fingers against his shoulders, and rock my hips into his, desperate for him, desperate to have him inside me. He has turned me into a sex-craving maniac and each caress, each kiss, each sweep of his tongue almost sends me over the edge.

Coming up for air, I stare at him, caressing his cheek with my thumb and forefinger. "I need you, please."

He smiles lovingly, moving his hands to the waistband of my thin sweatpants. His thumb moves to the bare skin that sits under the material and his eyes widen. "No panties either?"

I lift myself off his lap slightly, desperately wanting him to push his entire hand inside my sweatpants. He is happy to oblige, pressing his thumb deeper within the material until it brushes against my swollen clit.

"I'll let you into a little secret. I don't wear panties to bed."

I whimper as he circles his thumb against my protruding bud, a smirk lifting from his lips. "So you just go to bed in these very see through, very sexy pajamas?"

"Not all the time, sometimes I go to bed naked." I laugh, but it's quickly replaced with a soft moan when he eases a finger inside me.

"God," he growls, "where have you been all my life?"

"Waiting for you in panty-free pajamas," I breathlessly sigh. My eyes roll to the back of my head as the intensity of his finger sliding in and out tears through my body.

He chuckles again, placing a second finger inside me. "I love you. I love you so damn much."

"I love you too …"

And for the next mind-blowing twenty minutes, I am unable to utter another word.

# chapter 22

FINGERTIPS CRAWL DOWN THE side of my breast, along the ridge of my waist, over the curl of my hip and down the length of my thigh, reaching the apex of my knee. My body tingles in delicious shivers as Ashton repeats the process in reverse. I tangle my legs with his, pressing my delicate foot into the arch of his.

"This is my new favorite place," I sigh, pressing a kiss against his incredibly warm chest, just below his nipple. "Here in your arms. I could stay like this forever."

Ashton flips me on my back, the sudden movement causing the breath to catch at the back of my throat.

"I have to disagree. My favorite place is being buried deep inside of you." He thrusts his hips into mine, causing me to giggle. I playfully slap him on the shoulder. "You're insatiable."

"Just the way you like me, baby."

"Definitely."

He slides a piece of hair behind my ear, then gently strokes against my cheekbone with his thumb. "Are you going to tell me what happened earlier with Caleb?"

I stiffen at the reminder of our fight. "We had a fight. It was horrible," I confess.

"About what?" he inquires as he presses a lingering kiss on my shoulder.

"You."

He pulls away slightly, his eyes widening. "Me?"

I nod, stroking my fingers up and down his biceps. "Yeah, when you texted me earlier, I was in the kitchen cleaning up after dinner, and he read it."

He closes his eyes. "Shit. I'm so sorry, baby."

"It isn't your fault. I'm glad he knows. I just didn't want him to know tonight. I wanted at least one night without any bullshit. It's been such a long two days."

"I know." He ponders for a moment, then presses a kiss on my lips. "So what happened?"

I give him a running commentary of the fight. "I've never seen him so angry with me before, and the disgusted way he was glaring at me … it was as though he'd forgotten who I was. I've been friends with him for a decade, but it suddenly feels as though we're strangers." My bottom lip trembles and tears well in my eyes.

Ashton captures my trembling chin within his fingers and strokes over my lips with his thumb. "Hey, it's okay, don't cry. God, I could kick his ass for talking to you like that."

I love how protective he is of me. His possessiveness kind of turns me on.

"I get why he's so pissed. I've lied to him for weeks, I told him there was nothing to worry about. I've been telling him over and over there was nothing going on between us, even when I knew deep down that I was falling for you. You were unexpected, and I didn't know how to deal with these sudden new feelings." I caress his cheek. "Can I be totally honest with you?"

He nods his head, smiling down at me. "Yeah, of course, baby. All I want is honesty even if it kills me."

"It isn't anything bad, I swear." I smile. "I just want you to under-stand my life before I met you. Understand why I've been so resistant to you. A couple of years after I moved to Seattle, before I met Sebastian, I'd started dating for the very first time. It was a huge step for me to get out there, but I didn't want my past to continue to haunt my future, so I pushed myself to try dating. I was sick of being alone, sick of being a twenty-year-old virgin, so to speak. I wanted to be loved. But I hated it. I hated the way guys looked at me, the way they'd undress me with their eyes. They all reminded me of my brother. They only wanted one thing, and after everything I'd gone through, I couldn't let just any man have that part of me. To those guys I was just another notch on their bedpost, but to me it meant so much more.

"So when Sebastian came along, I thought he was the one. He was so different and I felt immediately at ease with him. It felt natural. It took a while, what with the insecurities of my past, but slowly I began to trust him and I fell in love with him. It was perfect. We moved in together, then I got pregnant. I was ecstatic. I mean, we hadn't spoken about having a family or even marriage, but we were in a committed relationship so it seemed perfect. But then a month after I told him I was pregnant, he got deployed to Afghanistan.

"Obviously I knew when we got together that the chances of him getting deployed were pretty high, so I was okay at first. It sucked knowing he wouldn't be here for Lily's birth, but I had Caleb, and I had my work to keep me busy. Then I went into labor, and I realized just how out of my depth I really was. My entire world was crashing around me and then, just to make everything a little more complicated, you came into my life."

I smile as I remember the first time I laid eyes on Ashton.

"You blew me away. At first I put it down to attraction, but I knew deep down it was more than that. I've always known it was more than that. Only I wouldn't admit it to myself. I thought I had everything set, but suddenly you appeared out of nowhere, and I started to question everything, and I mean *everything*. We became closer, and everything I'd ever felt with Sebastian was nothing compared to what I was feeling for you. I panicked. It was confusing. A touch from Sebastian would make my heart flutter, but a touch from you … I swear it feels as if my heart is going to explode right from my chest. Feel."

I grasp onto his right hand gently and place it directly over my chest so he can feel the erratic thumping of my heart.

"You see straight through me, deep within me." I clutch my own hand delicately over his keeping him close to my chest. "You understand me like nobody else, not even Caleb. I love Sebastian and I think I always will. He was my first love, the person who helped break through my barriers, but there has always been something missing, something I could never put my finger on until now. Last night you told me that I hadn't opened up to Sebastian like I've opened up to you and you're right, I haven't. He doesn't know about my past and my demons and I've never had any intention of telling him. I wanted to spend the rest of my life with him, yet I couldn't even tell him my secret. I spent a long time loathing myself for keeping something so big from him. I hated that I was lying to him, but I just couldn't part with it.

"You made me realize that maybe the reason I didn't want to tell him—that the reason I physically *couldn't* tell him—was because he wasn't the person I was supposed to tell. It was you. I know it sounds like some make believe crap, but it's true. I've spent four years of my life with him, unable to let go of my secret, but from the moment I met you, the words have just wanted to spill from me. I obviously didn't love him as much as I thought I did."

He gives me a gentle smile as his thumb strokes against my bottom lip. "He doesn't know you ran away from Miami?"

I shake my head and Ashton's eyes widen with surprise. "He knows I left, obviously, but he doesn't know that I ran away. I told him that we had a big family falling out and that we didn't speak anymore. He didn't question it."

"And you never worried that your brother would bump into Sebastian's family, or if he would get into contact with Sebastian through Facebook or some school reunion?"

"Yeah, of course, but Sebastian's family moved to Charlotte nine years ago, and have never been back to Miami, so I wasn't worried that they might cross paths. Sebastian doesn't have a Facebook account, and high school isn't something he'd like to relive. It was a dark time for him back then."

Ashton gives an understanding nod.

"Eventually the stress of Sebastian being in Afghanistan and then the birth of Lily, just became too much for me. The day you told me Lily had gotten pneumonia, I lost it, but then I was in the warmth of your arms, inhaling your perfect smell, wanting to pour my heart out to you. That scared me. The walls I so carefully built were quickly tumbling down and I knew that I was in deep trouble.

"I wouldn't admit it though. I just kept telling myself I was in love with Sebastian. That I wanted him, that I needed him. That I couldn't be with you because of my commitment to him. But there was always this little voice at the back of my head, taunting me, laughing at me. I was confused. I didn't want to love you because loving you meant hurting him and I wasn't okay with that. I'm not a cheat. That isn't me. I hate what I've done to him, but the moment I met you, I never stood a chance."

I pull Ashton closer to me, my fingertips caressing the ends of his hair, my legs wrapping around his muscular thighs. "I might have been battling with my feelings, but it was never a contest. Sebastian didn't even come close. I knew it the moment I laid eyes on you. I was just trying to do the right thing for Sebastian and Lily. You get that, right? I was never trying to hurt you. Ever."

My eyes flutter as he presses his lips to mine, taking my breath away.

"I know, baby... I get that. It was the same reason I tried to stay away from you. But like you said, I didn't stand a chance. I've been waiting a damn lifetime for you. I feel bad for the guy, I really do, but he doesn't deserve you. Hell, I don't deserve you. I don't think there's a man on the entire planet who is even close to being good enough for you."

"I don't know what I'm supposed to do though. How do you tell somebody that you've fallen in love with somebody else? What's the right way to break a person's heart?"

He gives me a pained smile. "I don't know, baby, I guess there isn't a right way. You're going to have to be honest. That's all you can be."

"I know, but I can't tell him yet. It's too dangerous. He'd get himself killed, but that isn't to say I'm not going to tell him. I will, just when he's back on US soil. Do you understand? He needs to hear this face to face. I owe him that much."

Ashton sighs. "I don't like it, but I understand."

I kiss him briefly on the lips. "Thank you. I do think maybe we shouldn't be doing this though," I say looking down at our naked bodies and entwined limbs. "Having sex behind his back like this ... it feels kind of wrong, don't you think?" My heart does a double somersault at his sudden devilish grin.

"Wrong? So this feels wrong?" He leans down and presses a delicate kiss against the corner of my lips, causing me to shiver at his touch.

"Or this." He presses tiny, luxurious kisses along my neck, towards the curve of my collarbone, and my legs subconsciously widen for him, his naked cock hardening against my inner thigh.

"How about this?" He brushes his lips to the top of my breast. "Does that feel wrong?" he whispers into my breast, sucking at the skin ever so gently. I can barely catch my breath when I feel the warmth of his wet tongue trace along the curve of my breast, circling around the nipple.

"I didn't ... I didn't mean it like that ..."

He smirks as he pulls away. "So what did you mean?" he asks innocently.

I laugh. "You know what I mean. No sex. Do you want me to spell it out for you?"

He wiggles his eyebrows with a sparkle in his eyes. "I like the sound of that."

He begins to nuzzle into the crux of my neck, then we both freeze at the sound of the front door closing shut. Ashton possessively pushes me deeper into the sofa, covering me as the sound of a man's booming voice hollers through the house.

"Asher ba-by! Where are you motherfucker?"

"Shit," Ashton curses, his muscular arms shield me. "Fuck man, don't you ever knock?"

I laugh nervously when I hear laughing from the other side of the room.

"Oh, my bad, man!" the guy says through a deep booming laughter. "It's about time, man. I was starting to think you forgot what a pussy even looked like."

"Get out!" Ashton growls.

"All right, all right. I'm leaving. You don't have to tell me twice."

My laughter abruptly stops when I see an attractive black man looking directly down at the both of us. I cower my body deeper into Ashton's, a blush covering my entire skin.

"Hey, you must be Ava. I'm Darnell."

Ashton's eyes turn a deadly black, his arms tensing around me. "Get the fuck out before I kick your ass!"

Darnell's eyebrow hitches up with surprise. "Like you could kick my ass. I'm ATF, man. You ain't got shit on me."

"Get out!"

Darnell backs away with his hands in surrender, a smirk splayed against his face. "Okay, okay … I'll let you get back to your hot *sex*. Nice to meet you, Ava." Darnell gives me a quick wink, leaving me utterly mortified when he walks away.

We stay in our intense embrace until we hear the sound of the door finally clicking shut, a clear indication that we are finally alone again. Ashton eases his hold on me, looking down with a mixture of apologetic turmoil and humor. "I'm sorry about that. I didn't know he'd be coming round."

"Asher?" I question.

"It's his nickname for me. He used to be my roommate, moved out about a year ago, but you'd think he still lived here with the way he strolled in as if he owned the place. I wish I'd locked the damn door."

His anger subsides when his eyes penetrate mine, dazzling me. "Enough of Darnell, where were we?" He places small kisses along the edge of my jaw.

"We were talking about not having sex," I try to say as coherently as possible before his kisses begin to overwhelm me.

"Oh, yes … no sex," he whispers with frustration against my neck, the stubble on his face scratching subtly against my skin, the roughness strangely turning me on.

"Yes, no sex," I confirm, smiling confidently.

"I'm not convinced."

"And why not?"

"Firstly, because your naked legs are still wrapped around my naked ass." He smirks while my smile falters. My feet press deeper against his ass of their own accord, my fingers clutching tighter against his biceps and my insides constricting as his palms move up my thighs, his masculine fingers kneading the muscles with expert precision. I forget almost instantly what we were talking about.

"Secondly, you're still naked." My breath hitches as his thumbs draw incredible soft circles against my inner thighs. I feel myself moistening as his fingers draw near to my core, and I push my hips out at the sudden tremor of arousal that rushes through my body.

"And third, if I moved just an inch higher I would be inside of you, deep … inside … of … you," he whispers slowly, the corner of his mouth turning up into a smile when a small moan audibly escapes from my lips. "But if you're sure, then yes, we can have *no sex*. When does he come back?" he asks as nonchalant as possible, his face impassive.

I swallow heavily as I calculate Sebastian's arrival and my heart sinks when I do the math. "Just under three months ..." I trail off with a pained whisper.

Ashton purses his lips as if trying to hold in his smirk. "Three months, no sex ... no ... sex," he repeats for heightened emphasis. His lips ascend along my shoulder, licking and nipping as he trails his mouth towards my ear. I gasp when his tongue swirls inside the dip of my ear.

"Okay," he says.

"Okay?" I breathe out with confusion. His tongue is very distracting.

"Okay, we won't have sex." I let off a frustrating sigh, but it comes out as a gasp when I feel his teeth clamp down on my ear. "Anything for you, baby." He starts to move out from my arms, but I cling to him.

"Where are you going?"

"To put some clothes on. You're too damn tempting all naked and beautiful, and if you don't want to have sex, then I need clothes."

I shake my head, pulling him closer to me. The idea of not having him in my arms like this for the next three months is too hard. "No."

"No?"

"No." I hungrily push my lips to his, grinding my body into his, desperate for him. "No, I want you to stay here. I want you," I whimper against his lips.

He chuckles inside my mouth, and I shiver as his laughter vibrates from the roof of my mouth. "I thought you might say that," he arrogantly whispers. He presses his mouth to mine and for the second time today, he makes love to me here on his sofa.

The next morning when I walk into the NICU room, I'm shocked to see Caleb in the rocking chair reading Lily a story. Silently I approach, placing my purse on the floor beside her cot.

"Hey, beautiful," I say in peaceful tones as I look at Lily, placing my forefinger in the palm of her hand. Smiling down at her, I watch as her beautiful brown eyes gaze around at her surroundings, each day becoming more alert. It's fascinating to watch. I glance up at Caleb the moment he stops reading out loud, and I notice he's looking straight at me.

"Hi," he whispers with a small smile, closing the book shut. Still angry with him, I look away from him, muttering a half-hearted hello. The atmosphere is thick with tension, and for the first time in years I feel awkward in his presence.

"Ava?"

"What?" I snap with a quiet whisper, staring daggers at him.

He sighs sadly and stands up from the chair. "I'm sorry."

"What for? The fight or turning against me?"

He takes one step closer to me, but I take one step back. "Both."

My body physically clenches when I feel his hand touch my arm. He flicks his head into the direction of the door. I follow him outside, quickly realizing Lily shouldn't have to be subjected to the tension that surrounds us.

He leads me to an empty corridor and turns to me when we come to a stop. "I'm really sorry. I shouldn't have spoken to you like that last night. I was more angry than anything, angry that you hadn't told me."

"And now?" I prompt him, crossing my arms over my chest.

"A little disappointed. I didn't think you had this kind of betrayal in you."

I look down at my feet as heavy guilt washes through me. "I know, neither did I." I close my eyes as turmoil seeps through my veins.

"Come here." I walk into Caleb's embrace, my head resting against his chest, my fingers clutching hold of him.

"I didn't mean for this to happen. I didn't mean to fall in love with somebody else … it just happened," I say with a shaky breath, a single teardrop rolling down my cheek.

"I know," he says softly against the softness of my hair, stroking the wavy strands through his fingertips.

"I fought it, I did, desperately but I couldn't stop it."

"And what now?"

I glance up to Caleb, and the next words crack my heart into two. "I break his heart."

"Hello," I say nervously as I answer the phone to Sebastian later on that evening, in the comfort of my own kitchen. I can't keep avoiding him forever. Plus, if I continue to ignore his calls he's going to become suspicious very quickly, and I need him to come home in one piece.

"Hi, babe. God, I've missed your voice so much." I clamp my eyes shut as guilt swims through my body, my chin trembling with remorse. "How are you?"

I have to take a deep breath before I answer but that seems difficult to do as the urge to vomit becomes prominent. "Yeah, I'm good, really g-good," I lie, chastising myself for the hesitation in my voice. "You okay?"

"Yeah, I'm fine, just missing my fiancée and my little girl. How is my little angel?"

"She's good, she's out of her incubator and finally in a crib."

"Holy shit, when did this happen? That's incredible," he says with excitement in his voice. I can't help but laugh along with his enthusiasm. The laughter momentarily calms my nerves, and for a moment I can pretend everything is okay.

"I know! I go away for two days and when I come back, she's in a crib."

*Shit!*

"What do you mean you went away for two days? Where did you go?"

I could kick myself for being so fucking stupid. My throat closes up as panic suffocates me to silence.

"Ava?"

"I … um …"

"Ava, what is it?"

When I still can't produce an explanation, his confusion quickly turns into irritation. "Goddamn it, Ava, will you just tell me?"

"My sister died," I spit out, my voice trembling. The line goes quiet, and for a moment I think I've lost the phone connection, but a loud exhale of breath on the other side of the line confirms he's still with me.

"Shit. Ava, I'm so sorry. Fuck. How? I mean what happened?"

"She … um, she took her own life." His gasp is audible through the receiver. "I was at her funeral in Miami."

"Alone?"

As calmly as possible I answer him, trying to make my lie as believable as possible. It isn't a difficult task. I've been lying to him for over four years. "Yes."

"Why didn't Caleb go with you?"

*Because he wasn't the person I wanted by my side …*

"I couldn't leave Lily on her own."

"Shit, baby, I hate how you had to go through that alone. How was it with your family?"

This dishonesty is exhausting work, but at least I can answer his next question with some kind of honesty. "Tense, to say the least."

"I wish I would have been there. I'm so sorry I haven't been there for you, but that's going to change soon. I promise. You just need to hold on for a little longer, babe. Can you do that for me?" His words swim hazily through my mind and I suddenly feel faint. I clumsily sit in an empty chair and bring my free hand to my head, my elbow resting against the table, taking in big soothing breaths.

"Of course I can," I lie through the skin of my teeth. I hate myself.

"It's just my paranoia talking, but I keep thinking that someone's going to swoop in and take my girl away from me." His words pierce straight through to my heart, and I have to fight the urge to burst into tears. He doesn't realize how accurate his paranoia actually is.

I am a truly horrible person.

"Don't be ridiculous." I clench my eyes shut as the words leave my mouth, my words that leave false hope.

"I know, baby, I just love you so much it makes me kind of crazy. I miss you, I miss you so much."

"I miss you too …"

I do miss him. I desperately want him to come home, safe and sound, I need him to come home for his daughter, but I don't miss him like I once did. I don't need him like I once did. I don't love him like I once did.

The moment we disconnect, the tears flow freely down my face, a mixture of guilt, hatred and nausea plunging into the deepest part of me. My body is drowning in a sea of deceit, waves of lies preventing me from resurfacing back to the top. I know I love Ashton, but I need to make sure I'm making the right decision. That I'm breaking Sebastian's heart for the right reasons. I need reassurance.

I grab my phone and with shaky hands I type out a quick text message to Ashton, a message full of trepidation and desperation.

**Ava**: *Tell me you love me.*

Thirty seconds later I'm pleasantly surprised to see Ashton's name flashing with an incoming call. Accepting the call, his voice fills my head with the three words I desperately needed to hear. "I love you."

"Say it again," I sigh, needing to hear it again.

"I love you," he says without an ounce of hesitation, and for good measure I ask him to say it out loud again.

He chuckles quietly. "I. Love. You. Do you need me to say it again because I will?"

Now it's my turn to laugh. "Yes, for the rest of my life."

"Done, done and done."

I can't keep the smile from my face. God, I love him.

"Good, because I love you too."

# chapter 23

HAPPY TEARS FALL AS I watch Caleb strap my daughter securely into her car seat. She's been in the hospital for thirteen weeks, three days, and today is the day I finally get to take her home. It's been a long time coming. She is one hundred percent healthy, weighing a perfect six pounds, four ounces. It's hard to believe that when she was born she only weighed two pounds and two ounces. She's faced Respiratory Distress Syndrome, jaundice, anemia, blood transfusions, pneumonia, constant apnea episodes, yet she has come out at the other end, still fighting. She's a force to be reckoned with.

She's incredible.

She looks as cute as a button in her little toasty-warm, white snowsuit, covering her from head to toe. The hand of the thumb she so desperately wants to put inside her mouth is trapped within the confinements of her mitten, so I crouch down in front of her.

"Hush, baby, I've got it."

I gently pull the mitten off her right hand, leaving the material to hang by a loose thread from the sleeve of the snowsuit. Immediately her hand goes back to her face, and she successfully manages to locate her mouth with her thumb and begins to suck. A new adorable trait she picked up a couple of weeks ago.

Her eyes flicker and almost immediately she falls asleep. I pull the handle bar of the car seat in an upright position until it locks into place. I stand back up and take the handle in my hand, lifting my daughter up. With a long inhale, I look to Caleb, tears lingering in my eyes. "Ready?"

"One second." He pulls out his phone to take a quick snapshot. "Say, happy coming home day."

I smile through my blissful tears as I get into position and lift Lily a little higher up in her car seat for the photo. "Happy coming home day," I say cheerily as he takes our photo.

"Do you want me to carry Lily?" he asks, placing his phone back into his pocket. I shake my head. "No, I can manage."

"Okay let's go, Mommy."

We say an emotional goodbye to the nursing staff. It's incredibly touching to see how emotionally involved they get with the babies. I can see it in their eyes. This part, saying goodbye, is the best part of their job.

They take a souvenir photo of Lily to put on the baby wall that hangs in the corridor, showing every single success story from the NICU. I promise to come and visit again. This place will always be Lily's first home, and the medical staff here did everything in their power to keep her alive and I will never forget that.

I follow Caleb in the direction of the exit, desperate to get my daughter home. Once we enter the foyer, my heart rate picks up when I hear the sound of my name being called. I turn around to see Ashton jogging towards us.

"Hey, I'm sorry I nearly missed you. I got caught up. How are my two favorite girls?" He looks between Lily and me before he acknowledges Caleb. "Caleb," he greets with a warm smile.

"Ashton." Caleb nods, barely reciprocating Ashton's smile. He's taking a while to warm to him and I can hardly blame him. He's caught in the middle of my betrayal, and lying behind Sebastian's back doesn't sit well with him. He accepts it but still doesn't condone my actions.

"That's okay. You're here now, and we're great," I say softly.

He steps forward, leaning over to give me a kiss, but Caleb's annoying cough cuts through our connection. Ashton steps back, a little irate.

"I can tolerate the two of you, but I don't want to see it," Caleb says.

Ashton nods, then crouches down to Lily's level, taking hold of her little mitten-covered hand.

I turn to Caleb. "Can you give us a minute, please?"

"Yeah, I'll be waiting for you outside." He walks away, leaving us alone.

"Still doesn't like me, huh?" Ashton questions, glancing up at me.

"He's getting there. He loves Sebastian like a brother, so it's hard for him."

He returns to a standing position, taking a step closer. "I don't know what I'm going to do without you here."

I smirk as he presses a quick kiss against my cheek. "How about do your work and stop hitting on vulnerable moms." I wink as I adjust the weight of my daughter in my arms

He smiles as he moves even closer to me, brushing his hand against mine, causing my heart to combust. "Correction. I hit on one vulnerable mom. I don't make a habit of falling in love with my patients' mothers. Just the really hot ones." He winks back, tightening his fingers against mine. The very touch is a direct line to every one of my senses as my body goes into frenzied shock. I become a hot, feverish mess when he is in such close proximity, and if it weren't for my daughter in my arms, I'd be begging him to take me somewhere private.

His eyes widen, and I shiver when his lips press against my ear. "I love how I can turn you on with just one touch."

I struggle to catch my breath, my heart racing. "How do you know I'm turned on?"

"Your pupils are dilated, your lips are parted, your breath has quickened and I can see that your nipples have hardened under your shirt."

He chuckles at my audible gasp. I clutch at my brown leather jacket with my free hand, hoping to hide the obvious arousal, but my jacket just gapes back open, leaving my bullet nipples on show for the entire hospital to see. I contemplate putting Lily on the floor for a second so I can zip myself up, but Ashton takes matters into his own hands, taking my zipper with his thumb and forefinger.

He zips my jacket up but can't resist brushing his fingertips over my breasts before he pulls away. My mouth gapes open at his audacity while my insides throb with sexual need. He smirks, amusement dancing in his eyes.

233

"And now we can add wet panties to your list."

I can hardly take a breath. I'm wildly turned on right now, and there isn't a damn thing I can do about it. *Tease.* "Haven't you got work to be getting on with?" I ask with humored frustration.

"Yes, another sixteen hours worth."

"Well, you better stop turning me on and get back to work."

He gives me a devilish grin, holding his hands up in defense. "Fine, I'm going. I just wanted to give you both a send-off. You got everything finished?"

The last two weeks he and Caleb helped with everything, including baby-proofing the apartment. Last night I set up the bassinet in my room and sterilized her bottles ready for feeding.

"Yeah, everything's ready. I even put a little welcome home banner up in the living room this morning. Not that she'll ever remember it, but it's a big day."

"I wish I could come with you, but I need to save more babies lives so they can go home too."

That makes me smile, and I press a kiss against his lips. It's a little risky, somebody could see us, but I can't stop myself. "I love you. Do you know that, Dr. Bailey?"

"I do, Miss Jacobson. I love you too."

"Call me when you've finished."

"Yes, ma'am." He looks down at a content sleeping Lily affectionately for a split second, then back up at me. "Catch you later, baby."

"Bye." I smile, then begin to walk away with Lily in tow.

I turn back around when Ashton calls out my name. "It suits you," he says.

"What does?" I ask with perplexed amusement.

He steps towards me until he is inches away from my face. "Being a mom. And I have to say you look sexy as hell right now. It's doing crazy things to me. I'm a lucky man." I'm smiling so hard it feels as though my face is about to split in half any second now. He leans down and whispers the words that shock me to my core. "And I can only imagine how sexy you will look carrying our child." He smirks, then walks away, leaving me even more turned on.

And confused.

Frozen to the spot, I glance down at Lily asleep in her car seat. I hope one day I can give her a brother or sister. I walk outside in a dream-like daze, picturing Lily and a mini Ashton running around in transcendent gardens, chasing after one another. I'm so caught up in my day-dream that I walk straight past Caleb, totally unaware of his presence.

He catches up to me, a look of concern on his face. "Are you okay? You look preoccupied."

"I'm perfect. Let's get my baby home."

"Welcome home, baby girl."

I take Lily-Mai out of her car seat and lift her gently into my hands, cradling her in my arms. I carry her from one room to the next, giving her an in-depth explanation of each room, and her bright eyes widen, almost as if my words are fascinating.

"And this is your nursery." The walls are painted in a plain pastel shade of pink, and a beautiful white silhouette Tinker Bell with tiny white stars twinkling from the end of her wand points to Lily-Mai's name in elegant handwriting above a traditional white pine crib. The crib complements the pure-white furniture and matching nursing swivel glider with an ottoman that sits in the corner of the room.

I walk her slowly around the nursery in a full circle, coming to a stop at the changing table.

"Let's get you out of your snow suit," I mutter gently to Lily as I lay her on the changing table. I zip her out of her snowsuit, smiling when I look down at her cute baby romper that says, 'My Mom Rocks' in pink rock and roll letters that Caleb picked up for her.

"Your mom totally does rock," I whisper in agreement as I lean down and lift her left hand into mine, placing a gentle kiss against her tiny fingers. Once her diaper has been changed, I bring her back into the living room and hand her over to Caleb, who is on the sofa flicking through the television channels. I walk into the kitchen to get her bottle ready, with her three different prescribed vitamins and medication.

A couple of minutes later I walk back into the living room with her bib and a warm bottle in hand as her shrieking cries echo through the apartment. "I'm here, baby, I'm here." I take a comfortable position beside Caleb and then gently place her bib around her neck. Placing the bottle between my legs, I take a wailing Lily from Caleb's arms and place her gently into the crux of my arms, cradling her. When I hold the bottle up to her mouth, she immediately takes the teat into her mouth and proceeds with her feed, the crying immediately being replaced with peaceful, eager gulps.

"And so it begins," Caleb says with an amused smirk. "You ready for sleepless nights for the next eighteen years?" I roll my eyes, smiling at his over exaggeration.

"Hell yeah, I've been waiting thirteen weeks for this. Bring it on."

As the weeks go by, I've had a few of Sebastian's friends drop by to see Lily, including Sebastian's dad and sister, and I've had to play the perfect wife-to-be. I'm just thankful none of them stopped by when Ashton was here because I'm not quite sure how I would have explained it. I hate all of this lying. I hate the guilt. I hate it all.

I just want to breathe freely again.

The only person who seems to be helping me from cracking up is my five-month-old baby, and that is possibly because she doesn't give me a moment's peace, giving me less of an opportunity to dwell on my poor decisions.

As I prepare Lily's bottle for her next feed, I take a glance at the calendar against the refrigerator and realize that in two days' time Sebastian finally comes home, and I'll get to break his heart into a million pieces, just days after Valentine's Day. I internally shiver, but the thought is quickly pushed to the side when I feel a warm set of arms slip around my waist and a pair of tantalizing lips press against my neck.

"You smell insanely good," he murmurs against my skin.

"Oh, that would be the smell of eau de parfum of baby vomit," I say in my best French accent.

I can feel Ashton press his chest firmly against my back as he pulls me closer to him. "That isn't it, trust me. It's the kind of smell that makes me want to lick you all over." I groan as I feel the shape of his erection pushing against my back. "But I can't," he says in mocking defeat. "I need to head into work. A woman in Olympia has given birth to twins at twenty-four weeks, and they're being transferred to Seattle as we speak."

I turn to face him, my hands caressing up his chest. "That's okay. You can lick me all over some other time," I say with a smile. "Go save the little babies."

He smiles and presses a gentle kiss against my lips. "I love you."

"I love you," I repeat, bringing him in for a hug and pressing a gentle kiss against his neck. "Go." I force him in the direction of the kitchen door and laugh as he pouts.

"Fine, I'm going." He blows me a kiss then leaves.

Smiling, I finish Lily's bottle and head into the living room for her afternoon feed. Once she has fallen asleep on my shoulder, I take her to the nursery and place her into her crib. I turn her baby monitor on beside the crib and head into the living room to resume my Sons of Anarchy marathon from last night. Exhaustion from the night before takes its toll and I close my eyes, unable to keep them open any longer.

I wake with a disorientated jolt when I hear the sound of my brother's voice. My heart is racing at a frantic rate as I listen for the voice again. After a few seconds of terrifying silence, I sigh with relief when I realize that it must have been a dream. I sit up and rest my face within my hands, taking deep calming breaths, trying to calm my heart rate. Then his death crippling voice echoes softly through my living room, freezing me on the spot. It's coming from the baby monitor. It wasn't a dream. It was real. He's here, in my home. He's in the nursery.

Fuck!

Lily!

I hastily run into the kitchen and grab the biggest knife I can find. A chill runs through my body when his voice comes through the baby monitor again.

"You're so beautiful, Lily-Mai. Just like your mom." As his words fill my head, I charge into the nursery, the knife held firmly in the palm of my right hand.

I physically choke as I skid to an immediate stop. My worst nightmare is before me with my daughter in his arms. I struggle to find my breath as I watch his evil eyes trace over Lily. In what seems like slow motion, he turns to face me with a vindictive smile etched along his face, and I physically have to hold myself back from charging at him and piercing this blade into his chest.

I watch him lean down and kiss my daughter against the softness of her head. The knife I held so steadily in my hand begins to shake. The ten years I've spent trying to bury him has been obliterated in seconds.

"Hi, *Ava*."

With two simple words, he has me crumbling into pieces. Suddenly, I'm no longer twenty-eight year old Ava Jacobson, the woman who is qualified in Krav Mega self-defense. Instead, I'm Ava Jacobson, the fifteen-year-old girl who is deemed useless against her brother's devices.

# chapter 24

## ASHTON

I SLUMP MYSELF AGAINST my open locker, burying my head into my hands with pent up frustration. I hate that I was the one who just had to tell the mother and father of their preemie twins that one baby didn't survive. The look of devastation on their face was pure hell when I explained how the genetic heart defect their baby boy was born with was too severe and that his little undeveloped body just failed on him. I did everything that was medically possible, but sometimes it isn't meant to be.

I hastily take my shirt off and throw it into the locker. I need to get out of here. Thank God, I was only on call and can head home. As I reach into my locker for my casual shirt and jeans, I notice my phone is flashing. Before I can answer, the call ends, but worry immediately picks up when I notice I have fourteen missed calls. Dialing the number, there's an answer after the first ring.

"Ashton, thank God. It's Caleb. Ava's missing."

I stop breathing.

"What do you mean Ava's missing?" My ears are pounding as the blood pumps vicariously through my veins.

"I mean Ava is missing," Caleb hisses through the phone. "I came home to Lily screaming the place down but there was no sign of Ava anywhere. She's not answering her phone either."

*Fuck!*

"I'll be with you soon." I hang up, and within ten seconds I'm dressed and out the door. That bastard has come for her. I just know it. If he so much as touches a hair on her head, I will kill him.

I break every traffic violation known to man, and a journey that should take twenty-five minutes, takes me only ten. Caleb buzzes me in, and I bypass the elevators and take the stairs two at a time. By the time I reach Ava's door on the eighth floor, I'm completely out of breath. I'm met by a distraught Caleb at the door, Lily in his arms.

"Is she okay? Is she hurt?" I ask, the pediatric doctor in me kicking in immediately. I stroke Lily's little head, tracing her entire face, looking for any sustained injury, neglect or concussion, but nothing screams out at me. That's a good sign.

"No, she's fine. I don't think she was left for long."

I sigh with relief as I kiss her gently on the top of her head. I follow Caleb into the living room and watch as he places Lily gently into the vibrating chair and straps her in.

"Do you think … do you think he has her?" he asks when he turns back to me.

"Yes." I pace around the living room, anger coursing through my veins. "I should have killed him when I had the chance," I murmur to myself.

"What are you talking about?"

I look up to the ceiling, pulling at my hair with unrestrained rage. I glance back down to Caleb, pursing my lips in anger. "I haven't told Ava this, but in Miami, after she told me what he'd done to her …" I grit my teeth at the very fucking thought. "I tracked that fucker down and beat him up."

He looks a little taken back at my admission. "Shit. How bad?"

"Felony bad." His eyes widen, half shocked, half amazed. "If it weren't for his wife being there, I probably would have killed him on the spot."

"So you think he's come back for some kind of revenge?"

I shake my head at his question. "No. You didn't see the look on his wife's face when she found out what that monster had done. He's come back because he has nothing left to lose."

Caleb lets out a long breath. "Fuck." He slouches on the floor with his back against the sofa, his elbows leaning against his bent knees.

"What's the plan then?"

"We find her and then we kill the fucker."

# Ava

I feel disorientated.

I try to move, but I'm physically bound to the spot. My eyes groggily flutter open as I wake from a deep sleep. Everything is blurry, and the flickering haze keeps pulling me under, keeping me in the dark. I can hear a faint voice in the background, but it's distorted,

"Ava ..."

A hand lingers against my face, but it feels wrong. Rough ... evil ... Avery.

Terror soars through my woozy consciousness, and I desperately try to pull away, but a sharp metallic slash against my wrists prevents me from moving, and I'm brought to a stand still from sheer pain. My eyes shoot open as I scream out loud, reviving me to my senses. With every blink, my vision improves until everything becomes very clear. My spread-eagled body is on top of a dirty hard mattress, my wrists and ankles chained to a bed.

I see my brother from out of the corner of my eye and instinctively I pull against the restraints again, but I cry out in pain as the chains bite into my skin. I glance up and wince as a trickle of blood drips from my left wrist.

"I was wondering when you'd wake." I shudder as his fingertip runs along my bare arm. My eyes fill with fear-induced tears as my entire body quakes with terror. "You've been out of it for a while. Two hours at least."

I clench my eyes shut as his fingers travel slowly over my shoulder.

"Where am I?" I croak as tears fall down my face.

"Where you belong. Where you've always belonged." I thrash my head away from him as he presses a kiss against my cheek.

*Wrong move.*

His hand flies to my throat and he squeezes my neck tight. I splutter as my air supply is abruptly cut off. "Now that's not the way to greet your beloved brother, is it, Ava?"

He angrily slams his lips onto mine, and I screw my face up in disgust. The moment his lips pull away, I spit aggressively into his face.

Again, *wrong move.*

I groan in pain as my face is whipped to the side by the almighty speed of his hand as he slaps me.

*Fuck!* That hurt.

He straddles me, gripping my mouth with forceful precision as he crushes my lips within his fingertips. "Someone needs to learn some manners." In one swift movement he rips my T-shirt and bra open, leaving the top half of my body vulnerable and bare.

"No! Please, no, no … please!" I desperately beg, not wanting him to touch me, not wanting him to …

"I'll be good. Please … I promise. Don't … not that … no … please."

His eyes linger down my chest, suddenly hungry, and I have to slam my eyes shut when his fingertips trail across my naked flesh. I brace myself for what I know will come next, but it doesn't come. Instead, it surprises me when he pulls away from me.

"If you double-cross me again, I will get angry. Very angry. Do you understand me?"

My body frantically shakes as I open my eyes, sighing inwardly with relief. "Yes, I understand. I'll behave, I promise," I rasp.

I watch him pick something up from the floor, and my dry mouth becomes almost unbearable when I realize it's bottled water. He holds it up for me to take a closer look.

"You thirsty?"

I nod numbly as he inches closer to me and places the bottle to my lips, pouring a little in my mouth. I swallow painfully as the water glides roughly down my throat.

"More?" I croak quietly.

"More what? Where are your manners?"

"Water, please."

"Seeing as you've asked so nicely …"

He lifts the bottle to my lips again, and I barely manage a small sip before he hastily pulls the bottle away, causing the water to dribble down my chin. He takes the bottle to his lips and licks the rim of the bottle with his tongue before taking a long swig.

"Your daughter looks just like you," he says after a few moments of silence.

I pull at my restraints in panic when I suddenly realize Lily isn't here, ignoring the pain that shoots across my wrists. "Where is she? What did you do to her?"

He vindictively smirks at my reaction and stands up from the bed, crouching down in front of me and stroking my hair. "Nothing. She's perfectly safe."

"If-f-f you did anything to her, I fucking swear to God …" I grit out venomously at the thought of anything happening to my sweet Lily.

He's suddenly right in front of me, his face contorted with anger. "You'll do what? What will you do?" My nostrils flare with each heavy breath I take as anger fills my veins, consuming me with hatred for this man. "You'll kill me, is that it? Is that what you were going to say?" I cower into the mattress as he straddles my waist, his fingertips stroking against my cheek. "Good luck with that."

Then without warning, my jeans and panties are ripped down my thighs and my legs forced open by his hands.

"I've changed my mind. I think you definitely need to be taught a lesson."

I cry out as his mouth slams against mine again, forcing entry. I desperately try to fight against him, screaming for my life, but he punches me so hard in the face that everything suddenly turns pitch black …

# ASHTON

I'm pretty sure I've covered every inch of this apartment from my constant pacing with anxious panic as I wait for Darnell and his wife, Brianna, to turn up. They are the only two people on this earth that I trust, other than my family, and Darnell was the first guy I called. He is an ATF special agent for the Seattle field division, so he's not to be messed with.

I'm relieved when I finally hear the buzzer and I'm engulfed in Brianna's arms. "Hey, boo, how you doing?" She presses a kiss against my cheek.

"All the better now that you're here."

Darnell pulls me into a hug, slapping my back. "Hey, man, we're going to find her, I promise." I nod once.

Caleb picks Lily up from the vibrating chair and passes her over to Brianna. She gushes over her instantly. "Oh, aren't you just the cutest?" She starts to bounce her in her arms, a smile plastered on her face.

"Will you be okay with her?"

"Yeah, we'll be fine. Won't we, beautiful?" she says to Lily with a smile.

"Her nursery is just through the corridor, the second door on the right," I say as I point her into the direction of the bedrooms. "I know she's just a baby, but I don't want her to be around all of this, so can you just keep her in there for the time being?"

"I've got this. Just go, find your girl. Find this baby's momma." I press a kiss against Brianna's cheek and a second kiss on top of Lily's head.

When Brianna takes Lily to the Nursery, Darnell gives Caleb and me the low down. "Okay, so I've put a call out to every police station within the entire Washington state area and they are fully aware of the severity of Ava's situation. I've made a call to all the local hospitals, airports, bus stations, train stations, you name it, but there have been absolutely no reports of them yet."

"That's a good thing, right? That means they're still in Seattle?" I ask.

"Well, not necessarily. They could be traveling by car, but from the time frame since the time you last saw her to Caleb coming home it is possible that they're still in the Washington area. I've given the authorities a description of Ava but what does this dick look like?"

I give him Avery's statistics to the best of my knowledge, and he radios over the information, not missing a beat.

"Are you packing?" He opens his jacket and pulls his shirt up to reveal a glock27 handgun attached to his belt. "Did you grab mine from the range?"

With a sigh and an eye roll, he reaches for the back of his jeans and pulls out my 9mm pistol, passing it to me. "I'm giving you this gun on two conditions. One, it's for emergency use only. And two, under no circumstances are you to shoot this bastard in the head. Got it?"

I hesitate. The second condition is one I'm not sure I can follow.

And he knows it.

"I'm serious, bro. I can't protect you from that shit. If you kill him, you'll go down for a long time and where does that leave you and your girl?" He's right, of course. I just hope he gets to him before I do because I'm not sure I'll be able to control myself.

"What if the kill is warranted as an emergency?"

"I'm gonna' pretend I didn't hear that, but I'm sure that would be justifiable in a court of law." He winks and I know he would back me up.

I bare the pistol within the palm of my hand, feeling the weight of it. I check the ammunition in the magazine release, then check the safety. As I put it away in the back pocket of my jeans, I notice the shocked look on Caleb's face.

"Relax, Caleb, I have a gun permit. I keep it locked up at the range."

He stares at me like I've suddenly grown two heads. "Is this some kind of Texas thing I won't understand?"

I groan, my patience quickly wearing thin. "I usually just use it to blow some steam off at the range now and again, but occasionally it's necessary when a psychopath abducts my fucking girlfriend." Immediately I feel terrible for speaking to him like shit, but I don't apologize.

"Okay, so what's the plan of action?" I ask Darnell.

"For now? We just sit and wait."

I almost pummel his pretty face. "Sit and fucking wait? Are you serious?"

"We don't have any leads, Ash. She could be anywhere. If we begin a search now, we'd just be clutching at straws. We need to be smart and let the authorities do their thing."

"No! I can't just sit here while that monster is doing God knows what to her! I need to find her. I can't just fucking sit here and do nothing!"

I'm losing my mind. The anger that is swirling around my body is almost at the explosive end of the spectrum and I'm moments away from losing my shit. Darnell grips my arms, almost shaking the crap out of me.

"I love you, bro, but you need to cool the fuck down. I have the best guys doing what they can, and I mean the best. I may only be ATF, and kidnap sure as hell isn't my area of expertise, but I have contacts in all the right places. We *will* find her, I can promise you that, and the moment we find a location we'll be out of here like a bat out of hell, but for now we need to sit tight."

With a fierce glare, he grips hold of my face with both hands. "And as for that motherfucker, it ain't over until he's in a fucking body bag." He slams a brotherly kiss on the top of my head, then pats my cheek a couple of times before pulling away. "Now get your balls out and stop being a fucking pussy."

He's right. I'm being a pussy.

But the moment I met Ava, she had me whipped.

God, baby, please be okay.

# Ava

I stir from my sleep as an intense pain ricochets across my head, awakening me from my confused stupor. It feels as if I have been hit by a freight train. My eyes flicker open to a dimly lit room, indicating nighttime has fallen. I squint through my heavily lidded eyes as I try and focus on my surroundings, my mind a muddled haze.

I try to stretch my aching limbs, but the sharp welts that cut into my skin are a painful reminder of my current nightmare from hell. My head pounds excruciatingly as I try to fight back the tears, my body still tied and bound to the bed, my shirt ripped to shreds and my jeans bunched around my ankles.

My stomach churns heavily as I notice an empty condom wrapper at my feet and the memory of my clothes being ripped from my body fills my mind. I have just enough time to turn my head to the side before I vomit violently on the mattress. A cold sweat covers my entire body and the pungent smell of vomit fills my nostrils as I empty the entire contents of my stomach. Spitting the last bits of vomit from my mouth, I turn away and close my eyes, taking slow methodic breaths to ease the abrasive stitch that is contracting along my diaphragm and my shoulders.

I can hear the sound of the bastard's footsteps, and I shift away from his voice, my eyes filling with tears, my heart thumping hysterically in my chest. "Shit, Ava. I leave you for one minute, and you vomit everywhere."

Unable to open my eyes through my lethargic haze, I hear his footsteps retreat further away from me, then the sound of a faucet running and his footsteps returning. My entire body clams up when I feel something wet and cold brush along my naked shoulder.

"I'm just cleaning you up," he says in a soft, almost-loving voice; the opposite of his angry rage from earlier. I hesitantly open my eyes to see him cleaning up the vomit beside my face and against the mattress with a damp towel. He smiles down at me when he notices I'm looking up at him. The smile alone is enough to send a chill along my spine.

"Why are you doing this?" I sob.

The softness of his eyes suddenly turns sinister, and I gulp in fear. "Because I'm taking back what belongs to me." I turn to look away from him in disgust, horrified at his words, but he grips my face, his fingers trembling in anger. "You ran away from me once, Ava. I'm not going to let you go again. You're mine. Do you hear me? Mine," he growls.

"What about your wife? Your baby?"

"She. Left. Me."

"I'm sorry," I feign sympathy, but the uncertainty in his eyes tells me he doesn't believe me. "What happened?" I probe gently, trying to take away his skepticism in the hope of calming him into a false sense of security. A security that could be the key to me getting the hell out of here now that I've spotted his cell phone in the front pocket of his opened shirt.

"Your boyfriend, that's what happened."

I blink in confusion. What has Ashton got to do with it? "I don't … I don't follow."

"Well, just in case you don't know which boyfriend I was talking about, try the one you're currently fucking, you little slut. He beat me

247

because you couldn't keep your motherfucking mouth shut."

I slam my eyes shut as his hand slaps me hard across the face for a second time. My eyes tear up at the sudden trauma. "I … I'm sorry," I stammer, my cheek developing a pulse of its own. I hiss as I feel the laceration against my cheek, causing the open air to cut through the moist gash.

Then suddenly everything falls into place. The night in Miami when Ashton came back with blood on his hands wasn't because he punched a wall at all. It was because he beat my brother up.

*Fuck* …

Avery's malicious voice interrupts my thoughts. "He's going to be sorry he ever fucking messed with me."

A cold chill shivers through me at the promise of his threat. "W-what are you g-g-going to d-do?"

"Nothing for your little head to worry about." He taps against my temple with his forefinger, but that does nothing for my cold-blooded panic.

"Please, don't hurt him. Please."

He sits beside me, dropping the vomit-laden towel onto the floor. "So two guys at the same time, huh? I've created a little monster in you haven't I? I must say it was a shock to see you at the funeral with some pretty boy, instead of Sebastian Gilbert. How in the world did that happen anyway? The last thing I knew, my old high school buddy had OD'd on cocaine, then ten years later he's shacking up with my baby sister. Small world, huh?" His angry tone doesn't match the calmness of his words. It's a dangerous combination. He moves in closer to me, so close I can smell his breath, and I have to fight the urge to heave.

"Who's the better fuck, Ava? Me, Sebastian or Ashton *Bailey*?" he says Ashton's second name with a mocking laugh.

As revulsion swirls around my stomach, I turn away from him, pushing the tears away at his sick and twisted question. "Fuck you."

His sinister chuckle fills the silence. "You have quite the potty mouth on you, don't you?"

I turn to face him with a sneer, wishing my death glare could kill him on the spot. "Well, I learned from the best."

After a moment, I glance up at the phone that is peeking out from his pocket, desperate to get my hands on it. I try to adjust my wrists in their constraints, my position starting to border on intolerable. "Is this really necessary?" I question, indicating the metal handcuffs that are keeping me in place. "They're really hurting," I cry, tears pricking my eyes.

"Yes," he says in a no-nonsense manner.

"Well, can I use the restroom, please? I need to wash the vomit out of my hair, and I need to use the toilet." He seems to ponder this for a moment and then much to my relief he reaches into the back pocket of his jeans and retrieves a key.

"Okay, but you've got ten minutes."

I moan in relief when my left arm is freed from its restraints, then once my right arm is free I desperately massage my delicate, wounded wrists. I clench my hands, trying to ease the pins and needles that tingle through them. He frees my ankles from the cuffs, and it's such a relief to have full control over my body again. He frees my ankles from the cuffs, and it's such a relief to have full control over my body again. He pulls me up to a sitting position and tugs my jeans over my hips.

As I stand up, I purposely fall into him, feigning imbalance and dizziness. He catches me so I don't fall and I manage to latch onto his phone, discretely pulling it from his pocket. My heart is pounding inside my chest, but I manage to conceal my harsh breathing as I slowly bring my hand down the side of my body, successfully placing the phone into the back pocket of my jeans without Avery's knowledge. I pull away from him with a shaky breath.

"Sorry, I lost my balance."

His eyes trace my face for a moment and for a split second I think he's figured out my plan, but he directs me to the restroom. I almost sag with relief when I enter the bathroom, but I keep it contained. Suddenly feeling a little light-headed, I take a seat on the toilet, placing my head within the palm of my hands and taking soothing, deep breaths. I glance up to see him standing in the middle of the bathroom, his arms crossed over his chest.

"Well, get to it then."

*Shit, he doesn't expect me to pee and shower in front of him, does he?*

"Can I have some privacy, please? It's not as if I can go anywhere is it? Please?"

"Fine. Ten minutes!" he barks, and storms out, slamming the door shut.

I inwardly take a breath of relief and rush up from the toilet seat to quietly lock the door. My heart is thumping furiously against my chest when I turn the shower on to block out any noise. I take the phone from my pocket, and fumble, praying it hasn't got a passcode on it when I unlock it. Instead, it has a surveillance type picture of me and my stomach threatens to spill again when I realize it was taken from inside my apartment only days ago.

*Holy shit.*

I lean against the edge of the bathtub and quickly type in Caleb's number. I would call Ashton, but I don't know his number off by heart.

My legs are twitching with apprehension as I wait for the call to connect and I can't keep my eyes from glancing to the door even though I locked it. My heart pounds with horror as I think of all the bad scenarios that would happen to me if Avery caught me right now.

Caleb answers on the first ring and my heart breaks when I can hear the obvious distress in his voice. "Hello?"

"Caleb, it's me," I whisper through a shuddering cry.

"Ava! Fuck. Are you okay? Where are you?"

I hear a muffled commotion on the other side of phone, and for a moment I think the call may have dropped, but to my relief Ashton's voice fills the phone and my eyes fill with more tears. "Baby, are you okay? Are you hurt? What's that bastard done to you?"

With a trembling breath, I whisper into the phone, "Yes, I'm … okay, just glad to hear your voice."

"Where are you?" he demands.

"I don't know. Avery ... he … he brought me to some motel. Where's Lily? Is she safe?"

"She's fine. She's safe."

I close my eyes and exhale a sign of relief. "Thank God. I don't have long. He thinks I'm showering but do you think you can track this phone? I managed to swipe it from him, but I don't know how long it's going to take him to realize it's missing."

"Yeah, baby, easy. Has he hurt you?"

I clench my eyes shut as the visions of the used condom come to the forefront of my mind and the silence that follows answers his question.

"Motherfucker," he hisses, but the sound suddenly seems faint. I assume he's already put me on speaker and is tracking the phone as we speak. Thank the Lord for the marvel of technology.

"Baby, I'm coming for you, just sit tight. I'm not going to let anything else happen to you. I promise."

"Okay," I say with a trembling cry.

"I love you," he exclaims fiercely, and my heart constricts inside my chest because I know he does.

"I love you too, and you, Caleb. I love you both. Please hurry," I say through a sob, tears falling down my face as I quickly disconnect the call. I stand and look for a hiding place for the phone, to help Ashton track my location easily through the GPS. My eyes land on the bathtub, and I notice it has a flimsy plastic panel against the tub. I gently push the panel inwards and with a small squeak it opens up, revealing a small gap. I quickly slide the phone through the gap and pull the panel back into place, barely avoiding trapping my fingers.

Realizing I'm quickly running out-of-time, I strip out of my shredded clothes and jump into the shower. Once I've scrubbed my entire body clean, washing the vomit from my hair in two minutes flat with a grainy bar of soap, I re-dress immediately into my torn shirt that looks more like a crop top and my jeans that chafe against my crotch, a painful reminder of what that *bastard* did to me.

I brush my wet hair through my fingers, and I gasp when I see my reflection in the murky mirror. I barely recognize myself. My eyes look empty and puffy, and both sides of my face are extremely inflamed and swollen. One side of my face is covered with multicolored bruises that fade just below my eye, and the other side of my face has a large, fresh laceration gaping open against my cheekbone. I wince when I notice purple bruised indents against my wrist where the cuffs cut into the skin. I go to touch the tender wounds when a fist bangs against the door causing me to jolt out of my skin. My heart thumps and crashes against my chest when my eyes fly to the door through the mirror in a panic.

"Ten minutes are up!"

I close my eyes, take a deep inhale and count to three. Then I unlock the door.

Without a moment's warning, I'm suddenly being pulled forward and knocked onto my ass. "Where the fuck is my cell?"

I cower against the wall as he screams viciously in my face. I grasp the thin strands of carpet, trying to hold myself upright. "I d-d-don't know." I groan out in pain when he grabs a clump of my hair into a tight fist and slams my head against the plasterboard wall.

"You're fucking lying to me! Who did you call?" I shake my head, wincing in pain when he tightens his grip against my hair, my hair burning against my scalp. "I d-d-don't know what your t-talking about! I haven't seen it. I haven't spoken to anybody. Check if y-you d-don't believe me!"

Letting go, he all but launches my head into the wall at full impact, causing me to gasp in pain when a crack tears through my neck. He flies off in search of his phone around the motel room and bathroom. To my relief he comes up empty handed. He didn't look under the bathtub.

"Shit! Where the fuck is it?" he shouts as he searches high and low.

I sit up from my slouching position, massaging my agonizing neck, but it only makes the pain even worse. He turns to look at me, a look of concern flickering in his eyes. Jesus, he has the psychotic personality of Jekyll and Hyde.

"Are you hurt?"

I grimace, but not from the agony. He moves to me, and it takes everything within my power not to shudder at his close proximity. He crouches to my level, gently reaching out to stroke my bruised face with his fingertips. "I'm sorry. I didn't mean it, baby, I didn't mean to hurt you, I just … I thought you took my cell."

He leans into me and presses a kiss against my tender face. My entire insides rattle with panic at his affection and I don't know how I manage to hold back the bile with the way his stubble irritates my skin.

"Hmm …" My heart crashes against my chest when I hear him inhale. "You smell incredibly good." He echoes the words Ashton had whispered to me before he left for work earlier. Those words held perfect memories, but now Avery has ruined them for me.

"I'm going to make it all better, I promise. As soon as we are on a plane and out of this shit hole. You'll see," he adds with another stomach hurling kiss.

"W-What do you mean plane? Where are we g-going?"

"Somewhere, where we can be together, just the two of us. It will be perfect."

Not only is he psychotic, he's delusional. I wish Ashton would hurry up. I need to escape this hellhole, right fucking now. Gently he lifts me up and guides me back over to the bed. "I need to head out to make a phone call, so I need to handcuff you again."

I shake my head hysterically. "No! Not back on the bed, please."

He gives me an exasperated glare, pushing me down on the bed with a little extra force. "It won't be long, I promise."

Helplessly, all I can do is sit back against the mattress while he fastens my wrist securely to the metal frame, but this time he leaves my ankles free.

"Don't miss me too much."

I scowl as he walks away from me. The moment the front door is locked securely, I hysterically pull against the cuffs, thrashing my entire body from side to side, angrily flailing my arms and pulling aggressively against the cuffs. But all I manage to achieve is slashing the cuffs further into my wrists and wasting vital energy. When I come to the realization that I don't have the muscle to break free from my cuffs, I give up and break down.

Please hurry, Ashton …

# chapter 25

## ASHTON

THE SOUND OF A phone ringing breaks through the silence.
*Ava!*
All three of us reach for our cell phones and my heart drops when I realize it isn't my phone. I watch Caleb from the edge of my seat as he fumbles with his cell, frowning at the flashing screen. "Who is it?" I growl as my mind goes into overdrive.

He shrugs his shoulders and answers without an ounce of hesitation. "Hello?"

*Please let this be Ava, please let her be safe.*

"Ava! Fuck. Are you okay? Where are you?"

I'm on my feet before my brain even registers the movement and I almost knock Caleb to the ground when I snatch the phone from him. My self-control has gone to shit, and it's down to this one girl. *My girl.*

"Baby, are you okay? Are you hurt? What's that bastard done to you?" My heart shoots out from my chest when I hear her voice, but that's not what has me nearly buckling to my knees; it's the timid, fragile tone to her trembling whisper. *Holy shit.*

"Yes, I'm ... okay, just glad to hear your voice." It's obvious that she is anything but okay.

"Where are you?"

"I don't know. Avery ... he ... he brought me to some motel. Where's Lily? Is she safe?"

"She's fine. She's safe."

I can hear the relief in her voice when she says, "Thank God," and I can imagine all too well how frantic she must have been knowing Lily had been left on her own for God knows how long. Jesus, I'm going to gun down that motherfucker when I see him. He's gonna' wish he never laid fucking eyes on me.

"I don't have long. He thinks I'm showering but do you think you can track this phone? I managed to swipe it from him, but I don't know how long it's going to take him to realize it's missing."

"Yeah, baby, easy. Has he hurt you?"

I can see Darnell in the corner of my eye mouthing, "Where the fuck is she?" so I put the phone on speaker, but I don't miss the silent reply from the other end. I'm going to kill him! Not only will I chop his body limb from limb until the bastard is a mountain of bloody body parts, but I will grate his dick off with a cheese grater until it resembles a pussy more than a cock. "Motherfucker," I furiously hiss as I search through Caleb's phone for the tracker Darnell installed a couple of hours ago. Reeling in my anger, I keep my shit together for the sake of Ava.

"Baby, I'm coming for you, just sit tight. I'm not going to let anything else happen to you. I promise." I click the tracking app open and allow the phone to track my beautiful girl.

"Okay," she says with a shuddering breath, and it kills me to hear her in such pain.

"I love you," I growl as if it will be the last time I'll get to say those words. But it won't be. I'm going to find her, and tell her that I love her. And then I'm going to spend the rest of my life telling her I love her over and over again until she gets tired of hearing it. And even then I won't stop telling her that I love her.

Ever.

I hold the phone out in Darnell's direction, indicating my girl's location with a point of my finger, and he is by my side in less than a second, his radio at the ready.

"I love you too, and you, Caleb. I love you both. Please hurry."

I grit my eyes closed as the phone call ends with the sound of Ava sobbing. Darnell claps me on the shoulder as he radios over to the authorities.

Then when you think shit can't get any worse …

Sebastian walks through the door with a confused look on his face.

"Oh fuck," Caleb mumbles from behind me, watching Sebastian place his duffle bag down beside the door. He takes a step closer, his eyes tracing over both Darnell and me before stopping on Caleb.

Darnell looks at me, raising his brows curiously. I briefly glance in his direction before returning my attention back to Sebastian. "Ava's fiancé," I whisper.

I don't miss the hearty chuckle from under his breath. "No, shit."

"What's going on, Caleb?"

Caleb steps out in front of me as if shielding me, protecting me. Although Sebastian might have a couple of inches on me, I can certainly handle myself, military training or not.

"We haven't got time to explain but Ava's been kidnapped."

Sebastian looks ready to blow when Caleb makes a desperate move to slide past him. He grabs Caleb by the arm. "What do you mean Ava's been kidnapped?"

"I mean she's been kidnapped, and we've just found her location, which we need to get to. Now." Caleb tries to push past him, but Sebastian steps out and pushes him back aggressively.

"Hold the fuck up! You can't just tell me the moment I get home after four months on tour that my fiancée has been kidnapped and expect me to understand what you guys are talking about." He looks between Darnell and me, keeping his eyes locked on mine for a second longer, almost as if he's trying to place me from somewhere.

"Who the fuck are these two chumps?"

I step forward, my fist clenched at my sides, but Darnell forces his hand to my chest and pushes me backwards, glaring at me to chill the fuck out. He's right. Fuck. I need to calm down. Sebastian doesn't know shit and for all he knows he's just wandered into a twilight fucking universe.

"What the hell's going on?"

I look at Caleb for guidance, but all he does is shrug his shoulders. "You need to tell him," Caleb says quietly.

"Tell me what!" he screams.

"Her brother has kidnapped her," I snap.

His eyes darken with confusion, taken back by my words. "Avery? I don't understand."

I sigh and turn my attention to Caleb. "I don't feel comfortable about this. This should come from Ava."

"Well, Ava isn't here to tell me is she?" Sebastian roars and it takes all my power not to zero my fist into his face. "So you better get talking. Now!"

With my anger levels rising, I turn into somebody I don't even recognize. "Who the hell do you think you're talking to, man?"

A panicked Caleb gets between us when he sees Sebastian take an angry step forward. "This is no time to get into a pissing contest, Ashton. Just fucking tell him what he needs to know, so we can go and get Ava!" This snaps me back into focus, and I nod with understanding.

"Who is this guy, Caleb?" Sebastian asks before a look of recollection ignites in his eyes.

"Look, Ava is in danger. We need to get to her before it's too late."

"I don't understand, how is she in danger? She's with her brother for Christ's sake. He's family."

"That motherfucker raped her!"

He pales on the spot when I scream in his face, shoving him back with full force. "Is this some kind of sick joke?"

Oh yeah, I just love making sick jokes about the woman I love getting raped by her brother. It's fucking hilarious.

"I wish! Do you want to know how old she was when she was raped for the first time? She was fifteen years old. Fifteen!"

"No! No, I don't believe you. She would have told me, I'm her fiancé." Caleb gives him a sad look. "Is this true?" he asks Caleb.

He answers Sebastian's question with a sad grimace. "Yeah, it's true."

A wounded look crosses Sebastian's features as the information outright punches him in the face. "I don't understand why she never told me, and why this guy seems to know more shit than I do! What the fuck's your deal?" he says, slamming his chest into mine. "Why are you in my house telling me shit about my girl?"

I make the mistake of raising my eyebrows up suggestively and he launches at me, swiping his fist against my jaw.

I stumble backwards a little disorientated from the heavy blow, but I don't retaliate. "I will let you kick my ass later, but right now we need to get to Ava! So you can either stay and lick your wounds or come with us. It's up to you, but I'm going. Come on, Darnell." I don't wait for a response. I charge out of the apartment with only two things on my mind.

One: save Ava

Two: kill the bastard

# Ava

Time feels as if it has come to a standstill as I watch the red digits on the digital clock that sits beside me on a grungy bedside table.

11:45

11:46

11:47

Every microsecond that ticks by feels like an eternity. Every second that passes by feels like the end of time. Every minute feels like a death sentence as I wait and wait and wait.

11:48

11:49

11:50

It has to be at least an hour ago since I called Caleb and spoke to Ashton. Where the hell are they? I have to close my eyes and exhale slowly to force my trembling tears at bay.

11:51

11:52

11:53

My line of vision traces from the clock to the front door developing a continuous pattern back and forth wondering who will come through the front door first.

11:54

11:55

11:56

As the minutes continue to tick by, the hope I have of Ashton coming to find me is diminishing and I convince myself he isn't coming.

My body jumps at the sound of a key turning in the door only to reveal my brother. I have to hold back my trembling tears again when he sits beside me, trailing his finger across my face, his eyes piercing fiercely into mine.

"Everything is sorted. We have a flight in a couple of hours. Then we can finally get out of here and be together without anybody interfering. Just you and me, baby."

*No, no, please no ... Ashton you need to hurry up, I need you ...*

He leaves me chained to the bed as he retrieves a bag from the other side of this tiny-boxed motel room. I watch as he unzips the rucksack and takes out a blond wig, the type that only a hooker would be seen dead in, along with some clothes and a passport.

*Shit.*

"You've been missing for a while, so I imagine you have people looking for you, especially your boyfriend and that faggot friend of yours."

My insides clench at the derogatory insult aimed at Caleb, and the vile hatred I feel for my brother has just quadrupled. I hate homophobic people, especially those who insult one of the most important people in my life.

"I imagine the police are already out there looking for you, so we need a disguise and we need to get rid of everything that screams *Ava.*" I shudder at the way his eyes travel down the curves of my body, and I have to stop the bile from rising when his fingertips trail down my breastbone.

"With a new disguise you need a new identity ..." He pauses to pick up the passport, opening it up to reveal an image that resembles me. Looking closer an inaudible gasp escapes me when I realize that the blonde girl in the photograph is, in fact, me.

*Jessica Walz ...*

I violently shake when my eye line follows the name on the passport. NO! He leans over, pressing his lips delicately against mine. I slam my eyes shut with disgust as the tears stream down my face.

"Look at me." My eyes flutter under his scrutiny, and the intense glare feels like a bullet to the chest as panic surges through me. "You're all I have now, Ava, and I love you so damn much."

Hearing those words leaves me wishing I had a sharp object so I could jam it directly into the artery I can see pumping in the side of his neck. I would twist and twist the blade, watching him bleed out until he became an unmoving corpse.

Through my disturbing thoughts, I don't even realize he's removed the cuffs from my wrists until I'm standing on my own two feet.

"Change," he commands, and under humiliating scrutinizing I have to dress in front of him. Once I have my panties and bra on, I move to put on the ridiculous leather pants when the sound of Macklemore's "Thrift Shop" comes from the bathroom.

My heart sinks.

*Oh fuck.*

His eyes turn black in a millisecond, and he is on me in an instant. I try to make a run for it, but I only make it to the door before my face is smashed forward into the wood. I scream out in agonizing pain at the impact.

"Bitch!" he screams as he rams my face into the door for a second time, the sound of my nose cracking evident over my screams. Blood gushes down my face as he hauls me up by the thick of my hair and throws me to the other side of the room. I scream, this time from the intense pain that tears through my neck from the earlier whiplash. He plows his fist into the side of my face, causing the blow to my neck to increase.

"You're fucking dead!"

Through the trembling strength of my muscles, I manage to use my bare feet to kick him in the face, making him lose balance. I scramble up on all fours when suddenly a swift kick to my abdomen causes me to fall flat on my face, and I scream out in more pain. I can barely breathe through the agony, but I continue to fight, desperately trying to remember what I learned in my self-defense class. He has me on my back, straddling my waist, and it's hard to remember anything when pain ricochets across my head from the speed of his fists.

"I'm going to kill you, and then I'm going to kill that motherfucking boyfriend of yours!"

Blood, sweat and tears cover my face, and for a moment I think he's going to win as unconsciousness begins to seep in. I can vaguely feel my panties being ripped apart as I claw my fingernails at his face, hitting and punching him until all I can feel is numbness. Through my distant screams and cries, my consciousness awakens to the sound of a gunshot and a heavy weight falling on top of me. My eyes blink open, and I see Darnell in an ATF bulletproof vest with a gun aimed at my brother. Armed police come barreling in and haul him off me.

He isn't moving.

He isn't breathing.

*Holy shit, he's dead.*

"Ava!"

Through my daze, I slowly look up to see Ashton running over to me. He drops down to his knees and gently pulls me into his arms. "Baby, baby, baby, thank God!" I gasp out in pain, and he pulls back in alarm.

My eyes fall on Avery as I see a paramedic working on him, resuscitating him. "Is he dead?"

"I don't know, baby." He brushes the matted hair from my face.

"I thought you weren't coming," I murmur through my tears.

"You had the fucking cavalry coming for you. I'm here, Caleb's here ... Se—"

I slam my lips onto his. The kiss is raw, full of desperation, and I put everything I physically have into this one kiss. Breathlessly I pull away. "I didn't think I'd ever see you again. You and Lily were all I could think about!" I cry.

"I'm here, baby, I'm here."

*Yes, yes he is.*

"I can breathe again," I say with a trembling cry, clutching him desperately to me.

"Yeah, baby, me too. Me too."

"I love you," I say breathlessly, pressing my lips gently onto his.

Suddenly, I feel Ashton freeze within my grip. "I'm sorry," he mumbles against my lips. I pull away, scrunching my eyes in confusion. "Sorry, sorry for what?" I follow his eye line, and the moment my eyes fall on the person stood in front of me, my world plunges back into the darkness.

*Oh fuck. Oh shit.*

"Ava?"

My lips tremble as I see Sebastian stood in front of me, the look of pain, confusion and devastation etched along his handsome face, and the physical pain is too much. Today is too much.

Everything is too much.

I close my eyes and allow my body to shut down, blackness enveloping me ...

# chapter 26

I BLINK THROUGH MY hazy sleep.

My eyelids feel heavy as a striking pain shoots across my forehead. I try to move my neck and groan in pain. It feels restricted, and my hands fly up to my neck in sheer panic.

"Shh, it's okay. It's just a neck brace," I hear Caleb whisper. I try to maneuver my head to look at him when suddenly he appears in front of me. "Hey, beautiful." I gently smile, as he takes my hand within his.

"Hi," I rasp, my throat feeling like raw sandpaper. A plastic cup and a straw appear in front of me, and Caleb gently places the end of the straw to my mouth. I take a small sip. "Thank you," I say after a second sip.

I trace my surroundings with my eyes, and I immediately recognize that I'm in a hospital room. I see Sebastian asleep in a chair to the left of the room, and Ashton asleep on the sofa to my right. My mind goes on red alert when I can't see Lily in sight anywhere. Fuck. Where's Lily?

"Lily?" I whisper in panic.

"She's fine. She's with my mom," Caleb says.

"She's okay?" I question, making sure I had heard him right.

"She's perfect," he says with a smile, immediately easing my panic. I breathe a sigh of relief, thankful that my baby girl is okay.

After a short moment, I trace my eyes over Sebastian again. As I look at his handsome face, the memories suddenly come flooding back to me. "How?" I say, shuddering at the memory.

"How can they both sit in the same room as each other? Because they both love you something fierce, and they're both stubborn. Neither would leave you."

I look between them, and the feeling that pierces my heart is crippling. I close my eyes as the guilt and shame swims through me. "I've made such a mess of everything."

"I know, but it's a mess you can fix. You just have to pick one."

"I have," I pause and concentrate my gaze on Ashton. I know irrevocably that he is the one I want to be with. I knew from the very moment my eyes fell on him that Sebastian didn't stand a chance. My gaze traces over to Sebastian and my heart drops, "But it doesn't hurt any less knowing that I'm going to break his heart. That I've already broken it."

I try to move into a comfortable position, but every muscle in my body screams out in blood-curdling agony and I can't keep the pained groan from escaping my lips.

"Let me grab a nurse. You're in a really bad way." I watch as he presses a small button on my buzzer.

"How bad is bad?"

He sits against the bed, gently holding onto my hand being careful of the cannula. "Well, you have two cracked ribs, a cervical fracture, deep wounds around your wrists, a broken nose and a broken cheek bone."

"And what about … you know?" I drop my eyes towards my groin area, once again becoming a victim of rape.

"There is no permanent damage, just a few tears that should heal up in time. They had to do a few tests, a hospital procedure following … rape." Pain is etched around his eyes and in the snarl of his voice. "Everything came back clean, but I wouldn't allow them to take a pregnancy test without your consent."

I clench my eyes shut, just imagining being riddled with *his* spawn, but then I remember the condom wrapper and relax, slightly. "I'm not. He used … a condom."

"Still, it wouldn't hurt to do one as a precaution."

I try to nod in agreement, but the mere movement in my neck has me groaning out in pain. "Okay," I mumble. After a short moment, I ask,

"Is he dead?"

"As much as I wish he were, no." My entire body freezes at the prospect of *him* still being able to hurt me. "The bastard is half way there though. He's on life support, and the doctors are unable to determine whether he'll make it through or not."

As I'm allowing this information to sink in, a nurse walks through the door, subsequently waking both Sebastian and Ashton, forcing me to deal with reality. Their eyes widen and they both stand at the same time, saying my name and bombarding me with questions.

"Boys, give the poor girl a chance to wake up," the nurse says, hushing them.

Sebastian and Ashton both sit back down. Unable to take their worried stares, I purposely avoid them as the nurse checks my vitals and adds more morphine.

When the nurse leaves the room, an awkward silence falls and I want to shout for her to come back. The tension in the room is so thick it could be cut with a knife. Finally finding the courage to look up at them both, I see Ashton's eyes are solely on me while Sebastian's eyes are currently staring daggers at Ashton, his hands balled up in fists. My heart sinks when I realize I did that. I'm the reason for the anger in his eyes.

"Can you give Sebastian and me a moment alone, please?" I ask, mostly to Ashton, trying to convey that everything is okay and that I love him with one look alone. He smiles, but before I can return his smile, the sound of a chair screeching across the floor breaks my gaze and I can see Sebastian looking between both Ashton and me, assessing our relationship. Caleb walks over to Sebastian and whispers something in his ear. With a brief glance in my direction, Sebastian nods. Caleb claps him on the back then walks out of the door, Ashton following behind him.

Hesitantly, Sebastian takes a seat beside me, and an awkward silence covers us. This is the moment that I have to break his heart. How do you begin with something like that?

I have to shift my body into his direction so I can get a good look at him without having to move my neck. "You changed?"

He blinks, his shoulders suddenly tensing at my words. "I'm not the one who changed, Ava."

I ignore the pain that rips through my heart and point towards his attire. "I mean your clothes. You were in your uniform."

"Oh," he says, looking down at his casual jeans and sweatshirt. "Um, yeah. You've been out of it for a couple of days. I've been home, showered, changed, spent some time with Lily-Mai."

I smile when I hear our daughter's name. "Good, she's missed you."

"Well, I'm glad somebody has." My heart lurches, and I feel physically sick with guilt.

"Sebastian ..." I sigh.

"Because from where I was standing it didn't look that way when you were declaring your love to somebody else." I close my eyes and take a deep, steadying breath. "I don't even know who you are anymore. Do you know how humiliating it was to find out that your own brother abused you from somebody else? More specifically from the man who has been sleeping with *my* fiancée? Were you ever going to tell me?"

I look down to my hands, unable to look him in the eye. "No," I answer gently and honestly.

"Didn't you trust me?" The pain in his voice is unmistakable, and it kills me.

"Of course I trusted you. I tried to tell you, so many times, but I just couldn't part with it. I'm so sorry."

He's quiet for a moment, and I can see the cogs turning in his mind. "Did you ever love me?"

My heart sinks at his question and it leads me to reach out for his hand. Thankfully, he lets me. "Of course I did. I *do* love you. You gave me my daughter, *our* daughter. You gave my life purpose. You brought me out of myself, gave me the confidence to love myself. You were my first love, my first everything." The tears run freely over my swollen face.

"But I wasn't enough," he whispers, a statement rather than a question, and I despise at how accurate he is.

"I thought you were, I truly did, but the day I met Ashton, my world shifted. I didn't mean for it to happen, it just did."

He wipes his eyes in frustration, disappointment clearly visible on his face. "I've been dreaming about coming home for months. Every night I would lie awake and instead of replaying the daily horrors that I was surrounded by, I would picture you and your beautiful smile. I'd visualize the moment I'd finally walk through our front door, and you would throw your arms around me, saying how much you loved me, how much you missed me. And I'd finally be able to be with my family and begin the rest of our lives together. It was the only thing that got me through all the shit, the deaths, the brutality of everything, and that's why I lied about the date I was coming home. I wanted to surprise you, but hell, it seemed that I was the one in for a surprise instead. It certainly wasn't the welcome home committee I had pictured in my mind, that's for sure."

He comes up for air for a moment, pressing the heel of his hands deep into his eye sockets as if desperately trying to push his emotions away.

"You wouldn't believe the amount of heartbreak I had to witness. Watching grown ass men cry because their wives or girlfriends were cheating on them back at home. It was disturbing to watch, but I thought I was one of the lucky ones. I would sit back and be so thankful that all this bullshit drama wasn't my drama and that my girl wasn't like that. Hell, infidelity hadn't even crossed my mind. It hadn't even registered on my radar that you would deceive me like that. I trusted you, but boy, how fucking wrong was I?"

"It wasn't like that. I—"

"What was it like? Tell me? Make me understand." I have to clench my eyes shut as the sudden reminders of my injuries begin to vibrate through me, and I hiss out in agonizing pain. "What's wrong?" he panics and suddenly jackknifes forward in his seat, clasping my hand.

"I just need a moment." I take deep breaths through the pain until it slowly begins to subside, allowing me to reopen my eyes.

"I'm sorry. You've been through hell, and I'm forcing shit on you when you should be resting," he says with remorse, rubbing his hand up and down his face.

"I have plenty of time to rest, but right now I need to explain." He doesn't argue, so I take that as my cue to continue.

"I didn't plan for it. I didn't plan to fall in love with somebody else … it just happened. I was lonely, vulnerable, and Ashton was the first person to make me smile again. I was in a really bad place. I was missing you like crazy, our daughter could have died at any moment, and he was there. I liked his company. Suddenly, I began to look forward to his presence just as much as I was looking forward to a call or a text message from you. It quickly escalated into something more than attraction, and I tried to ignore it, but the more I ignored it, the more I wanted him. I didn't want to want him, and I hated that I did want him."

"Were you seeing him behind my back when I came home on leave?"

"No, nothing happened. It wasn't until my sister passed away that things began to escalate." I take a jittery breath. "I lied to you when I said I went to Miami alone. I wasn't alone. Ashton was by my side the whole time."

I try to tread carefully with the next words that follow, but no matter how I word it, it's not going to shield him away from the pain. "It was in Florida when we first slept together." I tighten my grip against his hand, desperately wanting to comfort him, but he recoils away from me, snatching his hand away from mine. "I can stop if you want," I say in a pained voice, hating the sad and destroyed look on his face.

"No, I need to know." His jaw clenches.

"I didn't mean for it to happen. Just with the stress of the funeral, seeing my brother again ..." I see Sebastian visibly tense at the mention of my brother and I want to reach out to him, to wrap my hand around his clenched fists. But he doesn't want my touch, so I don't. "It all became too much, and I cracked under the strain. It happened so quickly. One minute I was blurting out my past and the next ... well, it just kind of happened. I despised myself afterwards. I locked myself inside the bathroom, sobbing, scrubbing myself down in the shower, just thinking about you and how I'd just deceived you. I hated myself, and I hated what I had just done to my family."

"You said when you first slept together? How many times were there?" His shoulders rise and fall quickly as he takes it all in.

"Sebastian ..." I breathe out, not feeling comfortable with his question.

"Tell me," he demands, his fist curling up so tightly that his knuckles begin to turn white.

"Only a few times," I manage to say. My audible heartbeat begins to race, through the heart-monitor.

"How many times are a few times?"

I close my eyes, unable to stomach looking at his broken face any longer. "I … um … no. Sebastian, no. I won't answer this question. I'm sorry."

"Shit!"

Still feeling edgy from the attack, I jolt out of my skin when I hear the sound of his chair slamming into the wall, and he kicks the side of my bed with rage. After a moment, I feel a dip in the bed. I slowly re-open my eyes, he is beside me, clutching my hands in his and leaning into me, his face inches away from mine.

"I want to get crazy mad with you. I want to hit him. I want to hit something. But damn it, I fucking can't," he finishes with a pained whisper that turns my insides out.

"You should hit me. It would make me feel better."

He looks down at my injured body, his eyes trace over my bandaged wrists, up to my neck brace and over my face. "I think you've suffered enough, don't you? And no matter how angry I am with you, I would never hit you, ever. You know that."

He lifts his hand up to my cheek, and his thumb gently traces my fragile skin. I close my eyes, welcoming his touch. It's comforting, it's familiar, and I've missed it. "I hate what he's done to you. Your pretty face … fuck," he says gently.

He stays quiet for a moment as if mulling things over, the cogs continuously turning. His next words shock me. "I don't blame you."

"What?" I blink through the confusion. What? Why wouldn't he blame me? I cheated on him. There is no one else to blame but me.

"You had to go through so much crap alone. I can't blame you for finding solace in somebody else. I wasn't here, and I'm sorry for that. But Jesus, Ava, you've broken my heart in the worst way possible. Of all of the people in the world who have ever hurt me, I didn't think you'd ever be one of them." He catches my single tear that escapes with the pad of his thumb. "Where do we go from here, Ava?" he speaks softly, his hand latching onto mine again.

"I have to follow my heart," I say honestly yet painfully.

"And what does your heart say?" I look into those hopeless eyes of his, eyes that say he would give me a second chance, and I desperately want to say, 'you, you're what's in my heart,' but I know deep down I'd be lying. It wouldn't be the truth, and I can't keep hurting him unnecessarily like that. It isn't fair. I need to be fearless and finally tell him what

I've been dreading to tell him for weeks now. I need to set him free.

"That Ashton's the one I want to be with."

I watch as his chin trembles and the tears begin to flow down his face. His cries turn into sobs as he brings his head down into my lap and mourns for our relationship. I bring my hand through his hair, brushing my fingers through the silky strands, and I join him with his mourning cries repeating the words, "I'm so sorry," over and over again. My heart is breaking along with his.

We stay in this embrace for what seems like hours. Once the tears have subsided, he shifts from me, his face red and swollen. "I should go," he whispers as he leans in and presses the gentlest of kisses against my lips. It suddenly occurs to me that this will be our last kiss and I don't want to let him go; I want to latch onto him and beg him to stay, but I don't. I won't. I have made my final decision, and I know it's for the best.

"I'm so sorry, Ava, for what you had to go through when you were younger," he begins when he pulls away from me. "If I'd have known, I would have ..." His eyes turn black with anger.

"I know."

"I hope that bastard dies for what he's done to you. He doesn't deserve to live. He deserves to rot in hell." He stands up and positions his hands into the front pocket of his sweatshirt.

"Will you be okay?" I know I'm asking a stupid question, but I need to make sure he isn't about to go and do something stupid.

He shakes his head. "Eventually, maybe, but no ... I've just lost the only woman I have ever truly loved." My lip trembles when he turns and starts for the door. As he starts to turn the doorknob he pauses for a moment. "I love you, Ava, I always will," he whispers without turning to look at me.

"I love you too." But he doesn't hear it because he's already out of the room.

And for the last time, I vow that this will be the final tear I will ever shed because I am exhausted and all cried out.

I fucking hate crying.

I take my fragile body and shuffle into the direction of *his* room. If Ashton and Caleb were here right now, they wouldn't have let me leave my goddamn bed, but I need to see him. I approach the room that is being guarded by a police officer. I expect the officer to stop me, to ask who I am, but he just smiles softly and pushes the door open for me.

"Thank you," I whisper, looking up at the kind police officer.

"My pleasure, ma'am."

I enter the room, clutching hold of my ribs, desperately trying to ignore the sharp, stabbing pain I feel with every step I take. It's eerily quiet in here, except for the continuous sounds of the machines.

Breathlessly, I come to a stop at the end of the bed and stare at his lifeless body. He's covered in wires, a ventilator tube in his mouth. I half expect him to open his eyes and taunt me, but other than the rise and fall of his chest he remains still.

I take a seat beside him, clutching my fidgeting hands together in my lap. I watch him, trying to understand why life decided to draw the short straw on the Jacobson family. I know they say everything happens for a reason, but the moment my father died, it was like we suddenly had a bad omen lurking over us and everything began to fall apart.

"I didn't ask for this. I didn't ask for my family to turn out like this," I say out loud, startling myself at the sound of my own voice, unaware that I was going to speak until I actually said the words out loud. "All I ever wanted was to be normal, to have a normal family. I had that. I had a loving mom and dad, a big brother, a baby sister, and it was perfect. Then when I turned eight years old, suddenly my life turned upside down, and it hasn't been the same since." I pause, forcing the tears back because I vowed never to cry ever again and I'm sticking to my promise.

"I didn't ask for my daddy to die. I didn't ask for my mom to become a drunken bitch. I didn't ask for my brother to touch me at fifteen years old. I didn't ask for my high school years to be taken away from me so I could spend three years looking over my shoulder, scared to have a conversation with a girl, let alone with a boy just in case you didn't approve. I didn't ask to run to Seattle just so I could get away from you. I didn't ask for my baby sister to take her own life. I didn't ask my asshole of a mother to disown me, to blame me for my sister's death. And I didn't ask to be kidnapped, abused and battered. To have my body covered in your blood after an ATF agent had to shoot you just to get you the hell off me. I didn't ask to be sitting here, speaking to my brother while he's on a life support machine, wishing he would just die because he's halfway there already. Wishing he would finally get out of my life. I didn't ask for any of this, but I got it anyway."

I'm trembling, anger coursing through my veins as I raise my voice, hoping that the bastard can still hear me through his coma induced sleep.

"I should just unplug the damn life support myself. It's what you deserve. You dead, face down, eating dirt from the evil grounds of hell, but I couldn't. I wouldn't because I didn't ask for this ..." I point to his unconscious body, "this bullshit in front of me. I never wanted a dead sibling, and I certainly don't want a second. I don't want to be the only family left, even if it is as dysfunctional as hell, but I guess we've already established we don't always get what we want in life." I take another breath.

"I don't know what happened to you, why you became the monster you are today, but it makes me sad. You could've become so much more, achieved so much more with your life, but it's too late. Your life is over, whether you live or die. But one thing changes today. I'm taking my life back, and you're not going to be a part of it. I'm going to live my life the way I want to live it, without you dictating it. You've dictated me my whole life. Today it stops. Die, don't die, I don't care. You are no longer going to be a blip on my radar. I'm done. You can't hurt me anymore, I won't let you."

I slowly stand, clutching carefully at my cracked ribs and careful not to make any sudden movements with my neck. I shuffle out of the room, and I don't look back. Wincing with every step I take, I head back into the direction of my room when I suddenly come face to face with the she-devil.

My mother.

"Ava," she gasps when she finally realizes it's me. Her eyes trace over my face, pausing briefly when they reach my neck brace, then tracing lower until she notices the black and blue bruises on various sections of my body, the ones that aren't hidden behind my hospital gown. When her teary eyes land on mine, I want to scream at the bitch.

"Oh, Ava." She goes to touch me, but I step back, pursing my lips with a snarl.

"Stay away from me," I hiss, tightening my hold on my ribs.

"Ava, I am so sorry."

"I guess you heard then," I snap, taking yet another step backwards, wanting to get away from her and her poison.

"I didn't know … I didn't … I had no idea … that he was … I …"

"Fucking save it, Carina." She visibly winces when I call her by her first name, but she lost the right to be called Mom a long time ago. "I'm not fucking interested. You're thirteen years too late." If it weren't for my broken neck and cracked ribs, I'd be ripping this bitch's hair out by now.

"Ava …" she trembles, tears rolling down her face.

"No!" I notice a couple of nurses turn their head in our direction, but I don't care. "You don't get to say anything. You lost the right to have an opinion the day you decided to pick boy toys and vacations over your own flesh and blood. My father would be turning in his damn grave at how this family has turned out. Fran is gone, Avery is on life support and look at me," I point down to myself, "beaten black and blue because of your son, because you didn't give a shit when we were growing up."

"Ava, I know I haven't been a great mother."

"You haven't been a great mother?" I question in disbelief, shocked at her audacity to call herself a mother in the first place. "You haven't been a mother at all! And it's pretty apparent considering one of your children is a rapist and the other killed herself!" Now I'm causing a scene and people are beginning to stare.

"Keep your voice down," she hisses in a hushed whisper and I want to shout even louder.

"You're not a mother, you're a fucking joke. Now stay out of my life. You're dead to me. Do you hear me? Dead," I spit out.

She physically blanches at my words, words she is very familiar with.

"What? They're your words, remember? It's the same thing you said to me at Fran's funeral, but this time they're directed at you instead. Have a nice life, Carina. I hope it's kind to you," I give her a feigned smile, my voice void of any emotion. I almost feel like curtsying at our gawking audience when I walk away from her, feeling as though I'm in my own version of a daytime soap opera.

The cliffhanger has already been and gone, but where the hell is my happy ending?

Two days later, the police inform me that Avery passed away. He was declared dead at 11:45 this morning. I don't say anything, I don't ask how and I don't ask why. I'm not happy. I'm not sad. I'm just numb. My unresponsive attitude makes it seem like I don't care and quite frankly I don't. Why should I? He's dead, end of story. I said goodbye to that life two days ago and now I'm desperately trying to focus on my future. However, that's easier said than done when he's still in my head, haunting me, taunting me. Every time I close my eyes all I can see is him. It's as if I am back in that motel room, feeling the pain soar through my body with every punch, every crack of my bones, every spilled drop of my blood, and I panic because it feels as if it's happening all over again.

I tell myself over and over that it's only been five days since my attack and that it will take some time to recover from it, but that doesn't make it any easier to cope with. As the days begin to roll by, my mind continues to struggle to get past the incident and it's making me more panicked, frightened, and tense.

I feel like at any moment he is going to appear out of nowhere, resurrected back from the dead, and it's an unnerving feeling. I'm constantly on edge. I can't even have Ashton look at me without any clothes on because I feel ashamed and disgusted with my own body. Like now for instance …

Ashton helps me out from the hospital bed and guides me into the ensuite so I can take a bath. I recoil the moment his hands touch my waist to steady my balance. He sighs sadly as he pulls his hands away from me and I grimace at his sadness.

"I'm not going to hurt you, baby. I promise. I'm not him."

A shiver runs through me when the sound of *his* voice echoes inside my head. Suddenly, I'm being transported back there, on the floor, crying out from the whiplash he caused by slamming me against the wall.

*"I'm sorry, I didn't mean it, baby, I didn't mean to hurt you …"*

"Don't call me baby," I snap, taking a hesitant step back, cowering away from the one person I desperately don't want to be frightened of.

Ashton holds his hand out to me, a sad smile placed on his lips. "Ava, bab—" he cuts himself off mid-speech and takes a calming breath before correcting himself. "Ava, I hate how terrified you look right now." He takes a cautious step forward. "Of how terrified you're looking at me. I'm not going to hurt you. I promise."

"I'm sorry, I just …"

He takes another step forward and gently grasps my fingers with his. This time I don't jump at his touch. "I know, you don't have to explain. It's just going to take time. We're going to get through this. It won't be like this forever, I promise."

He positions his hand fully in mine and gently pulls me into the direction of the bathroom. Once I'm standing in the middle of the steam-drizzled room, he locks the door behind him and turns to me. Panic and bile fill my throat at the possibility of Ashton seeing my naked, bruised, and repulsive body.

"Can you turn around, please?" I ask shakily, keeping a death-grip hold on the belt of my bathrobe.

His eyes widen at my request, then quickly fade into understanding. "You have nothing to be ashamed of," he states lovingly, but it doesn't stop me from clasping my fingers even tighter against the material, so tight that the belt begins to cut into my broken ribs. I gasp as a sharp pain shoots straight through my body, but the pain is not enough to ease my hold. My robe is my safety barrier, and I'm not ready to let go.

"Please?" I beg through labored breaths, my heart rate accelerating as the panic sets in.

He doesn't turn around. Instead, he keeps himself concreted to the spot, his eyes never once leaving mine. I feel lightheaded and nauseatingly ill. "Why?"

I take a frustrated breath and roll my eyes. "You know why," I whisper urgently, wrapping my arms around my body, feeling ashamed to be in my own skin.

He takes a slow step towards me. "I don't know why. Will you tell me, please?"

Without moving my neck, I trace my eyes down to my feet, clutching nervously at my robe, purposely avoiding his eye contact. "I'm disgusting. My body is revolting. I'm revolting," I whimper.

"Look at me." I flinch when I see his hand reach for my chin. He gently tilts my head up until my eyes meet his. "You're beautiful."

"No, I'm not. I'm ruined. He's ruined me," I whisper hoarsely. I try and look away from him, but he lifts my chin back up, training his eyes on mine.

"You're not ruined, you're beautiful. You're just a little wounded, nothing that your doctor can't fix." He smiles, tenderly stroking his thumb against my bottom lip. If I weren't so fucked up, I might have even laughed at his comment.

"I love you. Nothing will ever change that, ever. Do you understand me? I love you. I would never hurt you. You're my beautiful Ava. I just want to look after you. Will you let me?"

With a trembling smile, I begin to loosen my belt. "Okay, but can you keep your eyes on mine, please? It's the only thing that's keeping me calm right now."

"My eyes are going nowhere, beautiful. I promise."

Keeping my eyes transfixed on his, I unravel the belt and let the robe fall at my feet. He helps me into the tub, and true to his word his eyes never stray away from mine.

"Are you okay? Is it warm enough?" he asks once I've gently lowered myself into the soapy water and allowed the soothing heat to cover me from the chest down.

"I'm … it's perfect."

"Yes, you are," he says, kneeling down to my level. He leans forward and I cower away from him. I don't mean to do it, but it's an automatic reflex.

"I'm just going to place a kiss on your head," he warns gently. It immediately puts me at ease, and I relax under his touch when he reaches over and presses a gentle kiss at the top of my head. "We're going to get through this. I'm not going anywhere. I promise."

I hope so. I really fucking hope so.

# epilogue

Three Months Later - May 2014

SITTING ON THE SOFA in my therapist's office, waiting for my early morning appointment, I have to admit I've come a long way in just three months. After the incident, I spent a while locked within the confinements of my own head, struggling to come to terms with what happened to me, struggling to come to terms with life. And to make matters worse, I couldn't get the bastard out of my head. Whenever I closed my eyes, he was always there, constantly haunting me from the goddamn grave and I spent a full month suffering with insomnia.

The first month was one of the hardest months of my life. I may have been recovering physically, and my broken bones may have been healing, but emotionally? I was a mess. I was depressed, withdrawn; I didn't speak, I didn't do anything, except keep myself captive inside the dark surroundings of my bedroom. I didn't even mother or hold my own child. In fact, for a short period of time during my depression, I almost forgot Lily existed. I just became a living corpse, and I couldn't care less about anybody or anything around me.

I swore to myself I would never shed another tear for the rest of my existence, but a few weeks after the incident they began to fall and continued to do so for two weeks straight. They were tears of mourning;

mourning for my sister, something that my body never allowed me to do when she died six months ago. Of course, I cried, but I never physically mourned for her and accepted her death. No, instead I had to wait until I was at the absolute brink of darkness for them to erupt, and it was soul wrecking stuff. It nearly pushed me over the edge. I wanted the pain of it all to go away.

Thankfully, I was unsuccessful in my attempt at suicide by a long mile, but it was the one thing that shook me out of my depression. And the reason why it was unsuccessful is sat beside me right now.

My savior.

Ashton just knows when to be in the right place at the right time. Just the thought of not being here right now, especially for my beautiful eight-month-old daughter, is too hard to comprehend. It isn't even worth thinking about it.

I've been seeing Dr. Grace Campbell twice a week for the past nine weeks. It was intense at first, having a total stranger dissect my inner monsters, but eventually we began to work through them one by one and at the end of every week I can feel my spirit start to return. I can even say Avery's name without wanting to kill myself. It's hard, but it's something, I guess.

I'm still not fully recovered, but it's a work in progress and week-by-week my emotional state continues to improve. I don't think I will ever be my old self again, but that's fine. I don't want to be my old self. I'm focusing on being a new and improved self, a person who won't be buried by the demons of my past. This time I will be the one to bury them so deep in the ground that they will never be able to return.

The secretary pops her head over her desk with a bright smile. "Miss Jacobson, Dr. Campbell will see you now."

I turn to Ashton. "See you in an hour?"

"I'll be here waiting for you," Ashton replies. I smile as I stand and make my way to Dr. Campbell's office. Ashton has been with me to every one of these appointments. I have no idea how he manages to get time off from the hospital, but without fail, he is always by my side.

I knock on the door before I enter. When I hear a gentle, "Come in," I walk inside and take a seat on the leather sofa in the middle of her office.

Dr. Campbell takes a seat on the chair opposite me, crossing her legs with an electronic tablet perched lightly on her lap.

"Hello, Ava. You look well. How are you since our last session?" she asks in her usual, gentle tones, immediately creating a calming atmosphere within her office.

I sit further back in the leather interior with a genuine smile. "Yeah, I'm feeling really good at the moment."

"That's fantastic, Ava. Just what I like to hear." She looks down at her notes briefly on her tablet before returning her eyes back to me. "In today's session I want to discuss your relationship with Ashton." She pauses for a brief moment, and I nod with acceptance. "How is your relationship?"

"Yeah, it's really good. He's perfect. He's been my rock throughout all of this and the reason why I'm sat in your office right now. I feel very lucky to have him in my life."

She thinks thoughtfully for a moment. "Can you elaborate?"

"He's stood beside me through everything, even at the hardest of times. While most men would have just walked away, he didn't. He said we would get through this together, and he's been there for me every step of the way."

"Am I right in saying that you love him?"

"I'm madly in love with him. He's the one, you know? I knew it from the moment I met him."

"Tell me more about Ashton. Your face lights up at the mere mention of his name, and it's refreshing to see your face with such joy, especially after such a traumatic time."

*Well, I like this session even more if it means I get to talk about Ashton for a full hour.*

"What can I say? He's gorgeous. I could just sit and stare at him all day if I could get away with it." I chuckle. "He has a beautiful mind and an even more beautiful heart. And his eyes. He has these amazing green eyes, almost hypnotic, and I can lose myself in them in an instant. He makes me laugh when nobody else can, and he has this magic ability to make all the demons and bad shit disappear.

"Granted, he wasn't able to get through to me for a while during my mental breakdown but eventually his persistence paid off. He saved me from making a stupid decision. He loves me despite my baggage. He loves me for me. We've only been together for a short amount of time, but he's the one I see myself growing old and gray with. I don't know how I got so lucky to find him, but I'm going to cherish him for the rest of my life."

Wow, talk about Ashton 101. His ears must be burning right now.

Dr. Campbell smiles fondly at me. "Well, it seems you certainly have yourself a keeper there. We have established you have a strong emotional relationship with Ashton, but how is your sexual relationship?"

I let out a long breath and give her a sad grimace. "Not good at all. It's non-existent actually."

"Well, that is hardly surprising, Ava. You have suffered a tremendous ordeal. Sexual intercourse in general is a big step for any couple, but to add a history of sexual abuse into the mix makes a loving experience more complicated."

"I'm starting to feel that I'm ready. Three months ago, the very thought of Ashton seeing me without any clothes on scared me. I felt disgusting to be in my own skin. But recently, I've been feeling … you know …" I pause when the words become restricted at the back at my throat with embarrassment.

"Sexually aroused?" Dr. Campbell elaborates for me.

I feel absolutely ridiculous that I cannot discuss sex without turning crimson red. "Um … well, yeah. I mean is that healthy? I kind of feel like it should be too soon to feel this way after what I went through."

"There is no time scale on recovery. With some victims it can take only a matter of weeks, others it can take months. I have even known victims to be affected by their sexual abuse for years. It depends on each individual and their coping mechanism. Everybody is different. So to answer your question, yes, it is healthy. If you think you're ready to progress sexually with your relationship with Ashton, then I say what are you waiting for?"

I laugh. "Really?"

Her smile turns serious and she leans closer to me. "Yes, Ava. What I see is that you have spent your entire life letting one person dictate how you should live, and now that he isn't here to hurt you anymore, you have an opportunity to get your life back on track. It is your time for happiness. Your time to live your life the way you want to live it, and if I were you, Ava, I would grasp hold of it with both hands. You have come such a long way, and it is astonishing to see the strength you have gained in just nine weeks.

"You have fantastic instincts, so embrace them, trust them. You know your body better than anybody, and if your body is telling you that you're ready, then it most likely means that you are ready."

"What if the problem isn't with me What if the problem lies with Ashton?" I ask anxiously, biting the pad of my thumb.

"Are you saying he doesn't want a sexual relationship with you?"

"I don't really know. It's just we haven't done anything for such a long time. I worry he doesn't find me sexy anymore. He barely touches me, and when he kisses me it's as though he's kissing his aunt," I admit honestly.

"Have you discussed this with Ashton?"

"No."

"Have you discussed that you feel ready to progress your relationship to the next level?"

I cringe slightly as I murmur a gentle, "No."

"Well, that's your problem right there. He isn't a mind reader, Ava. You have to communicate with him, and you have to tell him what you're feeling. During our earlier sessions, weeks ago, you explained to me that you had a hard time letting him back in after the incident. It seems to me that he is trying to give you space, not forcing you into anything until you are one hundred percent ready. As far as he is concerned, you still aren't ready and he will continue to think that unless you tell him.

"Also, have you thought of how this could have affected him? Just put yourself in his shoes for a moment and imagine what he must have been going through the night he entered that motel room. Ashton was a witness and he would have seen everything. In some ways that can be just as traumatic and it is possible that he has his own insecurities and anxieties from that night as well. You need to be open with him, be open with each other."

I take a moment to absorb her information. I cringe inwardly at the image Ashton must have seen when he arrived in that motel room, watching how I was aggressively mauled and battered by Avery. And then to witness Avery get shot and go into cardiac arrest while bleeding out on top of me. I can't believe I'm only just contemplating what Ashton must have gone through; how he must have felt seeing me like that. God, it must have killed him. I know it would have killed me if the shoe were on the other foot.

"You're absolutely right. I've been so focused on me and getting myself back on track that I haven't even thought about how it could have affected him. He's been so strong through everything; I didn't even think to question how he was doing." My heart begins to pound against my chest, and I can feel myself becoming worked up.

"Ava, I can sense this upsets you, but what you have to remember is that you have been through a challenging time, emotionally and physically. Your mind has been solely concentrated on the past, and the incident. It is hardly surprising the focus has been on you. And as selfish as it might seem, you needed to be selfish to get to where you are today."

She's right. I have been selfish. I close my eyes as regret begins to suffocate me. "No wonder he's been so distant from me physically. And after what he witnessed … I'll be surprised he'll ever want to sleep with me again. I must repulse him." I frustratingly press the palm of my hands into my eyes, rubbing the tears away that are beginning to surface.

"You're doing it again, Ava. You are letting your insecurities run a million miles ahead of you," she says softly.

Gradually I remove my hands from my eyes and look up to the ceiling with an inhale. Shit, we've been through this so many times. Whenever I have doubts or bad thoughts, I automatically assume the worst, to the most unrealistic degree, but Dr. Campbell has been working me through it. She told me the moment I have an insecure thought I need to take a breather and count down from ten. Once my mind has calmed, I take a moment to rethink the insecurity through because nine out of ten times I'm overreacting.

So I do just that. I count down from ten. And once I've calmed down, I realize she's right. I was letting my insecurities take over.

"Feeling better?" Dr. Campbell asks when I finally look to her.

"Yeah." I sheepishly smile.

"And what are your thoughts now?"

"That I was being ridiculous to think that."

She shakes her head in disagreement. "You are not being ridiculous, Ava. After such a painful past where you have been continuously let down, your brain automatically assumes the worst, and that is absolutely understandable. It is a default you have become accustomed to, but seeing you take control of your insecurities and to be able to assess those insecurities rationally, shows me how much you have grown. You should be proud of yourself. It proves to me that you're becoming the strong woman you aim to be. We're not quite at the one hundred percent mark, but we'll get there."

After my session, I remain quiet until we arrive at Ashton's. Well, it's technically our house now, since Lily and I moved in officially a couple of weeks ago. Unofficially, we had been gradually moving in for weeks, considering we spent most nights here than we did at my apartment. Caleb thought we were moving a little too fast, but Ashton wouldn't have it any other way.

*"I've almost lost Ava twice now. I'm not going to let her out of my sight again."*

And well, here I am. My life is slowly getting back on track. My daughter is healthy and beautiful. I have the perfect man. I quit my job, and I'm slowly building up my own editing business for indie writers. I only have a few clients at the moment, but the clientele continues to grow day-by-day. Everything is amazing.

Everything except for the physical side.

I sit down in the corner of the sofa and watch as Ashton looks through the mail in front of me. "Are you okay?"

He looks at me and smiles. "Me? I'm fine, why do you ask?"

I fidget with my fingers when I answer. "Everything's kind of been about me recently. I just … I wanted to make sure you were doing okay with everything, with me."

The smile in his eyes is suddenly replaced with a look of concern. He takes a seat beside me on the sofa. "Why wouldn't everything be okay with you?"

Taking a deep breath, I push the insecurities aside and look him in the eyes. "Well, I haven't exactly been a great girlfriend lately, and it only came to light today that I haven't once asked how you were doing.

I kind of felt crappy after that."

He edges a little closer but refrains from touching me. It hurts, but I have to remember what Dr. Campbell said about him still assuming I don't want to be touched. "Please don't worry about me, I'm fine. And to be honest, I hadn't even noticed. I've just been concentrating on you and getting you better. I know things haven't been perfect, but I've never been happier. So you can stop thinking you haven't been a great girlfriend because you're the best girl a man could ask for, period."

I give him a hesitant smile. "Really? You're happy?"

"Yes, I'm as happy as a pig in mud." I laugh, feeling at ease instantly. "I'm happy, especially when your face lights up and you smile that beautiful smile of yours. You have nothing to worry about, okay? I love you."

He presses a fragile kiss against my lips, and before I can deepen the kiss he is already pulling away and my heart sinks. I need to tell him. I want him to kiss me the way he used to kiss me. I want him to hold me the way he used to hold me. I want him to love me the way he used to love me. I just want him back ...

"I'm gonna go take a shower before my shift."

I'm momentarily startled when he stands and heads upstairs to take his shower, leaving me on the verge of tears as I let another opportunity to open up to him slip away. Inhaling, I close my eyes, and count to ten, hoping the time out will calm my senses enough to stop the tears and draw some clarity on how to open up to him. I want the confidence to return so I can tell him exactly what I want.

One eye opens when I hear the shower running from upstairs, and I feel the telltale signs of my arousal when I imagine him naked while the warmth of the water covers every inch of his naked skin.

I glance towards the clock that sits just above the fireplace in the corner of the room. Caleb won't be back for another hour with Lily.

I find myself walking towards the stairs in the direction of the bathroom. By the time I reach the door, my palms are drenched with sweat and my heart is slamming against my chest. As I trace my eyes over the door, I have the sudden urge to turn around and run back down the stairs but realizing it is either now or never, I decide to rip the band-aid off and enter.

I'm met with a wall of steam, and it is instantly relaxing, and kind of erotic, a feeling quite foreign to me after such a long time. As I walk further into the bathroom, I stop at the sink and take a glance at my reflection in the mirror. Taking a deep breath, I watch myself as I remove my shoes, jeans and shirt. I trail my eyes along my slim body, bracing myself for what I'm about to do next. Breathing deeply, I reach behind my back to unclip the clasp of my bra and let the material fall away from my arms onto the tiled floor, leaving my eyes transfixed on my breasts. My heart is pounding at my vulnerable state, and even though I'm absolutely petrified, the sound of Ashton showering from behind the frosted shower partition calms the storm that is currently brewing inside my body.

The idea of removing my panties scares me slightly, so I decide to leave them in place for now. I count to three and step towards the shower, pushing myself to join forces with my sexual urges.

Inhaling heavily, I step into the walk-in shower, push away all the insecurities I have felt during the past three months and press my chest against his back. I swoop my arms around his waist and I'm immediately greeted with thrashing cascades of steaming hot water. His body jolts from under my touch and he freezes on the spot.

"Ava, what are you doing?" he asks panicked, pivoting his neck to look at me. I press my chest further into his back, trailing my hands up his chest and pressing a lingering kiss against the center of his neck.

"I want you," I mumble against his skin, and the feel of him against my lips sets my body on fire. It's strange but amazing. I have missed this so much.

"W-What?" he stutters with confusion. Feeling my confidence rising, I dig my fingers against his chest, causing him to hiss out loud at my touch.

"I've missed you," I say with a whisper of a kiss. "I've been trying to tell you that I'm ready."

He turns in my arms until he is facing me, his eyes widen at my half naked body. "You're ready?" he asks with a dumbfounded expression, and all I can do is nod. His eyes carefully trace my naked chest and my nipples harden under his stare. He cautiously moves closer to me, and tingles shoot along the ridge of my spine when his fingers caress my cheek. The sensation is so intense I have to grasp hold of his wrist just to keep upright.

"Are you sure?"

I lean into his hand, turning my head slightly and pressing a gentle kiss against his warm, wet arm. "One hundred percent yes."

He looks down at me with a look of adoration, his green eyes sparkling with worship. I trace my right hand up through his wet hair, and I love how the tendrils of his hair feel through my fingers. It's been so long since I've done this that I'd actually forgotten how incredible it felt. My heart skyrockets at the realization, but it isn't racing with terror; it's racing with exhilaration.

"Kiss me," I demand, and his eyes flutter with arousal. He seems frozen in time as he gazes at me with a look of awe, but when I whisper, "Kiss me," for a second time, he finally awakens from his stupor. I gasp with anticipation at the feel of his erection against my stomach. His fingers slide away from my cheek, up the back of my neck. With his fingers buried within my hair, he leans in towards me until his breath is only an inch away from my lips.

"Kiss you?" he whispers.

"Please, I need you," I reply breathlessly.

Then I forget how to breathe altogether when his wonderful moist lips press against mine and my entire world disappears in front of me. His tongue slips into my mouth, slowly and tenderly, and I fall further into his spell. Losing myself in this intimate moment, I caress my fingertips along his glistening back, grinding against his leg with my hips when my fingers trail along the softness of his ass cheeks. He grunts inside my mouth and breathlessly pulls away. "Baby … what are you doing?"

I smile when he calls me baby. He hasn't called me baby since I told him not to, three months ago after my brother tainted the word with his poison. But I don't hear Avery. I don't even think of him. I focus on the man in front of me and how he makes one word sound so damn sexy.

"You just called me baby," I whisper.

Regret instantly fills his eyes. "I'm sorry, I wasn't think—"

"Say it again." His eyes widen, and he seems conflicted by my words. I reassure him by pressing a tender kiss against his lips. "It's okay. I want you to say it."

His eyes assess my face, no doubt trying to find signs of reservations, but when he doesn't find any, I can see his distinct smirk curling at the corner of his mouth and his eyes sparkle with hunger.

"Baby …"

The way his husky voice drawls over the word is enough for me to lose control and I slam my lips onto his. I caress his tongue with my own and the taste of his tongue tantalizes every one of my senses. The hot shower falling over us, almost like a tropical waterfall, makes me want him in a way that I've never experienced before. For the first time in my life, I feel the breeze of freedom. I have nothing clouding up my mind. No demons from my past, no guilt of betrayal for Sebastian, no heartache of having my daughter in hospital, absolutely nothing.

And it's refreshingly freeing.

"Make love to me, please," I whisper against his lips. I nibble at his bottom lip, and his hands tighten against my hold as I physically feel his naked body begin to tremble against mine. "Show me how love is supposed to be."

With his eyes transfixed on mine, I feel his fingers caress over my hips until they trace under the edge of my panties and he gently pushes them past my hips, and over my ass. His eyes never leave mine as he crouches down in front of me, sliding my soaked panties down my legs, lifting my left leg and then my right until my panties have been success-fully removed and I am standing fully naked above him. I tilt my head back with a gasping moan when he presses a gentle kiss against my navel. When he stands back up, he lifts me up in his arms, and I instan-taneously wrap my legs around his thighs.

"Here or in the bedroom?" he whispers as he presses a kiss against my earlobe.

"I want you here … now."

Soundlessly he presses me up against the cold-tiled wall and I shiv-er at the impact. His cock presses against my sensitive opening, clutch-ing hold of me tightly as the water pounds endlessly over us. He rests his head against mine and presses a kiss along my bottom lip.

"Tell me you love me," I whimper against his lips, and he chuckles under his breath.

"I have fucking missed you, baby. I love you, I love you so damn much."

"I love you …"

He slides gently inside of me, and I let my head fall back against the tiled wall, allowing the sensation to ease through me. It's incredible. He inches his thickness inside me with gradual ease and he fits with perfect precision. He stills inside of me and looks me in the eyes with a mixture of hunger and affection, a look that has me tightening my hold against his muscular body.

"How does that feel?"

My heart throbs wildly as the sound of his burly voice sends an enchanting electric current to sweep through my body. "Hmm, it feels good ... it feels perfect."

Ashton's eyes pierce deeper into mine, placing me within his trance. "Hmm ... perfect ... just like you, baby." He presses his lips onto mine and begins to move in and out of me in a slow, loving, unhurried pace. I trail my hands across the top of his back, feeling everything begin to fade away at the glorious sensation of his cock sliding in and out of me.

Our moans become more frequent as the intense connection between us begins to spiral out of control and he begins to move a little faster. I feel the pressure begin to build at the sudden change in momentum. His lips pull away from mine, and I open my eyes to see his focus is solely on me and my entire body trembles under his gaze. I push my fingers through his hair into a tight grip when I feel the early signs of my climax peaking within the distance.

"So fucking beautiful."

His words add to my climax, and I cry out as he continues to bury himself inside of me, filling me with his unconditional love.

Usually within seconds my climax would peak, but after a short while the intensity of our intimacy completely overwhelms me and I feel myself become frustrated when my climax doesn't progress. A roadblock is stopping me from pushing over the edge, and I can't figure out why. Ashton senses my reluctance and holds my gaze, a gaze that captivates me in a split second.

"Baby, just relax ... just feel it, feel the love between us ... just feel it."

I close my eyes, listening to his seductive, calming voice and surprisingly his words soar through me enough to push through the hesitancy, but it still isn't enough to push all the way to the brink.

"I can't ... I can't," I cry out in frustration.

"Feel it, baby, feel it with me," he urges, and just when I think I'm unable to orgasm, he brings one hand between us and circles his thumb over my clit. I crumble in his arms as my climax finally hits. Through the steam filled bathroom, I scream out in a frenzy and lose all coherent thought.

Once I come down from my high, I open up my eyes to a thoroughly fucked Ashton. "Hi," he breathes.

The intensity of the love between us, the incredible act of love we just shared, causes me to become overwhelmed with emotions, and I'm unable to control the tears that fall. He catches my trembling chin within his thumb and forefinger.

"Baby, what's wrong?" he questions with a look of alarm on his face. I shake my head on a teary smile and let myself slide from his wet body, clutching his chest when I stand on both feet.

"Nothing, I'm just a little overwhelmed. I just … I love you so much, and I've missed you. It's been a long three months. So damn long."

He gently brings his knuckles up to my face, and even though my falling tears have been washed away by the water, he wipes the tears anyway, and I love him even more for it. "I know, baby, but you've fought through it, and I am so fucking proud of you."

I bury my face into the crux of his neck. "Just don't let me go back there. I don't ever want to go back there," I say as I feel his hands caress up and down my bare back, clutching me tight to his chest.

"You have nothing to worry about. I won't let you, I promise."

I pull my head away from his neck and look up to him. "Good because I couldn't bear the thought of losing you and Lily."

Sliding his hands through my hair, he leans down and brushes his lips against mine. "You won't lose us, I promise." The pressure of his mouth deepens against my already swollen lips and we greedily devour one another's mouths.

"Wow," I barely whisper through my gasping breaths. I bring the palm of my hands up to his chest and my breath hitches at the feel of his walloping heart against my parted fingers. Unable to resist the urge, I press my lips to his on a single kiss. "Do you *have* to go into work today?" I whisper against his lips. Now that I have opened up to him I just want to wrap myself around him and keep him to myself for the rest of the day.

Abruptly his lips are snatched from me, and a look of alarm replaces the look of lust. "Shit, work!" He jolts within my arms, but with the sudden momentum, he loses his footing against the slippery shower floor and falls flat on his ass, taking me with him.

"Oh my God, are you okay?" I take hold of his face with my hands as I straddle against his thighs, an amused grin on my face.

"I think I broke my ass."

I try to hold back the laughter, but it's useless when he starts chuckling. "It's a good job you're going to the hospital then ..." I laugh, and it takes everything in me not to collapse in a heap.

"Do you think this is funny?" He smirks with a humorous glint in his eyes.

"Oh yeah, definitely."

Slowly he lifts me from his lap and gently lays me on my back against the cold shower floor. Ashton, like a lion on the prowl, crawls on top of me until his face hovers over mine. "I'll give you something to laugh about ..."

The small bubble of laughter is cut off by the contact of his lips. Pulling away for a brief moment I mutter, "If you think that was funny, then I definitely want my money back." His lips vibrate above mine when I reconnect my lips to his.

Through a lingering kiss, he murmurs, "It was supposed to be metaphoric, baby, but how about I repay you in kisses?" He circles his tongue against my bottom lip, taking full advantage of my mouth, leaving me utterly breathless.

"Hmm, sounds good to me," I attempt, but it barely comes out as a moan, lost within the depths of each other again.


When Ashton and I finally manage to pry ourselves away from one another, wrinkled to a prune might I add, I leave Ashton to get changed for a shift that he's already fashionably late for. Hearing the sound of the doorbell ringing, I go downstairs to let Caleb and Lily in.

"Hey, beautiful girl," I say as I take her from Caleb's arms. "Did you have fun with Uncle Caleb?" She continues to smile as I plant a kiss against her tiny nose. I climb the three steps that lead into the sitting room.

"Yeah, we had fun. Didn't we, baby girl?" Caleb gently swings her arms to and fro and pulls a funny face, which she finds absolutely hilarious, and it earns Caleb a beautiful giggle. It has to be the most beautiful sound in the world. I still find it hard to believe she's my daughter. She's just incredible.

"How was therapy?" Caleb asks once I have his attention, and I can't keep the smile from my face.

"Yeah, it was good."

"What's with the shit-eating grin?"

I manage to cover my daughter's ears up by burying her head into my chest. "Caleb," I chastise him. "Lily, that's a grown up word. You don't ever say that."

"Ava, she isn't even talking yet."

"Yes, but I want her first word to be Momma, not S. H. I. T," I hiss out in a whisper, just in case my daughter is a genius child and will eventually pick up on the letters. It isn't something a mother wants their child saying.

He holds his hands up in the air on a chuckle, "Okay then ... what's with the S. H. I. T eating grin? In fact, you look different. Your hair's wet and ..." He looks closer at my shirt, and I shift nervously under his inspection. "Ava, why is your T-shirt inside out?"

I glance down at my T-shirt and immediately blush when I realize Caleb is right. I don't have time to answer when Ashton comes barreling down the stairs, with his backpack slung over one shoulder. His eyes fall on me as soon as he steps foot into the living room and my heart thuds at the heated intensity coming from his eyes.

"Oh, hey, Caleb," he says once he peels his eyes away from mine and hurries over to the coffee table to grab hold of his phone and keys.

"Hey, Ash, you in some kind of rush?" Caleb asks as he watches Ashton rush around like a headless chicken.

"Yes, for the first time in my life I am late for work, really late ... shit, where are my sneakers?"

Laughing, I walk with Lily in my arms and slide the sneakers into view with my feet, from behind the sofa.

"Thanks, baby," he murmurs as he shuffles his feet into his sneakers.

I hear Caleb from behind muttering about Ashton using the word 'shit' and not being reprimanded for it, but Ashton has an excuse. He's late, and it's all because of me.

He steps in front of me and presses a lingering kiss against my lips. "It was totally worth it though." I shiver at the very thought, and after a second breathtaking kiss he pulls away and proudly states, "I love you." He slowly pulls his gaze away from mine, and his smile widens as he looks down to Lily, who is staring animatedly at him. "And you too, beautiful. I love you too." He takes hold of her hand with his long forefinger and blows a raspberry kiss against the back of her tiny knuckles which has her wiggling her arms and legs excitedly on a screeching giggle. We all laugh along with her contagious laughter.

"Is that funny, baby girl?" He repeats the process, and a new set of giggles echo through the room. "Right, now you're making me late. Jeez, you Jacobson chicks are going to wreck me. I'm going now before I'm even more late."

I swoon with a goofy smile as I watch him rush out of the house and I begin to sway Lily in my arms like some lovesick fool.

"Well, I don't need any clue as to why Ashton was late for work. It's written all over your face." I burst out into laughter when Caleb begins to sing the kissing song. "Ava and Ashton, sitting in a tree, K-I-S-S-I-N-G …" He makes his way over to me on a jig. "First comes love, then comes marriage, then comes baby in a baby carriage."

He gets all into Lily's face, which has her erupting into hysterical giggles. When his laughter dies down, he pulls his arms around Lily and me, into a loving embrace.

"On a serious note, I am so damn proud of you. You've been through so much, yet you've come out of the other side, stronger. I'm so glad to see that pretty smile back on your face. I've missed it, and I've missed my best friend." I flutter my eyes with contentment as he presses a kiss against the top of my damp head.

"And whatever Ashton is doing, tell him to keep it up." He pauses for a brief moment. "I didn't like him at first. I thought he was just trying to take advantage of you, but I was wrong, and I'm so glad he came into your life when he did. Because not only did he save this little one's life," he says, smiling down at Lily before returning his attention back to me, "but he saved your life too. And for that I will always be thankful."

I feel a little teary, but luckily I manage to swallow the emotion down. "I'm so lucky to have him, but I wish my personal gain wasn't

Sebastian's misery. I hate what I did to him."

"You need to let that go, Ava ..."

"I know, and I'm getting there, but he's Lily-Mai's father. I still care for him and I hate how he can't even stand to be near me."

He looks me in the eye with determination. "Well, answer me this one question. The past eight months, minus the kidnap, the depression and the early arrival of this one," he says pointing down to Lily, "if you had a chance to turn back time, would you change what happened between you and Ashton if it meant not hurting Sebastian?"

I allow the past eight months to rewind inside my head, and I want to say yes, but the idea of not having Ashton in my life is too hard to comprehend. He's the one. I cannot imagine spending my life with anybody other than Ashton. "No," I answer, taking a painful swallow.

"That's what I thought. If you and Sebastian were meant to be, then you'd still be together. End of. You need to start forgiving yourself. You're finally in a place where you're happy, and that's where I want you to stay."

I still hate the way I treated him, but Caleb is right, I need to let it go, with everything else and begin a fresh. I just hope that one day, Sebastian can forgive me.

"You're right but do you think he will ever be okay?"

He purses his lips together in thought. "Yes, he just needs to find his true love like you found Ashton. And he will. I'm sure of it."

Lily starts to get a little fussy, so I set her down on her play gym and she instantly becomes fascinated with the overhead detailing. I kneel beside her on the floor and sit back on my heels.

"Talking of true love, isn't it about time you let somebody into your life ..." The small smirk that curls up at the side his mouth lets me on into a secret. "You have?" I ask, almost jumping on the spot with ecstatic enthusiasm.

"Yeah, but it isn't anything serious. It's just a guy I've been on a few dates with."

"Is he hot?" I ask with a smile.

"Hell, yeah. He's no Dr. Bailey though." He winks. His light smile turns serious for a moment, and he quickly turns the attention back to me. "That boy loves you something fierce and seeing first hand how protective he is of you, I know without a doubt he would take a bullet for you. Just promise me you will keep a tight hold of him, okay? He's one in a million."

I smile dreamily as I look up to a photo on the wall of Ashton and his two brothers, concentrating solely on Ashton. "I will, I promise. I'm never letting him go."

And when Ashton comes home waking me blissfully in the middle of the night, I do just that. He climbs under the sheets, and he is met with the warmth of my arms.

"Hey, baby, I was hoping you were going to be in our bed." I always opted for sleeping with Lily in the spare room, but from today that's going to change.

"I felt like trying something new."

"Well, I approve because I've missed you like crazy today and I've been dreaming of coming home to you all day. This is just an added bo-nus," he whispers into my neck. A comfortable silence covers us, and I embrace the tranquility it brings. It's the first time in nearly twenty-nine years that I finally feel the peace I've desperately been searching for my entire life.

"I love you so much. I'm never letting you go, ever," I say, sighing over the pattering sound of his heartbeat against my ear.

"But what if I need to pee?"

I bury my head into his chest as I burst out laughing. "I kind of meant in the forever sense," I say looking up at him.

"Good because you're stuck with me, baby. You're not going any-where."

"I wasn't planning on it but will you shut up and finally kiss me?" I can't see it, but I can definitely feel the smile radiating through the moonlit room.

"Yes, ma'am. It would be my pleasure."

*Get married, have children, travel the world, walk every step of the empire state building, get a tattoo, swim with dolphins, free fall from a plane, go skinny dipping. Anything. Everything. Just go, and live your life, grasp it with both hands and cherish it, please.*
Francesca Jacobson, 2013

The end

# acknowledgements

I would like to thank everybody who bought and read Look After You. I hope you enjoyed the story as much as I enjoyed writing it.

Thank you to my friends and family, which includes my Scottish family too. They have been extremely supportive since the moment I told them I was writing a book, especially my mum. She couldn't wait to start reading it after I'd written the first chapter. To say she is my biggest fan, would be putting it mildly.

I want to say a big thank you to Helen Stothard at Kinky Book Klub. She's been there since the moment I hit 'publish' on my Facebook page and she's helped with the promoting, and any author related questions that I've had.

Also, thank you to Tiffany Clark at Tiffany's Book Hangover, she became a friend and a fan in the matter of a day, and she is the first person to share anything I post on my Facebook page.

Thank you to neonatal nurse Helen Furness, who works at St Mary's Hospital in Greater Manchester. She is the reason for the accurate description of the NICU and she helped me tremendously with the hospital lingo, and medical technicalities

Another thank you to my beta readers and proofreaders, Vicky Johnson, Jennifer O'neill-Pantis, Amanda Jo James, Catherine Snelson, David Smith, Tara Louise Sharland at Beg me for beta and again, thank you to Helen Stothard and Tiffany Clark. Thank you for giving my story a chance and helping me turn it from a manuscript to a novel.

Now on to the woman who really makes magic happen: Sarah Hansen at Okay Creations. From the moment I set eyes on one of her book covers, I knew she had to design my book cover. In my eyes, nobody comes close enough to her art, and knowing the perfectionist that I am, I wouldn't be happy unless she designed my book cover. And oh boy, what a book cover she did design.

And on to the other woman who makes magic happen: my editor, Jennifer Roberts-Hall. That woman is amazing. She was always at my beck and call, always easing my anxieties, and always making me laugh. She stayed up until the late hours of the morning, working through the new edit of the manuscript and ensuring it was perfect. And she has. It's incredible. Thank you.

Finally, I would like to thank every single person who shared my Facebook and Twitter page and supported me, and my writing. It means the world to me.

Love, Elena XX

# about the author

Independent author Elena Matthews was born in Manchester, United Kingdom, where she lives with her other half, but even after eight wonderful years, she is still waiting for that *epic* proposal. Elena enjoys spending quality time with her friends and family, especially her four-year-old niece, Caitlin, who is the apple of her eye (She's a little monkey too!). Elena is positive Caitlin is the love child of Jekyll and Hyde. Thankfully, the joys of being an auntie, means she can hand Caitlin back over to her mum and dad when she's all tired out!

Elena spent three years of her life at Salford University studying media production, to decide at the end of her degree she no longer wanted to pursue a career in the media. Instead, it took her another two and a half years to realize her calling. Writing. Now she lives and breathes her writing. She even had to tell her colleagues at work whenever she is found daydreaming at her desk, it's because she is conversing with her characters.

# coming soon

**Look After Me** – Sebastian's story (Look After You series)
**Look After Us** – Ava & Ashton's Novella (Look After You series)


# connect with elena

Facebook: www.facebook.com/authorelenamatthews

Twitter: www.twitter.com/authorelenamatt

Goodreads: www.goodreads.com/authorelenamatthews

www.authorelenamatthews.co.uk

If you or somebody you know has been affected by sexual abuse, or needs information, please contact (USA) www.rainn.org or call 1.800.656.HOPE. (UK) www.rapecrisis.co.uk or call 0800 802 9999.

For suicide hotlines, please contact (USA) www.suicidepreventionlifeline.org or call 1-800-273-8255. (UK) www.samaritans.org or call 08457 909090.

For neonatal information, please visit www.bliss.org.uk

Made in the USA
Charleston, SC
08 January 2016